Marsha Hunt was born in 1946 and grew up in Philadelphia. She studied at the University of California, Berkeley, during the student riots of the sixties, but shortly afterwards came to Europe. In London she made her name in the hit musical *Hair*. Her celebrated career which followed includes fifteen years in rock music, work in radio, on stage and screen. She has been a member of both the Royal National Theatre (1983–1986) and the Royal Shakespeare Company (1989). Her autobiography *Real Life* was published in 1985 and her second novel will be published in 1991. She has a daughter, Karis.

# JOY

## Marsha Hunt

VIRAGO

Published by VIRAGO PRESS Limited 1990
20-23 Mandela Street, Camden Town, London NW1 0HQ

Copyright © Marsha Hunt 1990

First published in Great Britain by Random Century Group 1990

The right of Marsha Hunt to be identified as the author of this work has been
asserted by her in accordance with the Copyright, Designs and Patents Act 1988.

*A CIP catalogue record for this book is available from the British Library*

Printed in Great Britain by
The Guernsey Press Co. Ltd., C.I.

*For Eric and Bassam*
*But most of all for Karis*

# To Start With . . .

All families got secrets, but Joy's had more than their fair share. Like a fool, I went around thinking that she let me in on all of them, since I can't keep everything to myself and figured Joy was the same. But I found out she hoarded so many secrets, she kept them important ones from herself. So while I'm able to tell you what she did, ain't no use me pretending that I know why. I blame myself for some of it, although my husband Freddie B says it's wrong that I should shoulder all the blame for what done happened to Joy and her family, 'cause they was just born under bad moons. But I refuse to believe that God put some of his children on this earth to destroy theyselves.

What's troubling is no matter what Freddie B says, looking back I can see I had more to do with the mess Joy and them made of their lives than I realized. But it's way too late for 'I'm sorry'.

Like usual, a few mornings ago I was laying in the bed next to Freddie B, staring at the ceiling and listening to him snore while I waited for his 6:45 alarm to go off. I always wake 'fore it buzzes, and sometimes it's worrying to hear that old noisy clock of his tickety-tick by seconds that won't never get another chance. But I've resigned myself to listening to it, 'cause he can't rest good at night till he sees it set, even though he knows that for all them forty-some years we been married, I wake at least half an hour 'fore that alarm, don't matter what time it's set for. I rue the day I bought him that ugly square faced clock and wish I could throw it out sometimes.

What really don't make no sense is that he likes to set it on the little built in shelf by my side of the bed.

'What's the good of that,' I ask him, 'when I ain't the one needs waking.' But he don't bother to answer. That's his way. When he can't think up a good answer, he don't say nothing. Playing like he don't hear and he hears good as me and anybody else when he wants to.

I knew he wouldn't budge when our bedside phone started going, so the minute it did I reached over him quick to pick it up, though I was half tempted to leave it ringing, as I suspected it might of been that wicked wench in apartment 207 on the fourth floor calling for the umpteenth time to complain about the water pressure being too weak in her shower.

Not but the week before, I had to put her straight. I didn't mince my words neither 'cause tenants will sure take liberties if you do. 'Just 'cause we managing the building, Miss Gonzales, don't mean folks can ring us all hours of the day and night,' I said.

3

She tried to claim that with Freddie B usually holding down a day job she thought she best try to catch him 'fore work. But like I told her, 'My husband ain't no plumber and plumbing ain't what we're paid to do. Maintenance is all. And if you want a plumber, Miss Gonzales, call you one.'

We ain't nothing but glorified cleaners, and I don't mind saying it, 'cause though we took on a building this size, the man that interviewed Freddie B down at the real estate agency promised that my husband could keep his construction work as long as he could find time to put out the garbage and see to the halls, stairs and elevators for the sixteen apartments. And I'm the one to do most of that. If we had to mess with all else in this half baked building, there wouldn't be time to scrub your teeth in the morning. But the hussy in 207 seems determined to want to get my husband down in her place, 'cause she keeps calling 'fore daybreak about that shower of her'n.

So when I hauled the phone over to my side of the bed, I was right ready to give Miss Gonzales a mouthful, but luckily I didn't start straight in, 'cause it wasn't her. It was Tammy. Joy's mama.

I peered at the clock thinking that if it was 6:20 in San Francisco where we was, it wasn't but 9:20 for her over in Richmond, Virginia, and knowing how much she likes to sleep late, I figured she wasn't calling just to jaw. For a start, she wasn't pronounciating every word like usual. Though Tammy tries to give off like she's educated, she didn't get no further than high school like the rest of us. Don't make me no difference if she likes to take airs. That's always been her way, and since Joy told her years ago to stop correcting me all the time, I don't feel I got to watch every word with Tammy and just say out what I have a mind to.

'Tammy? What ch'you doing ringing my phone at this hour, girl? You ain't got nothing better to do than to be calling folks at the crack o'dawn,' I teased her.

There was a time when she was still living 'cross the bay in East Oakland that she used to try and phone me at least once a day, but ever since she got hitched up with that cop from Chicago after he retired and moved back to his home town in Virginia, she don't hardly bother to call no more. It's Joy who keeps me posted on what Tammy's doing, not that Joy stays in touch with her mama all that much.

'Baby Palatine, are you sitting down?' Tammy asked me.

'Girl, who are you kidding,' I laughed, 'my black behind is still in the bed and I'm proud of it.'

But me funning and bad talking didn't put her in no joky mood. 'Well, I've got bad news,' she said.

Tammy thrived on bad news and given half a chance could really spin a sad story out, especially if it was about somebody else. Listening to her could be more entertainment than them afternoon soap operas. But that early in the morning I wasn't ready to hear no long drawn out tale, so I asked her to make it quick 'cause I needed the toilet, which wasn't altogether a lie.

'I didn't know if you still turn on *Good Morning America* as soon as you get up, because I would hate to think you heard it first on the news,' Tammy said, 'because that would be terrible.'

I sat bolt upright and reached for my glasses but they wasn't where I thought I left them on the sidetable. I can't think good till I got 'em on. And from her sorry-sounding voice I suspected I needed to be in a clear mind.

'I got an unfortunate phone call a couple hours ago.'

'Tammy, what's up?' I interrupted, but what I really wanted to add was that I didn't need none of her suspense and it was way too early to put up with one of her melodramas. She can turn a cankersore into lip cancer or a pot burning into a four alarm fire and she's good at getting me going. Freddie B says that she should of been a politician or something, 'cause she's that sharp at getting folks riled up about nothing. Like the time she had me on the warpath hotfooting it to Alameda with her to complain about the county raising Bay Area land tax, when I didn't even own no land. When my husband seen me afterwards pacing up and down like a tiger in a cage he had to remind me that it was only Tammy that was gonna have to pay something extra anyway.

He says the only reason she bothers with me is that she can get me on a rampage so quick, but true as that may be, she's as much like family to me as her three girls. And I wouldn't of changed that for nothing even though I wasn't in the mood to have her calling at no 6:20 in the a.m.

'Tammy, my poor husband is trying to sleep next to me and it ain't fair me hanging on the phone with the cord stretched so tight across his neck, he's near to strangling while you don't say nothing.' Freddie B sleeps heavy as somebody in a coma, and I could of probably tied the telephone cord around his neck and been choking the breath out of him, and I bet he wouldn't of stirred. But Tammy wasn't to know that.

'It's Joy,' she said and waited just long enough for the tremor in her voice to give me goose flesh.

Joy was more like my daughter than she was hers, and for years it was usually me calling Tammy with news of Joy, 'cause Joy came to me 'fore she went to anybody, especially when she got into trouble which wasn't all that often. But it was often enough to keep me on my toes.

If I'd of had a child, I reckon it would have made me mad if she had always been rushing with her agitations and whispers to some other woman first. But then Tammy brought that on herself, 'cause there was a time when I was ready to listen to her children and she wasn't. And from back then, Joy took the habit of coming to me to share both the good and bad.

I prepared myself to hear Tammy say what I had long predicted which was that Joy'd got herself arrested, 'cause with all that gadding about she did down South with Rex Hightower, that rednecked, toothpick of a so-called boyfriend of hers, I warned Joy that it wouldn't be long before some of them Okies found reason to lock her up in a backwater jailhouse and throw away the key. She ran around like she thought she was some kinda blue-eyed blonde. 'Nigger,' I used to say to Joy and point my finger in her face so she knew I meant business, 'don't forget what you are and where you are.' But she let that good advice slide off her quicker than grease off a hot comb, 'cause she was always slow to listen to what she didn't want to hear. Miami, Atlanta, Memphis, Alabama . . . She wasn't scared to go none of them places, though she wouldn't always let on that's where she was calling from 'cause she knew I didn't hold with it.

That's why I figured Joy was in the South when she had phoned me at the weekend and wouldn't tell me where she was nor where she was headed. Though I'd got used to her being secretive about things like that when it suited her, it didn't make me feel no easier when she'd call me regular and refuse to say where she was. Being from down South myself, I don't have no illusions about what goes on. Don't matter what the newspapers say about how things is changing. They ain't changed all that much for no colored girl to be flaunting herself with no white man. 'Specially no hillbilly singer that's rich and famous as Rex and got girls throwing themselves at him. Like that great big fat woman I seen at the Mayfair supermarket wearing one of them 'Rex Is Better Than Sex' buttons that they give away with his last record. I was itching to tell her that I knew from reliable sources that he couldn't get it up, but my better self told me not to 'cause it wasn't Christian.

Soon as I knew it was Joy that Tammy'd telephoned about, I didn't want Freddie B's clock to tick another second till I knew exactly what was going on. And through my nightclothes, I could hear my heart thudding like a jack rabbit's waiting on Tammy to get to the point while she coughed a couple of times and cleared her throat. It's a nervous habit she claims, but I know it's her ruining her lungs with them cigarettes. Water filters or no water filters.

It wasn't but two words she finally eked out to end my Tuesday before it had a good chance to start.

'Joy's dead.'

I had to laugh. 'Say what?' I hadn't never heard of no such foolishness.

'Don't make me repeat it, Baby Palatine, because it was hard enough to say it. You're the first person I've had to utter those words to, because Jesse's not home and I haven't been able to contact either Anndora or Brenda. It so infuriates me to have daughters that I can never reach when I need them.'

I'd stopped listening to what she said. What was the point? Joy dead? It wasn't possible. She was light and life and sun and stars and everything glorious save God hisself, and to think that she wasn't somewhere on the planet was more than I could take in. So I didn't. With my free hand, I smoothed the covers over Freddie B and shifted him a bit to where he didn't snore so loud. He's better on his back. And while I didn't say nothing, neither did Tammy. We was both holding receivers that didn't seem to have anybody on the other end.

There was hardly light coming into my bedroom with the drapes closed, but I squinted to look from corner to corner. Wasn't much to take in but two easy chairs and a old dresser with the portable TV set on it. It was the same room where Joy'd slept last time she come to stay. Me and Freddie B hadn't been long moved into the apartment and hadn't nobody lived in it 'fore us. Even though it was a poky size and painted avocado green, she said she was real happy to see we'd settled in a brand new building with a nice view of the Bay Bridge. She was due for another visit in four days, and her and me were gonna take off for Reno. Freddie B said he didn't mind me tagging along with her. He was always generous about letting me go off with Joy and loved her near as much as I did. She was the child we could never have, my baby sister Helen used to say.

But odd as it sounds with me being practically old enough to be her granny, Joy was my best friend, right from the get-go. From back thirty-odd years ago when she wasn't but eight years old, I could have a better time with Joy than anybody. For a start she was always like somebody grown and had more common sense than most. And with my husband out working all the time and having to take on-site jobs that was fifty or sixty miles away from home, I didn't see him awake much except on weekends. So I spent a lot of time on my own till Tammy and her three little girls moved across the hall from us in Oakland that February of 57, right after my brother Caesar's birthday. Or maybe it was 56. Whenever it was, it was too long ago to think about.

Hearing Tammy's voice down the phone suddenly jarred me out my thoughts. 'Baby Palatine, are you still there?'

'Yeah.'

'Well, why don't you say something?' Tammy asked. I could hear her sucking away at a cigarette.

'Ain't nothing to say.' How could I tell her that I was mad 'cause Joy was supposed to be coming and I was really looking forward to the trip to Reno. It was way too soon for me to take in more than that. Pitiful as it sounds, I wasn't able to think beyond that one disappointment.

Tammy must of thought I'd lost my mind, and she wouldn't have been far wrong when I come to think that I wasn't crying or nothing and my voice didn't even crack like it do when I hold back tears.

I said, 'Listen, Sugar, you caught me 'fore I had chance to set on the toilet. Why don't you let me call you back.'

'Baby Palatine,' she asked disbelieving. 'Are you all right?'

'Yeah. Right as I can be under the circumstances. How 'bout you?'

She was the one had birthed Joy into the world and she wasn't crying neither, whereas most mothers would have been hysterical. But then

Tammy wasn't like most mothers. By her accounts feelings was things to keep to yourself, although she was known to let herself get well and truly revved up if anything happened to Anndora. But it seemed like a bus could run over Joy and Brenda, and Tammy wasn't fazed. She liked to claim it was 'cause Anndora was her youngest, but I wasn't never convinced. My baby sister Helen said from the first that she laid eyes on Tammy with them three girls that Anndora was favored 'cause she was the lightest skinned and the prettiest. But I didn't want to believe that, although as I got to know Tammy better, I grew to thinking Helen may not have been far off the mark. Crazy as she talks when she got that alcohol in her, ol' Helen can put her finger on the button about some things. A alcoholic can zoom in on the truth quick as a child 'cause they can't take in but the bare facts, and like Helen said, there's a whole lot of mothers that would have got to ignoring Brenda, homely as she was. So Tammy couldn't be chastised all that much for it.

Brenda was the eldest, and it was hard to believe looking at her big bulgy lips, eyes and forehead that she slipped out the same womb as Joy and Anndora. There was Anndora looking so beautiful – green eyed and olive skinned with that wavy auburn hair. So fine that it was easy for anybody to catch theyselves gaping at her even after they got to know her ugly ways. And Joy who wasn't just special to look at with her black almond eyes and perfect features, she had a wonderful way about her, always ready with a smile and something nice to say to somebody. That dark honey brown skin of hers just glowed, she was that bright in spirit, and when she walked in a room, frisky as a prancing puppy, strangers and everybody would want to talk to her. If Joy'd had of been born with a tail, it would have been wagging all the time, and it was more than once when she did them newspaper interviews while her and her sisters had that hit record of theirs that them writers described her as captivating. That was a perfect word for her, and I couldn't have said it better myself 'cause Joy could charm blue birds out of the cherry trees. And to see her in one of them slinky evening gowns they used to perform in . . . well couldn't nobody wear a gown like Joy Bang with her long legged self. She was queen.

'Baby! Baby Palatine! Hello! Are you still on the phone or am I just giving away money to A T & T?' Tammy's voice in my ear jolted me out of a vision of Joy in her red sequined gown. Glimmering. It was my favorite, out of all their stage outfits. 'Dammit, Baby Palatine, I know you're still there, because I can hear you wheezing.' Tammy was always making a to do about my touch of asthma. 'Now, I'll hold on while you go to the bathroom, because we have a lot to discuss.'

'Well I plan to be a few minutes,' I said, 'so I'll call you back.'

If I could of had things my way, I'd of turned back Freddie B's clock and tried to sleep off what I was wanting to believe was some kinda nightmare. 'Maybe I'm just dreaming this,' I tried to pretend, but something else kept saying, 'This is for real'.

Tammy's voice jumped in my ear again. 'My line's bound to be busy, because I have to call Brenda and Anndora somehow. So keep trying, if it is . . . Don't you want me to tell you how Joy died?'

No I didn't. So I just put the receiver back like I hadn't heard the question. That's a trick I learned off Freddie B who was still sound asleep next to me. I switched off his alarm 'cause if he didn't wake, I didn't need to tell him nothing.

Joy dead didn't make no more sense to me than if somebody'd said the sun fell out of the sky. It's no wonder I was pretending like it wasn't true.

I grabbed my upper plate from by the phone and put both feet firmly on the floor. My legs didn't feel like they was mine and I held on to the bedpost for a minute before I shuffled off to the bathroom like I do every morning first thing.

Thinking back on it, I guess I was in shock 'cause I acted like folks who been in a bad accident and ain't unconscious but might as well be, 'cause they try to keep going like didn't nothing happen. Once I seen a man act just that way after a motorcycle had hit him . . . the blood was gushing off his ear and he was laying on the ground wanting to talk about the weather.

I should of been boo-hooing hearing Joy was dead, but instead, I sat on the toilet cool as a cucumber and did my business. It wasn't till I reached for the toilet paper that I noticed my hand was shaking like somebody with St Vitus Dance.

'Joy's dead,' I heard myself say.

'Don't talk ridiculous, fool,' I answered back. 'She can't be dead. Y'all'll still be driving to Reno this Sunday night, you watch.'

I was really looking forward to spending a couple nights with her in a hotel, like in the old days when her and Brenda and Anndora was out on the road promoting the hit record they had out in 77. Bang Bang Bang they called theyselves.

I heard myself say to Joy like she was standing by me in the toilet, 'It was gonna be like better days. You and me in a nice hotel with room service and crispy, snow white sheets that I didn't iron myself. And me running you a hot bubble bath . . . Did you mess up, Joy? Your Uncle Freddie B's been laid off work two months, and we can't afford to have you go messing up on us now. So pull your socks up, child, and stop fooling 'round. Wherever you are and whatever you're doing, come on out.' I was hoping Joy was playing one of them hide and seek games that she was so good at when she was a bitty thing.

'Come on out, so we can head off to Reno,' I pleaded, while in my mind, I had a picture of her and her sisters, clear as if I was looking at a television set. They was waiting by the side of a stage in them red sequined dresses with the halter neck, and I was standing by with four face cloths. 'Cause Brenda sweated more than the others, I used to keep two on hand for her and one for Joy and Anndora who was there more for show. They sang the odd do-wops, but Brenda, singing the lead, got the sweatiest, so soon as they finished their stint, I'd hand 'em each a face cloth and rush on stage to collect up any of the big sequins that fell off while they was finger popping and dancing about. Them sequins was too hard to come by and way too expensive to just leave at every venue. So after I'd collected them up, I'd sew 'em back on 'fore the girls had to wear the dresses again. That was part of my job as their wardrobe mistress. But that was more the title their record company give me, so's the accountants knew what to put by my salary on the girls' weekly tour accounts. I did a whole lot else, including making sure Anndora and her sex-mad self turned up to the shows at all and seeing that Brenda had enough to eat when and if she wanted, though a diet wouldn't have hurt her one bit. She always was too big. Not roly-poly fat, but big like a mountain across the girth. Backside as well come to think of it.

Remembering how happy we all was back then is what got my eyes to tearing, and I was grateful when a few measly tears dribbled down my cheeks, 'cause as much as I don't hold with women crying, especially us colored 'cause we supposed to have more sense, it seemed right to show some emotions, though I wasn't making no sounds.

Sitting there on the toilet, my throat grew that tight, it nearly gagged me just to swallow. I knew a cream soda would of eased it straight away, but me and Freddie'd drunk the last of them six cans watching tag team wrestling on TV the night before.

But I dragged myself into the kitchen anyway, realizing full well as I headed down the hallway that I wasn't going to get no cream soda to drink. That was my pretend, but what my mind was actually set on was a kingsize box of Sugar Pops that I kept in a cupboard for Joy. They was left over from her last visit and even though the date on them had expired I didn't sling 'em in the trash, 'cause as long as I saw them everytime I opened the cupboard, I got the feeling Joy was coming any minute.

She didn't visit us but twice a year since she moved to New York from LA a few years back, 'cause she said Rex didn't like California. That was her excuse, but I reckoned that she used to sneak to LA and just not make it up to Frisco to see us. Not that I told her as much. She had her own life to lead and I never did want her to feel like she was obliged to come 'cause she owed me and Freddie B a visit. But still, I knew when she did turn up, she'd be expecting to find Sugar Pops like I always kept in store from when she was little and used to sit up at my table munching on 'em and reading the funny papers.

Even after she got grown and wanted to show off that she'd give up the funnies and didn't like to read nothing but the *New York Times*, she still couldn't pass up Sugar Pops with chocolate milk poured over 'em. She'd say, 'What you eat is one thing, but what you read is something else,' and I'd take that as my cue to slip the *National Enquirer* off the table 'fore she sat down, so I wouldn't have to sit through her lecturing me about reading rubbish. When the girls was touring, I didn't never get to read what I liked, 'cause if Joy caught me buying *Jet* or *Drum* in them airport lounges, she'd shoot me a look out the corner of her eye like she was the only one grown and I was a child, and I'd put them back.

While I stood there in my kitchen with my bare feet on the cold linoleum floor and tried to believe that Joy was coming like we'd planned, nothing would stop my mind from trailing back and forth over memories, and I caught myself hugging that box of Sugar Pops so tight that I'd crushed it. Both my cheeks was wet with tears, though I still wasn't crying out loud. Just sniffling like a big baby.

'Tears ain't never solved nothing,' I listened to my better self chastise 'fore I set it straight. 'Aw, shut up. You think you know everything. I can cry if I want. That child was as good as mine.'

And it was true. So much so that after Joy came along, thirty odd year back, it didn't never trouble me no more that I couldn't spawn none of my own.

But my better self was in a ornery mood and said, 'Don't shed no crocodile tears in here, and furthermore, you can throw out that old tired box of Sugar Pops 'cause neither you nor Freddie B eats that mess no way.'

I stuffed the box in the trash and headed for the living room with the sound of Tammy's voice on the phone singing in my head. Joy's dead . . . Joy's dead . . . Joy's dead . . .

With our living room drapes at the cleaners and with nothing but flimsy white nets up to the big picture window, it was shocking bright being that the window's south facing. The sun had the nerve to shine like it was gonna be a good day and it bounced off the brass planter that Joy'd sent me from Puerto Rico last Mother's Day and hit the mirror over the mantel. Usually San Francisco mornings is still dull and misty in late March, so I should of been glad it wasn't miserable and drizzling like it had been for the past week. But I was ready to be mad about anything.

All that buoyed my spirit for half a second was spotting my glasses on the teak dining table that Freddie B will insist on keeping pushed under the window that looks across to the Bay Bridge. I grabbed my ugly bifocals and shoved them on, and soon as I could see good, my head cleared up enough for me to say, 'Have you lost your mind throwing away that box of cereal when that may be all y'all got to eat 'fore you know what's hit you. You better fetch that mess out of the trash before God strikes you for being wasteful. And what if it's a mix-up and Joy ain't dead?'

That's how come I still couldn't bring myself to wake Freddie B with the news. What was the point telling him something that I didn't believe myself? And anyway, repeating tales can make them real.

I knew what not to think but not what to think, and turning to head back into the kitchen to retrieve them Sugar Pops my eyes fell on the one thing that I realized soon as I looked at it, they should of avoided. It was Joy's first grade picture taken a couple years 'fore her and her family moved to our building in Oakland from Wilmington, Delaware. It's such a cute picture. She got her hair in two braids and is smiling to beat the band with both front teeth missing, which she tried to pencil back in 'fore she gave it to me and which completely ruined the photo, but I still put it in a nice gold painted picture frame. At the time, though she wasn't but eight, it made me furious that she was childish enough to draw in her teeth, and I asked her why she did it. She could see I was in a temper and said she'd erase it, but like I said, 'Child, you can't be erasing on no picture. That's ridiculous.'

'Don't tell Mama. Please please don't tell my mama,' she all 'a sudden cried out with her eyes bucked like she was scared to death.

I hadn't never seen Joy crying, not that I'd known her more than a couple months, but she was happy natured and didn't never get into stews like children usually do. But she was sure scared that day that I'd tell Tammy.

It made me wonder whether Tammy beat on her or something, but I didn't never hear no whipping noises and didn't never see Tammy raise her hand to none of her children. Not even Anndora, who needed it 'cause she could get set on doing something and bring the house down till she got her own way. But Joy didn't never put a foot wrong at that age that I could see, so there wouldn't of been no reason to hit on her.

Anyway, that day Joy gave me her picture I made her a promise that I wouldn't never tell her mother. She made me say, 'Cross my heart to God or hope to die', 'cause she wouldn't believe me. Over the years I had to promise not to tell Tammy quite a few things. 'Don't Tell Mama ought to be your middle name,' I used to say to Joy.

Standing there in my living room looking down at that first grade picture, I said out loud, 'Miss Joy "Don't Tell Mama" Bang.'

The sound of it made me chuckle, though thinking back, I had many a sleepless night 'cause I was worried that Tammy should have been told something that Joy made me promise to keep back. Though most of the time, when she was little, them secrets was about kids' stuff. Like when her and Brenda'd been jumping up and down on their mama's bed and broke the springs.

But there was a few times I promised Joy that I wouldn't tell Tammy something that I knew I had to keep from Freddie too, 'cause although he's ready to turn a blind eye to most of what folks get up to, being a good Christian, he ain't ready to tolerate things that is well and truly wrong. Like the time Joy was s'posed to go to her eighth grade picnic, and I discovered she was hiding down the hall in Artie What's-his-name's apartment.

He was a ex-sailor that Freddie B didn't want to rent to no way, 'cause he was white. But like I told Freddie, Mr Houseman who owned the building was white, and it didn't make no sense that we'd work for white but not let 'em rent. But Freddie B is from New Orleans, same as me, and it took him a long time to trust white folk, and at that time we hadn't long been out the South.

Anyway, that morning of Joy's eighth grade picnic, I'd seen the girls off to school like usual, 'cause their mama was off to work before them, and I was setting in my place watching *The Heartline* on the TV when I smelled something burning. I got a real good nose, and no apartment house I'm managing will ever burn to the ground, 'cause when I get a whiff of something I don't wait a minute to check things. Soon as I opened my door, I knew the smell was coming from down Artie's 'cause his apartment was the onliest one down that end of the 'L' shaped hall. And like I thought, it was coming from his place, but when I knocked loud on his door , didn't nobody answer. And being as me and Freddie B was in charge of the building, I didn't have no choice but to open it with my spare key, 'cause I couldn't let the place burn down to the ground. But to my open-mouthed surprise I found Artie, bold as day, sprawled across his put-you-up in a nanky looking undershirt and puffing on a cigarette as nonchalant as if he couldn't smell nothing.

I could tell once I was inside the room that it wasn't nothing but some toast that had burned, but at least, like I said to him, he should have opened the window to let the smell out. Warm as it was that morning, he needed to let some air in anyways, which is what I was fixing to do when I marched over the other side of the room to his window.

That's how I spotted Joy's feet in her old red tennis sneakers peeking out from behind a brocade curtain in the corner of Artie's room where he kept his clothes hanging on a rail.

The shock of discovering that Joy was in there nearly give me a heart attack, and I felt a hot flush come over me so fast that I didn't know where I was and was rendered speechless with my mouth hanging wide open. But something told me to go and lay in wait outside the door instead of causing a ruckus right then and there in that white boy's room.

I couldn't hear nothing but myself breathing once I got outside his door, and I was standing there for what seemed like an hour 'fore Joy came creeping out on her tippy-toes shutting Artie's door real quiet behind her.

She had her hair in a chignon on top of her head with a red ribbon tied round it, and from the back she looked grown though she wasn't but thirteen.

I let her get ten paces away before I called out in a harsh whisper, 'Tipping ain't gon' help you none, Madam.'

Dim as it was in the hall with no window and no light on, I could still see she was so scared that she jumped a pace and looked ready to pee herself. The whites of her eyes was practically glowing, 'cause they had popped out so from fear of what I was gonna do to her, I reckon.

'What on God's name was you doing in that white boy's room?' I hissed at her like a alley cat. 'It wasn't but two hours ago I waved you off with your packed lunch and them cupcakes I baked for your picnic. So what on earth is you doing back here? And in there with Artie of all people!'

That day is the closest I ever came to hitting Joy, 'cause I was so mad she'd done something to leave me feeling like I didn't know her. Far as I knew, she hadn't taken no notice of Artie except to mention that she didn't understand why he never came to my place for the cups of coffee I offered him from time to time when we bumped into him. But standing there fussing at her in the hallway, it seemed I may just as well have been talking to a stranger though I'd known her 'bout five years by then.

She said, 'Don't get in a temper. I was just trying to help Artie.'

'Help him do what, pray tell!' I almost shouted though I was trying hard not to raise my voice.

She didn't answer right away which made me suspect she didn't have nothing reasonable to say and then she broke out crying by the time I'd escorted her 'round to our end of the passage.

'Don't tell Mama, will you?' she begged, falling down on her knees with her hands clasped together like somebody praying.

'That's supposed to mean something?' I asked her. 'Any ol' body can do that. I ain't fooled.'

'Please don't tell Mama,' she said like a four year old expecting a whipping.

'Joy, I can't keep something like this back from Tammy,' I said. But no sooner than I said it, I knew that there wasn't no way I could tell Tammy that I'd found Joy in Artie's room, 'cause Tammy had grown short of temper back in those days, and there wasn't no telling what she would of done.

'You know that Mama won't let me go to church with you anymore if you tell. And that'll be the end of choir practice and Sunday school and everything!' Joy cried.

I knew she was right, 'cause whenever Brenda did anything wrong, which was regular, the first thing Tammy would threaten was, 'That's it! Now I put my foot down. It's all that shit you're being taught in that damn backward ass church of Baby's that has you so you don't want to listen to me anymore. Well, damn the church! I'll keep you home, if you can't behave like a human being!'

I was the one that got the three girls inside a church for the first time, 'cause Tammy didn't believe in nothing and would have been happy if they didn't. My baby sister said Tammy wouldn't of let them girls of her'n go to Sunday meeting with me and Freddie at all, except Tammy was so happy to get some quiet and the apartment to herself on Sundays.

That morning of the Artie episode, I looked down at poor Joy, still pleading on her knees. 'Don't tell Mama, Baby Palatine? Please? Please? Pretty please!' She oozed them pleases out, spreading them on thick as molasses.

But I wasn't in the mood to sympathize when I asked, 'I want to know first off what you was doing up in Artie's. Don't you know it's dangerous to be in a man's apartment like that?'

Artie wasn't really a man. Wasn't but nineteen, but he was way too old for Joy to be keeping company with, no matter if it was only eleven o'clock in the morning.

'I wasn't doing anything bad,' Joy said before I made her get off her knees and go into my apartment. 'Artie's dying from cancer, so I said I'd make his breakfast this morning.' I thought I caught her crack a smile for a split second while she was wringing her hands and looking down at her feet, though I couldn't see her face all that good until I got her inside my apartment, 'cause there wasn't but one small window around our end of the hall and a couple of the light bulbs in the ceiling fixture was out that give off a decent light. She looked a mess with her red and white checked shirt half out her cotton skirt which was creased. Not nowheres near neat as I was used to seeing her.

'Stop all that crying, anyway,' I said to her pushing her away when she went to try to hug on me. 'That ain't gonna save you.'

I didn't know what to think. Joy didn't never step out of line that I knew of, and being kind hearted like she was and always ready to help folks, it didn't seem all that strange that if Artie was dying from cancer that she wouldn't have wanted to do something for him.

But the onliest problem I had believing her was that he looked strong as a ox. Artie was a big strapping blond thing from Idaho who had been a year in the navy 'fore he got discharged. 'Cause of having something wrong with his knee, he'd told Freddie B.

'Is it knee cancer?' I asked Joy. She had tears smeared across her face and with her nose running, she was a right sight.

'Maybe,' she said, and looked like she was ready to start crying again. 'He didn't say.'

I didn't know what to believe. Cancer seemed awful far fetched. It ain't like no cold you just catch in the night and I didn't know whether it was Joy lying to me or Artie lying to her. But I always thought the best of Joy, so I hated to believe she might not be telling the truth as she thought it to be.

'Now don't upset yourself. Calm down, and let me give you one of them nice chocolate cupcakes I got left over from that batch I baked for you to take to the picnic.' After she nibbled at it, slow and mournful, I gave her twenty-five cents to ride the bus back over to her junior high school. Wasn't no need of her missing the whole fun day where I was hoping she'd have a chance to make a girlfriend as she didn't seem to have one in particular like most girls her age.

'And stop worrying,' I said as she stepped out the door, after I made her wash her face. 'I won't tell.'

But no sooner than she was gone I headed straight down that hall to tell that Artie to get his duds and get out. Cancer or no cancer, I wasn't in the least bit interested and I didn't want no part of him if he was talking to them girls on the sly.

That was one of them times that I knew I had to keep the story back from my husband, 'cause he would have asked me questions that I didn't have no answers to neither then nor now. Him and me didn't have no secrets from each other till Joy come along. And it didn't feel right.

As I stood in my living room still in my nightdress that hot March 'Frisco sun was beating on me, and I looked down at Joy's snag-a-tooth picture that I was still holding in my hand, and then I wiped the glass in its frame to a high shine with the hem of my nightdress. Not that it was so needing it, 'cause I don't have no dust setting on things in my place. Never did. Never will.

Looking at Joy grinning in that picture made me so sad. She had a smile as big as a Dixie watermelon and could flash them perfect teeth of hers faster than any Marilyn Monroe. And like Freddie B who'd said it from the first he saw her, I believed Joy Bang was born to be a star. With her looks and personality, she could of had her own television show if she'd of had Brenda's voice. But then, everybody ain't born to have everything.

I thought about my poor husband laying peaceful in our bedroom and worried about how he would take hearing that something had happened to that girl that he so loved to spoil when she was a kid.

Freddie B would of give Joy the last dollar in his pocket if she'd of asked him for it, and she had in January which is exactly why we didn't have no savings to stretch over this last spell of his being laid off. Joy needed that $2700 more than we did at the time and I was glad Freddie B was quick to lend it to her with no questions asked, though it would have been nice if she'd been able to pay him back last month like she expected. But we both understood that she was still pinched herself 'cause some back-up singing she was booked for got cancelled.

I didn't like to say that it didn't make sense her borrowing from my husband when that bony faced Rex Hightower should have been seeing her over them tight periods. 'What's a boyfriend for,' I used to ask Joy, 'if he'll let you run around scrambling for your next meal and he's rich enough to buy the Golden Gate Bridge.' With her following him all 'round the globe and singing for free on his recording sessions, then claiming she couldn't charge her own boyfriend, I wasn't surprised he treated her any-which-a-way. 'Act like a dishrag and Rex will treat you like one,' I told her, but still she jumped everytime he called and that wasn't often enough from what I knew.

Smart and good looking as Joy was, who knows what she could have made of her life had she given herself half a chance to settle with one of her own kind. But she loved them white ones and I could see it right from when I had my very first talk with her. I remember that Saturday afternoon good. It was my day for cleaning the hallway and stairs of our building on Grange Street. Her and her mama and sisters hadn't long been living there, and Joy come out on the landing to watch me.

'Stand back, child,' I said to her. ' 'Cause you don't want to get none of this here dust on your dress.' As soon as I said it I was shamed of myself for sounding gruff. I didn't mean her no harm, but I didn't know her mama at all at that point, and I didn't want Mrs Tamasina Bang out fussing with me about getting her child's fancy dress dirty.

With the front door open downstairs there was enough light coming in on the landing where Joy was standing for me to see some of the fine detail on her pale yellow organdy dress which had a lacy starched smock with bits of deep yellow satin ribbon tied to it. It was that kind of party dress that all little girls wish they had at one time or another.

Joy was about eight and seemed shy, lolling there by the door of her mama's apartment, and though I'd bumped into her and her mother and sisters on the street, during their first month on Grange I hadn't had no time to take a good look at each of the children except to notice how different they was from one another. It was the youngest in her stroller that caught my eye, 'cause with them big green-grey eyes and mass of auburn curls, Anndora was a real heartbreaker. Not that Joy wasn't cute. It was just that as a toddler Anndora was perfect looking.

Anyway, seeing Joy that Saturday afternoon standing by herself on the landing, while I did the stairs, I was quick to see what a nice looking child she was. I don't have much time for children that's too forward, but she didn't even have to open her mouth for me to sense right off that she had a mild nature.

What was strange was how 'round about that time in my life I had been praying to the good Lord to send me a sweet little girl. True, I'd been praying for one of my own, but beggars can't be choosers, and I was prepared to get a child however I could. Even if it had to be one borrowed. Not that I knew right off that Joy was the one God sent.

While I peeked up at Joy on our hall landing that Saturday, Freddie B opened our apartment door to come out and saw Joy sparkling in that organdy dress. He whistled at her like them builders he worked with did at grown women passing 'em by and said, 'Hubba, hubba, ding-ding-dong!' When she hung her head blushing, I waved at Freddie to cut out making the child feel awkward. But once he gets going with the kids, it ain't no stopping him. He got a way with them anyhow, always has done which is why I felt bad back in them days that I couldn't bear him none.

Freddie B, all six foot four inches, looked like a beanpole giant towering next to little Joy.

'Wisht I had me a camera,' he said to her.

'Hi Mr Ross,' she said in a nice clear voice, as nectar sweet as some of them children I'd seen Art Linklater interviewing on his afternoon kiddie show.

'Baby Palatine,' Freddie B called down to me 'cause I was still sweeping, 'this girl looks good as Dorothy Dandridge, don't she?'

'She don't know nothing 'bout no Dorothy Dandridge, fool,' I told him.

'Yes I do,' Joy said to set me straight. 'She's a Negro movie star.'

'And quick as a whip she is too,' hooted Freddie B. 'You tell Baby just where to get off. You ain't been living in no cardboard box, tell her,' he laughed and his bottom lip drooped like the piece of snuff he had tucked in it was gonna fall out.

'Don't you let no snuff dribble on my clean floor, man,' I said to him.

But he was too busy monkey-shining for her to take any notice of what I said. Like a big kid he was back then 'fore old age got a hold of him. And me.

'You want to take a ride with me downtown so I can show you off at Capwell's Department Store?' he asked Joy. 'I bet you'd be the prettiest gal in there shopping today.'

I answered for her. 'Freddie B you know better than to be offering to take her someplace without offering them sisters of her'n. That's playing favorites, and what's her mother gonna say anyway.' He was always putting his size twelve foot in it. Right from that day forward he would forget and offer Joy what he didn't never give Brenda or Anndora.

Joy said, so polite-like, 'Thanks, Mr Ross, but I'm waiting to go to a party.'

'A party!' Freddie B yelled like he was invited. 'Is there gonna be some cake and ice cream?'

'I don't know,' said Joy bashful and hardly able to look up from her hands that she was wringing slow just to have something to do with 'em. 'It's a birthday party, so I guess . . .'

'You better not come back here without some cake for me,' he said, grinning to show off his big gold tooth before he run down the steps two at a time to get into his new Lincoln. It sat parked in our space in the lot by the side of the building.

I swatted him on his pea head as he passed me and chided, 'Stop worrying that poor child, 'cause she don't know what a fool you are. And stop by the barber shop 'fore you bring yourself home, 'cause you're needing a haircut.'

Just as he got out the door, that's when a little towhead white boy come up and got ready to put his finger on the bell like he couldn't see the door flung wide open and me bent over the bottom step with the pail and brush.

'Don't ring that,' I told him. 'What you wanting?' I was fed up with neighborhood children laying on the bell every afternoon while I watched the TV and begging money for everything from them same old tasteless brownie cookies year after year to school raffles. And not none of it did I ever need nor want.

Joy's little voice was practically singing when she piped up loud to say, 'That's Bernie and he's my best friend from class.' She was all 'a sudden rocking on both feet, she was so happy to see that knock kneeded boy. 'I'll be right down Bernie, but I have to get my present and tell my mama I'm leaving.'

She disappeared in the doorway and I gave him the once over like I would an untold number of straw headed boys that would come to that door looking for Joy over the next ten years.

Bernie's hair was near enough the color of Joy's organdy dress and though he was freckled and plain as any Tom Sawyer, you could tell by the way she got kinda giggly and giddy that she thought he was the cat's pajamas. And her not but eight.

That day, I watched her march off proud, swinging Bernie's arm to and fro as high as it would go. And I heard their small feet in their best party shoes crunching across gravel stones of the building's parking lot before they climbed into his daddy's blue De Soto. I'd be lying if I didn't say that them children made a pretty picture with him in a fresh pressed white long-sleeved shirt and bow tie. She had a white satin ribbon tied in a big bow and streaming down around her fat ponytail and both ponytail and ribbon swung back and forth with her and Bernie.

I got on with my Saturday chores and didn't think no more about little Joy that afternoon, so it surprised me when evening fell and she was ringing our apartment bell.

'You come visiting?' I asked her when I opened the door a crack to see but not be seen. Me and Freddie B was already in our bedclothes though it wasn't but six thirty, 'cause back in them days our treat on a Saturday night was to tuck up on the living room sofa and watch whatever was on the TV soon as we cleared away our supper dishes.

Joy didn't answer and looked sheepish when she handed me a wad of something wrapped in a children's party napkin. I could tell right away from the squidgy feel and sweet smell that it was fresh layered icing cake. 'What's this?' I asked her anyway, 'cause I was embarrassed that she'd brought us something. I wasn't use to getting no gifts, especially from no children.

'It's some cake from the party I've been to,' she told me. She was scared to look me in the eye when she said it.

'Lord, child, Mister Freddie B didn't mean for you to bring him back no cake. Not for real. He was just kidding you on!'

'I saved my piece for him and asked the lady to cut it in half, so there's a piece for you too. It has jellybeans on it too.'

It wasn't till Joy was grown that she owned up that she'd snitched that piece of cake, but at the time I thought she'd deprived herself for our sake and receiving it made my eyes tear up. Joy waited like she wanted to come in, standing at my door by herself like a little brown angel on a mission from heaven and what with the strong smell of sugar and vanilla coming off the paper napkin parcel in my hand and the sight of her in that yellow organdy dress in the dingy passage that I was forever sweeping, my mind drifted to Freddie B's favorite passage from the Bible that says 'Be not forgetful to entertain strangers, for thereby some have entertained angels unawares'.

I didn't ask her in that night 'cause we sure wasn't really dressed to take in company with me in pincurls readying for our service first thing Sunday, but I went down to the gadget store below us that following Monday and picked her up a little doll baby. It wasn't but a $2.98 one, but I decided that I would keep it in my place, so's in case I could coax her over for a visit, there'd be something to give her to play with.

I'd bought her a bat and ball as well but I'd broke it trying it out by the time she finally come to visit me proper, and I even had a twin cherry popsicle on hand in my freezer compartment, which I couldn't get her to take 'cause she said her mama didn't like her taking food from folks.

'But I ain't folks,' I said to her. 'I'm your buddy, and what's mine is yours.'

It didn't never matter to me that Joy wasn't my own flesh and blood. From the beginning, it brightened my spirits to have her to think about, and as Freddie B took to bringing little trinkets home for her like I did without me telling him to, I believed she was the little girl I'd prayed for and used to get him to call her our God-sent child.

It happened that about a month before Joy'd brought me and Freddie that birthday cake, I'd been to buy some new shoes in a flood warehouse sale at Hodgeson's which was the cheapest place in Oakland to get quality shoes. I ain't never been one for wasting my husband's money on clothes, but I'm partial to fancy shoes and have been since my school days in New Orleans when I had to walk a mile shoeless to the schoolhouse everyday, summer and winter. I swore then that when I got grown I'd have more shoes than the law should allow, and even though I usually like to wear a old pair of slip-slides around the house, I always got me at least half dozen nice dress shoes tucked in shoe lasts in the closet. I don't see it as waste, 'cause I can feel low spirited and put on a pair of pretty shoes that can get me smiling in no time like somebody that's got something to celebrate.

So, at Hodgeson's flood sale, when I laid eyes on a real unusual pair of royal blue lace-up high heels, I was determined that I was gonna have them, the only trouble being that they had just that one pair, size 3½. They wasn't but $5.95 which was even cheap for back then, and they had a beautiful 2½ inch splayed heel and was laced up with leather up the front from about a inch in from the toe. There wasn't no way I could get my big brogans in 'em, 'cause I been a size 8 since I was sixteen, but I bought them anyway. Luckily, it's snatch 'n' grab at them flood sales, so nobody from the sales department was around to ask me what I was doing buying them 3½ shoes for my big flat feet.

I knew Freddie B wouldn't of been proud of me spending his hard earned money on high heels too small for me or anybody I knew to wear, but I took a hankering for them that much that I bought them anyhow, and decided on the way home not to show him 'cause he'd of only had to see them come out their paisley box to be asking what I'd bought such weeny shoes for. Not that he complains about spending on clothes if he reckons I'll wear them. In fact it was me that fussed when he spent all that money on my real expensive red fox stole for our tenth wedding anniversary in '53.

Anyway, I didn't let him see them shoes and tucked the box they was in that said 'P-a-p-a-g-a-l-l-o, Made in Italy' all the way in the back of our deep clothes closet where he didn't never look. And some days, when I got fed up staring out the window at folks passing and there wasn't nothing good on the TV, I'd dig that shoebox out the closet. I felt like Grace Kelly or somebody just knowing the high heels was mine, and it didn't worry me one bit that I could only get my toes in them.

Anyway, one afternoon, about a week after Joy'd brought me and Freddie B that piece of birthday cake, I had 'em out when there was a knock at my apartment door. As wasn't nobody living in the building at the time but us and the Bangs directly across the hall, I figured it was one of them and opened the door more than a crack. I was real glad to discover it was Joy and got that excited at seeing her that I invited her in before I remembered that I had them shoes sitting out in the middle of my living room floor.

She'd come carrying the rent money for her mother and wanting a receipt, so I told her to have a seat on my sofa. Of course, being a girl after my own heart, the first thing her eyes fell on was them royal blue shoes.

'Golly, Mrs Ross, aren't they the swishiest high heels! Golly! Golly!' Joy cried out and plopped herself straight down by them on the floor, so she could oogle them up close.

I could tell from the fuss she made of the soft leather that she had a natural eye for a first class item, and it tickled me to see a little girl's eyes dance more excited that afternoon about them shoes than I was when I bought them.

'Papagallo,' she read out loud holding up the box lid. She was sure a good reader and didn't falter at that strange looking word like I did, and when I told Freddie B how good she could read it wasn't long before he was paying her twenty-five cents every Friday night to read him Psalms out the Bible. Joy's face beamed proud as she read the rest of what was on the shoebox lid. 'Made in Italy.' She looked at me. 'Made all the way in Italy where Mama says all the best shoemakes come from and they're my second favorite color after red.'

Boy, oh boy, my heart was doing a rumba to have that pretty child sitting on my living room floor grinning at them blue shoes like they was made of gold. The color of them heels actually clashed with the basic blue running through her plaid skirt and the baby blue blouse she was wearing, but I didn't mention that. Instead I said, 'They'd look good with that outfit of your'n. You want to try them on?'

'Mama says we mustn't put our feet in her new high heels, because we might break the bridge,' Joy said sounding woeful while she pulled her long, thick ponytail around to stick the end of it in her mouth.

'Don't go sticking dirty hair in your mouth,' I chastised her like I would of my own.

'Sorry,' she said right quick and her expression dipped from sunny to sad like she thought she'd done something real bad, all 'cause of what I'd said. Me. Miss Ham-Fisted.

'You don't have to say "sorry" 'cause there ain't nothing to be sorry about. I didn't mean to sound rough on you. Who am I to be telling you off. Stick that ol' hair in your mouth if'n it makes you feel better.'

But she didn't do it and shifted herself like she was fixing to get up and go.

'Well,' I said, dragging the word out and trying to think how I could stop her. 'It might be the rule over in your mama's place that you can't wear her high heels 'cause it breaks the bridge, but here in Baby

Palatine's you can try on any of my shoes that you like and even clump about in 'em.' With that I bent down to hand Joy the left Papagallo and curtsyed like I was a page giving Cinderella that glass slipper, and her face lit up like a Christmas tree.

'You'll really let me try them on, Mrs Ross?' She giggled all the while unbuckling her brown school shoes that somebody had given a good polish.

'Not only that,' I said heading for the bathroom and unhooking the big oblong mirror from off the wall 'cause we didn't have no full length one in the apartment, 'but Baby Palatine is gonna get you a mirror so's you can see yourself in 'em.' I set it at a angle against the living room wall, 'cause that's what I had to do anytime I wanted to see myself from the knees down.

Neither of us could believe how near them shoes came to fitting Joy's feet and she looked like a zillion dollars teetering around in them with her white cotton ankle socks still on. She only wobbled a bit though, she said 'cause the shoes was about a size too big.

'They belong to you now,' I told her and meant it. Though they was my newest and favoritest thing in the world, I wanted to give them to her way more than I ever wanted them myself. 'But,' I added, ' . . . and this is a big "but" . . . since your mama don't want you walking in high heels, I reckon you better leave these over here in their box at the back of my closet, and you can come over in the afternoons and wear them. But they gotta be our secret from everybody, 'cause I don't want your sisters getting jealous and Mr Freddie B don't know I got them.'

'I'm good at keeping secrets,' said Joy running her forefinger across her lips like she was sealing them up. 'I like secrets better than butter pecan ice cream.' Then she shared a couple with me no sooner than she said that. She whispered in my ear so not even the walls would hear that she was in love with Bernie Finkelstein and that she wanted to marry Alan Ladd, the movie star, she thought Bernie looked just like. I swore on the Bible that I wouldn't tell nobody.

Them secret Papagallo shoes was the first big bond me and Joy had between us, and the fact that nobody knew about 'em but us made Joy's afterschool visits seem all the more exciting to her when she would slip over and double lock my front door leaving Brenda by herself to watch the cartoons as Tammy didn't get in from work till six thirty by the time she'd also stopped off to pick Anndora up from the minder's.

Joy loved to hang over in my place playing with that $2.98 doll I'd got her and tipping around like she was grown in them royal blue high heels, licking a popsicle or sucking a toffee I'd got in for her.

After her first few visits, I went to the dime store and bought some more for her to play with, 'cause I didn't want her to get bored and that little cheap doll neither walked or talked and wasn't that much fun. Remembering how I liked jacks when I was her age, I got her some and the woman in the dime store sold me a board game she said was popular with her own daughter called Chinese checkers that had pretty colored marbles. Lots of 'em in six different colors.

But Joy's favorite turned out to be the ball and jacks. She'd sit cross-legged on my polished parquet floor and want to play game after game with me. I pretended not to notice if she cheated, and as my hand was way bigger than hers for scooping up the jacks, I had a advantage over her anyway. So I figured it was fair enough if'n she needed to cheat to win.

When I'd slip a saucer full of homemade lemon drop cookies over to Brenda, she'd hardly look up from the noisy TV set and didn't seem to mind that my God-sent child played over with me. Though Tammy'd told the kids not to take food off folks, I told Brenda, like I'd told Joy, I wasn't just folks, and if we didn't tell Tammy about the cookies, she wouldn't have nothing to get mad at no way. Both the girls seemed scared of her, but Joy more than Brenda, and it worried me.

Whereas I did a lot of mooning out the window at other women in the streets with their kids 'fore Joy and me got to be pals, I suddenly had her afterschool visits to look forward to, and like I told Freddie B who noticed how I'd perked up and kept my hair combed, I hadn't never met no child as well behaved as Joy before. 'You can be bad in here if you want,' I'd say 'cause she was almost too good and could get so quiet I'd tell her, 'Go on and bang some pots and pans if you want.' She was so like a grown woman sometimes though, telling me how good my cakes and cookies was and how much nicer I kept my place than her mother did theirs as she didn't bother to collect up Anndora's toys. And Joy had perfect manners and didn't never forget her pleases and thank yous neither.

My baby sister Helen was kind of jealous that Joy came into my life, 'cause 'fore Joy, I used to put up with Helen laying in a stupor around my apartment when it suited her. Her and my brother Caesar used to come and drink each other under the table, but I lost tolerance for their street corner shenanigans when I thought Joy was likely to pop by, 'cause I don't hold with getting drunk in front of kids. And neither Helen nor Caesar was content unless they had a bottle of whiskey or wine at their lips.

Helen tried at first to poison my mind about Joy and claimed that the child was too good to be true, and that she wouldn't trust no eight year old that was so full of compliments for everybody and didn't never put a foot wrong. She said she had a second sense that Joy wasn't all she seemed, but with drink in her, Helen's got a mean streak and it ain't wise to listen to what she says. 'There's Joy telling you how much she likes the gold tooth you got in the front, and there's you mouthing bad about the child. Now I'll tell you straight Miss Helen D'Orleans you're just jealous 'cause I got me a little girl.'

She'd stick out her tongue at me like she was five years old whenever I said something mean to her and had been doing it since she was a kid, but at twenty-seven it didn't suit her no more.

'You don't know where that woman and them kids don' come from,' slurred Helen, 'nor where they're going to. 'S'pose it's hell and back,' she said, and laughed that drunken laugh of her'n. Ever since she was little Helen knew just what to say to vexate me. She could be like a mosquito buzzing 'round my ear, driving me to distraction, and what she said got my thoughts going.

Not knowing nothing of Joy and her family before they moved to Oakland left me brimming over with questions that little Joy acted like she wasn't supposed to answer. So I figured her mother'd had warned her not to go spreading their business, though I did find out that her daddy had had nice dark brown wavy hair like Joy's and a thin mustache and was young when he died unexpected not long before they'd up and moved West from Wilmington, Delaware. But Joy would go quiet and find an excuse to slip home if I asked about her when she was little, so I stopped prying, till curiosity got the better of me during one of her afternoon visits a couple of months after she'd started coming over.

She was setting in the middle of my living room floor on her fivesies in our third straight game of jacks, when I told her to pop over to her place and bring me some of her baby pictures so I could see what she looked like growing up. I figured that wasn't nosying in with questions, but was just about looking at photos. That's when she came back with her snag-a-tooth picture and we had that to-do, 'cause she drew in her two front missing teeth with a pencil and then got terrified that I'd tell her mama.

But like I explained to Joy, it was real baby, baby pictures that I was interested in, and when she claimed her mama didn't have none, I refused to believe it. 'Can't you let me have a see, please, please pretty please,' I begged like a agitating child. 'I don't know no mother in the world that don't keep her hands on a few baby pictures.' And I didn't. Every woman I knew that had a child had some pictures to brag on when they was babies.

So the next day Joy come visiting, I asked her again for a see of some pictures while she was playing herself a game of Chinese checkers and I was ironing Freddie B's shirts.

'Don't you got just one?' I asked. 'Not just one bitty, bitty one even?' I longed to know what my God-sent looked like when she was one or two or three even. 'Who you was as a baby is important to me, Joy. And the less you tell me the more I itch to want to know 'cause pals is supposed to know everything about each other. Your mama hasn't got just one?' I said, showing her that a picture the size of my thumbnail would do me fine.

'Honest Injun,' Joy answered like I'd taught her to say instead of 'Swear to God' which is what she made me say before she'd tell me something that I wasn't suppose to know, like how much her mother paid for that pair of beige high heels she bought at Hodgeson's that I really liked.

'Honest, Baby Palatine, honest, honest, honest, honest!' she hollered banging her balled up fist on the floor. It was as close as she got to showing spunk, 'cause up to then she was as polite with me as kids are with strangers, though I'd got her to stop calling me Mrs Ross like I was some old fogy. 'I only have that first grade picture and I already gave you one,' she said emphatic and pointing to where I'd tucked it in Corinthians in Freddie B's big black Bible on the sideboard.

'It ain't like you was born during the war when didn't nobody have the time to think about taking no pictures. I bet it's that you don't want me to see 'em.' Then I took to teasing her. 'What's the matter, you was a ugly baby and you're scared I'll make fun of you?'

The minute I said that her eyes watered up like she was going to cry, and she rushed to put all the marbles and the Chinese checkers board in their box and put them back careful in the broom cupboard where I kept all her play things.

I was annoyed with myself for upsetting Joy and did my best to make it up by saying, 'I was just joshing. Any fool can see that . . .' Then I stepped away from the ironing board to do a shuffle and swing Freddie B's work shirt in front of me while I broke out singing, 'You Must have been a Beautiful Baby' that I'd heard many a time on the radio. But as toneless as my deep voice is, it's no wonder that it didn't make her smile. I wasn't good with kids in them days. Not like Freddie, 'cause I was too quick to talk to them like they was grown and say things in too harsh a way. Hadn't nobody taught me better, and funny enough, it was Joy, little as she was, who used to tell me that it was best not to say exactly what was on your mind, 'cause people like to hear compliments and not what you was really thinking. Not but eight and she already knew grown folks' tricks that I didn't know. That's what living in the city can do for kids.

Though she had beat me at jacks for the third time that afternoon before she started playing Chinese checkers, I said, 'Come on Joy, let's have another game of jacks. I don't care about no ol' baby pictures.'

But they stayed on my mind, so later that evening when her mother had give her and Brenda and Anndora their supper and let 'em go downstairs to play out in our parking lot, I settled down with Tammy for a cup of coffee and asked if she had any old family albums I could see. By then, I'd got up a regular habit of popping over to her place to keep her company after the kids' supper, 'cause she didn't know nobody else in the neighborhood and hadn't made no friends at work.

'Both my husband and I were orphans,' she said, 'so we had no families. I'm sure I told you that we'd met in the orphanage in upstate New York when we were sixteen.'

True enough she'd mentioned it when I asked her for references for renting the apartment, but at the time I didn't take no notice, 'cause when she said she had three kids I didn't figure we would end up taking her no way, 'cause the last thing I wanted was somebody's brood of bad-assed, nappy-headed children to have to scrub up behind. She had also said at the time that her husband didn't leave her nothing and got hisself killed when a crate fell on him in the shipyard warehouse where they was both working for which her and them kids didn't get but $5500 compensation from the company.

But setting there cosy in Tammy's place with a steaming cup of milky coffee in my hand, when I asked to see family photos, she walked straight over to a bureau and unlocked the top drawer and brought out a whole stack of pictures which she seemed quite happy at first to show off. And I got so excited I didn't know where to put my face.

I don't know how many umpteen baby pictures of Brenda and Anndora I skimmed over, though I ooohed and aaaahed loud at every single one thinking I'd best be polite. But nice as they were, I was really only wanting to see the ones of Joy, 'cause them other two children didn't mean so much to me like she did, 'cause Brenda was often broody and Anndora was so spoiled that it was impossible to like her, cute though she was.

When me and Tammy had sifted through nearly the whole pile, about thirty-five pictures in all, and I hadn't seen one of Joy, I lost patience and asked Tammy in a backhanded way why Joy got missed out. 'How come you got so many beautiful pictures of your eldest and your youngest?'

'Sherman. That was my late husband . . . Sherman.' Her expression clouded over and she sounded scornful when she seeped out his name that second time, like he didn't bear her no happy memories. 'He liked to think of himself as an amateur photographer and loved to use the children as his subjects. He could even do his own developing,' she added brightening up a bit. 'I would definitely have encouraged him to start up a photography business but with his depressions, I wasn't sure that he'd be able to deal with the public.'

I could see her bite her tongue for letting go of that much in front of me. It was easy to tell that Tammy didn't like to talk about him, and whereas I first thought it was 'cause she was still mourning, I began to wonder. His body hadn't long been in the ground 'fore she picked up and decided to give herself and them girls a fresh start by moving West on the advice, so she claimed, of a girl in her typing pool in Wilmington, who had an aunt in Oakland.

As Tammy handed me a shiny black and white photo, about eight by ten inches of her holding Brenda as a toddler, she said, 'Sherman was really good, wasn't he? I think so many of them look professional.'

She was right. The way he used the lights made a soft halo around both mother and child in the picture I was holding and he'd got them to sit semi-profile but still look straight at the camera. It looked like he took 'em in a studio, but Tammy said they was actually setting on the toilet seat with a gray wool blanket tacked on the wall behind them.

It was abvious the picture had been taken after the war, 'cause Tammy had her hair swept up in a smooth fat pompadour roll at the side that was fashionable in them days. And she was wearing a dark box shoulder dress that had big white cloth buttons down the front and a square scooped neckline with heavy white broderie lace trim around it that made me notice for the first time that she had a swan's neck. There wasn't a blemish to be seen on her young, wide-eyed face, and if they'd had colored calendar girls back in the forties, Tammy would for sure have been eligible.

Looking at that picture, it was easy to see where Joy and Anndora got their best features from.

Their mother had Anndora's delicate bone structure and perfectly shaped Kewpie doll lips, Joy's big slanted almond eyes and pointy nose and Brenda's only redeeming feature, skin as smooth as a baby's butt. Although Tammy wasn't ebony like Brenda and had a unusual skin tone halfway between Anndora's pale complexion and Joy's rich dark chestnut color.

In fact, anybody looking at that picture Tammy'd handed me of her and Brenda would have assumed that the sorry looking baby on Tammy's lap was somebody else's, except that Brenda did get her mother's high forehead and widow's peak. It was two shames though that on Brenda they were so oversized, they didn't flatter, so whereas Tammy's high forehead and widow's peak was a beauty feature with the way she wore her hair swept back, on Brenda the forehead was so broad and her hair was so thin and scraggly like chicken fluff, that Brenda's widow's peak looked more like a receding hairline. Which ain't too helpful on a girl.

Poor Brenda didn't never grow enough hair to sweep it back off her face so it looked neat nor could she comb it down on her forehead in a bang to make her forehead look smaller, and I would have said that it was cruel of God to birth any girl child so plain that had such a pretty mama. But to his credit, he did make up the difference with them diamond vocal cords he lavished on Brenda. Not that any of us knew it at that time or they showed in that baby picture of her with Tammy that I was meant to be admiring that evening sitting over at Tammy's.

All that my naked eye and anybody else's could of seen was a super pretty young girl half smiling and a verging on ugly baby grinning with not but four teeth in her whole mouth.

'This is sure a pretty picture of you and Brenda,' I lied a little like Joy had taught me, and handed it back to Tammy. 'And don't kid yourself,' I added to sprinkle some truth on what I'd said, 'Sherman wasn't all that clever with the camera. You got God to thank some too, 'cause you was fine as you wanted to be.' That made her happy, and while it was true of the young Tammy in the photograph, the actual one sitting by me, though good looking, had aged quite a bit, though it couldn't have been more than nine years since that picture was taken, 'cause Brenda wasn't but ten. Tammy's sweet innocent look that she had in the picture was gone and it wasn't just because of the sophisticated blond streak at the side of her temple. Pretty features ain't all that makes a woman beautiful. How she holds them counts for something too, and from the first that I met Tammy when she came to look at the furnished apartment we had advertised in the *Tribune* she always looked worried and under strain, even when from time to time she'd belt out that barroom laugh of hers if something on the television'd give her something to laugh at.

But that evening setting in her place in Oakland, I'd finished my coffee, it was getting dark and I still didn't have what I'd come for which was a baby picture of Joy.

'I can't wait for you to show me the ones Sherman took of Joy,' I said, but no sooner than them words petered out of my big mouth, Tammy's friendly air iced over and she gave me a chilly look which unnerved me about as much as I expect she wanted it to.

'Sherman never took any of Joy,' she said in that tight-lipped way folks'll try on whenever they mean not to be questioned no further. But

I was ready to bite the bullet, because why would a father take all them wonderful pictures of two of his children and not take none of the third? Seeing as Joy was born between Brenda and Anndora, it took some explaining for Joy's sake if nobody else's.

'That's a doggone disgrace,' I said daring to push the point further. I say dared 'cause not but a week before we was setting there going through them pictures, Tammy had been over my place and showed herself to have a sharp, ugly tongue when she cussed out my baby sister Helen twice in a night. I got to admit that Helen was blind falling down drunk and deserved a tongue lashing. So setting there in Tammy's living room while the sweet sounds of her three children playing below drifted through the kitchen window, I tried to laugh a bit to make out that what I was about to say to her was a joke. But I figure she could tell that I meant it.

'Didn't Sherman favor Joy?' I asked.

She didn't let me finish her daughter's name before her lip curled back like a dog about ready to bite. 'You have one big damn big hell of a nerve to say something as nasty as that,' she said. Then she yanked back the few pictures I was still holding in my hand. I'd been kneeling down on her wine rug in front of the coffee table which was piled with the photos that we'd been through and she was perched on the edge of the naughahyde grey-green sofa bed that had a tear in it, so I leapt up quick thinking that I best go home 'fore she said something that would make me do something that wasn't Christian. Like hit her. 'Cause if I want to, I can have as much temper as the next one. So forcing myself to sound friendly and polite I said, 'Freddie B will be expecting his Friday night fry-up to be on the table when he gets home from work, so I best do my duty and get to cleaning that mackerel I bought him this morning.'

Tammy didn't try to fake no pleasantries like I did that evening. Without saying so much as 'goodbye' or 'dog kiss my foot' she stalked off into her bedroom through the double doors and slammed them so hard it's a wonder the full length mirrors screwed on them didn't crack. I was stunned 'cause it wasn't like I'd said nothing all that bad about her husband, so it didn't make no sense that she got as mad as she did, but I put it down to her caring more about Sherman than I'd realized, 'cause I wouldn't of put up with no woman making no remark about

Freddie B if he was dead neither. But still, 'fore I let myself out, I went to the kitchen window and called the children in 'cause I feared their mama was in such a temper she'd forgot she'd left them out playing in the night air.

After that ding dong with Tammy, for the whole month of April, she wouldn't say nothing but a begrudging 'morning' and 'evening' to either me or Freddie B if she happened on us in the hall, and I got tired of him asking me what she could have been in such a huff about. But something told me not to tell him how I'd been trying to get a picture of Joy and had said something to Tammy about her husband not favoring Joy like he did Brenda and Anndora that got Tammy so mad.

It perplexed my poor husband to see me mope around when he'd come in from work, but what I couldn't explain was that once Tammy stopped speaking, Joy stopped slipping in to see me in the afternoons, and she wouldn't even take none of the cookies I'd baked for her if I offered it to her and Brenda in the hall after school. She'd give a meek smile and say, 'We can't take food from strangers,' like she did when we first got to be pals.

Brenda acted like she was scared to look at me when she'd say, 'Hello Mrs Ross,' hardly loud enough for me to hear and all formal after I'd got so used to all of 'em calling me Baby Palatine. Even Anndora, who I suspect was born with her nose stuck up in the air, and didn't never take notice of me anyhow, so when she didn't give me a smile, I was used to it. She didn't take to nobody outside her immediate family and her mama didn't teach her that it was rude to look through people like she didn't see them.

My baby sister Helen said not to pay it no mind at first. Then she got mad when Tammy wouldn't bother to speak to her neither. 'Evict her black ass!' Helen said one day loud enough for the entire neighborhood to hear. 'Throw 'em all in the street! You don't have to put up with that uppity mess.'

As the Bangs' apartment door was directly opposite ours, it made me feel real uncomfortable with them not being neighborly, 'cause wasn't nobody else living in the fourplex but them and us, since Mr Houseman wouldn't get the plumbing fixed in them two studio apartments up at the front. But I just prayed night and day that things would get to rights, so that I could have Joy back.

All that April, at about half past three on weekdays, I would hear Joy
and Brenda let themselves into the main door downstairs, and then
leave it to slam shut as they raced each other to our landing to unlock
the door to their place. With my ear cupped to my front door, I could
hear that they was whispering and trying to be real quiet while they got
their door open, and I knew they was scared that I'd come out and
either embarrass them by saying 'hi' or offering them something. Once,
I got the idea to leave the Papagallos in the box outside my door to
remind Joy of the good times we'd had, but common sense got the
better of me and I baked my baby sister her favorite lemon meringue
pie instead.

But that month and a bit of us not speaking must have been way
harder on Tammy than it was on me, 'cause I'm sure she'd got used to
me doing things for her children. Not just Joy neither. 'Cause me and
Freddie did try to remember them other two everytime we handed out
quarters and bought double decker ice cream cones downstairs at the
soda fountain in the drugstore that Mr Houseman's son-in-law ran
below us. And while Tammy didn't have neither the time, inclination
nor know-how to bake cakes and cookies like I did every week, her
children must have been missing them goodies I'd always had for after
dinner and weekend surprises.

Me and Freddie B was always buying the girls expensive treats on his
pay day like eskimo pies, 'cause we knew that Tammy couldn't really
afford them extras on her stenographer's salary. She couldn't earn half
as much doing office work as Freddie B did for bricklaying back in them
fifties. So we had way more money to sling around than she did, and to
top it off, we wasn't hardly paying no rent to old man Houseman in
exchange for managing his building.

Anyway, one Sunday in May, about five weeks after the photo mess
with Tammy, when me and Freddie B'd been back from our church
meeting for a couple of hours, long enough for him to fall asleep as usual
in front of the television, Tammy come banging on our door. Hysterical
she was with Anndora sniveling in her arms 'cause Anndora had cut
her hand pretty bad playing restaurant and trying to open a can of
Spam with a sharp can opener.

Tammy needed for Freddie B to rush her and the children over to
Oakland General which was way on the other side of town, but I offered

to let her leave Joy and Brenda with me which she did gladly. I was sure glad that I had on my Sunday best when they came and didn't have my hair nappy. And I could see that Joy was glad to be setting back in my place even though she wasn't saying nothing to me.

Since the emergency ward was as crowded as I warned Freddie B it would be on a Sunday afternoon with it starting to get real hot in our part of the world, they had to wait around for hours at the hospital 'fore Anndora got them three catgut stitches that the doctor said she had to have.

Expecting they would take as long, while Joy played Brenda a game of Chinese checkers that I told her to take out the broom closet, I made the two big ones their favorite snack of a thick wad of grape jelly, between slices of nice fresh soft white bread and left two covered plates full of pork roast, crackling and greens in the warm oven for Tammy and Freddie B coming in, 'cause him and me was due back to the church at five as usual. And I was determined to be there as the whole congregation was planning to turn out 'cause Sister Hall's brother Tommy was in town from New York City and was gonna sit in with the choir. He was a jazz trumpeter that showed up from time to time, to play for our church when he was working some clubs in San Fran. Them little bips and bops he added to sweeten Miss Scott's piano playing always transformed the music and inspired our choir times before when he'd come, and I didn't want to miss it.

Naturally I was also excited that I had a excuse to have to take Joy and Brenda along with me not knowing how late their mama would be held up at the hospital. I was shocked when they admitted while I was getting them into their best dresses that they hadn't never been inside no church.

'Not neither for wedding nor funeral!' I didn't bother to ask how they missed getting to church when their daddy died, 'cause it wasn't my business, but I thought that Mrs Tamasina Bang needed her backside slapped for not attending to them children's souls. And with all the hoo-ha she sometimes made about colored people being backward, there she was acting backwards herself.

Like I explained to Brenda and Joy 'fore we climbed the bus heading for the meeting, at the First Tabernacle of Saint Barnabus where me and Freddie was members and he was a deacon, the actual building wasn't nothing but a ol' grocery store that we was renting till the congregation could collect up enough to do better. But I didn't tell them that by no way of apology, 'cause I was proud of our church. And with that choir of twelve, including Sister Hall who'd done some gospel recordings, First Tabernacle didn't need my apologies nor nobody else's.

Once we was on the bus, Joy was acting back to her usual and it was nice to hear her say I looked real pretty, although pretty is one thing I ain't never really been. Not bad looking, but not much better than ordinary 'cause of my teeth being too long and my cheeks being pudgy even when I ain't carrying no extra weight which I wasn't back in them days. I was wearing my white felt hat with the black and white mesh veil and had pressed, waved and curled my hair, 'cause it didn't matter how I used to go around looking on weekdays, I didn't mess on Sundays. And still don't. I had a good figure all through them fifties and in that chartreuse suit with the short waisted bolero jacket I had on that Sunday I showed it off, I think, though the skirt kept riding up 'cause any skirt that fitted me snug around the waist like that chartreuse one did was always too tight for me round the backside and didn't want to stay down. And I knew I had to warn Joy and Brenda 'fore we got to church that a few ladies might get to fainting if the spirit hit them, but the girls wasn't to worry 'cause that was a powerful sign that the Lord was with us.

From the minute we arrived outside First Tabernacle, the girls had themselves a high time. The church was located on the corner of 7th and Front in a part of town where nobody bothered to sweep the streets and it was tucked between a tailor shop and a bakery, but since neither was open on a Sunday, if it was too hot to wait inside the church before Reverend Earl and his wife Naomi turned up, folks with little children used to congregate outside and some of us could sit on the big wooden ledge of the bakery window which had a big awning that cut out the sun that set in our direction.

Joy and Brenda was my pride wearing their organdy party frocks and out there playing tag with the other children when the pastor drove up. When I introduced her and her sister to him and his wife Joy said, like she'd rehearsed it, 'Good evening, Reverend and Mrs Earl, I'm very pleased to meet you.' All that was missing was a curtsy.

He sure worked up a lively sermon that evening and I was thankful that it brought a couple Sisters to their feet. 'Vengeance must be the Lord's' was the theme, and Joy asked me what vengeance meant while the choir was getting situated. I did the best I could to explain. 'I think it means don't try to get back at folks if they do something bad to you.' She smiled and nodded but I could tell she didn't take it in. Remembering that Joy and Brenda wouldn't know none of the songs that we'd be asked to join in on with the choir, I whispered to Joy to tell Brenda just to clap her hands.

After the choir got to singing the fourth verse of 'My Father's House has Many Rooms', and Sister what's-her-name with the dyed red hair started to sing her solo with some trumpet accompaniment by Tommy Hall, Brenda got to waving her arms and hopping from foot to foot like she got a little spirit, but soon as I saw Joy swat her with her Bible study manual, I figured Brenda wasn't doing nothing but mocking some of my congregation and I chewed her out about it soon as we got outside. Though she swore blind that the spirit had actually hit her. I got to admit she was the one that begged me to take her again and tried to tell her mama all about the choir, and Sister Hall's brother playing the trumpet and Reverend Earl's message about vengeance and how Sister Slater broke and run up to him in the middle of his sermon and tried to pull him off the pulpit 'cause the spirit got to her so.

But Tammy was too caught up telling her own story to me about what had happened in the hospital to take any notice of what Brenda had to say. And whereas I would of expected Tammy to be het up with worry about Anndora who was passed out 'sleep in her mama's lap from the day's excitement, Tammy had her mouth full to overflowing with the name of John Dagwood who she'd met in the emergency ward.

'I felt so sorry for the poor guy,' she said. 'His first day in town after driving all the way from Detroit and he had the bad luck to have a truck back into him at a stop light. He said he thought he only had a little whiplash, but being in the insurance business he thought he'd get a hospital x-ray on his back because John Dagwood said if you don't handle things in the right way you never get any compensation. And after the trouble I had getting compensation for Sherman, I know what he means. Of course, Mr Dagwood said had Sherman been white things might have been different.' I listened with one ear, 'cause I was too busy noticing how strange and quiet Joy got sitting next to her mama and stroking her baby sister's little fair arm that was tucked under Tammy's while Anndora was laying 'sleep with her perfect lips parted looking every bit like one of them baby beauties that was on the Ivory soap commercial. Joy was slowly running one finger up and down Anndora's forearm and hedging as close as she seemed to dare to sit by her mama who tensed up when Joy got near to her. Tammy acted like somebody who don't want to be touched and she was not trying to give Joy none of the hug that her Anndora was hogging all to herself.

'You want to come over here and sit on Baby Palatine's lap?' I asked Joy in the middle of Tammy saying that John Dagwood had asked for her phone number, because he didn't know many people in Oakland and thought it might be a good place to settle while he waited for a job with some national insurance firm in San Francisco.

Couldn't nobody blame Brenda when she gave up trying to tell her mother about our First Tabernacle choir and slumped over to sprawl herself in front of the TV which was blaring all the while her and Tammy had talked at cross purposes. I was glad that Joy'd sidled over to sit on my lap, but at eight she was already a bit too long limbed for cuddling which is why I figured that her mother didn't like to bother.

'Did Mr Ross like John Dagwood?' Joy asked her mama like a grown person trying hard to make conversation with somebody they ain't got nothing in common with. Nothing like when Joy and me was together and could have us a laugh about Dennis the Menace in the funny papers or what Bernie had told her in the playground at school or her pencil drawings of girls in evening gowns. She was always drawing the same looking white girls with a flip-up hair-do wearing fancy evening gowns designed different, though they had the same heart shaped bodice.

Tammy answered Joy with, 'Freddie fell asleep after the first hour's wait and I was very happy to have someone to talk to that looked decent and spoke like he had some education.' I hoped she wasn't referring to my husband being one of them who didn't look nor talk right and she could see I was taking it wrong, 'cause she was careful to add, 'Of course that emergency ward was as full of riffraff and alcoholics as you predicted it would be, Baby, and I'm glad we won't have to go back there again, because that young doctor said that any qualified MD can take out Anndora's stitches as the cut was not serious.' She lit up a cigarette and without drawing a breath she said, smiling down at Anndora, 'Can you believe that when John Dagwood asked Anndora her name, she told him and even took the chicklets he offered her. I've never seen her take to anyone like that, and I had to mention it to John Dagwood in as much as Anndora wouldn't even allow Freddie B to touch her. "You must really have a way with children, because my daughter refuses to talk to just any ol' body. She obviously likes you. You must have kids of your own," I said to him, and was surprised to hear he's not even married.'

As soon as Tammy said that, I could see the writing on the wall, 'cause while she was quick to claim that she wasn't interested in meeting none of them nice young Christian men from First Tabernacle when I offered to set up some introductions, the glisten in her eyes every time she said John Dagwood's name told the tale of a woman ripe and ready for romance.

'Sounds like you already sweet on Mr John Dagwood,' I said. No sooner than I heard myself say it, I knew I was spilling too much of what was in my mind. But Tammy was feeling gay and looking girlish, and didn't take offense, 'cause she was so relaxed setting there in a pair of black toreador pants with a grey and black striped short sleeved blouse to match. She looked like the kind of girl any stranger new to a big city like Oakland would have been happy to be bumping into his first night in town, and I told her, 'I wouldn't be surprised if that fella thought he was pretty lucky to meet the likes of you.'

She blushed and soon as she did Joy turned to me and whispered 'Mama's got a boyfriend, Mama's got a boyfriend,' in a sing songy voice but not loud enough for Tammy to hear who was off in a daydream anyway, till I reminded her that them little girls of her'n was gonna be needing something to eat 'fore they went to bed, 'cause I hadn't give 'em nothing but grape jelly sandwiches.

'Oh gosh,' Tammy yawned and sighed, 'I guess I'd better get up and take Anndora to bed.'

'I'll do it,' Joy said like she couldn't offer fast enough. 'Do you want me to put on her pajamas like she likes me to, Mama?' Ain't many children as willing to help as Joy was, but Tammy took her for granted.

'Thank you, Joy,' she said like she was talking to hired help. And Joy straight away slid off my lap to collect Anndora off her mother's.

Didn't nobody think that Anndora had been listening to what we was talking about, but soon as Joy rustled her up in her arms Anndora said she wanted to go hear the choir at my church next time Joy and Brenda went.

I didn't have a minute to be pleased, 'cause Tammy harped up, 'We won't be having anymore church visits in here. And Brenda,' she called loud enough to be heard over the *Lassie* episode that Brenda was watching like it was her life in danger up there on the screen instead of Lassie's master, Tommy, 'Brenda! Turn that doggone TV off and go take that good dress off before you ruin it. I don't know what on earth possessed you to put on something like that anyway.' Neither Joy nor Brenda was tattle-tale enough to say I was the one that picked them dresses out the closet for going to church in.

At ten years old Brenda could sulk better than any child in the world and she kicked the leg of the coffee table on purpose just to let us all know that while she was about to take off her dress like she'd been told, she wasn't happy about having to do it in the middle of *Lassie* and if a commercial hadn't come on when her mama told her to get up, I don't reckon she'd of done it no way.

Tammy still didn't get up herself to make a effort to fix nothing for them girls, so I offered to let them come over to my place for a snack. 'I'm willing to rustle up some roast pork sandwiches, if anybody's interested,' I said, and quite honestly would have emptied my fridge I was so happy just to be setting with Tammy and the children and talking like normal neighbors.

Tammy stretched. 'Oh would you, Baby? You've done so much already today, but it would be wonderful if you'd fix something for Joy and Brenda.' They was likely only to get a can of Heinz hot dogs and baked beans off her anyway, 'cause Tammy wasn't much for fooling around in the kitchen. On the one hand I could understand it, 'cause she worked all day. But on the other, there was a lot of women holding down jobs way harder than Tammy's in a office and had more kids to feed when they got in than she did, and they still managed to put a proper cooked meal on their table every night. What surprised me was that she would make the effort too, once she had that John Dagwood to fool with. But I wasn't to know that then. At the time, I lifted myself up from the hard wooden upright chair I'd been sitting on for that hour and called into the bedroom for Brenda and Joy to follow me over to my place for a bit of something to eat.

'Y'all ready to tuck into some of my chocolate cake with butter cream icing?' I called.

They come tumbling out of that bedroom lickety-split and as we walked out the front door, Tammy's phone rung.

I hadn't never heard Tammy talking on the telephone in the three months that she'd been renting that apartment and I figured that what Joy had whispered to me about 'Mama having a boyfriend' was exactly right.

'I bet that's that John Dagwood,' Joy told me as her, me and Brenda took the three steps across the hall into my place.

I was singing that night in my kitchen while I dished up two plates of supper for the girls, and was about as happy as I recalled being the morning in '45 when Freddie come back to me in New Orleans from overseas after the war. Both times my feet wasn't touching the ground, and both times Freddie B noticed.

'Happy as a sandboy, ain't ch'you, wife?' he said slapping me on my behind, and Joy blushed as she caught him doing it, 'cause she had just walked in the kitchen. 'You wasn't s'posed to see that,' he said swooping her off her feet and lifting her on his shoulders. 'Baby Palatine –' Freddie talked like Joy, who had taken off her party dress when Brenda did and was in her flannelet pajamas, wasn't there.

He practically had her head touching the ceiling 'cause she was so high up perched on my husband's shoulders – 'you reckon Dorothy Dandridge looked like Joy Bang when she was little? I bet Dorothy wasn't as pretty,' he said and reached his long arm up to tickle Joy under her armpits 'cause that's where he knew she was the most ticklish.

She got to giggling and struggling so, I feared she was gonna fall, and said, 'Y'all get out of my kitchen with that foolishness, 'cause next thing you know there'll be a accident and Tammy'll want to tan my hide.'

And the whole truth was that I didn't want to never do nothing again that could upset Tammy, 'cause I saw how easy it was for her to turn her children against me.

After that breakup we'd had, I vowed to watch my mouth, hold my tongue and never ask too many questions or say nothing that would make Tammy force Joy to stop being friends with me again. So I didn't dare breathe another word about Joy not having baby pictures, though it was still puzzling why her daddy didn't take none, and I wasn't goofy enough to mention Sherman's name, even if Tammy brought him up, 'cause she made it plain she didn't want him talked about unless she was doing the talking. And as I noticed that the kids never mentioned him, nor Wilmington, I sure wasn't gonna stick both feet in my mouth neither.

With that call that Sunday evening being from John Dagwood, just like Miss Joy suspected, Sherman didn't get mentioned much therein after no way.

Tammy was spellbound with 'John Dagwood this' and 'John Dagwood that'. If she'd of been a Catholic, I reckon she should of bowed her head everytime she said Dagwood's name, like them Catholics is suppose to when they mention Jesus Christ.

I didn't meet Dagwood right away, but Freddie'd give me a good enough description of him 'fore he ever set foot through Tammy's door, 'cause soon as Joy and Brenda'd had themselves something to eat and went home, I couldn't wait to hear Freddie B tell me all about this man that they'd met in the emergency ward.

'He seemed a nice enough fella,' Freddie said dragging every word out like he'd said something worth spending a minute over. 'I think he was from Chicago.'

'Tammy said Detroit,' I corrected him. 'And if you ain't gonna get it right, don't tell it,' I scolded Freddie B. 'Was he nice looking?'

'How'm I 'sposed to know that,' Freddie said, like a blind man.

' 'Cause you saw him, didn't you?'

'Yeah, I saw him, but then I saw a whole lot of people setting round that emergency room, and I'd be a' lyin' if I told you I knew what any of them looked like.'

I think Freddie B can be ridiculous when he's so busy minding what he claims is his own business that he don't know what's going on around him. He was that way back then when Tammy met Dagwood, and he's still that way.

But I wasn't gonna let him get away with not describing the man that Tammy had been talking to, 'cause inasmuch as she kept saying she wasn't interested in no men, it was kind of juicy to think that she'd stumbled on something at that hospital.

'Was he brown skinned,' I asked my husband who had his head stuck in the paper.

' 'Bout my color,' said Freddie B without looking up.

'I don't believe that Tammy'd have no eyes for a nigger black as you,' I said. And I didn't. She struck me as the sort that was color conscious and would have shied away from any man as deep chocolate as my husband.

'Okay then,' said Freddie just to aggravate. 'He was white. White as this here tablecloth.' Which was on the dining table where Freddie B had the funnies spread out beside the sports page.

'Freddie B! Stop fooling around, now, and pay attention,' I fussed.

'Okay.' He didn't never have the nerve to tease me too long 'cause he knew I'd get in a huff and wouldn't say nothing to him for a whole hour and he couldn't stand it. 'Okay. He was about my color. Honest, Baby, and he had him a thick mustache that looked like he'd been combing some Brylcreem on it cause it was shining.'

'Nice looking?'

'Yeah. What you women would call nice looking, but his hands felt like he ain't never done a day's work. Soft as Tammy's they was when he stood up and shook mine as we was leaving the hospital. I heard him tell Tammy that he was looking for work and I told him to come down on the site I'm working in Palo Alto, but he said he hadn't never done no building work. I believe it too with hands like a woman's. I told him all he had to know how to do was use a shovel if he didn't have no bricking trade like me, but he still wasn't interested.'

'Tall?' I didn't care as much about John Dagwood's employment details as I did about if he was good looking. Some women, and I took Tammy rightly to be one of them, only want them a handsome man, but I listened to my mama who told me never to get hooked up with no pretty niggers 'cause they wasn't nothing but trouble, and thought their asses weighed a ton. That's how come I was glad to end up with Freddie B, 'cause even when he was young, he looked like the Sad Sack with his slow lanky self. Not that he was dim-witted. Just snail slow. But give him some arithmetic and he could add sums faster than all us, including my brother Caesar who used to get As in math'matics all the time.

'That Dagwood fella wasn't tall as me,' said Freddie B, still with his head in the paper.

'Well that don't mean nothing, 'cause who is tall as you but them basketball players?'

'Wasn't tall, wasn't short,' Freddie B added.

'Thank God she ain't taking up with no short ass,' I said, 'cause that was something else my mama warned me off. 'Short ass men got a chip on they shoulder,' she used to tell me and Helen.

'If you sit patient,' said Freddie B, 'you're likely to see him for yourself, 'cause Tammy told him to come on by whenever he wanted, and with as much jawing as they did in them three hours we was hanging 'round that hospital, I don't guess he'll keep her waiting long.'

'Why didn't you tell me that! You knew that all along, and was gonna keep it back!'

Remembering back on that evening when I was setting with my husband who didn't have his bald patch on the crown and wasn't wearing spectacles yet 'cause he was still young, reminded me that I wasn't in Oakland in our old place on Grange but was standing in our apartment in San Francisco in such a trance thinking 'bout the past, I hadn't told Freddie nothing yet and was forgetting to deal with Tammy.

If something bad really had happened to Joy, it wasn't Christian of me to be feeling sorry for myself when I should have been on the phone giving her mama some comfort and telling my husband that our God-sent child was dead. It didn't matter what I thought about Tammy's brand of mothering, wasn't a woman living that wanted to bury her own child.

So I stood Joy's snag-a-tooth picture that I was still holding back on the mantelpiece and let the morning sun hit it, and picked up my pale green dogeared telephone file card that was laying by it. That card's usually in my wallet, 'cause I won't use no handbag except on Sundays which is why I never use the nice leatherbound address book that Joy give me last Christmas. I peered down at the card as I carried it to the kitchen phone, and after I took that box of Sugar Pops out the trash, I dialed the code for Richmond. Then all 'a sudden something told me to try ringing Joy's instead which is what I did.

We got one of them fancy-ass phones that chimes out a different music tone for every digit you tap. It aggravates me every time I ring out on it, but it come with the apartment, and we ain't suppose to change nothing. I tapped out 1-2-1-2 for New York City and traced my finger down my file card to Joy's number which I don't know off by heart, 'cause she changed it quite regular, and I didn't know the new one. But I lost my confidence after it rang once and put the receiver back. 'S'pose Rex picks up the phone?' the devil in me said, though I hadn't ever known it to happen during all the years Joy'd been knowing him. Spoiled as he was with secretaries and assistants and God-knows-who-all he employed to wipe his nose and his behind, he probably ain't picked up his own phone in them twenty years. All that fame and money can affect a man like two worms boring their way through a apple and leaving it rotten to the core, so ain't no place for it but the garbage heap. Which is what must of happened to Rex.

When he was young, I understood what Joy saw in him 'cause he was a nice looking boy, being half Comanche. That rudey color he had in his cheeks all the year round made them strange turquoise blue eyes of his stand out even though they was set way back in his deep eye sockets and seemed even more so cause of his high cheekbones. But as he got older, he got gaunt looking and the big dark circles 'round his eyes made him look sickly to me, though it seems that half the white women in the South would shout me down disagreeing.

There's been times when I've seen him singing on the television wearing a cowboy hat and it's been hard to tell that he's past forty. But when his gray hair is showing his age is a dead giveaway, though like Joy says, he's had some gray strands since she met him when he was twenty-five or so. But nowadays when I take a close up look with my magnifying glasses at pictures of him in the *Enquirer*, it shows that his skin is starting to sag around the jawline, and all the cowboy hats in Texas can't hide that.

In the beginning I was relieved that Joy took to somebody that was as nice to her as Rex was, 'cause he was always buying her things though not expensive and had that limo of his pick her up and drop her off anytime she was with him. But like I reminded Joy at the time, don't go falling in love with no limousine, 'cause it won't never propose to you. But when Tammy told me not to discourage Joy from going around with Rex, I knew all Tammy was seeing was them dollar signs hanging over Rex's head. 'Cause I agreed with my baby sister Helen who said wasn't no white guy with that much money gonna do nothing for Joy but fill her full of baby and run off. And to tell the truth, she'd of been lucky if he'd of done that much.

Joy should have found herself a nice colored fella and been married and driving a stationwagon full of her own children. But she was always trying to appease her mama somehow, though as far as I could see Tammy didn't try to do nothing to please Joy. Tammy didn't want daughters, she wanted stars: somebody to make her feel important, so she could act like she was a big shot herself. I could see that soon as the girls had their hit 'Chocolate Chip', and all 'a sudden she was bragging about 'my three daughters this, and my three daughters that'.

I stood looking out my kitchen window with the phone at my ear, and I was feeling both mad and numb. Looking but not seeing and listening but not hearing, and whereas the sight of folks seven stories down heading for their work usually got me raring to get into gear and start my chores, I didn't feel up to doing nothing. It seemed like there wasn't enough strength in me to tap out Tammy's phone number and I was staring blank not wanting to talk or be talked to. So when I did finally ring Tammy's, I was praying her line would be busy. But it wasn't and I got agitated to hear a man's voice saying, 'Hello. O'Mara residence.'

'Is that you Jesse?' I asked.

'Baby Palatine?' I normally liked to hear Jesse's furry Southern voice, because something about the tone reminded me of my brother Caesar's voice. Though Caesar's been dead sixteen years, I can still remember what he sounded like everytime I talk to Jesse.

'Baby Palatine?' Is that you?' Jesse asked again, 'cause I still hadn't answered.

I didn't want to talk to him and had to try to think of what to say. I can't stand for somebody I don't know good to be giving me sympathy, and I was nervous he would say something mushy about me losing Joy.

Meaning to sound spry, like wasn't nothing upsetting me, I said, 'I thought Tammy said you wasn't home?'

'A few of us retired dudes that used to go to school together have a regular rummy game on Monday nights, and if we have a few beers, I sometimes feel like I shouldn't get behind the wheel to drive home.'

Joy once told me that the only thing that irritated her about her mama's husband was that he wanted to do everything by the book and never stopped being a cop. Not even at the breakfast table, 'cause the things he wanted to talk about that he spotted in the morning papers was all cop stuff. And she said he was always going on about being law-abiding and wanting his family to be. And while Joy wasn't one to rush around breaking rules for the sake of it, she didn't pay taxes, nor parking tickets and would speed anytime she thought she could get away with it. 'Cause she didn't never do nothing that she wasn't sure she could get away with.

Jesse's voice wouldn't quit in my ear. 'I'd knocked back a few scotches and thought I should bed down on my buddy Edgar's sofa which is where I was sleeping when Tammy tracked me down, so I don't know why she made such a big deal of my not coming home like some great mystery was involved. I often don't come home or call after the rummy game, and leave the number of whoever's house I'm playing at on the kitchen table. Just like I did last night before I drove the car out of the garage.'

He could have rambled on talking about nothing for a hour, as long as I didn't have to answer. For one thing, I was relieved not to have to talk to Tammy . . . until he explained that I couldn't even if I wanted to.

'I gave Tammy a sedative and put her to bed,' he said. 'She laid there watching the news before she finally dozed off. I think she's expecting to hear a report about Joy dying, and I didn't want to tell her that I think that with the girls not having a hit in ten years, it's unlikely that anybody even remembers them. Let alone will report it on the television.' For somebody who, according to Joy, was supposed to be quiet, I was surprised Jesse didn't draw breath. 'Tammy told me that you'd be phoning and that she'd managed to tell you the shocking news. Sad. So sad, when young people die.'

Tammy's husband or not, I hadn't never set eyes on Jesse and though I didn't want to be mean and think on him as no stranger since him and Tammy'd been married over two years, I wasn't ready to think on him as family neither, and definitely didn't want him telling me the details about Joy.

So when he said, 'I can only tell you what I know myself which is not a hell of a lot,' I wanted to stop him, 'cause he didn't know Joy good enough to have real feeling for her. Though Richmond ain't far from New York City, she didn't bother to visit him and her mama but three times in as many years. What I was wanting to say didn't come out though, 'cause another lump was welling up in my throat so I couldn't speak, and while I pretended to listen to Jesse mouth on, what I was actually thinking about was that he was the only man I knew of that Tammy let into her life or her bed after John Dagwood up and left her in the middle of the first year when her and the kids lived opposite me and Freddie B in Oakland. She never said as much, but a blind man could of seen that she pined and nursed her broken heart like somebody normal would nurse a coronary thrombosis. I thought it was selfish and a waste with them children needing them a nice stepdaddy . . . somebody decent to help her give them the extras that they had to do without unless they got 'em off me and Freddie.

All these thirty years, I haven't breathed a word to nobody about the reason Dagwood disappeared or what I'd said to him to make him leave. As it was me, who didn't have no choice but to send him packing, I felt positive all along that he wasn't never coming back. But had I told Tammy as much she would of known that I had something to do with him leaving, and much as she was wishing him back, I was praying for him to stay away. And praying is stronger than wishing.

Like my mama warned me and Helen, 'A pretty nigger will run you into the ground and you won't never know what he's up to nor who he's up to it with.' That was John Dagwood. Wasn't no question that he was a real looker and wasn't only me and Tammy that had thought it neither. Even Freddie B had to own up that he was nice looking after Freddie'd seen John Dagwood in that emergency ward the time Anndora'd cut her hand. And I had me a girlfriend back then, Tondalayah Hayes her name was, who acted like she couldn't believe what a heavenly vision loomed before her eyes the first time she spotted Dagwood. And considering her line of work, Toni, as I nicknamed her for short, wasn't one for falling over backwards over no man. But I recall that's exactly what she almost did trying to sneak a peek at him from my bathroom window in Oakland after I'd told her that Tammy had taken up with somebody that even Freddie B, not one for noticing things, had said was nice looking.

While Jesse's voice was still chatting in my ear, I was remembering that conversation I'd had with Toni that took place two weeks after Anndora's Sunday visit to the emergency ward. Tondalayah had come for a Friday afternoon visit and I told her if she stood in my bathtub she could just about see Dagwood. So Tondalayah was bent over, peering out of the two inches I had opened for her to be able to see him out my bathroom window while he was shirtless down in the parking lot, busy scrubbing down the white walls of his tyres of that little two seater convertible he had that I hadn't never heard of. She said 'Nice looking, shit! That's the understatement of the year! That nigger's a black prince.'

'Doggone it, Toni,' I whispered standing behind her. 'Keep your voice down, girl.'

'Oh, you're so nervous about everything, Palatine. You give yourself the jim-jam-jimmies. The man can't hear me, and so what if he can? I haven't said anything bad.' As Tondalayah stepped out of the bathtub, I could see that she'd left black scuff marks from the rubber soles of her ankle boots, so I reached behind the tub to get a rag and the Dutch cleanser. It wasn't likely that she'd think to do it herself, 'cause she claimed she had better things on her mind, miles away from housework. What with her being a stripper, I could excuse her for it.

'He's got black pearls for eyes and white pearls for teeth.' She laughed high notes and threw her head back like she was about to go into one of them belly dances I used to see her do when we first met while I was cleaning a strip joint where she worked for a spell down Bakersfield way. Though some of them Sisters at my church used to turn their nose up at her when I'd drag her to First Tabernacle from time to time, me and Toni was real good friends.

'And who said he was dark?' She was still rampaging on about John Dagwood. 'Black as that Turkish coffee they serve me down at the Souk's Cafe,' she said and sipped at her beer glass full of red wine. What I liked about her was she could hold her liquor and knew when to stop. Not like my baby sister.

'He looks hard and supple in all the right places too,' she said moving over to check her fake chignon bun in the mirror. 'Body like a welterweight . . . Shit, Palatine, tell your husband when you see him that Miss Tondalayah Hayes said John Dagwood ain't just nice looking. No-sirreee-Bob. That nigger is fine as a motherfucking Georgia pine, and I better not get a chance to run my fingers through that good hair, 'cause I could get dangerous.'

'Aw shut up, Toni, he ain't even got no hair to speak of.' He kept it close cut so that you could practically see his scalp and it showed that his head had a perfect shape. 'And long as them red fingernails of yours is, you'd probably draw blood if you run your fingers 'cross his head anyway.'

'Dan-ang-ger-ooze,' laughed Toni and popped her fingers with each syllable, before she let out a squeal and shook like somebody had walked over her grave, and got ready to stand in the bathtub again so she could take another look out the window.

'You don't know when to stop, do you?' I said and closed it shut in case the sound of her voice carried and John Dagwood and everybody else in the neighborhood could hear her.

Tondalayah was so loud she reminded me of country folk which is one of the things I liked the most about her. Good looking as she was, she was down home. No airs. And the other thing I liked was that she was the most generous person I'd ever met in my life. Way more than Freddie B even, 'cause whereas he would give the shirt off his back to kin, Toni would give what she had to any ol' body that needed it. And not just her money neither. Like the first time she come up from Bakersfield to spend the night in my apartment and my baby sister Helen was setting on the toilet so drunk that she thought she was setting on a chair. So when Toni went in there to have a pee and couldn't get Helen to move, she run a lukewarm bath and took the trouble to get my baby sister in it. With my help, of course, but the idea was Toni's and so was the underwear and navy blue pedal pushers that she loaned Helen to put on when we finally got her out the tub. Her and Helen was both five foot three inches and narrow hipped though Helen done put on a bunch of weight since then. Tondalayah had Helen looking like somebody else by the time she got the blue eye shadow and pale orange lipstick on her. And I couldn't believe Helen was quiet as a lamb while it was going on till Toni went to put a comb through Helen's hair.

'I don't want you combing on my hair,' Helen told her, trying to pull away.

'You better shut the hell up, before I beat you to death with this comb,' said Toni which made me laugh, and made my baby sister take a swing at Toni who didn't pay Helen no mind and kept combing 'cause no sooner Helen tried to take that swipe she passed out 'sleep.

But big hearted as Toni was, she took that thing of 'what's mines is yours and what's yours is mines' to the extreme, meaning that as far as she was concerned, it included men. Not that I was scared she wanted mine, 'cause apart from a couple spinster Sisters at the church wasn't nobody rushing to get their hands on my husband back in them days. But from the ruckus Tondalayah was making about John Dagwood while she was standing there in my bathroom, I could tell that it wouldn't of taken no more than a wink of his eye to have her up in his face. And Lord knows I didn't want no argument with Tammy over

Tondalayah fooling with Dagwood 'cause hardly two weeks had passed since Tammy and me'd made up after the mess over Joy's pictures.

The Tammy-Dagwood courtship started way too fast for me, and Tammy was quick to think that the sun rose out of his behind, 'cause he had some college education and wore a clean shirt and tie every day. But I was itching to tell her that some pimps did too.

Partly what bothered me about Dagwood was that he didn't have no job and wasn't out looking for none, though he claimed he was waiting on a position at a insurance company or other. And though I heard Freddie B offer a couple times to take John Dagwood over to the building site where he was working, so Dagwood could pick up some cash for working as casual labor, the guy had the nerve to say flat out that he wasn't interested.

'Here is a list of don't dos,' little Joy told me she overheard him telling her mother. 'Don't porter, don't garbage collect, don't work in a hotel, and don't get your hands dirty.' And Joy showed me how Tammy doubled up laughing when he said it.

Dagwood . . . that was what Tammy'd called him for short instead of John. She said it sounded cute 'cause it was like Blondie's husband in the Sunday funny papers. Dagwood always carried him a dark brown pigskin briefcase, but I told Freddie B that I didn't believe that nothing was in it but a bottle of VAT 69 whiskey. That's all he would drink which seemed way too select for a man with no job, but Tammy said that he'd told her that his grand-daddy'd left him a fourplex in Detroit and he collected enough rent off that to pay for the studio apartment he was in over by the Lake District and keep that foreign sports car of his and have extra left over for living off.

I didn't take Dagwood to be the sort that would steal or ponce or be hanging out on street corners in the middle of the day, but I figured him to be that sort of drifter that's easy to come, 'specially between some woman's legs, and easier to go. But I didn't never say as much to Tammy, 'cause I could see she was crazy about him from the first time I run up on 'em setting together two evenings after Anndora'd got her hand sewed up. I know it was a Tuesday 'cause it was the night for putting garbage out. I'd peeped my head in the Bangs' front door 'cause it was left ajar like Tammy said she would leave it 'case I wanted to pop in for a chat after the kids was in bed. But I got a big shock when

I stepped quiet into her living room from her entrance hall, careful not to wake the kids, and found her with John Dagwood. He was setting with his stocking feet parked on the coffee table and Tammy was there on his lap smooching him with a couple of her sweater buttons undone so her white brassiere was showing. There was a fifth of whiskey, half finished, tucked between them and the arm of the sofa, and seemed like there wasn't no place safe for me to rest my eyes.

Tammy's little two bedroom furnished apartment didn't have nothing in it but second hand furniture that Mr Houseman had picked up at St Vincent de Paul's, and there wasn't much of it, thank goodness, 'Cause with the rooms being medium size and Tammy's brood of three with their toys and whatnot, wouldn't of been standing room in there had Mr Houseman put more furniture in the lounge in particular. Apart from the naughahyde sofabed, there was just three hardback chairs and two lamp tables that I thought should of matched the coffee table, but Tammy said she didn't mind they was different. But me and Freddie B'd slapped a couple fresh coats of cream paint on the walls not but a month 'fore Tammy'd rented it and with the overhead light off and the two wine bottle lamps on either side of the sofa that Tammy'd bought switched on, the living room didn't look bad. And that evening, with the half dozen red roses stuffed in the cutglass vase Tammy'd borrowed from me soon as she got in from work, the place looked homey, even though she'd taken down the framed pictures of Jesus that I had hanging between the two lounge windows that overlooked the side street. Feeling uncomfortable, I was ready to examine every inch of every wall as I stood there and shifted from foot to foot.

'Come on Baby Palatine. Sit and let me introduce you to Dagwood,' Tammy said, patting at the free space on her sofa like it was either the time for me to sit or her to be introducing him.

He didn't even make the effort to stand up when I reached to shake his hand, so right away I knew what kind of hometraining he had. 'Cause any man raised right knew to stand up to greet a woman, 'specially as I was obviously older than him, though I reckoned it couldn't of been more than ten years.

He flashed me a smile and I tried to smile back and said, 'How d'you do,' and got my rusty dusty out of there quick as I could, 'cause no sooner than we'd exchanged hellos, Tammy had the nerve to lay a big kiss on his cheek like I wasn't still there. If he didn't know no better, she did, and what with them kids right there in that apartment 'sleep, I thought it was a disgrace that they was carrying on so that anybody could walk in on 'em.

'I'll latch the door behind me,' I said, hinting that they should of done as I walked out. But I don't reckon that they heard me or knew that the door was open or cared, 'cause Tammy was a goner once Dagwood came on the scene.

It was two weeks after that that Tondalayah come visiting and spotted Dagwood down washing his car, and I'll give her credit that she didn't never bat her eyes at Dagwood once I'd made her swear she'd keep to herself and respect that he was Tammy property. When Tondalayah died fifteen years later from liver cancer, it nearly broke my heart, and I'll give Tammy her due, she cried near as much as me and her girls did. Including Anndora. 'Cause Toni did a lot more for them girls than Tammy ever knew about over the years, and it was Tondalayah Hayes they had to thank when time came for them to take to the stage and do things right from knowing what to wear to hip shaking.

I hated that she died with no family to mourn her. But we did the best we could, and I kept a black armband on for a whole month after she passed, I loved that woman so. Near as much as I loved Joy, but different. 'Cause Toni was like my sister and Joy was like my child which is exactly why I didn't want nobody as distant as Tammy's husband Jesse talking to me about Joy and relating either that she was dead or how it come to pass.

But how I want things to be and how they often is, are two different kettles of fish so there I was still holding onto my telephone with Jesse's husky voice dripping down the line. Richmond to San Francisco.

'Tammy told me that you'd be calling, but I must admit when the phone rang I thought it was the Sante Fe police department calling me back, because I had just left a message with a fellow I know that moved to that precinct from Chicago.'

'Why were you calling him?' I sure do hate it when my curiosity gets the best of me and I start asking questions when I want to be quiet.

'Because that's where Joy fell dead from a massive heart attack on that tennis court, and I figured he might help out with dealing with all the paper work so that we can get her body back to New York without a lot of extra cost. Actually, it wasn't in Santa Fe she died. It was Taos.'

'Where's that supposed to be,' I said, asking a question I didn't much need a answer to 'cause the 'where' wasn't half as important as the 'how' of Joy dying.

'In the mountains above Sante Fe, that's why I got on to the Santa Fe police department.'

'Now I realize that you didn't know nothing much about Joy, but I can set you straight on one thing. She had enough energy to bury Hitler's army, and I find it completely impossible to believe that she died from playing no tennis. She took good care of her body. Ate right . . . used to drive me half crazy reading them food packages before she'd eat something that wasn't fresh. Exercised. Jogged most every day since she turned thirty, so it don't make a blind bit of sense that she'd of dropped dead playing no tennis. I refuse to believe it, and if I had the money I'd be right on the plane to see what done happened for real.'

'I've spoken to the coroner himself, and I didn' get the impression that anything happened other than what he told me which is that Joy was having a tennis lesson, and in the middle of a serve she fell to the ground, in a way that made the tennis instructor first think she'd had a bad cramp. But when Joy didn' get up and seemed to have a convulsion, this girl that was teaching her called for an ambulance. But Joy was dead before it got to her. Massive coronary is the verdict, and while I can understand that both you and her mother find it unbelievable, it sounded like the truth to me. Why would the coroner have a reason to lie? Joy was nothing to him.'

Just like my mind had told me from the first I heard Jesse's voice, he wasn't the person that should of been telling me none of this, 'cause he didn't have no special feeling for Joy. I could hear that in his voice. It was Tammy I wanted to be speaking to and I asked him to get her.

'I told you Baby Palatine that she's asleep, and with that sedative that I gave her, there's no way in the world that I could get her to come to the phone now. She couldn't make any sense if she did anyway,' Jesse added.

The idea that Joy was laying somewhere dead with nobody with her made me feel sick, and I wanted to talk to Tammy to find out how Rex Hightower figured in it.

'What the hell is Tammy doing in the bed if her child is dead,' I asked Jesse. That second I got over feeling sad 'cause the thought of Tammy laying in the bed while Joy was laying in a morgue made me so mad.

All the time I knew her, Tammy'd been so concerned with how she was feeling that she didn't never let them girls of hers come first. Not even Anndora for all the fuss Tammy made about her. Tammy's girls didn't get raised. They just drug themselves up once she got to feeling sorry for herself after Dagwood left in '56 . . . maybe it was '57 . . . I ain't never been good on dates, but Freddie B probably can remember exactly, 'cause it was the same year the Yankees lost the world series and he'd bet on 'em. Whatever year it was, I did what any Christian would and didn't let them girls run wild. As Freddie B and me couldn't have none of our own, it suited me. But like my baby sister said at the time, that wasn't the point. True enough, it's the mama who's s'posed to take time to mother, but if'n it hadn't of been for me and Freddie B ain't no telling what would have happened to them. 'Cause from the time Dagwood walked out, Tammy stopped caring about everything, and her kids was the first on the list to go.

But it was real obvious me and this new husband of Tammy's didn't see eye to eye about what her duties was supposed to be, 'cause Jesse said, in answer to my question about why she was in bed, 'There's not a lot Tammy can do from here, Baby Palatine. Her sitting when she's exhausted won't bring Joy back and since Santa Fe will be shut down until nine a.m., she can't even go ahead organizing the funeral.'

Tammy was probably the last person Joy would have wanted doing that, but how could I tell him as much.

'You got Brenda's number?' I asked him, 'cause I would of rather talked to her than him, since he sounded like Tammy probably had him hoodwinked into thinking that she was suffering. She was good at that. Even I fell for it for a time after Dagwood left and Tammy took to her bed surrounded by any kind of bottle that was made – from hot water bottle to pill bottle to whiskey bottle, though I'd by lying if I said she ever became a alcoholic. But she might as well have been since she stayed in the bed for months with me waiting her hand and foot till I got fed up and stopped bringing her in food, although I kept up fixing meals for them children. Though I have to say Brenda and Joy did a lot for theyselves. And for Anndora.

'Brenda's phone's been disconnected,' Jesse said.

'Again!'

'Yes again,' he sighed. 'Her girlfriend Latrice moved to Phoenix for six months for some job training scheme with the Federal Government and Brenda'd run up a big seven hundred dollar phone bill calling her every night.'

'Seven hundred dollars!'

Joy had told me that Brenda had taken up with a new woman but I was only half listening to her when she said it, because Brenda'd been through so many women it didn't seem worth taking in the details about her latest at the time, since I'd had enough about Brenda and women from the first she let it out. In fact, if Brenda hadn't started that ruckus in the papers about being a lesbian, things might have worked out real different for Bang Bang Bang. Although I reckon it was Anndora's fault as much as Brenda's that the group split up 'cause Anndora had a tantrum and stopped speaking to Brenda when the story about Brenda hit all the papers. 'Cause they had a number one record and wasn't nobody admitting back then that they was gay, it caused a big stir. Not like these days. Everybody in San Francisco is gay seems to me when they turn out in the thousands for them gay parades. I didn't blame Brenda, when the fuss started, to take it upon herself to quit. Not that I hold with her laying up with women, 'cause as far as I'm concerned that's uncalled for. But since she was the one doing all the singing and getting none of the glory, 'cause Joy and Anndora had all of it, she said she didn't have to put up with Anndora giving her attitude.

Anndora being the youngest was used to having her way. Children born pretty as Anndora got people smiling up in their faces before they've earned it, so they start out thinking that life's a pushover.

Which brought to mind that as much as I didn't have time for Anndora, I would of rather been talking to her even than to Jesse.

'How 'bout giving me Anndora's number,' I asked him.

'Hang on, sweetheart,' he said. 'I'll see if I could put my hands on it. Tammy's probably got it in her book somewhere, though I know Anndora's like quicksilver the way she rushes from place to place. On planes and off planes more than Joy she was.'

I didn't like to hear him mention Joy in the past tense. It was like he'd buried her already.

Last I'd heard, Anndora had been living in Milan, Italy, and it wouldn't of surprised me to hear she'd shacked up with some gangster, 'cause all that ever interested her was brassy clothes and flashy cars and she didn't care how she came by them. Joy said I didn't give Anndora a chance, but then Joy was the main one who ruined her. When they was little, Joy used to dress Anndora up like a china doll and pull her up and down the streets in a red wagon so that folks would stop 'em to ooh and aaah. Joy wasn't but four years older than Anndora, but once Tammy went off the rails over John Dagwood, Joy played mother. She had sense but she was too soft, so little as Anndora was, she walked all over Joy and that didn't never change that I could see even after they got big. Kindness is one thing but you ain't 'sposed to let people treat you like a door mat.

Helen used to say that she thought part of Anndora's problem was that she looked too white and thought she was too good to be with coloreds, and it's true enough that she didn't never have no colored friends at school, not that there was many of them there to choose from, 'cause Tammy'd got her into a school out of our district and whereas Anndora should have been going to Grange Elementary two blocks away which was almost all colored, Tammy'd put her into a school over by the library, six blocks from the house where wasn't nothing but white folks and Mexicans living then, though I hear it's all colored now.

But when I'd go to collect Anndora out the school yard and she'd be standing with them little Mexican children that she was always making friends with, I couldn't hardly see no difference between her and them.

I hated to think it, but Joy seemed proud that her baby sister didn't have no color to her. Even Anndora's fingernails and toenails was thin and brittle like white folks'.

When Bang Bang Bang was touring in Europe, all heads turned when that girl sashayed down the street with them green speckly eyes of hers and that dark reddy brown hair hanging down her back in big waves and ringlets. Them folks in Europe couldn't believe it was hers and was always asking if she had on a wig and what country she come from. Anndora lapped it up, but over the years, she got to look way older than Joy. I expected as much, and was always telling Joy to be thankful she was brown, 'cause that light skin wrinkles up quick.

Jesse had come back to the phone. 'Baby Palatine, either I'm not concentrating well enough or it's actually not in Tammy's book, because I can't see Anndora's number or her address. But I know she's living in Milan, if you want me to see if I can get her telephone number from the international operator.'

'Ain't no need going to all that trouble,' I told Jesse. 'When d'you think I should phone back to speak to Tammy?'

'Give it a few hours.'

'A few! I'm setting in San Francisco at my wits' end and I got to wait around a few hours to find out what's going on?'

'I understand how you feel, but we're all helpless. Life takes an unexpected turn like this, and as much as we want and expect the world to stop, everything goes on. That's something I learned working in the police department. Life goes on.'

I didn't want no policeman's lecture, I wanted to know what had happened and why, and I wasn't gonna get no satisfaction out of Jesse, but I figured Rex might have some answers.

Jesse hadn't finished talking. 'Baby Palatine, we plan to drive to New York as soon as Tammy wakes up, because she thinks that's the best place for us to all be. She asked me to ask you to meet us there if you phoned, and I assume you have Joy's address.'

With Freddie B out of work two months I didn't hardly have the money to get across the Bay Bridge on a bus, so getting to New York was gonna take some doing, but I didn't let on to Jesse.

'Okay, I'll meet y'all there. I don't know nothing about the planes and that, but I'll get myself there.'

'I'm sure that's where the funeral's going to be held,' Jesse said, and as I was worried that he would start in talking about Joy again I hurried to get rid of him.

'You've been a big help, Jesse. Thanks. And I'm looking forward to meeting you proper. Bye, now,' I said and hung up.

Petty things can set me off, but when I got to deal with the big ones, I even surprise myself.

Dry-eyed, I opened my kitchen cupboard and took out that box of Sugar Pops and kissed it before I slung it in the trash.

I ain't claiming I was thinking completely straight though, 'cause if I had of been, the thing I always say when anybody passes would have come to my mind which is that 'the Lord giveth and the Lord taketh away', 'cause don't nobody know as good as him when your train's come to the end of the line.

But my pea brain didn't settle on no thoughts as clear as that, 'cause it do often let me down when I'm trying to think sensible, and I needed a clear head to figure out how I was gonna get to New York when the money jar I kept for rainy days was lower than I'd seen it for donkeys' years partly 'cause Freddie'd been putting his big hand in it to dole out money every Sunday for the organ fund at the church.

That's the onliest bad habit Freddie B's got which is trying to act like we can do more than he can afford to when it come to the church collection. I tell him, 'There ain't no shame to you being broke and out of work, and all you got to say to Deacon Penrose when they ask for our organ donation is, "I ain't got it. Pure and simple," 'cause he probably been out of work hisself and knows that if you could be out earning a wage packet, you would be.'

But Freddie B thinks it ain't Christian not to give when we get asked.

'Shoot,' I tell him. 'What kind of a mean so-and-so do you think God is, if he held it against a man that worked hard all his life for being a bit short on the church collection from time to time. Anyway, the organ ain't for God, it's for Deacon Penrose who claims that organ music is so important for lifting up our souls. A guitar and a tambourine would do just as well, and he knows it good as I do! Like when Brenda and Joy was singing up at First Tabernacle and all we had was that jangly ol' upright that Sister Fletcher's sister bequeathed to the church. Brenda still sang good and won them gospel contests, and wasn't nobody jumping up to the pulpit in the middle of her solos to say, "She ain't got the spirit 'cause we ain't got no organ".'

But I can talk to Freddie B sometimes till I'm blue in the face and he don't listen. So his hands been in my money jar so many Sundays that there was nothing left in it but sixty dollars. Which ain't nothing, so I tried to think on who I could call and borrow some money off and not leave them short, and the onliest person who came to mind was Sebastian Egerton.

Much as I harped on that Joy would of been better off to stay with her own kind and leave them white boys alone, I would have been more than happy if she'd of settled with Sebastian, 'cause if a man loves a woman crazy, like Sebastian did Joy, that's who you put down roots with. Don't matter what color he is. Like me turning up with Freddie B. I didn't take a mind to marry him 'cause he was either smart nor cute nor light with his lanky self. I married him 'cause he was plum loco about me and with him heading out for the war, I figured I wasn't gonna find nobody living or dead that loved me as much as Freddie B did. And thank God I did the right thing. Which is more than I can say for how wrong Joy did by shining Sebastian on. She said he was too tall and thin to be sexy.

'What's that got to do with anything,' I tried to say, but even my countrified eyes could see Sebastian didn't have nothing but a young boy's body though he must of been twenty-two at least. And though that was six years younger than what Joy was, I reminded her that Freddie's younger than me by two years but that didn't stop us from getting hitched up.

'Here comes Mister Too-Lean-to-be-Seen,' Brenda used to holler at Sebastian when he climbed on stage with them other three musicians that played back-up for Bang Bang Bang. And Sebastian would just laugh with that shy way he had and pop a toffee in his mouth and walk on over to his keyboards. I hadn't never seen nobody but my brother Caesar eat as much candy as Sebastian and have a full set of healthy looking teeth and still be the size of a rail. It gave the impression that he was way taller than six foot one inch and what with him being long limbed as well, in body he reminded me of Freddie B when we was young. But that's where the similarities stopped.

Sebastian was always pushing that flop of blond heavy hair of his back, 'cause it was always falling in his eyes, and from where his hair separated into a natural parting, I could see it was his natural color though Joy was always teasing him that he got that perfect straw color out a peroxide bottle. There's no denying Joy sure knew her blonds, and when we was all working down in LA for the first promotion tour, Joy said she preferred them tan, blond surfer boys to Sebastian 'cause they had some meat on their bones. It was a shame that she said that in front of Sebastian, 'cause even though he would laugh like he saw the joke in it, I know it probably hurt his feelings with him being so gone on Joy.

Brenda said there was two things that put Joy off him. The first being that he was too crazy about her and the second being that he didn't have nothing but the wages he made off playing for the Bang sisters. But with that said, I could see he didn't love nothing living better than a black Bechstein he got to play when we was recording in the LA studio and a silver and brass trumpet he carted everywhere like it was his only child. He'd named it Sunshine and kept the silver and brass on it gleaming better than I could.

Seeing him around them Southern California boys, Joy said you could tell right off that Sebastian was foreign. And it was true. He didn't even have to open his mouth for you to hear that English accent of his that I liked so much. Though Freddie B thought he talked like a fairy. But like I said to Freddie B to put him straight, them English soldiers that Freddie said he met when he was fighting overseas during the war must of sounded just like Sebastian, and Freddie had told me when he come home how brave he thought they was for white boys. They wasn't no sissies. And neither was David Niven that Sebastian sounded just like to me.

Sebastian had him a college education. In fact he explained to me one night when he was setting in my room waiting on Joy that he had him two college educations, 'cause he'd been picked out special from all the people at his music college to get him a degree from a university at the same time he was taking a special musician's course. I didn't get all the gist of it, and I had a hard time trying to picture him being at two different schools at the same time, but I believed him, 'cause even though he was a atheist, I could tell he wasn't no liar, and in spite of him throwing cuss words around all the time, even when he wasn't mad, you could kinda tell he was real smart and from good people. He would just cuss for the sake of it, and like other folks would say good morning, with Sebastian it was always 'F' this and 'F' that.

It put me off him at first, but Joy told me not to take no notice 'cause he didn't mean nothing by it, no more than them other musicians did. But I didn't never cotton to it. But seeing as he wasn't no child of mine, wasn't nothing much I could say to him. He was nice enough otherwise and had a gentle way about him that I liked.

Seeing Joy standing with him reminded me of the first time I saw her walk out swinging Bernie Finkelstein's arm when we was living on Grange. Her and Sebastian looked made for each other, and the few times I saw her let him put his arms 'round her, I could see that he didn't want nobody else in the world but Joy. He'd kiss her on the cheek with his lips just about grazing that rouge she wore to go with her fire engine red lipstick that was all the rage then. His lips would just barely touch her like he thought she was too delicate to kiss harder which used to make me want to laugh, 'cause delicate was one of them things Joy wasn't. And sometimes when we'd be waiting, the whole crowd of us, the girls, the musicians and the roadies, waiting to check into some hotel where we was staying on tour, I'd see Sebastian stand just close enough to Joy for their shoulders to touch, but he wasn't never bold enough to put his arms 'round her unless she put her arms 'round him first which she didn't do unless she wanted something off him.

Joy charmed Sebastian into loving her when he first started working with the girls. But I think it was 'cause she was antsy, with Rex off touring in Europe. She said she was bored and needed a diversion.

'A diversion! Sebastian Egerton ain't no road re-route. He's a man, Joy, and you can't get him all excited about you if you don't mean to do right by him, 'cause that stuff comes back on you.' And sure enough she got the same treatment from Rex Hightower.

I know Joy had Sebastian in her room all night for two nights once. But I didn't hear no sounds like they was having no sex. 'Cause with me always in the room by hers and thin as some of them walls was in them hotels and motels we stayed in while we was traveling, I could hear if she had somebody in there and was actually doing something with all that noise she liked to make. Whooping it up like a mule on the run or a hog getting murdered. A few times I got up out the bed and took a shoe to the wall. Not that I was bothered to hear her having sex since she was grown and what she did with her body was her business, but she was s'posed to be a star. Folks got to recognizing the girls in them hotels and I didn't think all that noise was dignified and didn't want nobody putting it out that Joy was fast, 'cause Anndora had that reputation and deserved it.

It was Anndora said Sebastian's dick was too small for him to be any use to her or Joy and I wanted so bad to slap her face not only for talking dirty, but for knowing in the first place what he had between his legs. I reckon she only got in the bed with him to spite Joy, and whereas Joy said after she caught 'em together that it didn't bother her one way or t'other, I felt Sebastian had a chance with Joy before that. Anndora didn't care where she put herself and I never thought I'd see the day when I met a woman that I felt took advantage of men when it come to sex. But there came Anndora to prove that it was possible.

I was there the night she dragged Sebastian to her room. They'd both been sitting with me in the bar of a hotel we was staying at one night on East Pleasant Street in Baltimore, and Anndora handed him one of her sleeping pills to pop in his mouth, 'cause he said he couldn't rest after them shows. Next thing I knew the boy was slurring his words and spilling his Wild Turkey that he always ordered wherever he went but never drank. Them pills didn't affect Anndora like they did other folks. They was supposed to be sleeping pills, but no sooner than she had one, she was wanting to lay on her back and throw her legs up in the air. It was Brenda that saw Anndora lead Sebastian off and told Joy when she come to set with us that Anndora'd took Sebastian up to her room. I know she just told it to stir things up. And that's the exact results she got, 'cause Joy went and got a key from the porter claiming she was Anndora and walked straight into Anndora's room at that ritzy hotel and caught Sebastian sleeping there in her sister's bed. Joy said she just walked in on 'em for a joke, but I knew that in her heart she was hurt, 'cause much as she said Sebastian didn't mean nothing to her, he had that thing about him that made you trust him and I don't think she ever thought that he'd be one to do no dirt like mess with her sister when he claimed he had eyes for Joy.

Sebastian tried to explain what happened and him and Joy finally had a little set to about it, 'cause I heard him say to her the next night 'fore they went out on stage, 'You're hot and cold. Interested but not interested. I don't know what the fuck you want and I don't think that you do.' She turned her back on him and he whirled her 'round to face him. 'If I wait for you after the gigs to make sure you don't get hassled,' Sebastian said, 'you're annoyed because you say I'm hovering around too much, and now just because I passed out in your sister's room, you're not speaking and moody and want to give me a hard time.' But Joy didn't never like to be disturbed before she went out on that stage, and always wanted to go on there smiling like the world was hers, so I wasn't surprised that I didn't hear her answer. She was checking herself in the mirror 'cause that's what she did last thing and she acted like he wasn't talking to her.

Sebastian and the other musicians always went on before the girls and did a couple songs to warm theyselves up and gee the audience up, and then Sebastian would yell to them other three players 'Jump for Joy',which was the title of the song he wrote that they played to bring the girls out. I used to stand by and watch 'cause didn't matter how hot it was, I enjoyed seeing them fans get excited when Bang Bang Bang hit the stage. Sebastian always had a Camel cigarette lit, perched on the edge of the electric keyboards he played, and I never knew why he bothered to light it. Maybe just to give him some honky tonk atmosphere, so he could see the smoke drift up in front of his eyes 'cause with all that dancing his fingers did 'cross them keys, there wasn't no time for him to smoke, he had that piano burning up so. When his fingers hopped around them keys like they was hot to the touch, Brenda used to laugh and come off and say, 'You had that piano smoking again white boy.'

It always surprised me that Sebastian's hands wasn't nothing special to look at. Long as the rest of his body was, his hands was smallish for a man's, and fingers maybe even on the short side.

I agreed with Joy that I didn't know what all them little white girls was screaming at everytime Sebastian stepped out on the stage, 'cause wasn't nothing manly about him but his manners and them fans wasn't to know that. He had a girl's face and looked too soft. Except for that square chin of his that had a dimple in it, wasn't much sign of man, and from off stage there was no way they could of seen them long black eyelashes he had that I always teased him I wanted to borrow when he finished with them.

There was two numbers that Sebastian got to play trumpet on and when he stepped from behind his keyboards and synthesizer that was always lined up in a 'L' shape at the far side of the band left of the drummer to walk over and take over and take centre stage with Brenda, them girls used to get theyselves in a frenzy like somebody sanctified that had caught the spirit, screaming 'Seb! Seb! *Seb*-astian' like they was calling God. I used to get to giggling till I couldn't catch my breath at them simpleton girls acting so crazy.

Brenda said it near broke her heart to hear a white boy playing trumpet as good as Sebastian could and especially with him being so English at that. She used to say she had a good ear for trumpet solos and

I believed it, since she had stayed partial to the trumpet from that time I took her and Joy to First Tabernacle and she heard Sister Hall's brother Tommy playing. Anyway, she used to grab the mike in the middle of that second trumpet solo Sebastian played and yell, 'The white boy's got soul,' and Brenda could really howl it like some preacher and get the crowd to chanting it too. And Sebastian, shy as he was, used to always flush pink and slip back behind his piano like he didn't have them wild young white girls screaming to yank his drawers off him.

Then as part of their stage routine, he would give a loud count into the next number. 'TWO – THREE – FOUR – JOY, JOY, JOY!' he'd call across to them other musicians and Brenda would start in on a real pretty slow tune, sounded like a spiritual that Sebastian said he wrote special for Brenda, but any fool knew he wrote it for Miss Joy as well. And I thought he liked to play that one after his trumpet solo to show that however many of them girls in the audience that was hollering out his name, Joy was all that was on his mind. And I believe she was all that was in his heart. Yes indeedy. Sebastian Egerton was in love with the whole of Miss Joyce Clarissa Bang. Every fart. Every bruise. Every hangnail. Every period pain. Every dark mood. And I noticed she had more than a few when we was on the road . . . he loved her for all of what she was. Not like them boys she met down them places where the girls played who was only interested in the glamorous, smiling Joy; the one they figured had some money in the bank, which wasn't nothing but a illusion 'cause that music business is a pot of gold with a hole in the bottom of it for most of them people struggling to get by in it. Though Sebastian, unbeknownst to Joy at the time, was one of them with better luck.

Joy said the love flowed so from Sebastian Egerton's eyes when he looked at her, it was like staring into full beam headlights and she had to look away to keep him from blinding her. And at them rehearsals, I'd catch him sometimes staring so hard at Joy it's wonder he didn't bore a hole into her while her and Anndora'd be practicing their back-up steps.

One time when we was setting in a hotel bar by ourselves and there was a piano, he played me a instrumental he wrote for Joy called 'Without You'. Way before it ever got recorded. Then later he showed me all the music that he wrote out for it. I couldn't believe it.

'You did this by yourself,' I asked him. It looked as much Greek to me as them pages of Hebrew I see written in the front of Freddie B's big Bible.

'Yeah,' said Sebastian holding them thirty or so music sheets like they wasn't nothing. But every line was filled in so neat with music notes and dots and dashes and I don't know what all. 'It's a concerto,' he told me, and showed how all the parts was for different instruments, violins, violas, flutes and a harp, that he believed he would one day get to play it.

'Child, you a genius! Did you let Joy see this here that you done?' I asked 'cause I thought that seeing how smart he was might warm her to him a bit more.

'No. It's no big deal. I learned to do it at college. It passes the time,' he said and sifted them all back in the big brown envelope they come out of. He wasn't one to brag about nothing and the onliest time I heard him brass his buttons was the night that he come to sit in my room and told me about his two younger sisters that he raved about and who was still living in some place in England near Birmingham. He didn't talk all that much about his folks and I didn't get the feeling he had a lot of time for his daddy who was a retired physics professor.

I loved that boy like a son by the time we'd been out on the road a few months, 'cause I noticed he always made sure I wasn't stuck nowhere by myself and got me anything that was handed out free. Course I realized part of it was to do with him knowing that I was closer to Joy than even Brenda and Anndora, and he probably figured that getting to me was a way of getting through to Joy. But for all that, the boy was special and I even respected him for leaving us when he did 'cause it showed he had heart.

It happened after our big show at the Buzz Club in Chicago. The next day we was driving fast out of south-side headed for a club we was playing in Rockford and our limo hit a dog. Joy told the driver to keep going which wasn't like her 'cause she liked animals. But she liked being on time more. Then Sebastian chimed in and said he rather be late for a gig than to hit a dog and leave it in the middle of the road.

That poor limo driver that come with the car we was renting for that day didn't know what to do when Sebastian pulled back the window separating driver from passengers and told the man to stop after Joy'd just told the man to keep going.

Only Sebastian, me and Joy was in the car, 'cause the rest of 'em had gone in another car with Danny Lagerfield who was managing the girls.

'Stop the fucking car,' Sebastian said like he wasn't in no temper but was about to be. 'I'll get out and take care of the fucking dog and you can stuff your fucking gigs, Joy. See how well they'll play tonight without me, you cold-hearted bitch, because I couldn't play anyway if I had to think about that poor fucking animal we left in the road.'

Joy was used to having her way with him, and I was kinda glad to see him putting his foot down, 'cause I thought he was right and it was the Christian thing to do, although his cussing and name calling wasn't necessary.

'Don't be ridiculous,' Joy said in that sweet way that had him wrapped 'round her finger. 'We haven't got time to stop, Seb, and as hard as we hit it, he's probably dead anyway.' Sometimes she could be as good as Tammy at making sense out of nonsense.

Sebastian wasn't listening to her. 'Stop the car,' he said again to the driver. 'I'm out of here!'

I didn't think he had it in him, 'cause he was always so easy going which I forget and mistake for weakness.

Wasn't no way in the world that we could of got through a show that night without that boy, and Joy knew it good as he did, 'cause he was band leader and apart from that, he had made a name for hisself working for Bang Bang Bang, and a lot of them girls come just to see him.

Joy didn't never let herself get mad if she didn't figure being mad was the best way 'round a situation. Otherwise, I guess she would of told him where to go then and there, 'cause I saw the thought flash through her eyes. Her lips was pursed tight like they always was when she was thinking hard, though she let common sense guide her, and I let out a sigh of relief.

'Please turn around and pick up the dog,' she said to the driver like the idea'd been hers all along. But I knew she was already steaming and scheming which is how she did if she thought somebody got the best of her. She was setting quiet in that limo planning vengeance, and I think she knew I knew it. 'Cause I knew her good.

I used to always try and tell her when she was growing up not to forget that vengeance was the Lord's. It was in Joy's right ear and out her left.

That poor cocker spaniel was still laying out there in a pool of his blood and whining though it didn't look like there was much left of it to be conscious, and Sebastian lifted it careful up in his arms like it was his sick child and he couldn't see the blood. Then when he climbed back in the car with it, he insisted on sitting up in the front with the driver so we didn't have to look at it, and made the driver circle slow round that slum till we found a kid on a bike who knew where there was a vet. Sebastian paid the boy five dollars to have the kid lead us there on his two wheeler, but all that boy was interested in was getting Joy's autograph and since we had a few records of 'Chocolate Chip' we gave the child that as well as the money.

Though Joy got to smiling and acting friendly, she was still in a heat, I could tell from her pursed lips, which meant that even if it didn't look like nothing was eating her, she was actually setting there figuring out a way to get back at Sebastian. It was pitiful to see her wanting vengeance, 'cause her mind would get set on that one track and she couldn't hardly think of nothing else. That was her only big weakness and I couldn't train her out of it from when she was a kid.

Even though Sebastian was in the right that afternoon, I could tell that Joy wasn't gonna let him get away with backing her in a corner and wasn't but a week later that she convinced Danny, the girls' manager, that Sebastian had too much to say in things and made sure she'd found a replacement before Danny fired Sebastian.

I was sure sorry to see Sebastian have to leave and he took the guitar player, little Jimmy Fraser, with him which Brenda said was to be expected as him and Jimmy was best friends and it was Sebastian that had introduced little Jimmy to Bang Bang Bang in the first place. I didn't let Joy know that I got 'em both a going away present and when I give Sebastian the ashtray I got for him, I told him that I knew good as he did why he was really getting fired. He squeezed my hand, but didn't say nothing.

No sooner they was gone, they put their own group together . . . I think it was called Margarine. No. Maybe it was called Butter, I can't remember but it was something that you could spread on bread, and whatever the name of it was they had a great big ol' hit with the song Sebastian wrote called 'Too Old to Boogey, Too Young to Die'. Couldn't hear nothing else on the radio. They put it out after Bang Bang Bang broke up over that mess about Brenda being a lesbian. And since Joy knew I liked Sebastian a whole lot she made me a tape with that song on it and the one that was on the flip side which had that instrumental on it Sebastian'd wrote for Joy, 'Without You'. It was beautiful, and I didn't dare tell her that I knew he'd wrote it for her. 'Cause whereas on the one hand she was thoughtful enough to tape it for me, Sebastian didn't never get mentioned again after he got fired. She'd erased him which wasn't easy to do seeing how big that band of his and Jimmy's got. Hit after hit they had and got way bigger than Rex Hightower ever thought to be.

Sebastian rang me a few years later when he was getting ready to go on a solo tour of Japan and asked if I would tag along with him to look after the back-up singers that he was taking. I was wanting to 'cause he was offering me a lot of money and Freddie B was out of work, but I felt that Joy would have been upset with me if I had of gone, 'cause she was used to me siding with her over everything. Including her firing Sebastian Egerton like she did. When he asked on the phone about Joy, I reckoned he wasn't over her 'cause he was so salty when I said that she was on the road with Rex. Sebastian said, 'What's she still doing wasting her time with that fucking no-talent coke head?' I took coke to mean Coca-Cola, naive as I was, and thought that Sebastian was smarting over Joy choosing Rex over him. But I should of listened. Sebastian give me different numbers I could ring if I wanted to change my mind and go out touring with him, and though I scratched them down in pencil in the back of Freddie's Bible, I didn't reckon I'd ever put them to use.

But Sebastian Egerton was the onliest person I knew of in the record business that would of cared as much as I did about how Joy got buried and I toyed with the idea of calling him to see if he could help me get to New York. Out of all them rich folk that Joy claimed she knew including 'Lord this' and the 'Earl of that' she met over in England, if any of them would mourn her passing, it was him.

And Freddie B of course who was still laying sleep and none the wiser . . .

I peered out my kitchen window again down to the San Francisco streets and wondered why everything hadn't stopped, but like Jesse had said, life goes on. And though I wanted to stick my head out that window and let out a long roar over San Francisco to raise the spirits of my mama, and brother Caesar, and Tondalayah Hayes that I had lost to death, and beg them to stand together and wait on my Joy who was coming, I didn't. I just cried.

Fifteen minutes later I had wiped so many tears away on the hem of my nightgown that it was near to sopping wet. I decided to get dressed and to pull myself together for my husband's sake.

I thought I should put on something cheerful, so I would look bright even if I didn't feel it. 'Least it would make me feel better when I caught myself passing the hall mirror. So I went and stared into the hall cupboard where I kept my good clothes and wondered what was gonna be right for me to wear to tell Freddie B that Joy was dead.

Pink ain't what I call my color, but Joy once surprised me when she said I looked my best in baby pink 'cause dark as I was, it lifted my complexion, and Freddie B sat there with a lump of snuff in his mouth agreeing with her. At the time, I didn't know they was conniving me and that what was really about to happen was that Joy was planning to buy me a pink silk trouser suit as a Easter present. It was made in France, 'cause she didn't bother with nothing made in America if she could help it, and Freddie B loved that it had a floppy long buttoned down shirt that hung over the baggy pants to hide my backside.

I pulled that suit off the hanger and took it in the bathroom to put it on, trying all the while not to let myself get to crying again 'cause it seemed like I'd lost control of them tears and they was starting and stopping when they felt like it. Like I myself didn't have a bit of say in it.

While I washed and slipped on my things, I was practicing the best way to tell Freddie B about Joy but however I put them words together they didn't come out no easier and said the same pitiful thing. Our God-sent child was dead.

First off I thought I'd say, 'Listen, Freddie B, why don't you have you something to eat 'fore I tell you something bad that's happened.' But he didn't like me beating about the bush over nothing important so I thought he'd better have the direct approach. 'Listen Freddie,' I said out loud, 'ain't no use me mincing words, 'cause Joy is dead and I might as well let you have it straight.' But that seemed too mean, so I was thinking I'd say something soothing with it, so I said, 'I can stay home and keep you company watching the wrestling on Sunday night like you like, 'cause Joy's dead and I won't be going to Reno.' But that didn't sound like I was telling him no more than that he had pork chops for dinner. Then I figured that the nicest way to tell him was by taking him a mug of coffee and setting at the end of the bed to say 'I got sorriful news Freddie B from Tammy that you ain't gonna want to hear no more than I did . . .'

But all the while I was practicing and dressing, them tears flowed so I couldn't believe I had fluid in my body for no more, and I was wiping them and blowing my nose when Freddie B popped his head 'round the bathroom door to say, 'Wife, I done told you about talking to yourself all the time. Next thing you know them men in white'll be knocking on our door to take you out of here.' He's always in a good mood from the minute he gets up and it took me off my guard him sounding so perky, which got me to boo-hooing out loud.

'Hey now, girl, I was only joshing. You keep talking to yourself if'n it makes you happy. Ain't nobody gonna come in pass me and drag you out of here,' he said trying to be nice.

He ain't one for cuddling but he come and stood by me and took my left hand in his 'fore he slipped off my spectacles and pulled some toilet paper off the roll to wipe my face.

For all that practicing I did, wouldn't nothing come out my mouth but a croaky whisper.

'Our God-sent child is on her way to heaven, Freddie B.'

'Well, if that was what was meant to be, Palatine, it's wrong for you to be crying like you mad about what God done willed. Joy'll be all right. Least off she ain't gonna get no rheumatism like I'm getting and no lumbago like you got. So calm yourself and let's give thanks that you had her for as long as you did.'

'You mean "we" 'cause she was yours too,' I said reminding him.

'Joy was everybody's,' he said steering me by my shoulders into the kitchen. 'Let me heat you some coffee.'

Freddie B believes you got to live and let live, die and let die, and whereas I was worried that he would take Joy's dying as hard as I did, seemed like as if he was expecting it. Which is just what he was like when his mama passed though it was unexpected 'fore we moved West from Louisiana. At the time, I was scared I had married somebody who didn't have no natural feelings, 'cause he didn't show none, but he told me standing by him at his mother's grave, "Cause you don't see no tears on the outside, don't mean I ain't got none flowing in.'

He ain't easy to figure, as easy as he is by nature.

'Who's taking charge of Joy's funeral?' Freddie B asked after I watched him fix two mugs of coffee and head back to the kitchen doorway where he stopped and beckoned me to follow with a jerk of his head. I trailed behind him to the living room like his old mutt.

'Tammy's s'posed to be,' I said as I set myself down opposite him at the table, 'but from the sounds of it, she done gone to bed . . . again!'

I added that again 'cause when Dagwood left her she took to her bed with nothing but a bitty temperature which she used as her excuse not to get up afterwards for months. And while I didn't expect for a minute that losing Joy would affect her near as much as losing Dagwood, I didn't know what to expect from her and was worried about what I could do with no money, if Tammy took a mind to play at being sick 'fore she got Joy buried proper.

Freddie B asked, 'You spoke to Tammy?'

Of course the half truth was yes. But all a' sudden I didn't want to tell my husband nothing but the whole truth about that and a lot of other things that I'd kept from him for years 'cause of Joy. They had piled up. And setting there at the table with him, I felt guilty about all that I had kept back. So I tried to answer his question honest as I could though I knew he wasn't gonna be happy about what I said.

'When Tammy phoned I didn't want to believe something bad could'a happened to Joy. But then, by the time I was up to hearing about it and phoned her back, Jesse picked up and I didn't want to get the story off him.'

Freddie B looked over at me blank. Like I knew he would. Not able to understand why I didn't cotton to Jesse telling me about how Joy died. And he give me a man's answer. Like I knew he would. 'Jesse ain't no stranger. He married to Tammy and treats her fair too from what we done heard off Joy.'

'Heard *from* Joy, Freddie B.' I try to correct him, but it don't do no good, and sometimes I just have to throw my hands up in the air and give up on him.

'Heard off her or heard from her . . . it amounts to the same thing which is that the man is married to Joy's mama and he got just as much right to talk about Joy dead or alive as anybody, I reckon. I betcha it'll be him that'll have to pay for the funeral come to that, 'cause Tammy ain't worked in years and don't have no money of her own.'

'If she's working or not, or if Jesse is or not ain't the point. Rex Hightower ought to be paying for Joy's funeral. And giving her eulogy as well. That's exactly why I wanted to have words with Tammy and tell her to make sure that the man does something for Joy now, 'cause she been doing for him all these years. Running after him. And waiting for him to marry her when she could of done something with her life.'

'He wasn't holding no gun at her head, now wife.'

'But Freddie B it ain't fair that that Rex with his ooh-boo-coos of money don't do nothing for Joy.'

'Well he ain't never been doing for her that I can see, so it's late to expect him to start up now. Zebras don't change stripes. A man born stingy'll die stingy.'

Sometimes there wasn't no getting sense out of Freddie B. He saw things like a man, so I decided not to say nothing else to him 'fore he made me mad about Rex. My nerves was too worn out to be disagreeing with anybody about anything. And what really had me on edge was the worry as to how I was gonna get the fare to New York which is why I was ready to fuss with my husband. He's always nearest at hand for me to pick on when I get niggly, poor man.

So I tried to think of something nice to say, something that would shift some of the money worry off of him, 'cause no doubt it come to Freddie's mind quick as it come to mine that a funeral meant money. ' 'Member that English kid I told you about? Sebastian Egerton? I'm thinking on calling him to see if he'll lend us the fare to get us to New York where Tammy told Jesse she wants us all to meet up at Joy's.'

Freddie B is funny about borrowing and though he's quick to lend, I ain't never known him borrow off nobody but his eldest brother Harold who had a chicken farm in Louisiana and did not bad and loaned us the money in '49 to get to California. So it didn't surprise me all that much when Freddie give me a funny look over the top of his spectacles like he do when he's fixing to lay into me about something. But first he stuck a pinch of snuff in his bottom lip and hawked a big spit in that aluminum can I keep for him down by the table leg, since he always takes him a wad of snuff in the morning. My baby sister's the same.

'After all these years of paying my dues on time,' Freddie B said, 'I figure I can borrow some off the union. Maybe not enough to get us both back East, but sure enough they'll lend me fare for one, 'cause this is a emergency.' That was his way of telling me that I wasn't calling no Sebastian Egerton, and slow as Freddie B is to getting things said most times, the words spill out his mouth quick when he ain't in the mood to be disagreed with.

With my husband creeping through his whole life like a snail, I used to ponder how he managed to keep up at work. But my brother Caesar once told me that Freddie B had him a fine reputation on a industrial site Freddie'd got Caesar some work at one time. Caesar said Freddie was known not for fast bricklaying but for bricking sure, so's when he did something, that foreman didn't never need somebody to follow behind to rebrick a second time.

I give my husband a long look. He sat still. N'ere muscle moved and he stared out the picture window that took up half the wall in our poky little living room. Staring west, across all them flat roofs, he reminded me of that skyscraper three blocks away that we could see hovering in the sky. Lean and narrow as he is Freddie B ain't nothing substantial to look at, but it would take a mighty earthquake to bring him down. I was sure glad to have him setting there with me and when a few tears dribbled down my cheeks before I could stop them from settling in splotches down the front of my pink silk blouse, he reached 'cross the table and put his hand over my two that was clasped in a fist on the table in front of me like my first grade teacher used to make me do. Freddie's rough palms was twice the size of mine and they covered my hands like a blanket to make me feel safe enough to weep louder than I had done all the morning, and when I got to sobbing till my shoulders rocked, he just tightened his grip. Since he ain't never been one for cuddling, I grew not to need it over the years till his way of showing care come to be enough for me. Like it was that morning with the San Francisco sun beating through the window on both of us, till he stood up to say, 'I best get myself ready to head over to my union. Won't take no time to sign for a loan. I'll be back here 'fore you can say Jackie Robinson.' He smiled and winked 'cause he ain't able to be serious about nothing for too long.

'Ain't you planning to come to New York with me? If we took the Greyhound back, I reckon we might . . .'

He stopped me before I could finish. 'Girl, will you go ahead and book you a roundtrip ticket on a jet plane, 'cause I don't want you straggling all across the country on no bus.'

'Nothing's wrong with the Greyhound,' I said sniffing back the last of them tears.

'Roundtrip, Baby, and I mean that,' he said and bent over to take another spit into that aluminum can. He don't never order me to do nothing and I kinda like it when he does.

I asked him, 'Why ain't you coming?'

''Cause I got to stay here and wait on work. S'posed to be tomorrow or Thursday that they'll be calling fellas for that building that's going up in San Leandro, and if I ain't here when they call, we'll miss out. Our God-sent child will understand, and seems to me like you got enough howling and that in you for both of us,' he laughed.

'What's gonna happen about your dinner while I'm gone?'

'You didn't never worry about that when you took off all them times before,' Freddie said. 'I can open me a can of something. I'm sixty-four years old. If I can't help myself now, when I'm gon' start.' Freddie B Ross is still lying 'bout his age. He's near seventy and just don't want to give up work. So he puts his age back and refuses to draw his pension.

Sometimes it's a worry that he don't look but fifty, fifty-five, 'cause I reckon they got him doing more on them building sites than he should be. Not that he ain't in good health, but he's working up next to them young fellas in their twenties and thirties and knowing him, he wouldn't raise a whisper to say if the load they give him to do is too heavy.

I stood up to give him a peck on the cheek. He hadn't shaved but wasn't but two little patches where hair grew on his face no way. And when I reached up to run my hands across the baldy patch I like on the crown of his head, he ducked so I couldn't reach it.

'Don't go mussing up my hair now, woman,' he said.

The joke is that he don't have none to muss. Them tight black and gray kinks sit solid as alabaster on his head and separate into teeny-weeny beads at the nape of his neck. I could remember when he was young and folks laughed at his nappy hair and pea head. 'Folks' was mostly my baby sister, and now even she come to admit that since most his hair is grayed and the dentist pulled out Freddie's gold tooth when he fixed him up with new bridge work in front, that Freddie B's starting to be kinda nice looking. Which is exactly why I suspect Miss Gonzales in 207 keeps calling like she does.

'You coming with me? Maybe you oughtn't set c'here by yourself,' he said.

'No, I best stay by the phone in case Tammy calls,' I told him, and no sooner than them words slid out my mouth, the phone went, like telepathy. It spooks me when that happens, though it does a lot.

'I'll take it in the kitchen,' I said rushing to get there 'fore the ringing stopped.

'All I got to do is get my shoes on, and I'll be out the door,' Freddie B told me.

Hurrying to pick up the phone, I stubbed my toe on the corner of one of them kitchen cupboard units and was so busy cussing myself for being careless that I was still hobbling like a cripple and mumbling when I yanked the receiver off the wall.

'Them durn cupboards, catching my foot all the time,' I was saying when a voice interrupted.

'Baby Palatine Ross?' the man's voice give me the shock of my life so that I had to pull out the stool and sit down while I said, 'Yeah? This is her.'

I didn't have to think for a second about who it was, 'cause I had picked up many a receiver back in the old days and heard Rex Hightower asking for Joy. I knew it was him before he said it.

Mr Rex Hightower hisself was sobbing down my telephone, and only for Joy's sake did I not hang up.

'Hell, Baby Palatine. I don't know if you remember me.'

How could anybody forget him with his pasty-face plastered all over every place. I never understood what the big fuss was about. Plain as the day was long with them dark circles underneath his eyes, his hair in a ponytail like a woman's, and no more tune to his voice than Freddie B got. And Freddie B's so tone deaf, they recently had to pull him aside and ask him not to sing out so during the hymns up at our church.

Rex went on trying to introduce hisself. 'I'm an old friend of Joy's.' If he had of been more of one, I thought, maybe she wouldn't of been stretched out nowhere on a slab, by herself. I told her right from the first I noticed she was too quick to jump when he called, that there wasn't no way in the world that a white boy from Oklahoma could do more than wave his dick at a colored girl. Part Comanche or not, Rex wasn't gonna marry Joy. Deep down, I felt the same way about it my baby sister Helen did, though I'll grant that for a minute there I liked the way he treated Joy. But I held my tongue and watched her hang on for him year in and year out, twenty in all from when her, Brenda and Anndora started out singing back-up on some of Rex's third hit album. That ol' jingle-jangle hillybilly stuff that reminds me of broken down barns and dusty hen yards soon as I hear it.

Rex was close on hysterical, and though it didn't sound like he was putting it on, I'd seen him do a couple cowboy movies that he cried in, so I wasn't all that sure he wasn't faking it.

'Calm yourself, now.' I tried to sound soothing but I probably sounded mad 'cause that's how I actually felt. I didn't trust Rex, and though it hurts me to hear a grown man cry, something told me maybe he wasn't crying for real. And even if he was, wasn't no more I could do for him than listen to his sobs.

He kept saying, 'Sorry.'

I told him, 'There ain't nothing to be sorry about,' but I only meant as far as his crying was concerned, 'cause on some other counts, I reckoned he had a whole lot to be sorry for, especially where stringing Joy along was concerned. But who was I to judge and chastise? I figured the good Lord could take care of that side of it.

Rex excused hisself to go blow his nose, and when he went off I could hear his voice mingling with another man's while I sat waiting on him to come back to the phone. It made me mad that I was doing just what I saw Joy do. Wait. And waste her precious time on Rex. So I was tempted to hang up, but I suspected he would have too much to tell for me not to hear him out.

Standing in my kitchen with the receiver at my ear, I could hear Freddie B rustling around by the front door in the hall 'fore he yelled 'See ya' and slam the door. I wanted him to stick his head in the kitchen so's I could tell him that Rex Hightower was on the phone, but it wouldn't have interested him all that much no way, I guess, 'cause Freddie B is happy not to mix in nobody's business but his own.

I stared out the window. The sky was that true blue color you only get in pictures, and after them rains that we'd been having I wasn't used to seeing it. With me and Freddie B being at the top of our building, up there with the birds, sometimes I feel cut off from things, like I ain't part of what was going on on the ground. And while some mornings, I didn't like feeling set apart, that morning it was right. I didn't feel part of nothing nor want to. I felt like the last decoration that somebody forgot one time and left hanging on the Christmas tree when they stuck the thing out by the trash on garbage day, 'cause whereas I had been counting the days and getting more and more excited as Joy's arrival day got nearer, suddenly I didn't have nothing to wait for nor be happy about. I wasn't ready for the bad feeling that I had come over me. I suddenly realized that my phone wouldn't never ring again with her giggling and chatting on the other end. Them phone calls that kept me a part of her world which, for a whole year almost when Bang Bang Bang was going, got to be mine. Day after day of excitement, not just 'cause of the shows and the glitter, but 'cause I was sharing it with Joy who was one of them people that walked around believing that any minute something good might happen. And she got me to feeling the same way, especially when she'd drop me a letter every once and a while with a hundred dollar bill in it, when she didn't owe me one and I wasn't waiting on it. She gave me that feeling that pennies did truly drop from Heaven, and I liked to think that was what Rex did for her.

Ever so often when she wasn't expecting it when they was younger, he'd ring her to say 'There's a plane ticket for you at my office,' and she'd be off in his world of limos and parties with folks she thought was important. But the sad part of it was she believed they was better than she was. 'Cause they was white. Like that was supposed to mean something. It did to her I guess. Joy wanted to be white. From when she was small, I suspect, Joy harbored a suspicion that it was better, easier to be white and when she got older and would sit at the back stage mirror painting on mounds of fire engine red lipstick and lining her eyes with black kohl, she'd sneak a glance at Anndora, and I could see that envy sidle up on her like a black widow spider. Joy'd glance back at the mirror and pinch her nostrils tight to make her nose thinner. As it was thin as a post already, them nostrils would of had to stay stuck together to get her nose as narrow as she wanted it to be. And she'd smooth her hair back till there wasn't a crease to be found in it as it slid back slick across her scalp. Partly she claimed it was fashion she was after, but I reckoned that it was looking colored that she was wishing to leave behind. Since she ain't on her own in that judging from them white looking brown-skin gals they pick to be in the high fashion magazines, there wasn't much to hold Joy guilty for. But I knew she hankered to be something she wasn't.

Tondalayah noticed it too. And one time when she was watching Joy put on her makeup to go out with Rex one night, Toni noticed how Joy painted on her lipstick to make her lips look thinner than they was and then pinch her nose. 'You can pinch that nose all you want, Miss Thing,' Tondalayah laughed at her, 'but you never pinch all the nigger out of it nor you. It bounces back like a boomerang and you better thank God for it.'

'Leave the child alone,' I told Toni to shut her up 'cause I could see Joy was annoyed. 'Don't you never get tired of postulating.'

'What's postulating?' Tondalayah asked me.

'You know, playing like what you got to say is the be all and end all of everything.'

'That's called postulating? Says who?'

'Tammy.' I wasn't lying neither. Tammy used to use big words and if I didn't know what they meant, she'd explain 'em and then keep testing me on them till I could use 'em right. But they was way easier to use than to explain, so Tondalayah used to get mad at me if I put her straight with one of them Tammy words 'cause I could feel what they meant better than I could explain them.

It was the sound of Rex's voice back on the phone reminded me that Joy being dead was fact and that I was gonna have to hold myself together while he weeped.

'Sorry, sorry,' he said, determined to wear that word out. Seemed like I'd been hanging on the phone five minutes and he still hadn't said no more to me than who he was.

'Baby Palatine, I'm sorry to say that I'm calling you about Joy. She's had an accident.'

Didn't Jesse say she'd had a heart attack? 'What kinda accident?' It seemed fishy that what one was calling a heart attack another was calling a accident.

'Well not exactly an accident,' he said, slipping and tripping over every word like he couldn't get a grip on what he had to say which made me more suspicious.

It was strain enough to have to talk to Rex at all and it was made worse with him not able to finish a whole sentence.

'Well maybe I shouldn't be the one to tell you,' he said. 'But I know that Joy would have wanted you to know and she always used to say, "If anything happens to me, make sure you contact Baby P." I wasn't sure if anybody else would bother to get in touch with you. Ma'am are you sitting down?'

Why was everybody wanting me to be sitting down. First Tammy. Now him. And neither me sitting nor standing would make a blind bit of difference to the facts. I couldn't listen to him wrestling with the words no more, so I cut him short.

'Her Mama already called me, Rex,' I said. 'But I 'preciate you taking trouble to ring.'

'Oh.' He let out a big sigh. 'Okay,' he said. 'Well it's good that you already know. I'm so shocked. I can't get over it. Who would have thought it? . . . Joy. But I just want you to know that if you need anything, anything at all to get things organized, just pick up the phone. Don't hesitate.'

He didn't do hardly nothing for Joy and now he had the nerve to be trying to talk like somebody generous. Asking *me* if I needed something. I wanted to know why he didn't never ask her that? It made me so mad that I all a' sudden felt like I didn't want nothing from him. Not for her funeral. Not for her family. Not for nothing. Twice she'd got in trouble and had to come to Freddie B and me. I couldn't understand how it was that she had him and all them high faluting friends and had to come to us for $1000 loan last year and then that $2700 in January which wasn't but a crumb to him.

'Thanks all the same, but my husband don't let me want for nothing.' I hoped I was shaming Rex by saying that but seems like folks like him don't have no shame.

'Well I'd like to help if I can.' His voice made me want to scream and rail. What was this white man doing on my phone playing the big shot with a heart when I knew he didn't have one. I tried not to sound mad. 'Thanks all the same, but I don't need your help.'

I'd of seen myself crawl on my hands and knees to New York City 'fore I took a dime off a him. I wanted to say something nasty like 'I don't want your money, 'cause ain't no telling where it's been.' What I really needed was for Helen to have been standing by me. She'd of been quick to know what to say, but I can't never think of nothing snide till it's too late sometimes.

'Joy's mother is dealing with the funeral arrangements, so why don't I give you her number so you can talk to her direct.' I knew he must of had Tammy's number if he had mine. She couldn't stand him after she realized he was just stringing Joy along and she told him exactly what she thought about him more than once though it made Joy mad. Who could blame Tammy? She knew as well as I did that Joy could have had somebody nice if she hadn't been waiting around for his long faced, skinny assed self.

I thought about the time Joy was thinking to go back to college to try to become a teacher after the mess with Brenda telling the paper she was a lesbian had spoiled Bang Bang Bang's chances. I was so glad that she seemed ready to settle down and I got Freddie B to tell her hisself that we'd pay her tuition and books, 'cause she hadn't been able to save nothing while she was on the road with her sisters.

Joy was smart and always got her As all through school and I figured that group or no group, she had all the stuff to make something of herself. But no sooner than she'd applied to Frisco State and got herself a place, along come Rex sticking his two cents in.

So he told Joy to come by the apartment to tell me she wasn't gonna be needing to borrow money for books. Like I was supposed to be excited.

'You got to learn to get your priorities straight,' I told her, ' 'cause Rex ought to be encouraging you to get yourself a vocation.'

'But he said teaching is just going to be a drudge and I won't have time for him. And I can earn a fortune doing back-up work once it starts coming in regularly. Don't you see!' She was bubbling and had the nerve to think I was gonna.

'No I don't,' I told her.

'Think big,' she said and tried to tickle me 'cause she could see I was upset with her. 'Think white!' she said, laughing. She was always telling me that white folks had a brighter outlook on things. 'More hopeful. More adventurous,' she'd say.

'But you ain't white and won't never be, Joy. And when all them rich white friends you done made while you had that hit, fall by the way side, you won't be left with nothing but the want ad column of that *New York Times*. And all you'll be ready for is domestic work. Cleaning their houses. When you could be somebody. Get your priorities right.'

My baby sister was setting there in my apartment that morning and I didn't think she was listening to me and Joy 'cause she'd already had a few nips at the bottle of Thunderbird wine she hadn't taken out of the brown paper bag it'd come from the liquor store in. But she said to Joy, 'Don't let no white boy be messing with your priorities, girl. 'Cause priorities is like shoes. *You* the one's got to wear 'em and if they don't fit, don't nobody suffer with 'em pinching and ruining your feet for life but you.' Though I knew what she was trying to say, Joy wasn't the one to tell nothing in no down homey way like Helen liked to talk, so I told my sister, 'Stop talking through your wine, Helen, and go lay yourself down somewhere,' and like a tired hound she sauntered round the living room a couple times 'fore she found her a spot on a dark brown sofa I had at the time and curled up and fell asleep. Much as Joy liked Helen, she wouldn't of listened no more to what Helen had to say than she did to me. Unless it was what Joy wanted to hear. It wasn't often that I tried to sway her, 'cause I knew it didn't do no good, and I knew there wasn't no way that Joy would of listened to me over Rex, so I saved my breath, and let her give her tuition money back to Freddie B like she'd come to do.

But it was like Freddie B had said to me 'fore he went to his union to borrow that plane money for my trip to New York, Rex didn't hold no gun at her head. Not that I could see anyway. And it bothered me why she gave up so much to be with somebody who didn't want to do right by her. And still he wasn't making much effort with her dead, 'cause when he told me on the phone, 'Let me give you my New York office number, 'cause y'all might find you're short,' I knew Joy couldn't of meant no more to him than one of them secretaries that lapped up his every word and licked his behind.

'You sure you don't want to call her mama?' I asked Rex, 'cause much as I didn't want his help I had to remember maybe Tammy needed it.

'I really don't plan to get involved with Mrs Bang again, because we don't see eye to eye, you may recall.'

I figured he was talking about the time Tammy'd phoned his record company to say that she knew he was hanging with a colored girl and if he didn't stop she was going to turn the story in to the papers that he was messing with her daughter. Her daughter being Anndora who had tried to push Joy out the picture and slid her behind in Rex's face. That's when Joy told me that Rex couldn't do nothing in the bed no way, so she wasn't worried about Anndora trying to gain his favor. But much as Tammy didn't care all that much about him stringing Joy along, she wasn't ready to see her favorite chasing his tail. But self serving as Anndora was, I reckon Tammy was doing Rex the favor when she called his manager.

'Mrs Bang is Mrs O'Mara nowdays,' I told Rex to set him straight. 'But go 'head and give me your office number, 'cause ain't no telling how much a funeral is gonna cost in no New York City and I maybe will have to call you for Tammy.' Wild horses wouldn't have been able to get me to phone Tammy with a number for Rex. But I acted like I was taking it down anyways.

'First, I should give you this number here at the hotel though. I don't know the area code, but I'm in Santa Fe and the number is 555–1212.'

'Did you just get there?' I asked him. It wasn't my place to stick my nose in, but Santa Fe was sure popular all 'a sudden. Did he get there before Joy died is what I really wanted to know. But I asked otherwise. 'Did you see Joy's body?' I knew he didn't never want his name linked with Joy's and so if they was traveling together she always stayed in one hotel and he stayed in another. But for all I knew he'd been with her when she died and wasn't letting on.

'Lord no. View the body! I'm too squeamish to do anything like that and anyway, I didn't find out she was dead until a couple hours ago when a mutual acquaintance of ours bumped into me at this hotel I'm in. He told me that he was at the tennis club when it happened. But I'm down in Santa Fe. Joy died up in Taos.'

In my mind I pictured Taos to be a suburb of Santa Fe. 'What's the difference, it's all in the same place ain't it?'

'No Ma'am,' Rex said and blew his nose again. 'Taos is up in the mountains. To be honest, I found it a strange coincidence that Joy turned up there anyway while I was here. I mean . . . Taos?' Rex said like he was trying to figure it out himself. But I wasn't fooled. He couldn't pull the wool over my eyes like he did other folks. Making out Joy wasn't no more to him than a friend. He went on, 'There's not a whole lot to do up there at this time of year but ski, and she didn't do much of that as far as I know. But as you of all people should know with Joy, there's no telling what she was up to. She was a lady with her fingers in many pies.' I didn't know what he was insinuating and didn't like the sly way he laughed, after he'd said what he did.

'Do you have Joy's things?' I asked hoping to jar his conscience into going over to the morgue and seeing about her. If he had a conscience to jar.

'No. I can't be seen to be involved because the press would be down on me like flies. But I can send somebody to find out what's happened to her effects if you want.'

'Her mama's probably seeing to that.' I wanted to get off the phone 'cause the fact that I was being polite to him made me mad at myself. But before I went to say goodbye, I said, 'You will be coming to Joy's funeral? You know she would have wanted that.'

'Well, you did understand people didn't realize what sort of arrangement I had with Joy, didn't you. But this time I had to come here to check a location for a video shoot, and I don't know why Joy was here. Do you?'

I realized there wasn't nothing Rex had to say that I wanted to hear, but it didn't make a bit of sense that Joy was in Santa Fe the same time he was without they was together but booked in separate hotels. Her in his shadow. Like always.

'Will you call my office and let my secretary know where to send the wreath? And maybe we can meet soon and talk about everything. If you know what I mean. But I can't now. I've got too much on the boil.' Him talking in riddles gave me a headache.

'Ain't you coming to New York?' I had to ask again 'cause from the way he was talking, I got the feeling he wasn't.

'I'll have to think about it. Now's not a good time for me. There's so much work on with this new album out and the tour about to start. But I'll be in touch. Promise. Don't worry. You'll have everything you need and Joy's owed. Just call my office.' She was owed a wedding band, but what would I do with it.

I didn't want to hear no more. I had to get off the phone before I said things to him that I was wanting to but oughtn't.

Rex did everything he could to keep their 'thing' quiet, although from time to time his name would be linked to Joy's in the papers. Joy said it wasn't her color that made him so scared to let on he was going with her. But that was her fantasy. When they started up, with Rex being a country and western singer, her and him both knew that them redneck fans wasn't going to tolerate him having no colored girlfriend and soon as his manager heard about Joy he tried to put a stop to it, but Rex was kinda reckless when he was young and seemed proud to show Joy off at first. But he sure wasn't about to let her get away neither. One time when we was on the road, I heard her tell him on the phone, 'If you don't want it in the newspapers, that's the price you'll have to pay.' But seemed to me from where I was looking she was the one paying the price.

When Rex started doing the odd movie and tried to stray some from that ol' yokel music, he still kept her hid. And why Joy put up with it shall remain a mystery to me. 'Cause the fact that even she admitted that he had problems in the bed meant that she wasn't getting neither wedding ring nor sex, nor that sugar daddy treatment that a whole lot of women ruin their lives behind.

I guess that when somebody spends their whole life doing without, they don't know no better and maybe that was Joy's problem. She didn't actually believe it was her right to have. And yet at the same time, she believed it was so much that she went around with her head in the clouds.

Right from when she was little, it broke my heart to see her have to do without, especially when I knew I could give to her. But usually I drew the line at buying her the big things for Christmas and Easter and birthdays. Except the time when she was ten and I got her a two wheeler. I noticed all the kids down the block from us had bicycles 'cept her and Brenda. But Brenda didn't want one noway, 'cause all she ever wanted to do was either play with a streety girl called Sarah Jane Henderson or watch the television set in the apartment by herself. It was lucky for me Brenda didn't want one, 'cause second hand or not, that bike set me back some pocket money, 'cause I knew that if I had of asked Freddie B to get it for Joy he'd of said we had to ask Tammy first. He was always doing that, making me ask Tammy if'n I could give something before I gave it and like or not she'd take and say no. So I didn't bother to mention it to him, when I took a mind to pick up a two wheeler for Joy that one of the Sisters at my church was selling.

It was red and silver and had a basket on the front handle bars, so Joy could put the shopping in that Tammy was always sending her for. Being as she said after work she was too tired to get groceries.

I reckon that's the onliest reason Tammy let Joy keep that bike. 'Cause it was useful to Tammy indirectly. Otherwise, she'd of probably made Joy hand it back. She was that proud. And it was them children that suffered for it.

I understood with her being on her own that there was a lot she couldn't do, but even when she could, she'd grind her feet in about something and say no when it would of been just as easy to say yes. Like the time Tondalayah needed for somebody to mind her dog while she went to Texas with some man or t'other that May after Tammy and the girls had moved in.

The girls had been begging their mother for a puppy, so they got real excited the Friday that Tondalayah phoned me up to ask me to ask around and see if somebody at my church could babysit her dog, a great big dalmation named Josie, 'cause Toni was sneaking off to Houston for a couple of weeks. She said she'd pay somebody and leave money enough for food, 'cause the dog ate more red meat than a grown man. Joy and Brenda got so excited. Anndora too come to think on it. They wanted to do it and was jumping up and down when their mama got home. Tammy said to me and them, 'We can't have a dog the size of a man staying in this apartment, Baby Palatine. What'll Mr Houseman say?'

I said to her, 'Don't worry 'bout ol' man Houseman. What he don't know won't hurt him, and anyway, them two apartments up the front's still vacant, waiting on him to have the plumbing done. We could leave Josie in there of a night time and I can walk her in the mornings when the kids is at school. Come on, let the girls babysit her.'

Tammy looked unwilling and seemed like she wasn't in no mood to be bargained with, so I said to Joy, 'If y'all can't have Josie over to your place, how 'bout you take care of her over mine and y'all can still get paid for babysitting her.' Well, them children was that excited that I didn't know what to do 'cause I had said it before I'd asked Freddie B whether it was all right with him.

He come in tired from work that night and I said, 'Honey, what would you say to having Tondalayah's dalmation in here for a couple of weeks?'

I said it serving up his favorite spaghetti and meat ball supper which I cooked special to win him over. 'Tondalayah's in a fix, Freddie B, and needs for us to take care of that dog so she can go home.' Her home was in Georgia, not no Texas. But I needed for him to think Tondalayah had a good excuse for setting off. Not just another man.

Freddie B don't get mad at much, but I could see he wasn't happy about that dog coming till he heard that Tondalayah was gonna pay the kids to mind it. He would've spoiled them girls rotten if I'd 'a let him. Anything they wanted to do was all right by Freddie B and Helen used to say he was worse than me for ruining them. Joy especially.

When the time come for Toni to come to collect that dog back after the two weeks, Joy was heartbroken. But like I told her, babysitting somebody's dog was one thing and keeping one for real was another. So I said I'd get her a mouse instead and we went down the pet store. It didn't cost us but a quarter for the little thing. It had pink eyes and white whiskers and I pretended I liked it, but I'm like most women when I see a mouse. Though I guessed as long as the thing was clean I wasn't bothered, and seeing as it had been born at the pet shop and not in some sewer, I didn't mind it so much. We bought a little cage for it and set him right on my kitchen window sill. I told her, 'Give it a name, 'cause naming a thing is important.' Joy wanted me to help her pick one.

'No,' I said. 'Now this here is your mouse and you got to give it a name just like my mama give me one, and your mama give you your'n.'

So she thought on it for a whole day before she come back to me and said, 'I either wanna name him Leftie, David or Samson.'

'Leftie, David or Samson?' I said. 'Them's some funny names for a mouse.'

She said, 'Well Leftie, because when he stands up in his cage he always has his left paw up or David and Samson both out of the Bible since they're who I've been learning about at Bible studies on Sunday.'

She asked me which name I liked the best.

I said, 'Well I think Samson's pretty good,' and it made me laugh 'cause the mouse was everything but a Samson. 'David's too much like a real person's name and Leftie sounds like a criminal out of one of them Edward G. Robinson movies. So I reckon that somebody's name out of the Bible would be the best.'

We got Samson a exercise wheel and he used to 'bout drive me crazy running 'round and 'round and 'round on the squeaky thing while I was cooking.

Joy sure did love that mouse of her'n and every day for weeks she'd come in and clean up his cage and give him something to eat and sit there talking to him like he was a person.

Then I don't know what happened, but one afternoon I come home from grocery shopping and though he hadn't been sick nor nothing, Samson was laying stiff in his cage on his back with his feet straight up in the air. I put a little piece of pink toilet paper over him, as his shroud. First off I was gonna throw him down the toilet, but I thought maybe she'd wanna see him dead. It's important to see a thing's dead, so you know they ain't no more; ain't lost, ain't misplaced, just finished in that body and ain't coming back.

Joy cried and cried and cried over Samson and I said, 'What you crying for, baby?'

She said, 'Because he's gone and he was my friend.'

'You know what you got to remember, child?' I said. 'Love is stronger than death.'

She said, 'How do you know?'

I said, 'You don't stop loving a thing 'cause it's dead. Love is forever, so love is stronger than death. That mouse of yours will be stronger in your heart now he's gone. He hasn't gone nowhere except out his body. So now you can take him round even better than you could before 'cause he's in your heart for all time if that's what you want.'

We tried to have a funeral for Samson down in the parking lot. Brenda was out somewhere or other playing so she couldn't come sing a hymn with us, and Anndora refused to come out 'cause she was watching her favorite cartoons. So me and Joy went down with a couple of popsicle sticks she had decorated with some water paints I'd got her and she made his cross. We found a little patch right back in the corner of the parking lot that wasn't all gravelly for his grave. We put a couple dandylions on top of the grave and we had a 'safe journey Samson' ceremony that must of lasted all of fifteen minutes including the twenty-third Psalm, Lord's prayer, eulogy and two hymns.

After that for about a week I used to see the tears well up in her eyes when she'd come in my kitchen. I used to tell her, 'Miss Joy, don't forget . . . love is stronger than death.'

There was a lot that went on at our building in Oakland that made that first year that the Bangs moved there unforgettable. Most of it was good, but what was bad was real bad, and I reckon that none of us got right after it, although from the outside everything looked normal. Funny how you can look back on things and everything is clear, but when you in the middle of it, it's like a haze and you can't believe you'll ever find your way out.

By dinnertime, I was packed ready for the last night-flight to New York. Freddie B was able to borrow $650 off his union, which was about what I needed for a two-way ticket, a decent wreath and some food and taxi money.

'Don't you be fooling with none of them gals at the church,' I teased Freddie B when he dropped me at the airport. He must of needed to see Joy buried as much as I did, but the difference between him and me is he never thinks about hisself first.

Summer, fall, winter or spring, New York makes me feel like a tick crawling 'round on a mangy dog covered in sores. And as soon as I took a whiff of the nanky air when I got off the plane, I was reminded of it and wanted to turn back and go home. You got to be a Olympic sprinter to catch a bus out of JFK airport. The mix up and chaos with them buses and the cars and taxis and rent-a-car shuttles reminds me of a movie I seen once about Shanghai where there wasn't no lanes for driving. Traffic every which-a-way with horns honking.

I only had one bag, but there was a young Chinese girl I seen had four and wasn't a redcap in sight to help her from the sidewalk to board the bus. She looked a whole lot spryer than me but I helped her climb on with 'em anyway, which she really seemed to appreciate, 'cause she waved at me when I got off at the World Trade Center and caught a cab from the bus stop over to Joy's.

I hate as much as anybody to throw hard earned dollars away on taxis, but I'd rather suffer having to watch that fare meter click away than lose my life down them subways where I read how them hoodlums will stab you quick as look at you. I was always scared something was going to happen to Joy down one, so I told her don't ride 'em. When she called all excited to tell me she'd bought a ten-speed bicycle, I said, 'A bike in that god forsaken place!' Thinking about her pedalling around through the pit holes and filth and past knife attackers high on crack it's a miracle she lived as long as she did.

My feet swell on planes, so I was glad to kick my shoes off in the cab but I couldn't get them red pumps back on when we pulled up outside

Joy's tall apartment building. But could tell the taxi driver was wanting to get rid of me, so I finally got out with the shoes off. I don't know what the doorman musta thought when I walked into Joy's smoke-mirrored lobby at dawn in March with my pumps in one hand and suitcase in the other.

I was sure glad when he pointed me in the direction of that elevator, 'cause he'd of had to carry me up to Joy's sixth floor split level apartment otherwise. Not that I got nothing against stairs under normal circumstances. Being as I'm used to cleaning them, they don't usually bother me except when my lumbago acts up, but as I didn't sleep none on the plane and they had that air conditioning blowing on my neck, I never closed my eyes. Between feeling the cold and my mind rummaging through the past, there wasn't hope of me sleeping, so I tried hard to read Matthew out of the New Testament. But some of them strange Bible names look like gobble-dee-gook when my mind ain't clear.

The elevator was mirrored three sides, so I didn't have much choice but to look at myself. I noticed my forehead glistening but couldn't be bothered to take my puff out of my handbag and powder it, and I looked about as worn out as an old brown felt hat my baby sister used to shove on her head. But I had on my charcoal gray Christian Dior suit and matching red and gray paisley silk blouse that Joy got me. Creased though my outfit was from sitting on the plane, nobody woulda took me for a scrub woman. Freddie B hates for me to call myself that, but that's all being a apartment manager is these days, 'cause we don't pick and choose who's gonna live in the building nor collect the rent like we did in the old days.

My plaid suitcase didn't have nothing but expensive clothes in it, 'cause Joy was always sending 'em for birthdays and whatnot and I took real good care of 'em. So a few things I'd had years, some that she'd passed down when she got fed up with wearing them. We was a different shape but with her being not but a inch taller than my five foot seven, there was a lot of her stuff I could make good use of.

I was glad I didn't put on nothing black and didn't pack none for the funeral, 'cause Joy didn't like to see me in it. She said with me being dark, black didn't look dramatic like it was s'posed to, it just looked lifeless and made me look lifeless with it. But Freddie B wouldn't settle till I packed his black armband, 'cause he was vexated by me not packing no mourning clothes. 'Joy didn't believe in mourning,' I said to remind him and myself, 'she always said if she died, throw a party and celebrate.' But I let him watch me open my case and put his armband in it, so he wouldn't fret the whole time I was gone that I didn't have nothing proper to be setting with the family at Joy's funeral.

'It ain't right you wearing that light gray suit. What's Tammy gonna think,' he asked me 'cause he was used to me being worried about what she thought. And that's when it come to me that for the first time in all the time I knew the Bang family that I didn't care a hoot about what Tammy thought and wouldn't have been scared to tell her so. Without Joy, she didn't have no hold over me and I wasn't so sure I owed her nothing, like I had convinced myself I did 'cause of what happened with Dagwood. Without Joy to hold me to her family, I felt free.

The security at Joy's apartment house was tight, which surprised me 'cause from what I could see that neighborhood wasn't nothing fancy. Chelsea, Joy said it was called. But dirty as the sidewalk was, it could of been Harlem though I didn't expect for a minute that Joy would of been living in no colored neighborhood. The white doorman had him two walkie-talkies and there was little cameras tucked in some of the corners and even one tucked in a corner of the ceiling on the elevator. I hoped nobody was looking at me looking at myself on a screen by the elevator door.

It was real early but I wasn't sure of the exact time. I didn't need no watch usually, as I can tell it from the light. But I was confused 'cause of the time change. The lights was on in the lobby and hallway. I hadn't never been to Joy's new place, 'cause although she'd asked me to visit a couple times, I wasn't my old globe-trotting self. I didn't like to tell her I was getting too set in my ways to be hanging around them airports and Freddie B deserved some consideration. Especially after he let me be away from home almost the whole year Bang Bang Bang was touring. And didn't complain once.

I checked myself again in the mirror and wondered if I should of put some lipstick on at least, 'cause I knew Tammy was gonna be dolled up. Didn't matter how old she got, she used to put herself together real good from the time the girls had that 'Chocolate Chip' hit. She kept expecting folks to snap her picture, even when we was at the supermarket, and I used to laugh to myself but not say nothing. You'd of thought it was Tammy'd had that record out. Anyway, by the time I got through mulling over lipstick or no lipstick, it was too late and the elevator had stopped at Joy's floor.

Whatever Joy's neighborhood looked like, there wasn't no doubting that somebody had been spending money decorating the halls and whatnot. They wasn't playing around with no lino; them floors had a thick dark gray wool carpet that was better quality than what our Corporation in San Francisco put in our apartment. And there was gray and white marble skirting the walls and expensive lighting sunk into the ceilings, with all of 'em blaring like electricity was free. Not that I wasn't glad of the bright lights, 'cause there's something spooky about hallways in apartment blocks when ain't nobody walking around in them. Don't matter whether it's day or night.

I got myself ready for Tammy to answer Joy's apartment door when I buzzed the buzzer. I hadn't seen her for a few years, not since before she married, and got rid of the bungalow she rented in Walnut Creek, back of the Oakland Hills and moved over there with Jesse 'cause he owned his own home. I told her when she moved that I didn't know how she was going to manage in no Richmond, Virginia, 'cause the South takes some getting used to 'specially for coloreds from the North. But like she said herself, she's unpredictable.

I was ready to make a special effort not to get into nothing with Tammy and them, being that my blood pressure is quick to shoot up when I get aggravated. I didn't know who all was going to be in Joy's, but I figured there wasn't nothing I couldn't cope with for three days. My ticket home was booked.

The Bangs didn't know how to get along together when Joy wasn't with them, and I hated the way they didn't treat each other with due respect. Brenda didn't never have much time for Anndora, even when they was growing up, and then when they had the group, Brenda hated that Anndora didn't give Brenda no credit for doing the singing that made the record worth listening to in the first place. It was Joy that played go-between, so that it seemed like Brenda and Anndora was getting on when all that was actually happening was that Anndora would talk to Joy and Brenda would talk to Joy, but Brenda and Anndora didn't have to make no effort to talk to each other. I figured it was their mama's fault for not training them to care nothing 'bout one another. 'Cause families ain't just born, you got to work at 'em, even when there ain't much to work with like I feel sometimes with my baby sister.

I don't know what exactly I expected when Brenda opened the door. But for a start, it wasn't her, who I hadn't seen for years. I didn't have chance to get a good look at her 'fore she grabbed me and my bag. She was her same loud self and her voice booming in my ear kinda lifted my spirits.

'Come let me give you a hug!' she shouted. 'It's been too long, girl. But wait, let me look at you first.' She stood back and gave me a good once over up and down and turned me round. 'All right, Miss Baby Palatine Ross, Herself-in-Person. Go 'head and work that suit, Miss Thing!' It sounded like something Joy would have said, and as soon as I heard it, I broke down.

'Hey now. Come on. You know Joy wouldn't want you upset. We have to rejoice. Get it? R-E-J-O-Y-C-E.' Brenda spelled it. 'She would have like that. Re-Joyce.' Actually Joy hated for anybody to call her by her full name and kept meaning to change it on her passport.

Brenda made me sit on the sofa, and I tried to pull my nerves together while she went to heat up some coffee in the microwave. She brought it back scalding, and waiting on it to cool gave me a chance to look around.

Nothing but beige and white everywhere my eyes fell, from pinky beige carpets to eggshell colored walls and white doors that led to what I knew not. I opened and closed doors, peeking in everywhere. On the quiet, I was looking for Joy to jump out a cupboard and yell 'BOO' like she did when she was little. She was too alive in me to be dead. I still couldn't believe it.

'What do you think?' Brenda asked, just as it was crossing my mind that there wasn't nothing of Joy in the apartment, and I wondered if she'd paid somebody to do it up for her, 'cause it didn't look like no place she'd ever had that I knew of. Whereas I loved that first apartment she had in Oakland after she left home 'cause she'd lined the walls with photographs and old pictures she picked up from junk shops. The first place of her'n wasn't fancy and didn't have much furniture in it, but with the plants she had growing everywhere, it was alive. It was Joy.

Brenda asked me a second time. 'Come on, what do you think?' I knew she was talking about what I thought of Joy's place, but I didn't let on, 'cause I figured she wanted me to say I didn't like it 'cause it was cold looking. But I didn't give her the satisfaction of hearing me put nothing of Joy's down, never.

'What do I think about what?' I answered.

'Well this apartment for one thing.'

'I haven't had time to think nothing. I just come in off the street.' Brenda was jealous of Joy and it was understandable 'cause although Joy went out her way to act nice to Brenda, it didn't seem fair that one sister had so much and the other seemed to have nothing.

'Haven't you been here before either?' Brenda asked.

'Joy's been to see me and Freddie B a few times since she moved from LA so there wasn't no need,' I told her. 'She's only had the place a couple years and what did I need to be spending my husband's money for, coming all the way to New York when Joy come to us twice a year?'

'How's Uncle Freddie B taking it?'

'His usual. You know he don't never show his feelings. We done buried his whole family over the years, his mama and three brothers and sister and he didn't show nothing 'cept when his eldest brother Harold died and Freddie B was mad 'cause he hadn't paid him back some money we'd borrowed off him.'

Brenda wasn't listening, she was too busy walking round Joy's living room inspecting it. 'So what do you think?' she asked again which annoyed me, 'cause I didn't know what to think but didn't want to tell her. For Joy's sake I hated to admit to myself or Brenda that her great big living room with its high ceilings and pale bare walls was too modern for me. I wasn't impressed with the floor to ceiling white venetian blinds. Nor the spindly curved neck metal lamps. Nor the silver metal end tables that looked more like upside down milk crates than furniture, I want a place to be homey, but Joy's looked like something off one of them TV ads. Hardly no furnishing to speak of save a huge glass table with eight see-through plastic chairs and a great big sofa and a whole bunch of fancy lights sunk in the walls which Brenda played with from a control panel till I made her stop. She had them blaring and dimmed, on and off, like she was lighting up a stage or something.

Forty-one years old and acting like a child. It was that childish thing I used to like most about Brenda, but the thing that could also always drive me to distraction. Didn't matter how old she got, she was a little girl, wanting to play and looking for attention, though she didn't never get none except from Dagwood and when she had that mouth of hers opened to sing.

'Brenda don't play with that, 'cause what'll happen if it breaks,' I said, taking the control panel out her hand. I lose patience quick when I'm tired. 'Come on,' I said to her, 'let's snoop and see what all is here.'

But soon as I said it, I knew that it was gonna be like walking around a new hotel suite, nice to look at, but no sign that anybody had been or was coming back. It wasn't nothing like I thought it would be. Somehow I saw Joy in a place with red walls and fancy Turkish carpets with vases everywhere overflowing with flowers like she used to oogle over in them *House and Gardens* books she bought in her teenage days when she thought she might one day be a Mrs Somebody or T'other.

Me and Brenda checked the hallway by the kitchen and the cute little toilet come dressing room that was off it. Every wall was snow white and bare and Joy had three big walk-in cupboards chockerblock with more clothes that the law should allow. All I really liked was the gray green painted wood staircase leading to her upstairs.

Joy always kept her places real nice. Mostly I think for Rex's benefit, since she claimed he could of popped in any minute. Not that he ever did that I knew of.

Her white kitchen floor tiles was spic 'n' span, sparkling brighter than the plates I take out the dishwasher to eat off at home. Joy's floor shined like nobody'd walked on it and if I hadn't seen her clothes in the cupboards I'd of wondered if she could of been living elsewhere. I never thought I'd see a place I thought was too clean. The oomph was polished off it and if there'd be one crumb or speck of dust, it would of stood out like a fly laying dead on the kitchen counter. The apartment didn't feel nothing like Joy. It was so squared up and didn't have no personality. Not even a book to be seen and she loved to read.

When you know somebody good, you don't want 'em to show change and I'd always known Joy to keep her walls covered in picture posters and photos of everybody. And neat as she was, she didn't fuss with dusting all that much.

'Have you ever seen a sofa this long?' Brenda asked me before she plopped her wide behind down on it. Beige. Suede. And expensive no doubt. It must of been the length of two sofas. I'm surprised the thing didn't collapse with Brenda dropping her full weight down on it, sturdy though it looked.

'Mind!' I yelled 'cause the only plant in the room, a ten foot tall willowy thing behind the sofa, started to sway like it was going to keel over. It wasn't ready for Brenda. Nor was I, tired as I was.

At my age, I can't pretend it's no easy thing to be jumping on and off planes in the night, and I had a bit of a headache coming, made worse by Brenda when she had been flicking them lights. But I know that impatience don't never get me nowhere but in trouble, so I tried to say nicer, 'Come on, let's have us another snoop 'round.'

Then we noseyed about together, poking in the little there was to poke in without going up to the next floor 'cause Brenda said her mother and stepfather was sleeping up there in Joy's room above. It sounded funny to hear her say 'stepfather', but I could tell she liked the sound of it.

'Stepfather,' I laughed. 'You call Jesse your stepfather?' Joy didn't. She liked Jesse well enough, but she didn't try to pretend that he was nothing more to her than her mama's husband. For all I could remember of Joy pandering to Tammy to keep her happy when we all lived on Grange, as Joy got older and Tammy got sweeter to her, Joy didn't seem to have no time for her mother.

I used to say to her, 'I don't care what you think about your mama, it's in the Bible that you supposed to show her respect.' Not that she wasn't respectful, but there didn't seem to be no real love in them things she did for Tammy like paying her rent and giving her an allowance after Bang Bang Bang had their record out. I was proud of Joy for taking care of her mama, but it peeved me that whereas Tammy could of gone out and got herself a job, she was happy to live off Joy which is why Joy was relieved more than anything when Tammy finally settled with Jesse and Joy didn't have to foot her mama's bills no more.

'He *is* my stepfather,' said Brenda like Jesse was some kinda medal that she could of worn on her cotton blouse. I never could make head nor tail of her thing about men, but thinking back, when Tammy was with Dagwood, it was Brenda out the three girls who was the most excited that Tammy'd taken up with a man. Freddie B said it was 'cause she probably missed her daddy more than Joy and Anndora.

Since she was a child, Brenda was overgrown, but seeing her standing in Joy's, I realized that it was worse than I remembered. She was a mannish size and even her hands was broad like they was meant for heavy labor. Though her hair was Jeri curled and she'd obviously taken some trouble with it, it looked more a man's style than woman's. And any middeweight would of been proud of biceps as big as Brenda's. Not a ounce of it looked like fat. She was just big . . . Like Man Mountain, one of the wrestlers Freddie B love to hate on TV.

'Brenda, you been working out down that gymnasium?' I asked kinda sheepish as she was stroking the suede on the sofa. She had on a short sleeve blouse with lacy collar and cuffs and pearl buttons. It pulled a bit across the bust like she could of done with a bit more fabric in it. I don't know why she ever thought she should wear frilly things being six feet and Lord knows how many pounds. They didn't never suit her. But even in high school she wanted to be in ginghams and lace, poor thing.

Brenda said, 'I don't have money to fool around at a proper gym, but my girlfriend Latrice bought me a bull-worker to tighten up the flab on my arms. They look good, don't they.' She flexed her muscles and I winced. 'Latrice says it's a big improvement.' A bull-worker? What next, I thought.

'You better give that thing a rest unless you fixing to take up lady wrestling,' I said and couldn't keep a straight face. Brenda didn't never mind me laughing at her, 'cause I didn't mean no harm. I was thankful to have something to laugh about to tell the truth, 'cause I hadn't found nothing to even crack a smile over since I'd heard about Joy.

'It's too quiet in here,' Brenda said as she stood up to cross the room and try to get the record player going that was on a tall metal shelf standing against the wall by the fireplace. The record player and tape deck had umpteen black buttons and knobs on it and I watched her jiggle every one. Nothing happened and she got mad and banged the top of the amplifier with her big man-hands.

'You're gonna break that thing,' I chided her.

'I can't get it to go on,' she said and banged on it again. Brenda hadn't changed. And just like she hammered on Joy's record player, she seemed to hammer at life which didn't work for her neither.

I had hoped that when she got to singing and had folks praising her for having a special talent, that Brenda would of put her life into some order. But from them Dagwood days, Brenda proved herself to be unpredictable and stayed that way.

Like I said, Freddie B claimed her problem was that she might have been missing her daddy more than the other two. But I couldn't see how he figured that, 'cause Brenda didn't mention her father no more than Joy did. And once Dagwood slipped into the picture, you would of thought that Tammy hadn't never heard of no Sherman Bang and that them girls of her'n must of come via immaculate conception.

It was 'Dagwood this' and 'Dagwood that' and 'Dagwood t'other' as far as Tammy was concerned, and I hold that to be the reason that Brenda made way more of the man than she should of done. And the reason she got herself into the trouble with him that she did which turned all our lives upside down, so that nothing came after including that hit record to shift things right again. Especially for Brenda.

But it was Tammy to my mind that set the stage for the trouble. 'Cause girls will do what they see their mama do. And Brenda proved the point too well as far as Dagwood was concerned.

I never heard Tammy say a word against Dagwood till she spotted him early one morning coming out the beauty shop on Grange with the red headed gal named Bobbie that owned the place. She was a brown skin, birdy-like woman who always wore a white uniform and seemed to be running in and out the corner delicatessen ordering ham and Swiss cheese sandwiches for her customers and the operators in her shop. I knew her to say hello to, 'cause when she first took over the beautician's not long after me and Freddie got the job managing for Houseman, Bobbie stopped me in the street and wanted to hire me to clean her beauty shop, part time. She was looking for somebody to sweep up all the hairs of a nighttime, scrub the five cubicles her operators rented off her and do the mirrors and combs and brushes and whatnot. I wasn't interested and since we didn't need the money, Freddie told me don't do it. Naps on the floor and grease on everything. Scrubbing the burnt grease off them hot combs and curling irons was bound to be some work and Bobbie didn't want to pay nothing but $1.75 an hour. Besides, I had enough to do running Houseman's building 'cause whereas wasn't nobody renting but Tammy, it was still work with the hall, stairs and shops below and my husband was bringing in good money. But I was glad to get a opportunity to take a good look around Bobbie's shop before I turned the job down, because I used to see a whole lot of fancy looking colored girls going in there and I didn't feel it was the sort of place I'd be comfortable in to get my hair done. Being the owner and having her name on the neon sign that sat in the window, Bobbie charged higher than the rest of her operators, so she got the 'five hundreds' and used to stay open late for them. She was the first hairdresser I knew of to do a cold press.

At that time there wasn't nobody living in either of the two small front apartments of Houseman's building, so I used to go into the biggest one in the afternoons and sit by the window. It overlooked Grange where there was shops on both sides of the street. Bobbie's, the tonsorial parlor, the launderette, the deli beside the drugstore and Mrs Kitchen's odds and sods shop below us. When I had time to sit there watching out long enough, sometimes I'd see some women come and go from Bobbie's, but that didn't happen much 'cause I had my soap operas to catch at one o'clock and a wash, straighten and curl could take a few hours.

The afternoon I saw Dagwood walk in and out of there something told me not to tell Tammy 'cause it might start something, though I mentioned it to Freddie B. Men stick together and mine ain't no different 'cause first thing he said was, 'Don't be busybodying.' It made me wonder what my husband was turning my scent off Dagwood for unless Freddie B had something to hide hisself. I wouldn't put it pass n'ere one of 'em to be out creeping.

'You got something to hide,' I asked Freddie B. 'Cause it's us busybodies, Mister, that come up with the information.'

'No,' he said, shifting like I'd made him uncomfortable though he didn't look up from reading his evening *Tribune*. I told him, 'There's enough Sisters up the church if you're looking for trouble, they'll be quick to help you make some. How 'bout Sister Fletcher with her bandy-legged self who's always grinning up in your face? You know the one with the gold tooth in front that come from that backwater in Lou'siana but tells everybody she's from New Orleans?' I was just stirring it 'cause Freddie B would of been the last man on earth skirtchasing.

'The Lord is gonna strike you for talking that mess.' He didn't like me to say a bad word about nobody and sometimes it took all the fun out of life.

If Tammy had seen Freddie B coming out the hairdresser's with a woman, I sure would of wanted for Tammy to tell me. So, as I always practice 'do unto others as you would have them do unto you', I figured I would have to wait and pick the right time to tell her. But Dagwood spared me the trouble, 'cause Tammy was coming home off the bus and caught him herself the next evening. He was standing in the doorway of the beauty parlor with his arm around Bobbie's waist, Tammy said. Right out in broad daylight. Where folks could see.

The day it happened Anndora was home from the minder's with a cold, so I was setting babysitting on her in Tammy's apartment with the other two children. I'd had Anndora acting up on me all the durn day and was glad to hear Tammy coming up the steps. But the three girls was so busy watching *Howdy Doody* or something when their mama come in and threw her things down, they hardly said 'Good evening'. She was trying to act normal but I could see something was bugging her. Her eyes was flashing and she was blowing that cigarette smoke out her nostrils like a dragon.

'You coming down with Anndora's cold?' I asked her.

'No. I'm not sick, but I am sick of somebody,' she said, and took me in the bedroom and shut the door so she could tell me she saw Dagwood with Bobbie. Something stopped me from telling her it wasn't the first time, because without me putting my two cents in she was mad enough, with her nostrils flaring, blowing that cigarette smoke and cussing worse than my baby sister. I tried to peek out the window when she went down and waited for Dagwood in the parking lot to tell him she didn't want him in her place no more. But I couldn't see nothing. Nor hear. When she come storming up the steps half an hour after she went down, she was by herself. But Dagwood wouldn't take no for an answer and stayed in his car waiting on Tammy to come back out. I know he had him a decent apartment to go to judging from the neighborhood he said it was in, but he sat in that car. As it was a Wednesday night and I had to go out to check the shops was all locked, I spotted him sitting behind the wheel with the top down, there in the dark. I don't care how hot it is by day, California gets chilly at night, and I couldn't stand to see him huddled without no blanket or nothing. He said that he had him a bottle, that he had a bit of whiskey to warm hisself up on, but I went up and brought him down one of our ol' army blankets anyway.

When I went to the toilet at three in the morning, I peeked out and saw him still there. He sat in that sports car the whole night and when Tammy went to work the next morning, she said he followed her bus to Alameda to that federal government agency where she worked but he didn't have no pass to get in the government precinct. They don't mess at them government places, and he had to stay outside.

I was hoping Tammy wasn't gonna take Dagwood back, but the kids kept asking her why he was sitting down in the parking lot, 'cause that's where he stayed for two days.

She told me not to let them out to play down in the parking lot while he was down there, and when he disappeared during the second day, I was relieved to see we was rid of him, so the kids didn't have to stay cooped up indoors. But he showed up again just before Tammy was due home. To tell the truth I wouldn't of been sorry for Tammy to of seen the last of him that day 'cause the nice widowman Mr Thigpen from my church had dropped past that very afternoon asking after Tammy. I didn't know Mr Thigpen good, but he had a regular job and a bungalow. Didn't many people own nothing back then, so I knew he was a good catch.

It was Brenda was the most miserable the whole time Dagwood was out in the car. She was the one that favored him, always begging to brush on his hair and set on his lap while he listened to them ol' timey blues records and she used to hate to go to bed when he was there. Joy used to tease her and say that Brenda acted like she thought Dagwood was some kinda movie star.

If Brenda been Anndora's size, it might of seemed cute, her following behind a grown man like Dagwood, but Brenda was nearly tall as me, though not but ten, and plain as the day was long. With her feet big as mine in a pair of Mary Janes, she looked flam-footed. I ain't saying it to be mean. It was true, and there wasn't much her mama could do about how she looked; 'cause if Tammy'd dressed her up older, Brenda would of looked better since she had a fullblown woman's figure, but wasn't no way to put a child her age in women's clothes. And in children's dresses, Brenda looked backward. Like them folks that's slow-witted.

When the three of them girls was together, nobody took notice of Brenda, they was so busy admiring Anndora for being cute and Joy for being so sweet natured and smart, and I'll give Dagwood his due, he seemed to go out of his way to show Brenda favor. Always saying she looked nice with such-and-such ribbon in her hair and asking her questions about what she was watching on the TV. Just to make conversation I reckon. 'Cause ain't no way in the world that he could of wanted to know nothing about them cartoons and that, she liked to watch.

Dagwood was the only body I ever saw make a fuss over Brenda, and I thought it was 'cause she treated him like he was God. One time, when he bought each of the girls Golden Story books, he got *The Ugly Duckling* for Brenda and she moped about it. Said to his face that she didn't want a baby book and tried to give it back. But he sat down and read the story out to her and said if she minded her Ps and Qs that the same thing could happen to her. And had her believing she could be a swan. I won't lie: ain't many would of taken the time.

Anyway, when Tammy gave Dagwood the push, anybody might have guessed it was Brenda's own flesh and blood setting out in the car for them two days. And I believed that Tammy might of held off on Dagwood if it hadn't been for Brenda begging and pleading for her mama to give him another chance. Which is all Tammy needed to hear. So she gave in. And we had Dagwooditis in the Bangs' household again. Tammy was worse than Brenda, so I didn't go in and out of there much in the evenings. If he stayed the night, Dagwood would get up mornings and drive Tammy all that way to work and drop Anndora at Miss Otis', claiming he was glad to do it. And then we wouldn't see him again till he picked them up.

Though I was glad Tammy had her somebody, I didn't take to Dagwood who I heard tell Tammy straight that marriage wasn't in his scheme of things. He wasn't my sort and I knew exactly why when Joy come bursting in my place late one morning. The weatherman'd predicted it was going to be a scorcher and I was already sitting at my kitchen table drinking a cold grape soda with the fan blowing directly in my face. I didn't have on nothing but a flimsy green cotton washdress and was wondering what nice surprise I was gonna fix the children for lunch as it was their second day home from school for summer vacation. I'd got used to making 'em cakes and pies once their mama heard both Freddie B and me say that we didn't mind the girls eating us out of house and home.

When Joy come rushing in all a'buster and a'fluster I hadn't never seen her cry outright in the time I knew her, so it scared me half to death when she come flying at me to bury her head on my bare shoulder. I could feel tears and she was hopping from foot to foot. Either anxious or frustrated and I figured Brenda must of hit her.

'What's the matter? Tell Baby,' I said to coax her into telling me what was wrong.

'I can't,' she said and looked up at me blinking back the tears from her big black almond eyes. 'I don't want to get Brenda into trouble.'

'Brenda done done something to you?' I asked Joy. ''Cause I'll give her what for!' With her being way bigger than Joy there wasn't no way that it would of been fair for Brenda to hit on her.

'I can't tell,' she said and then started crying so loud I took her on my lap though she was getting too big. I rocked her back and forth and said, 'Come on now, you can tell me. Ain't we buddies no more?' I wiped them few tears. 'Cause loud as the noise was she was making, the tears were few.

I could feel her whole body trembling when she said, 'I don't want Brenda to go to reform school.'

'Don't talk foolish, child. You been watching too much TV. Brenda ain't killed nobody, has she? That's the onliest reason they send kids to reform school.' Joy got it from her mother to make a mountain out of a molehill, so I told her to get down off my lap and I'd go to see what Brenda was up to.

'No,' she said, and sobbed some more, hardly able to catch her breath. And clung on to me tight with her arms locked about my neck and wouldn't get down.

'Joy, it's too hot for a commotion. If Brenda ain't killed nobody and ain't burning the place down, ain't nothing that she could be up to that's all that bad.' Like children do, Joy used to think the world was going to end if a glass got broke. It was her mother'd started her worrying about that kind of foolishness.

'Well, I'll tell you something,' she said and got off my lap to fetch the Bible off the mantelpiece. She brought it in for me to put my hand on. 'But I'll only tell you if you swear not to tell. Or make Brenda get in trouble with Mama.'

'How'm I gonna swear 'fore I know what I'm swearing about.'

'Well,' she said, looking like she was ready to put the Bible back, 'then I can't tell you and you'll never find out!' She quit her blubbering so quick, for a minute I thought she had just been kidding me on and all that crying was just for show. Not that she did none of that kind of performing for which Miss Anndora should of had her a Academy Award.

'Joy! You and your bad self had me worried for a minute,' I said and give her a tap on her behind to scoot her over to her place. 'Let's go see to Brenda. 'Cause if whatever she's doing got you that upset, I better check on her.'

'Dagwood's in there, so maybe you better not,' she said blocking me from opening the front door.

'Your mama didn't go to work this morning?' Dagwood didn't never stay behind after Tammy left for work, and I'd hoped he wasn't starting.

Joy shook her head. 'Mama's gone already. She left us some candy money on the kitchen counter.'

'Well why didn't Dagwood drive her?'

'Because she told him he was better off to stay in bed. I heard her say that if he had a hangover she didn't want to ride with him. So he didn't take her. Or Anndora. Mama said she'd been with Anndora to Miss Otis' on foot enough before and she could again.'

'Well no doubt if Brenda's up to something, he'll put a stop to it.'

'But he didn't,' she started up crying again, and I got worried and carted her over to the bureau where she'd put the Bible back.

'Lookahere, I've got the Bible and I'm swearing on it,' I said. She ran to make sure the front door was shut and tiptoed back and started to whisper in my ear.

She loved secrets, it's true, better than anything else but butter pecan ice cream.

'Brenda got in bed with Mr Dagwood,' she whispered soft but wasn't no mistaking what she'd said.

'Don't play, now, Joy. That ain't nice,' I scolded.

'She did. She snuck under the sheet he had covering him. I saw her.'

'And what did he do?'

'He was sleeping.'

'You sure?' I went back to the kitchen and turned off the fan so I could hear her good.

'Yep,' she said. 'He was sleeping at first. You know how he does with the pillow over his head. Then he woke up while Brenda was still covered up.'

'Well what's such a big secret about that. I'll tan Brenda's hide, 'cause she ought to know better than to be getting in the bed with a grown man. That's dangerous. You know better than that don't you?' She looked up at me and her eyes filled up again.

'I think Brenda did bad things. You know like you-know-what.'

'What ch'you mean by you-know-what?' I hoped she wasn't meaning what I thought she was.

'You know. The bad thing.'

I pulled her in front of me and looked dead in her eyes. I hadn't never known her to lie to me. 'I thought you said he was sleeping.'

'He was at first. But Brenda pretended she was Mama and then he woke up and made these noises. Groaning noises.'

'How do you know that?' My jaws was clinched tight and I broke out into a sweat, 'cause with the heat and my heart pounding it was enough to make a body faint.

'Because while she was under the sheets she peeped out and stuck her tongue out at me and threw her pajama top on the floor.'

'You sure! You ain't just funning, Joyce Clarissa Bang, and making this up is you?'

She shook her head again and I didn't know what to think. One minute she was in a tizzy crying and hotfooting, and the next minute telling me something I was afraid to believe.

'Oh my God, Joy. You sure you ain't fooling me?'

'I saw her, Baby Palatine. Honest Injun. And then I got scared she'd have to go to reform school, because that's where they have to send girls don't they when they have a baby?'

'You sure that Dagwood wasn't sleeping?'

'Well, I'm not positive. But I did see him take the pillow off his head after Brenda had been playing around under the sheets for a while. With her bottom in the air.'

'Then what happened?'

'He called out Mama's name, sort of romantic. Like in the movies and then he said, "Tammy, you shouldn't have stayed off work, but I like it. Darling I like it." He said "Darling" twice, then he stretched out his arms and when he did, the pillow fell on the floor and he screamed and moaned like he was dying, but Brenda was still hiding under the sheets. Then he pulled them back and said, "Oh my God, oh my God, Brenda. No." When he jumped upright he didn't have any pajamas on.'

'Why didn't you come here sooner? You gone crazy or something?'

'I didn't want to get Brenda into trouble,' said Joy dry-eyed.

Brenda and Dagwood. For all I knew what Joy saw wasn't the first time. It was only about the week before that we was all walking down the street and a teenager walked by us and I overheard Brenda say to Joy, 'That nigger was fine as a Georgia pine!' Tammy wasn't with us, so I slapped Brenda's behind and told her we wouldn't have no more fast talk and she shouldn't be calling nobody a nigger 'less she wanted to be called one her own self.

I figured she'd been listening to Tondalayah who was always saying that this somebody or that somebody was fine as a Georgia pine.

While I wanted not to believe Joy, I thought with her being a child, even if she didn't know all the ins and outs of all that had gone on, she couldn't of made up the bit she told me. In my head I was begging and praying, 'Jesus, show me the way.' I ain't never felt that lost, but I tried not to show it for Joy's sake.

It wasn't but two big steps between my door and Tammy's. When you stepped in her hallway their bathroom was on the right, while the living room was straight ahead with the bedrooms off it, left. The place wasn't big enough for all of 'em, specially when Dagwood was there, but they managed, 'cause with Tammy at work and the big 'uns at school, and Anndora with the minder, Miss Otis, none of 'em was in it that much till school had let out.

'Brenda!' I called out and stayed stood in the hall which wasn't no more than a four by four with two closets. It didn't have no window, being a internal hall, so the only light it got came from the bathroom window. Otherwise you had to switch on the electricity, but soon as Brenda opened up the bathroom door there wasn't no need.

Joy had come with me and was trying to hang on to my hand, but my palms was sweating so that everytime she got a grip, her hand would slip out and she'd have to grab mine again. Joy'd stopped crying by the time Brenda'd opened the door with her hair standing on end like she'd been tussling. She come out wearing nothing but her underpants.

I hadn't never seen her bare bosom and couldn't believe what I was seeing. There was girls in that strip joint I used to clean down Bakersfield where Tondalayah had worked that wasn't as well endowed, and woulda given eye teeth for the two full mounds Brenda was toting. I was shamed to look at her and told Joy to cover her eyes.

'Where's your clothes, child?' I asked Brenda. She wouldn't look at me. With head bowed, she just pointed to the bedrooms. I knew that wasn't no place for her with Dagwood in there. I could hear him rustling round. 'Well wrap a towel or something round you and come 'cross to my place. You in big trouble,' I told her before I heard the bedroom door open.

The apartment was laid out so you had to come from the adjoining bedrooms through the living room to get to the toilet. And Dagwood come through with his shirt off and no shoes or socks on and his trousers half done up. I turned my back to try and act like I didn't notice him coming but he spoke my name. 'Palatine!'

Only he had a way of speaking to women that made me mad 'fore he had chance to say two words. There was something commanding in his voice like folks take on when you work for them. It gets my goat as soon as I hear it.

'Palatine,' he said again. Dagwood didn't never call me by my full name and I didn't like it. I wanted to say, 'You can talk familiar to them other wenches, but don't come in my face calling me no Palatine, 'cause my husband's the onliest one ever calls me that.'

But instead, I just threw him a look over my shoulder and said, 'We ain't got nary a word to say to you.'

The hateful way I said it set Joy off. Tears and everything. She started creating. 'You promised you wouldn't fuss, Baby, you promised me.'

Sure enough she'd made me put my hand on the Bible and swear that I wouldn't start fussing if she told me what she was crying for. But Bible or no, that was too much of a promise.

'Don't make me have to go outside and find me a switch,' I scolded her.

She was howling the place down. 'You promised. You promised.' She was looking past me at Dagwood and had a hold o' my thumb that I couldn't shake loose.

'Brenda! If you don't put something over yourself, you gonna get a beating too!' I couldn't believe that she was exposing herself with Dagwood standing right there. The hall light was off so it was dim what with Brenda blocking what light was coming out the bathroom. But you couldn't miss her titties, and from where we was, I could see beads of sweat on Dagwood's chest which didn't have no hair on it, and I couldn't help but notice he had him a natural sheen to his skin. Like dark polished oak, his muscles had that high a shine.

'It's Brenda you ought to take a strap to first, Palatine. In fact I should have slapped her hiney myself!' he shouted.

'Don't be telling me who to hit, Mister. That ain't your place. And if you lay your hands on one of these here children, you'll be a dead sonuvabitch.' I was trying to see what I could grab to hit him with if I had to.

'I know what you're thinking,' Dagwood said. 'But you can stop. It was Brenda who got in bed with me. On top of me and under the covers and was doing I don't know what.'

'You grown! You shoulda made her quit.'

'Hell,' he said. 'I thought it was Tammy!'

'I'm s'posed to believe that?'

'Don't go taking Brenda's side.' He looked at Joy. 'You saw her didn't you, Joy. Tell Palatine,' he told her. Then he said to me, 'It was Joy shouting, "Brenda, I'm gonna tell Mama!" that woke me up.'

'Don't draw Joy into this,' I said. 'You done enough already.' Then I asked Joy, 'Where was you when it was happening?'

'Peeking through the door in there.' She pointed to the living room. It bothered me that she didn't come to tell me soon as she saw Brenda climb into the bed, but I had too much on my mind to say as much.

Dagwood looked mad more than scared. Not guilty like somebody who's been caught out. 'I haven't done a damn thing,' he said. 'I had a few drinks when I came in this morning at about three o'clock. Then Tammy and I went to sleep. When I woke up with somebody all over me, I didn't even open my eyes. I naturally assumed it was her.'

That was the same story Joy told, but I didn't want to think that Brenda would do something like that. It was upsetting. She wasn't the sweetest child, nor the cutest, but she wasn't bad.

'If you didn't treat this place like a brothel, that child wouldn't know nothing 'bout laying up with no man,' I told him.

'Well I think there's something seriously wrong with that girl. That's what I think. And I'm calling her mother to tell her to come straight home so that we can get this nightmare sorted out. Because,' he broke off and leaned up against the wall and put his head in both hands, 'because I'm not the kind that would mess with a ten year old. I've got women lined up around the block waiting for me.' I knew that was true enough. 'You've seen me with these kids. Do you believe I'd harm them?'

'I don't know what to believe,' I said. 'But you shouldn't be standing in front of no little girls with your shirt off. My husband wouldn't do it.'

Joy rushed at him like a panther with her fists balled up and started to hammer on him. He grabbed her flailing arms, and as I went to stop him, his head butted up against my cheek. Soon as it happened I felt my face start throbbing and held my hand up to it to ease the pain.

'Get back here, Joy. Get back,' I yelled at her. Dagwood had her in a hold. Her eyes was wild.

'Don't you tell Mama,' she kept on kicking and shouting. 'I'll kill you, if you tell, I'll kill you.' She was near on hysterical while Brenda was watching like all of it was on the TV and she didn't have nothing to do with the noise and wrestling going on.

I pulled Joy off Dagwood and pushed her and Brenda into the bathroom.

'How the hell did I get caught up in a mess like this,' he asked me. 'Now you can believe me or not, but I'm telling you for Brenda's good as well as mine, that child was doing things that I can't get her mother to do. So where did she learn that?'

'Off you and Tammy. Who else! Y'all ain't supposed to be laying up in no bed together in front of these children. You ain't married and ain't thinking 'bout it. I seen you necking in front of 'em myself.'

'There's nothing wrong with kissing. They can see that on the TV. And whatever else we do, we do in the bedroom. I haven't been making it with Tammy in front of her little girls. I'd have to be out of my mind.'

'I don't live in here, so I don't know what goes on, but it don't seem natural that no Brenda climbed in the bed on top o' you less you been encouraging it.' Where I got hit under my eye was pounding like a tom tom.

'We'd better call Tammy,' he said.

'You best wait on that,' I told him. I was scared. Tammy had a bad temper and gone as she was on Dagwood, there wasn't no telling what she would have done to Brenda.

'Come out the bathroom, now, y'all,' I said to Joy and Brenda.

Brenda looked sheepish and didn't cast her eyes in the direction of Dagwood when she went out the door.

I didn't know what to think. Nor what to say. Or who to say it to.

Nowadays, you hear every kinda story 'bout folks taking advantage of children. Everytime you open the papers seems like some poor child done had somebody fooling with them. Daddies, Uncles, Brothers. Teachers. Preachers. The whole shooting match. But I still ain't read nothing 'bout no children taking advantage of grown men, although I did hear something just a while ago about some little nine year old boys raping some old woman. But back then it was different. I didn't even know nothing 'bout no man till I got married. My mama used to tell me you got pregnant from swallowing a watermelon seed.

Anyway, Joy came out the bathroom sniffling. 'Don't let them take her to reform school,' she kept repeating. Over and over. Over and over she kept saying that. She was taking it all worse than anybody.

'Reform school would be a good place for Brenda,' Dagwood said under his breath. But Joy heard him and flew at him like she had lost her mind.

'You leave my sister alone, leave her alone. You nigger!' I hadn't never heard her say nothing bad to anybody before and it took me by surpise. I'm 'shamed to say I laughed. Nerves, I think it was.

Dagwood held Joy off him and said, 'Well I think there's something wrong with every one of you. That little girl got in bed with me and did things that some grown women won't do, and you're laughing!'

I couldn't explain that I wasn't laughing at the situation. It was Joy that got me going. She looked like a wildcat, her bangs sticking up in the air and face smeared with tears and dirt. I don't know how her face got that dirty. I hadn't never seen her like it. She was real careful about herself. They all was for that matter. Tammy had raised them that way.

Dagwood said, 'Tammy'd been telling Brenda all along to stop sitting on my lap every time I sat down. I thought she was worried about me taking Brenda's weight and was making an unnecessary fuss about nothing when she would say Brenda was the size of a woman and shouldn't be on my lap. But maybe she knew something that I didn't. I see now that she definitely knows a lot that *you* don't.'

I didn't know what he was referring to nor much care at that moment. Poor Brenda was scrounging around for love and affection. That was all. The child needed a hug from time to time. And Tammy saved hers for Dagwood and Anndora.

'I'll be back,' I told him, all the while pushing Joy out the door and into my place. But something said not to go in and let the children see me confused. I was supposed to be grown and know what to do. But I was still my mama's child and wanted to cry out for her help.

'Joy, go sit quiet with your sister. I'll be in there in a minute.'

Standing alone in the dim passage didn't clear my mind. Instead it give me time to realize my legs was like jelly, and dwell on Brenda. She wasn't much different from other little girls her age. She played jacks and tag sometimes, but mostly she ate too much candy and watched too much television. Brenda's problem was just that she was way bigger than most and developed. She wasn't fast, though. She liked to fool with nail polish, but it was Anndora who couldn't wait to get into Tammy's Maybelline and blue iridescent eye shadow. Brenda had to do some cooking and cleaning, but I knew of kids from the church who did way more.

She didn't make friends easy and didn't like to go to school, and I saw one report card where her teacher said Brenda couldn't sit still long enough to take things in. So anytime she could figure a way to stay home, she did. Tammy would tell me to keep an eye on her, but I had other things to do and a husband to look after.

When she stayed home from school, Brenda said she liked to be over in the 'partment by herself, and one day I found out why. I caught her reading a dirty book in the bathroom. '*Peyton Place!*' I said. 'Child, have you lost your mind!'

I showed it to Tammy that night and she shrugged it off. 'That devil's been in my bottom drawer,' she laughed. I didn't see nothing funny and told Tammy to hide that mess better. I didn't think she should of had no nasty books like that around, but I didn't say nothing. Tammy thought the Bible did more harm than them ol' dirty books she bought and told me that to my face.

Brenda only had one friend to speak of who was the sorriest child on the block. Sarah Jane Henderson her name was. Big as Brenda but she was twelve and shouldn't of been in Brenda's class, but she'd been held back a couple of times. Her mother'd spawned seven children and didn't have two dimes to rub together, and kept their place like the neighborhood junk yard. Some rusty bikes and a broken down baby carriage stayed crammed on the front yard and not a blade of grass grew where it was meant to. Every stray dog passing used it like a public lavatory. Didn't nobody come out to clean the turds away neither, so they dried to dust in the summer and smelled to high hell in winter. What winter we had.

Sarah Jane was always walking 'round with scabs on her legs and no matter what nanktie dress I saw her in, the hem was half hanging out. I asked at the church if we shouldn't donate food and clothes to the Hendersons, but didn't none of the sisters wanted nothing to do with 'em 'cause they said the Henderson woman laid up with anybody that come along, as did her two oldest girls.

First I thought it was Christian of Brenda to bring Sarah Jane home. She looked like she had bed bug bites and every kind of sore. And stank. I had to air the place after she'd been in it, and it wasn't just her clothes. I couldn't wait to get her in my tub and put some of Brenda's clean things on her. But it didn't take but one afternoon with her in my place to tell she was a bad influence; she was fast and I didn't want Brenda hanging with her.

They was going through one of my *Jet* magazines and I heard her say to Brenda, 'Ain't he fine. I bet he got a big dick too.'

I didn't say nothing to her, 'cause I figured she didn't know no better. But soon as she was gone, I told Brenda not to play out with her no more. But I used to see her in our parking lot from time to time waiting for Brenda to come out when Tammy was home. Tammy said she thought it was good for Brenda to make friends with somebody real poor. I'm ready to be Christian as the next one, but you still got to show good sense. No telling what Brenda had learned off her. But it crossed my mind that with Brenda spending her time with a girl like Sarah Jane, wasn't no telling what Brenda knew or would do.

When I had mulled over things a few minutes and went to open the door to my place, I was surprised to find Joy plaiting Brenda's hair. I expected the girls to look different . . . changed . . . like folks do after they been in a calamity. But they seemed like they normal selves sitting at the table playing hairdresser. I made Joy go wash her face, but couldn't actually look direct at Brenda when I gave her my new blue housecoat to put on. She had the nerve to smile like a chessy cat.

'Joy,' I said, 'I think I got some cherry Kool-Aid in one o' them kitchen drawers. Make it up so y'all can have some. And I'll be back in a sec. I got to go deal with something.' I meant Dagwood. 'Watch some TV if you want and don't be sticking your heads out the window.'

Brenda run to switch on the television before I could get back to my front door, and if I didn't know that she'd been doing what she had, I wouldn't of believed it from looking at her. It flummoxed me. I wasn't sure if I was s'pose to hit her or punish her or just let her be.

'Can't we go outside to play?' Joy called from the kitchen.

'No. It's too hot,' I shouted back. 'If y'all behave for five minutes while I'm over cleaning up your mother's, maybe I'll take you to my church hall this afternoon.'

'Oh goody, goody, goody,' Brenda yelled, and started jumping up and down. Since Joy hadn't finished combing Brenda's hair, one side was sticking up and the other was plaited in a tight braid that was no bigger than my baby finger.

'Don't go getting excited,' I said loud enough for Joy to hear as well, "cause y'all ain't going no place if you don't promise Baby Palatine here and now that we won't never tell nobody about this that happened this morning. And Brenda, I don't want you to make no mistake about! What you did is a sin 'fore God and if you was mine, I woulda beat you till you couldn't sit down. But you ain't, so I'm gonna let it slide. But there can't be no next time for nothing like this, 'cause the penitentiary is exactly where you'll end up.'

'Un uhn,' called Joy. 'Not the penitentiary. Reform school. They don't let kids in the penitentiary.'

'Who asked you, Miss Fancy Pants. I'm doing the talking. Anyway, that's why we ain't gonna tell your mother.' Brenda looked buck-eyed and I was glad I scared her 'cause kids forget too easy.

'Joy! Come,' I called. 'I'm gonna have both y'all put your hand on Uncle Freddie B's Bible. It's in there on the table where we had it a little while ago.'

Joy come in hopping on one foot with the Bible under her arm.

'Don't play up now. This is serious.' Both of 'em giggled as I grabbed their right hands to make them swear eternal secrecy and everlasting silence.

'Shouldn't we prick our fingers and swear in blood?' Joy asked. She loved all that mess that she used to see on *Lassie* and *Rin Tin Tin*. I didn't even bother to answer.

First I read them the twenty-fourth Psalm, and when I got to the passage that says 'and does not swear deceitfully', I eyed each of 'em separate and repeated it again so it would sink in. Joy thought I didn't see her sneak a glance over at Brenda.

'Y'all can play around all you want, when I get out the door, but it ain't asking too much for you to concentrate for half a minute more, now is it?' She was good at getting Brenda going.

The Bible gave me a bit of strength and I felt better till I got back out in the hall and knocked on Tammy's door. I was nervous, but I was determined not to let Dagwood see as much when I marched in.

The heat hit me, 'cause their place caught the morning sun before mine. It was like a oven.

I got used to Dagwood having a bright expression, but he looked dull and ashen when he came out the bedroom. He hadn't finished dressing and had his hands jugged down in his pants pockets.

Whatever Tammy saw in him, she wasn't gonna find no easy replacement, 'cause I hadn't never come across nobody like him in all my born days. Didn't want to watch the sports. Couldn't do much of nothing with his hands. Was always wasting his money on old timey blues records that didn't nobody want to hear, and always prosthetizing 'bout how to make a million off one bit of foolishness or another.

'Fore he'd come along, wasn't nothing in Tammy's life but kids, work and TV if you don't count me and Freddie B. She looked lonesome to me a couple times when I popped over to visit and the kids was in bed, but I didn't say nothing 'bout it, cause it wasn't my business to butt in. But soon as she took up with John Dagwood she was smiling from morning till night. Didn't nothing bother her, and if he just walked in the room, the heat and light coming off her was strong as the sun that day.

Tondalayah used to say that some men's only put on God's earth to be lovers, and from the way I figured it, that was probably Dagwood's claim to fame. It didn't make me feel easy to think about what Tammy was gonna do without him, but that's how it had to be. It gave me the jim-jam-jimmies to stand there and face him. But I did.

He saw me poke at my cheek to make sure it hadn't come up from when he'd butted me in the face and I breathed heavy when I said, 'Dagwood, ain't but one thing you can do. And that's head straight out of here and don't come back.'

I watched the sweat trickle down his temples. 'I'm not sure that's the right way to handle this,' he said. 'What about Brenda?'

'Why worry all 'a sudden. Not but ten minutes ago, you was telling me to beat her!' To see his sorry face made me mad and I wanted to ring my hands round his neck and choke the life out of him.

'I wasn't thinking straight, I was so angry, but of course I'm worried about that kid,' he said. 'And if I disappear it'll make Tammy think I have a reason to hide.' He stared at me with his big deer's eyes like a innocent boy found guilty. He kept biting on his bottom lip till I thought he would draw blood.

'Tammy don't never have to know nothing 'bout this,' I said. 'I sure ain't gonna tell. And the kids ain't.'

Dagwood paced back and forth like he was the only one burdened with the whole world's troubles. He come up and laid a hand on my bare shoulder. I wanted to shake it loose 'cause it didn't have no more weight to it than a woman's, but I stood still and kept my eyes down.

'Are you going to talk to Brenda to find out why she did it?' he asked.

I let that go in one ear and out the other. Back then decent folk didn't speak to kids about no sex. Not even no husbands and wives did that I knew.

It was way different in them days . . . I hadn't never even seen Freddie B naked. And didn't expect to. 'Cause I believed it wasn't respectable . . . So when me and him did what married folks do we kept lights out and nightclothes on. It sounds old fogyish to say it nowadays but back then Freddie B and me didn't feel right about it on the Sabbath. That's one of the reasons I couldn't understand how Tammy and Dagwood was wanting to go at it every chance they got.

'Palatine? Are you going to talk to Brenda?' Dagwood was waiting on some kinda answer, and I didn't want him to have the satisfaction of getting it.

'Why didn't you have a job to go to? Wouldn't none of this mess of happened,' I said and pushed his hand off my shoulder.

'Just because I won't take the first damn menial thing that comes along, you want to act like I'm a layabout. Hell! It's not a crime to be out of work when you get to a new town. I've worked all my goddamn life!' He was yelling and I got a whiff of the whiskey stale on his breath from the night before.

'Keep your voice down,' I said and walked over to the window and looked out to make sure nobody'd heard him in the street. We wasn't but one story off the ground and the window was a quarter open in the living room where we was standing.

'I swear to you, I was asleep.' He raised his hand to God, but it was too late for that, and stared into my eyes when he said, 'Believe me. I was dreaming. In and out of sleep, and I could feel warm hands on me. A wet mouth.'

'A child's lips was kissing on you and you didn't know it wasn't no Tammy up in your face! Mister, you are shucking 'n' jiving me. I don't believe that,' I shouted, figuring he took me for a numbskull.

'It wasn't my mouth. It was . . .' I didn't wait on him to finish, 'cause I didn't want to hear and laid up side his head with my right fist to stop his nasty talk. As strong as I was, it surprised me I didn't knock him down.

Dagwood didn't hit back. But he wavered and then shook his head like he was trying to put his brains back into place 'fore he said, 'You want to hit me again?' He stuck his chin up in my face. 'Go on, if it makes you feel any better. I wish it could do the same for me. Nothing can hurt me like Brenda has.' He could see I wasn't gonna take another swipe and he slumped off into the bedroom.

When the double doors was left open between the living room and the big bedroom, it was like one great big open play space, and that's how Tammy kept it in the daytime. Till Dagwood came along, and she stopped bothering to open them. So the kids got to acting like even their little bedroom was off limits till bedtime.

But during them first days of the girls' summer vacation when I was in and out of there checking on Joy and Brenda, I used to open both doors again till Tammy was about due to come home. I knew she wouldn't mind.

That morning just one was open. The bedroom drapes was drawn but the sun was that powerful that the flimsy bit of lined bottle green cloth up at the window calling itself a drape couldn't keep out neither heat or light. Dagwood yanked it back and threw the window right up. He needed to 'cause there was a heavy smell in the room. Part sleep, part something I refused to think on.

'You brung this on yourself,' I said. I was standing in the doorway. 'all that attention you give Brenda wasn't no good for her. That's what probably done it.'

'There was nothing wrong with giving her some love. I couldn't stand to see her an outsider in her own family. I left my father's house because of that kind of treatment. I always got the short end of the stick too, being darkest like she is.' He stood by the window looking out, so a bright sun ray cut cross his cheek bone which was baby smooth and deep chocolate colored. 'My two brothers used to always tease me and say "Step aside coal wagon, and let a high brown pass." It was supposed to be a joke, but I was little and it hurt because I knew they meant it. I grew up thinking they were better than I was because their skin was a few shades lighter.'He looked down at the back of his hand and kinda laughed but not a bit like he was enjoying hisself. 'It was "black niggers ain't worth this" and "black niggers ain't worth that" all the time in my old man's house, and I had to turn a deaf ear to it and pretend it didn't affect me. But the mirror said, "You ain't worth shit." And my family treated me like I wasn't.' He turned to me. 'Brenda needs a bit of that kindness Anndora gets from Tammy and you give Joy.'

'Color ain't got nothing to do with it,' I said. 'I'm just as black as Brenda almost. So's Joy.'

'But not quite, and Joy's hair grows long enough to make the difference, doesn't it?' His deep set eyes pierced me till I looked away. 'You know it as well as I do,' Dagwood said.

'You trying to blame all this that done happened on Brenda being dark skinned?' I had never heard of no such foolishness. 'That's bull, Mister, and I ain't crazy enough to buy it.'

I'd been treated the same at my mama's but I wouldn't of never said so to Dagwood. In mama's house she taught a rhyme to us children to keep us alert and alive living down South that went, 'If you're white, you're right, if you're brown, you'll get around, but if you're black, get back.' Anybody colored had to learn that quick enough. They say it's changed but I don't know. I still see it. Don't make me no never-mind. I was born black as the ace of spades and I'm gonna die just that way, and I'm proud of it. They'll always let a few of us slip through, but not many, and nary one looking like me with big lips, flat nose and hair that don't grow but a few inches every hundred years. No indeedy. Not in my lifetime.

Dagwood started up again. 'I don't feel . . .'

'We ain't got no time for feelings, boy. We done talked this backwards and forwards long enough, and I can't leave them children sitting by themselves no longer, so finish putting your duds on and get out of here, so I can figure a way out of this.'

He set hisself down on the wood chair to lace up his shoes and then dropped his head in his lap like he wasn't gonna get right up. So I put in my final word.

'I don't like you and ain't got no reason to trust you, but I believe you ain't been fooling with Brenda which is the onliest reason I'm letting you to walk out of here and not look back. 'Cause Joy wasn't far wrong when she was up screaming about reform school. Brenda can't be in the same room again with you, and when you get out in the street and give it thought, you'll understand what I mean.'

'Doing nothing makes you as guilty as pulling the trigger on Brenda. To encourage those kids not to tell their mother is wrong.' Dagwood stopped for a second like he had something important to say, then began throwing his few things into a brown paper sack that come from Leo's supermarket. 'Things are not what they seem. You should know that . . . Tammy should tell you . . . Look, Palatine. Tammy and I have such a good thing going. Don't you understand? That's why I wouldn't let her give me no for an answer after she saw me over at the beauty shop with my father's third cousin's wife.'

It was the first I heard that Bobbie was 'supposed' to be a relation but cousin or no cousin, Dagwood had to go. I stepped into the bedroom to pick up the sheet that was thrown on the floor. Shaking it out I spotted a yellowish wet patch against the bleached white.

'What's on this here sheet, man?' My voice come back ringing in my ears.

He didn't have to look. 'You want me to take it over to the laundry?'

'The hell with the laundry. You spunked in that child and she ain't but ten!'

'No,' he said not able to look me in the eye.

'No, my mama! It don't take Dick Tracey to see it on this here.' I threw the sheet down and fell to kneeling at the foot of the bed. 'Sweet Jesus, please save us.' I bowed my head and started to pray, because Brenda was already getting her monthly and a picture come into my mind of her pregnant.

'Didn't you hear what I've been saying.' Dagwood half spoke, half whimpered. 'I was asleep with the pillow over my head to keep out the light and I thought it was Tammy. I thought I was dreaming.' When I looked at him, his face was winced up like somebody in pain.

'One minute you say you was dreaming and the next you claim you thought it was Tammy,' I cried.

'You know how it feels when you're asleep and somebody's got their mouth all over you. Licking and biting you in and out of a dream. It was like sleeping on a roller coaster, and it felt . . . oh God! However I explain it, it sounds bad,' he said and started to sob. 'I didn't want it to stop because Tammy had never taken me out of myself like that before. Then when I heard Joy calling, "Brenda, Brenda, I'm going to tell if you don't stop," I thought the kids were playing in the living room. So I laid still and tried not to come. And when Joy's voice called again it was so loud it really woke me and I put my hand under the sheet to try to stop Tammy who still had her mouth on me to tell her to see to the kids, but the pillow fell to the floor . . . I . . . couldn't . . . I . . . not able to control myself, and at the same time I saw it was Brenda. Brenda beneath the sheet. Not Tammy. And I felt myself screaming but had no control left. God forgive me. But I didn't know it had been Brenda. I swear, I swear, Palatine.' He sobbed and sobbed. I hadn't never seen no man in a state like it. 'Pray for her.' He sucked his breath and said real quiet, 'Pray for all of us. But it can't erase what's happened.'

I pulled myself up and wiped at my eyes. 'I got to see to them children. I expect they'll be all right.' I figured I ought not tell him about how they was playing hairdresser when I checked them.

'And what will you say to Tammy?' Dagwood asked me as I was fixing to walk out. I hadn't thought about it. To tell the truth, I hadn't thought about nothing. I was just bumping in and out of the whole upset like a blind man pretending to know where he's headed but with no hope of seeing his way. I watched Dagwood open a drawer and put a couple more things in the paper sack. Then he took a ring off his finger. It wasn't nothing flashy. Just a signet ring like they give kids graduating high school. 'Give this to Brenda,' he said.

'What for? So she can think she gets a prize for acting like a whore! She can't have nothing from you,' I told him.

'I know what she did was wrong, but she has to live with it and that'll be punishment enough. You know what I mean, Palatine. Brenda's only a baby. Let me show her that I've forgiven her.' He was holding out his palm to me with the ring, but I wouldn't take it.

'Just go about your business, man. And promise me and yourself you won't never breathe a word of this and it will pass.' I believed that.

When I watched him walk down the hall stairs I whispered at his back, just loud enough for him to hear but not Joy and Brenda,

'Promise me, please, that you won't never come back. So I can tell the children . . .' He wouldn't turn 'round. 'Promise for Brenda's sake,' I begged.

He paused at the front door with his hand on the latch and turned to look back at me at the top of the stairs. He didn't say nothing for about a minute that seemed like two days. Then he nodded and slipped out.

It seemed to me that Tammy was the biggest loser that day, 'cause the kids got to playing and roughhousing like they plum forgot all about what had happened that morning. But time proved we all lost something. Tammy just showed hers more.

When she got home that evening with Anndora in tow, I was real nervous and didn't know what to say, but Tammy said it for me when she told me that Dagwood phoned her at work to tell her a job had come up in Detroit and he was taking off 'cause there wasn't nothing to stay for. She didn't bother with supper. She swigged a bit of VAT 69 she found that Dagwood had left in the kitchen and went straight to bed not noticing it was my clean sheets she was laying on. When I brought the kids back later that night, I looked in on her. She had a fever. I suspected it was heartache she was suffering, but I told her it was probably a summer cold and she should call in sick the next day as it was Friday and she'd have all the weekend to strengthen up. I watched her get up out of bed to grab Dagwood's tie that I forgot to hide when I found it on the back of the chair. She sniffed at it and rubbed it on her cheek and kissed it. Held on to it night after night like I seen children do with a piece of silky trim off a blanket. She kept it by her pillow, till she finally wore it out, so it wasn't nothing but a piece of rag the day she got rid of it. I wanted to shout 'Hallelujah' when I spotted it in a rubbish bag in her kitchenette. I remember that afternoon good, 'cause me and Freddie B'd picked up a little Christmas tree for the kids and she tried to make us take it back. But I told Tammy, 'Whatever's was wrong with you, Christmas is coming day after tomorrow whether you ready or not.' She'd been off work nearly six months and didn't never admit to me nor herself that it had to do with Dagwood leaving. But that's what it was. Love sick. My Christmas present from her that year was to hear her say, 'I'm going back to work.'

That secret I shared with her two children built a wall between me and Tammy, and whereas it locked me and Joy in together 'cause we had to trust each other, it blocked Brenda out. I couldn't trust her, much as I tried. 'Specially round my brother. I was scared for Brenda to be with Caesar so when he'd come to stay, I made excuses why Brenda couldn't play in my place. What with him and the drink and her being a child in a woman's body, wasn't no telling what coulda happened, I thought.

From the minute her mother took to the bed, Brenda had to do most of the cooking and cleaning. I hated to see a girl her age with all that housework, but she seemed to come into her own with them chores. Like it was a penance that unburdened her. I helped as much as Tammy's pride would let me. She laid up pining and called it sickness while Brenda slaved. But like Tammy, I had to admit the more Brenda did the happier she looked. She was able for her age and Freddie B used to marvel at her. Of course, he didn't know the whole story . . .

With the children off school when Dagwood disappeared, I begged Tammy to let me take 'em to the First Tabernacle Sunday school. I think she finally let them go more to have some peace and quiet than to encourage them to respect our Lord, because she still wouldn't have no talk about the Scriptures nor Bible reading in her place.

I used to say, 'What you got against Jesus Christ? He ain't harmed you that I can see.'

'He hasn't done a damn bit of good for me either.'

The louder she blasphemed the harder I prayed for her. And them children. I burnt enough divinity candles over that six months to light up the Oakland Coliseum.

Tammy didn't have no pact with the devil or nothing. It was that them Jehovah's Witnesses back in Wilmington put her off God she said when they used to knock on her door every Thursday night and refuse to leave till she had a *Watch Tower* pamphlet off them and let them in to preach gospel. I reckon they saw her need which I could see myself. 'Goddamn religious fanatics. I've had them up to here,' Tammy'd say reaching her hand to her chin. 'I haven't got a bit of time for all that shit. If you niggers would stop praying long enough to learn to speak English properly you wouldn't need no damn God. Look at the Russians. They closed down those doggone churches when the Communists came into power!'

I run outa there a couple times when she said more than I reckoned I could pray away, but I used to always end up going back. I'd keep her company a lot. Mostly she watched soap operas in the afternoons and helped the kids with homework once they was back from school. Anndora'd started first grade that September.

Tammy knew that I wasn't partial to Dagwood from the get-go, so she didn't never mention him. But she did a lot of weeping when she was first laid up that June while her girls played in the streets from dawn right up to bedtime. They was out shouting with the morning glories.

Hard as my poor husband worked, wasn't a dime saved what with Helen, my brother Caesar and them children eating his pay check up. But I couldn't watch n'ere one of them go without, 'cause Tammy's sick leave pay ran out after three months. She had her a old white doctor, Dr Cobbs, that used to come give her prescriptions and the certificates she had to send in to the job, but he wasn't nothing but a debt collector hiding behind a stethoscope. His bill ate up her sick leave pay.

If it hadn't been for Joy, I don't know how I woulda got through that year. She was always bringing me dandylions and saving me a piece of her bubble gum. It worried me that she was around Brenda so much, but there you are, ain't no way to separate sisters so I just used to keep my worrying to myself. Joy was leader anyway, and Brenda used to follow behind like Joy was the eldest. I used to tell Brenda, 'Child, you better start thinking for your self, 'cause you ain't always gonna have Joy to watch over you.' Little did I know it was a prophecy.

My mind shifted from the past and that sorry time on Grange Street to Brenda standing by Joy's record machine determined to bang on it till she broke it, and I wondered what I could do to help her get the music going, but I ain't never been handy with no electrical things.

'We best leave it be then, if you can't get it going,' I said.

'What d'you think I'm gonna do, sit here for three days without music while Mama tries to drive me crazy? Can you believe she hasn't said a word to me since I arrived. Mama should've at least come down to say hello.'

'She ain't said hi to me neither and I ain't ready to storm the troops. She's probably sleeping. Calm down, Brenda, and stop acting like you ready for Custer's last stand.'

She was standing with both broad hands on both broad hips and legs astride. All was missing was a six gun. 'I've drug myself all the way down here from Roxbury on a broken down, clapped out overnight bus and my mother can't drag herself down half a flight of stairs to say "Good morning". Mama hasn't set eyes on me since I took the time and spent money I didn't have to visit her and Jesse two years ago in Richmond. I didn't have to bother. Joy and Anndora didn't.' Forty-one years old and Brenda was still comparing herself to her sisters like a child would.

'Your mama's grieving, Brenda, and I know her and Jesse drove all the way from Richmond so maybe they're too tired to move,' I said to ease her aggravation, but it didn't do no good.

'We're all grieving, goddamit. Mama can't play like she's got grabs on it. Not this time. We all lost somebody,' she said and threw herself on the sofa. 'And what about you? What about me? Joy was the only one in the family that remembered I had a birthday and with it being the first day of the year, it shouldn't be all that easy to forget. Of course I wouldn't have expected any better from Anndora, but wouldn't you think your own mother could send you a card. Or call at least. When did I last get a birthday card from Mama?'

Even when the girls were little Tammy used to forget their birthdays –and I used to run around trying to make up for it. But she didn't appreciate it and said it made her look bad when I fixed a birthday cake. But I figured all that was water under the bridge and why Brenda wanted to bring up birthday cards with her sister dead was beyond me. It never did take much to get Brenda going, and for a minute I couldn't understand why she suddenly flared up. I was just forgetting that was her way.

'Maybe there's an instruction book for that record machine,' I said thinking to distract her.

Strange as it was that Tammy didn't shout down a hello at least, there didn't seem much point in fussing about it.

'Don't try to change the subject, Baby Palatine.'

'Well, hollering ain't never done no good, and there's a whole lot else for you to swell up about if'n you're in the mood to, like how it happened that Joy's supposed to be dead from a heart attack.'

'Sometimes it's best to get things off your chest,' said Brenda referring to her ruckus, and while that may have been true, it was her chest getting the relief and mine bearing the burden. And I was too tired to listen to her rant on about her mama when there was more important things, like arrangements for Joy's funeral, to put mind to.

If I could have had my way, I'd of stayed in a hotel, 'cause I wasn't in the right frame of mind to put up with Brenda and Tammy arguing with each other and about each other when some folks would of been fraught with mourning. But they was always doing it and no matter how many times I heard it, I still found it upsetting that a mother and grown daughter didn't try to get on better. Neither one had no respect for t'other and I'd seen times when Brenda was politer to the gas meter man than to her own mama.

I tried to get the record machine going while Brenda looked out one of the tall double glazed windows that made the living room seem way larger than it was. With both of them floor to ceiling and situated on adjoining walls opposite the front door, it made the room seem real big even though there wasn't nothing worth looking at outside 'em. One looked directly over a parking lot and the other look across to a six story red brick building with filthy windows and a ugly maroon door. Not much to see at that hour of the morning either way. I had been on my knees fidgeting with the record machine and trying not to notice how uncomfortable I felt to be in Joy's place without her there. Maybe if she'd of been there, it wouldn't of felt so empty and lifeless to me.

'What's the red light mean?' I called over to Brenda, when all a' sudden a light the size of a pinhead started throbbing.

'Did you get it working?'

'I'm the wrong one to ask about these new fangled machines,' I said but I was relieved that it hummed like I'd got it going, 'cause for as long as I'd known her, Brenda always cheered up when music played.

'You did better with it than I did,' she said turning knobs again. 'What do you want to hear?'

'Joy used to always keep some Nat King Cole around.'

'It's a bit early for cocktail hour music,' she said

'Nat King Cole ain't cocktail music. He's soothing. That's how come the radio plays him all the time of the day and night.'

'Well let me look.' Brenda bent over to sift through the records. She was poured into a pair of tie dyed blue jeans and her behind was that broad that I wondered what factory had the nerve to turn out a pants size to fit her. The funny thing was that she had shape. Bust, waist, and hips didn't drop in one straight line, thickset as she was. Brenda had her a waistline though I woulda been scared to guess how many inches around it was.

Brenda was born sloppy I imagine and whereas the few albums and tapes Joy had was in a neat stack in a special metal cabinet, it didn't take Brenda but a minute to sling 'em all about her on the floor. She was still messy as ever.

'Will you settle for Billy?' she asked me.

'Eckstine?'

'No, Baby, Holiday.'

'She's too depressing.' That's all I needed was Billie Holiday singing one of them 'Gloomy Sundays' or 'Strange Fruits' to finish me off. Much as I liked her voice when I was young, it reminded me too much of Southern lynchings.

'How about some Motown?' Brenda's face brightened no sooner than she had the record out the sleeve, so I didn't try to stop her though I would of liked something quieter. What did I care? If it wasn't Nat King Cole I would only be half-hearted listening anyway. And certain music has a way of bringing back too many memories.

Brenda didn't seem so out of place when she started dancing around Joy's living room. I thought she'd stopped stewing, but then she turned around to me and said, 'Can you believe that Mama didn't even leave a light on for me and she knew I was getting in at five. How was I supposed to find my way around. It took me ten minutes to work out how to turn the lights on. I was so mad.'

I thought hunger might have been her problem so I offered to fix her some breakfast. Food could always solve Brenda's agitations and usually it didn't matter what she put in her mouth. If she could chew on it she was satisfied. But it surprised me when she answered, 'Naw. I'm too ruffled. I'll have some beer.'

There was a big clock tower I could just about see from one of the windows. 'It ain't even midday. You can't start up drinking this early.' I can't stand to see folks abuse theyselves with alcohol.

Brenda said, 'Okay. I spotted some Aunt Jemima in one of the cupboards before you got here, but don' ask me which one.' They all looked exactly the same. I like a kitchen to look like a kitchen, but Joy's had everything hid away so you couldn't see nothing but white laminated cabinet doors. Even her double door fridge freezer was disguised behind one of them fake door fronts. Only thing out was a white percolator and the toaster to match. I can only do pancakes right in an old fashion iron skillet, but I was sure Joy would of had some kinda fancy frying pan though I don't suspect it ever got used, 'cause she didn't like to cook nor want to learn to, and her stove told the tale. It was spotless. Like brand new off the showroom floor.

We found the pancake mix after Brenda opened every door in the kitchen. Though I was trying to go along with the rhythm of conversation Brenda was setting, I wanted to talk about Joy, but I didn't want to upset Brenda again so I raised my voice above the music to test the waters.

'Do you know what's happening about your sister's funeral?'

I had my jacket off and my blouse sleeves pushed up, and Brenda was leaning on the sink watching me mix batter. I was dying to slip off my roll-on and relax, 'cause nobody was there to put on a show for.

'Mama found an undertaker in the yellow pages. Some guy that's over in Harlem. She asked me to get here in time to go over there with her. That's why I had to take the bus last night. The appointment's at eleven.'

'I can't hardly believe it,' I said. 'Joy was the picture of good health with more energy than a football team. 'Member her always giving herself them B12 shots? Up and dying from heart failure . . .'

'You think it was drugs?'

'Joy didn't mess with no drugs,' I said stirring in some more milk, 'cause the batter didn't look runny enough.

'She used to. Although I seem to remember how you turned a blind eye to it.'

'That stopped a long time ago when she gave up smoking cigarettes.'

'I'm not talking about marjuana. Nobody dies from that.'

'What else is there, 'cause you know Joy wouldn't fool about with no heroin. She was kinda wild, but she wasn't crazy.'

'Baby, there's a whole lot of other things to play with these days. PCP. Coke. Crack. Smack ain't the only way to go, and Joy dabbled and took her taste like everybody else in the record business. That's one of the things that I didn't like about all those backing sessions. Half of those musicians were high all the time.'

'Not Joy.' She had a few little faults but she was the first one to take her some vitamins and be exercising and worrying 'bout chemicals in the food.

'We all have secrets,' said Brenda. I guess she knew that better than anybody, I thought, as I grabbed her hand to stop her from sticking her finger in my batter.

'There's no telling what people get up to behind closed doors. I knew a guy worked at the post office. He was real nice and seemed as normal as anybody else. Wife. Couple kids. I took him for straight, you know. But out of the blue he didn't come to work for a few days and didn't call in. Next thing we knew he'd turned up, dead of course, but the catch was the cops found him down an alleyway in Cambridge dressed in women's clothes. Suspender belt, bra, the whole shebang. And that was a lesson to me, that you never know people.' Brenda looked at her watch. 'You think I should call Mama?'

'She'll wake up in her own good time. Tammy don't like the mornings no way.'

Brenda opened and closed the frigerator. I could tell she was restless. I said, 'Look in my pocketbook and take out some money and get yourself some beer, if you want.'

'I've got money!' She was always proud. 'Do we need anything else?' She opened the fridge again and checked the freezer. 'Ice cubes. Joy must have been on a starvation diet. I've never seen a freezer compartment this empty, 'Brenda said and only half shut it.

I didn't want to tell her that the place didn't look lived in to me 'cause I didn't want to get Brenda thinking.

'Well, take twenty dollars from me, please, and get some bacon and whatnot, 'cause we all have to eat before nightfall and there is only milk, eggs and orange juice. And I bet Tammy brought that with her 'cause the juice has a Virginia label on it,' I said.

'You think I should ask Mama if she wants something? I think I can hear the television going in their room.' Brenda was itching to see her mother. I don't know why, because they never did get along, not in all the time I'd known them.

'Let Brenda worry about Brenda. Your mother's got a husband up there. Maybe they want a minute to themselves.'

She wasn't happy, and slammed the front door on her way out to the store. There was no need frying pancakes till she was back, so I went to the living room and looked out the window. There was a big black and white weatherbeaten sign above the parking lot that said Valet Parking $17 per day, $60 a week. 'Hmph,' I said out loud. 'I can remember when you could rent a whole house for that much.' Freddie B gets cross when I refer back on what things used to cost, so I try to stop myself from doing it in front of him, 'cause I think he likes to forget about how much we used to could afford but can't no more. We was rich back in them days in Oakland and didn't know it. I used to check prices on things to be cute back then, but now I have to, and whereas Freddie B loved having him a new car every few years, we ain't changed that Chevy since the girls had that hit record.

Joy sent money when she could, a hundred dollars here and there when we wasn't expecting it, and she didn't wait for no birthdays or anniversaries to do it neither. She said she just liked to surprise us, but I don't reckon she realized what a big difference it made. It wasn't the money, it was that it got me waking up in the morning throwing open them living room drapes with a feeling something good could happen. Either it could come with the post, or the phone could ring and it'd be my God-sent child laughing and ready to gab from wherever for half hour about nothing.

Joy was a good name for her, but she might just as easy been called Hope. To hear her talk about what she expected to get out of life, you'd of thought she had blond hair and blue eyes. Her head was way up in the clouds and I used to try and pull her back to earth, 'cause I wanted her to dream big but I didn't want her dreaming for more than she was gonna get. I used to say, 'You was born the wrong color to get you all them things you want to believe you got a right to.'

She'd say, 'White's not a color, Baby, it's a state of mind and all you have to do is think white.'

'What's that s'posed to mean?' I asked her one time.

'Believe that the world is yours and you can have anything in it. Think that the world turns for you,' she laughed. She was always laughing which I loved.

Then she got to dancing with her arms flailing all over the place and her legs and feet going every whichaway. All out of step like we used to see them white kids do when they danced in the clubs we worked when Bang Bang Bang was on tour. Joy'd say, 'See, Baby! I can even dance white.' She'd nearly have me peeing myself laughing.

It didn't seem possible she was gone, and I walked across her living room to look in her closets again. Like I expected to find her there. She always wore a real expensive perfume called Bal à Versailles that would creep all over you when you'd been sitting in a room with her for a while. I could smell it on some of the clothes in her closet. To get a sniff of it felt more real to me than anything that had happened that morning and I would of shut myself up in there with them if I coulda done 'cause the closet was deep enough. But instead, I pulled a see-through plastic chair over to the door of it and set myself down. There was two tall cardboard boxes setting on the closet floor, and I decided to have me a good wade through them both while I waited on Brenda.

The first thing I checked was full of nothing but papers. When it came to bills and receipts and old letters, Joy was a hoarder and refused to throw them things out. I used to ask her, 'What you saving all that mess for?'

'There might be some information on some of them to make them come in handy one day,' she'd say. 'Especially those letters.'

As few as she'd had from Rex, she'd saved every single solitary one, I expect, though I didn't plan to sift through the pile to seek 'em out.

The other box was full of rubbishy things, like she'd cleared her drawers and threw everything into that one big box. It was full of junk couldn't nobody give away. Old brassieres. Sunglasses. A deck of cards. Broken scissors. A whistle, a couple of dirty magazines, including that one Brenda gave that interview about being a lesbian. The silly thing is that the magazine was called *Queen for a Day* but it was full of pictures with boys with nothing on and I don't know why Joy bothered to keep the nasty thing.

Right down at the bottom of the box I laid my hand on a whole stack of pictures that I didn't realize I was looking for till I'd found them, and I couldn't help grinning. Family, friends, publicity shots and all mixed in a big batch together with a big thick rubber band 'round them. I put 'em by and pulled the box out into the room to get a better look in it, but when I did, my nose caught wind of something in the closet smelling like old sneaks. It wasn't strong enough to kill the perfume scent, but it was strong enough to make me curious about what it was coming off, so I found the switch on the wall in there to turn some light on to get a look right in the corners. That's when I spotted a nasty looking gray rag chucked way at the back like somebody'd just tossed it in there. Good thing I had light, 'cause if I woulda put my hand on it without knowing what it was I suspect I'd of thought it was a dead rat or something. It was dampish, like it hadn't been laying in there long, and I picked it up between my thumb and forefinger 'cause I didn't want to grab hold of the dirty, smelly thing and carried it through to plop it in the kitchen sink. Then I went back about my business looking through them pictures.

Some I remembered like the one of Joy, Brenda and Anndora when they had the group. They looked fabulous decked out in identical skin-tight see-through dresses with sequins clustered up together to cover their private parts. Them dresses was murder to take care of. Brenda and Joy had on wigs to match up to Anndora's hair and Brenda was kind of leant over with her behind sticking out to hide her being taller than her sisters.

Joy always did Brenda's makeup and would have her looking like somebody else, but still if Joy or Anndora hadn't been in the photo with her you mighta took Brenda to be one of them men turned out to look like a woman like the ones they got billed outside that transvesterite club in North Beach.

There was one nice shot I hadn't never seen of Brenda standing outside the First Tabernacle, and there was a whole bunch of pictures of the girls growing up.

I wanted to take my time to go through 'em, but first I went to look out of the window to see if I could spot Brenda coming out of the grocery store over near the corner opposite. It bothered me that she wasn't back, 'cause folks can be getting hit in the head on their doorsteps in New York. Then I went to check the little TV monitor in the narrow passage by the kitchen. It showed who was in the lobby or at the double fronted door which was glass and had two huge palms standing either side of it. No Brenda. I'd of hated to be that doorman setting there all the day where everybody in the place could see what you was up to every minute, and seeing him on that monitor looking half dozy made me want to doze myself. It crossed my mind to stretch out on Joy's sofa and have a five minute nap, though I was scared that I'd sleep through Brenda ringing on the door bell.

So instead I went and opened the cupboard in the passage opposite the toilet and stared in. It was all clothes. Mostly coats and some riding clothes hanging neat and pretty. I spotted a stack of shoeboxes on the floor and amongst them I was shocked to see that paisley box them Papagallos had come in way back when. Helen'd found 'em one time tucked in the far corner of my closet on Grange and tried to tell me she thought Freddie B was keeping him a young woman somewhere 'cause they was so small. So I lied to Helen and said they was Joy's graduating present from junior high and actually gave 'em to Joy outright though by that time they didn't fit her no more 'cause she was fourteen and had shot up both in height and shoe size from them early days when her and me kept the Papagallos a secret. It gave me a real big surprise that Joy still had the box, and when I pulled it out and opened it them blue shoes was in there, still smelling like brand new leather. Not a scratch on 'em. Wrapped careful in the same black tissue paper they'd come in originally. Seeing them Papagallos like to broke my heart, and I got a big lump in my throat when I took them out the box. I tried to push my foot in the left one, far as it would go, which wasn't no further than my big toe with my feet still swollen from that plane. I figured that the little ball of polythene Joy'd put in the toe was to hold the shape 'cause the toe was so pointed, but when I took it out I saw it was actually a little plastic sandwich bag balled up which had a itty-bitty piece of paper folded up neat inside it.

I decided Joy wouldn't mind me snooping as she wasn't gonna be coming back, but I still felt guilty all the same about inspecting what was on the piece of paper. It had some numbers scratched on it in Joy's writing, so small I had to take a good long look to figure out what they was. I said out loud, 'One five, nine zero, three six,' and didn't know what she would of been bothering to hide no number for.

I'd heard tell of people playing the numbers when I was living in

Louisiana, but you didn't hear nothing about the numbers racket in California. I guessed if you could play 'em anywhere you could play 'em in New York. Gotham City as Batman calls it. Joy always did like to gamble which is why we was supposed to be heading for Reno, but she couldn't get me to bet her a dime in all the time I knew her 'cause although she was quick to say, 'I'll betcha a dollar for this or five dollars on that,' I'd tell her, 'We supposed to be friends, how I'm gonna take money off you, even if I do win.'

'Cause the number was written in Joy's hand, I stuck the paper in the change purse in my pocketbook and kissed them blue Papagallos 'fore I put them in my suitcase. I was about to collect up them pictures too that I'd found and stick them in my suitcase, but something said, 'Be fair. Everybody'll be wanting dibs on them.' So I left the pile still setting on the floor by the cupboard door.

I was that tired all 'a sudden that I was punchy. Jet lag gets me that way, and I thought I'd better put my head down for a minute at least 'fore I got a headache with forcing myself to keep my eyes open. I couldn't wait no more for Brenda and took a camel hair coat out the closet to cover myself up while I stretched out on the sofa. Needless to say, I didn't get no more than two snores out good 'fore the bell went.

'This ain't no barn,' I told Brenda when she come in and left the front door wide open. I took two of the four shopping bags she was toting off her and went with them in the kitchen. She slammed the door so hard I thought she was going to take it off its hinges.

'Sorry that took me so long,' she said.

I was glad for the peace and quiet, I thought to myself soon as she started banging them cupboard doors. 'Brenda, Brenda, let me put the messages away.'

'Has Mama been down?' she asked looking at her watch.

'No.'

'We have to be at the undertaker's soon. I bet she doesn't have a clue how to get there. Harlem's not just around the corner you know. This is Chelsea. It's way across other side of town.'

The first bag I emptied was full of stuff we didn't need like cinnamon and cornmeal, canned pumpkin. Brenda could really cook but she never bothered to economize when she shopped.

'Brenda, what all did you buy?'

'Half the store,' she laughed. 'They're going to deliver the rest. I couldn't carry it all.'

'How much did you spend?'

'Only twenty dollars of yours.'

'I hope you didn't go mad. Nobody's going to be in the mood to eat. My ulcer feels like it's 'bout ready to start up as it is. In fact I meant for you to get me some Pepto Bismol.'

'What about the wake? You know how people need to eat at the wake.'

'Is there going to be a wake?' Tammy wasn't a bit God fearing and I didn't think that she'd do more than invite a few of Joy's friends for a simple service at the funeral parlor. I should say I was hoping she'd do as much.

'See, this is the what we should be working out, because Mama'll do her usual and leave everything till the last minute so nobody's going to know what's going on. Yesterday she couldn't decide whether she wanted Joy buried or cremated.'

'Cremated! For what, pray tell!' I hadn't heard no foolishness like that in my life. 'I thought Joy'd have her a pretty white satin lined open casket. You know how she liked to dress up and show herself. Don't you think that's how we ought to do it?'

'What makes you think that? That means somebody'll have to dress the body and do her makeup.'

'Lord, child, don't you want to see your sister for the last time? I sure do!'

'What for? She can't wave back, and I don't particularly want to remember Joy as lying dead. I never did like viewings. People always look too weird. Nothing like they usually look with that powder on their faces. Anyway Joy's the type that would like her ashes thrown in the ocean or something romantic like that.'

'Don't talk ridiculous. What's romantic about having some fish eat on you?'

'Oh Baby, don't ask so many questions. I don't know! I don't know,' she said in a hushed voice, and then burst out crying. Brenda wasn't never one for weeping, so it took me off guard.

I followed her to the living room and sat right up close to her on the sofa. She'd plopped down on the coat I left and I had to push her off it.

There was too much of Brenda for me to put my arms 'round, so I took her hand and kept patting on it.

'What about R-E-J-O-Y-C-E. I'll tell you like you told me, Joy wouldn't want you upset.'

'I'm not crying for her. I'm crying for me.'

'Go on and cry then,' I told her. Whatever she was crying for, holding it in wasn't gonna do her no good. Brenda didn't try to wipe her face and I didn't have a handkerchief, so I sat there and watched the tears stream down. Good thing she wasn't wearing no makeup.

There's a big import store down on San Francisco wharf that sells them wood carvings and statues that look like they come from Africa but they got 'Made in Taiwan' stickers on most of 'em. Years ago Tondalayah went in there and bought me a carved head made from some kinda dark wood and it's of a African woman who got a great big high forehead like Brenda. So watching Brenda weep, I kept seeing that carved face with its big bulgy eyes weeping too. Part, I guessed it was 'cause Brenda's dark smooth face reminded me of that one I'd been putting polish on everyday. Brenda's hair-do didn't match up to her face, but everybody young got 'em a Jeri curl nowadays whether it suits or not.

I kept patting Brenda's hand and said, 'Joy'll keep watch over you. Don't worry. She can do a better job of it now than she did before.'

Brenda didn't even make a sniffing sound. Just sat there staring out into space. I got up to re-start that record she played before she went to the store. I don't know what young colored boy was singing, but his high voice lit up the room and backed sorrow in the corner again so we could try to forget death for another little bit.

'You still ain't had nothing to eat, Miss Brenda, and I know you got to be hungry from traveling all night. I am. I could eat me a whale.' I pulled her with me. 'Come on,' I said, 'let's get you a paper towel and I'll fry up them pancakes.'

She tagged behind me to the kitchen like a little child.

'I can't eat,' she said. 'I've lost all my appetite.' She took a sixpack of Colt '45 out the brown paper sack I hadn't finished unpacking from her trip to the store. It was still too early to drink, but Brenda was grown and it was her kidneys.

'How 'bout we wake up that mother of your'n.' I knew it was what Brenda wanted. 'You think Tammy still takes her a sweet black coffee first thing?'

Brenda tried to keep looking sad but I could see she wanted to smile. She was opposites. Lion one minute. Lamb the next. When she was growing up it was a job to keep up with her for just that reason, and she wasted most days acting hard done by. I knew it wasn't just in her imagination that her mama showed favorites, but I used to try and tell Brenda you can't go through life licking on the same wound. When you see something that aggravates ain't gon' change, that's the time to decide to learn to live with it.

'Why don't you go up and ask her,' Brenda said and knocked back that beer like it was gonna be her last.

I didn't really want to go, but I could see it would make Brenda feel better, so I tippy-toed up the wooden staircase to the floor above. Joy's was more the size of a house than a apartment. But no sooner I was on the landing, when I got up close to the bedroom door I heard the television going with the door cracked open enough for me to just about peep in.

Tammy was sitting on the edge of a great big bed with gray sheets, eiderdown and matching pillowcases. It must of been what they call a queen size bed, I thought, 'cause it was twice the size of mine's and Freddie B's. The thin stripped white venetian blinds wasn't drawn and so I could see Tammy was in a thick white terrycloth dressing gown and was wearing a short curly-haired wig that had slipped a bit where she was sleeping on it I guessed. It was cocksided. She was glued to the television, which didn't seem right under the circumstances but Tammy was always a bit of a TV addict. I figured she was best left alone, 'specially as I couldn't see the whole bed and assumed her husband must of been on it somewhere in the corner where I couldn't see, so I tiptoed back downstairs as quiet as I went up.

Brenda was waiting in the kitchen with her hands stuck on her hip which was not what I call a good Brenda sign. It used to mean she was fixing to start something and I suspected that it still meant that very thing. So I tried to sound bright to lift the mood of gloom she'd been whipping up in the kitchen instead of getting on and frying them pancakes.

'Your mama's watching the TV,' I told her, knowing it's exactly what Brenda did and didn't want to hear. She'd want to so she could say she was right, and didn't so she could coax Tammy downstairs.

'She's crazy. There's no way in the world that they're going to mention Joy's dead on breakfast TV. You know that's why she's got it turned on, don't you?'

'Shush up, Brenda. You can understand at a time like this 'un your mother's disturbed.' It only takes one beer with some folks. I hoped Brenda could hold her liquor.

'Mama's got to get her head in gear. We're supposed to be at the undertaker's. Who's gonna sort out this funeral?' Maybe that was what was really worrying Brenda. With her being the eldest and all of forty-one years old, lots of folks would have said organizing Joy's funeral was Brenda's job.

She was ready for a fight when she tore up the stairs taking them two at a time calling all the while like a banshee, 'Mama! . . . Mama!' I thought the whole building would collapse, and I'm sure the people downstairs hadn't never heard nothing like it.

Brenda rapped at the bedroom door so hard it's a wonder she didn't bust her knuckles and as it wasn't shut, I guessed it must of flung wide open with that bashing she give it.

'Just turn that damn thing off,' she was hollering. I couldn't make out what Tammy answered. Poor Jesse. I bet he didn't know what he was getting into when he hitched up with Mrs Tamasina Bang and her brood.

No sooner than she'd hollered something or other that wasn't all that clear to me, Brenda stomped back down in a huff. 'Miss Greedy Guts said she'll be right down.'

I didn't know what that remark was in aid of and had to ask. Brenda said she saw a empty king size bag of bar-b-que potato chips and a empty box of jelly donuts up there.

'Well the woman can't starve herself,' I said. 'And there is the two of 'em.' I hadn't seen Jesse when I peeked through the door but I knew Tammy was definitely planning to bring him.

'She might have thought about somebody else.' Brenda was like a five-year-old sometimes. I couldn't believe it. Joy dead and Brenda worrying over some potato chips.

'Mama didn't even look at me when I was talking to her. She had the remote control in her hand and just kept switching from channel to channel. Didn't say "good morning". "How was your trip." Nothing.'

Tammy knew just how to irritate Brenda. And got pleasure out of it, I reckon, 'cause it was so easy for her to wind Brenda up into a rage.

'I told her,' said Brenda. 'Mama, pry yourself away from that goddam television long enough to tell us what's going on. She's like somebody crazy sitting up there.'

'Where was Jesse?'

'He was sticking up for Mama like you'd expect. What does he care . . . he hardly even knew Joy.'

'Yes I did,' a voice said from the staircase. It was him. I wanted the floor to open up and swallow me, but it didn't so I faked a weedy smile when he come into the kitchen. Brenda wasn't embarrassed like I was. She looked ready to stir trouble and the bad atmosphere was sticking to everybody and everything. It didn't seem right that me and Jesse should get off on a wrong footing 'cause of Brenda, so I tried my best to be friendly, but 'Hi Jesse' came out meeker than I wanted for it to. I didn't think it was going to do the trick for a minute 'cause he looked me dead in the eye.

'Baby Palatine?' He yawned and rubbed his chin like he was just waking up. When he smiled I felt easier. 'Somehow I pictured you as a great big woman.'

My roll-on girdle was digging into my waist but I was glad I didn't take it off 'cause it makes your clothes hang better.

'I used to be a lot skinnier than this . . . didn't I, Brenda?' I tried to bring her into it 'cause she was still scowling.

Jesse's younger looking than I thought he'd be, and slighter. Brown skin men sure do look dignified when all their hair turns white, 'specially when they got a head full, like him. Freddie B lost some of his before he turned fifty, and although I love to rub the bald patch on his crown, it ain't nothing to look at. Not like Jesse's head full that was about two inches long but cropped real neat all over.

When Joy told me Jesse's hair and mustache was white I imagined a old fossil of a man. But when the whites of folks eyes are clear as Jesse's and they stand upright like him though he ain't tall, they don't never look old. Something 'bout Jesse's narrow face and smooth darkish brown complexion reminded me of them Ethiopians they showed starving on the TV day and night a couple years back.

I didn't know if Jesse was asking me or Brenda when he said, 'Any coffee on the brew?' It was a tight squeeze in Joy's kitchen with the three of us in there, like too many crowded on the bus. So I stepped out in the hallway and told him, 'I made some fresh a while back and stuck it in the fridge. It's in that white pitcher.' He had a twinkle in his eyes that I first took to be him flirting. But then I soon realized he probably twinkled the same way when he was sitting on the pot.

'You Californians are something,' Jesse laughed. 'Don't you think it's a bit early in the year for iced coffee?'

I figured he was kidding me on. Any fool knows you have to pour it in a cup and microwave it. 'I'll fix it. How 'bout you, Brenda?'

She still looked mad and was trying to get the frigerator door open without asking Jesse to move since she wasn't speaking to him or me. He couldn't help but be in the way, 'cause with two people in that little space, wherever you put yourself, you was blocking either the sink or stove or something. Didn't make no kinda sense a great big apartment like that with a kitchen not big enough to swing a cat in. Without intending to be helpful, Jesse shifted his weight from his right foot to his left and that gave an inch so the frigerator door could swing past him.

Brenda said, 'Praise god, Amen, and thank you Jesus!' all in one breath. I thought she was being snidy about him moving out her way 'cause there wasn't too much else for her to be all that thankful for at that point in time.

She said, 'I just saw that Colt '45 that I put on ice. It completely slipped my mind that I'd bought it. Now I don't have to have that ol' coffee.'

'It's not old. I told you I made it fresh. Didn't you see me switch on the percolator while you stood there watching me mix up the pancakes?'

'There's pancakes?' Jesse's eyes opened twice their size. He was a jokester, I could tell. I got a lot of time for a man with a sense of humor and he made me feel easy.

'Batter,' Brenda answered while she popped open beer can number two.

'I can't remember when I last had some homemade pancakes,' he said, licking his lips and rubbing both hands together.

Before I could offer, Brenda said, 'Why don't you two go sit down and I'll rustle some up.' It was the first nice thing she'd said. 'That's if you think we have time.' She was forever checking that watch o' hers.

'Tammy's just went in the bathroom as I came down,' said Jesse.

'That gives us an hour stuck here then,' Brenda sighed in her orneriest voice, definitely meaning to be sarcastic.

Me and Jesse both cast a look at one another, as much as to say, 'Let's not let her get started,' and we shied off to sit down at the big glass top dining table pushed up against the wall in the living room. Wasn't a fingerprint on it. Joy must have had her a daily, but she'd claimed she only had a man come once a week when I talked to her about saving money.

I couldn't hardly believe I heard Brenda pop open another beer no sooner than me and Jesse set ourselves down.

'That ain't water you're drinking, y'know,' I yelled in to her. She didn't answer. 'Brenda? You listening to what I say?'

My baby sister Helen's been a alcoholic most her life and I seen how it ruins women especially. Helen's been busted up more times than I care to count. Falling down drunk one day. Getting knocked down by somebody the next. She been cut on, both inside the jailhouse and out. Looking at all them cuts on her face now, wouldn't nobody believe she used to have them boys lined up waiting out by my mama's porch every Saturday night. So I ain't got no patience with drinking.

When Brenda called back, 'I hear you,' I wanted to remind her that hearing and listening is real different.

She called out again, 'Baby Palatine, you want to put on some music for me?'

'What for? So I can't hear you opening them beer cans?' I was joking. But I meant it.

'No, Ma'am. Just wanna hear Stevie Wonder.'

'Where will I find him?' I called in to her.

'He's already on there. Just swing the arm over on the turntable.'

The groceries turned up while I was getting the record machine sorted out and fetching my Bible out the front pocket of my suitcase. Brenda had bought all the newspapers. They was on top of the bags with the shopping. 'What ch'you needing with all of them papers?' I asked.

'I wanted to see if there was anything about Joy in any of them, although I didn't actually intend buying quite so many. I tried to stand in the store and skim through them which is why I was gone so long, but the guy made me buy them. Goddam Chinamen. They always act like you're trying to steal something.'

I didn't offer to help Brenda put the groceries away, 'cause big as she was, there wasn't space for me in the kitchen while she cooked.

Jesse sat at the table and thumbed through the papers, and I was wanting to look over his shoulder. My girl hadn't been a nobody all her life, right enough, though I wasn't fool enough to think they was going to mention Joy on no *Good Morning America*. But it crossed my mind she might of had her a line or two in one of the papers.

'You see anything?' I asked Jesse.

'Like what?'

'Something about Joy.'

'I already told Tammy that nobody is interested in niggers dying of a heart attack. Now if it had been a drug overdose it would have probably been on the front page with pictures, but the only coons they report dying of heart attacks are tycoons.' Jesse smiled and offered me a back section. 'You want to check the obituary?'

'No thanks. I might as well stick to the Good Book.'

I turned to my favorite passage in Jeremiah and read a bit out aloud:

'Why does the way of the wicked prosper
Why do all who are treacherous thrive?'

'So you can have pancakes,' said Brenda. She put down a plate in front of me and shimmied over to the record player so she could flip the record over before she danced back into the kitchen.

Jesse eyed her over the top of the newspaper and said, 'I hope they already arrested the fella that made those jeans.'

I laughed with my hand up at my mouth, but Brenda still heard and yelled out, 'The joke's gonna be on one of y'all if I come out there in that living room and bop somebody.'

I could tell Brenda was feeling brighter. Might of been the food. It would have been like her to eat two pancakes while she was cooking for every one she brought through, but like Freddie B says, 'Whatever makes you happy'. She was singing and snapping her fingers in the kitchen and it's a wonder Jesse didn't complain about the record player volume. I liked the boy's voice singing on the record, but the thumpety-thump of the bass and drums was about to give me indigestion which I'll admit ain't nothing but a sign of old age, 'cause I can remember not all that long ago when I was the first to holler 'Turn it up' and be ready on the dance floor to shake and finger pop.

'Listen . . .' said Jesse. He stopped eating and put down his fork. I thought he'd found something about Joy and was going to read it out, but he wanted me to hear Brenda singing along with the music. Her voice was dipping in and out, and even just singing in the kitchen wasn't no doubt that that girl was endowed with a blessed talent.

'You never heard Brenda sing?' I asked Jesse whose ears was perked.

'Tammy's got an old record of the girls but it's scratched and has honey on it in a couple places so I've never heard it.' He put his finger to his mouth to hush me from talking while Brenda sang along in the kitchen with the backing vocals. She sailed across them notes like a eagle, singing the bottom parts and then jumping straight to the top notes.

Jesse said, 'She probably could have been a opera singer if she'd had the training,' and went back to reading his newspaper.

'Didn't nobody care nothing 'bout no opera back in the fifties when I took her up my church and she joined the children's choir. I only did it so that her and Joy could get some religion, 'cause Tammy didn't see to it they had none. Anyhow, when our pastor asked if Brenda could join the grown ups' choir after she'd been singing in the children's choir six months, it meant me taking her twice a week for choir practice, but I didn't mind since it keep her out the street and from in front of the television.' I could tell Jesse was back to listening to her singing and not me talking which was fair enough 'cause don't many get to hear a voice like Brenda's. 'You think that's something. You oughta hear her break free on that gospel stuff,' I said.

'She could be making money with a voice like that. Ella can't sing as good as that.'

'I don't want to hear 'bout no Ella Fitzgerald, nor none of them new ones, 'cause nary one got a pair of vocal cords on them like her. We tried to tell her . . . but you can only drag a nag to water, you can't make it drink,' I said before Brenda came in and sat down with her plate piled high with sandwiches.

'You didn't want pancakes?' I asked her.

'Not enough batter, so I fixed a couple sandwiches.'

Triple deckers is what she meant by sandwich. One was a tuna salad with mayonnaise, lettuce, tomatoes, onion and pickles, and the other was a peanut butter-grape jelly with banana, nuts and raisins. Jesse looked up from his newspaper to hear what all the chomping was and shook his head.

'Do you think that's a good idea,' asked Jesse. 'Good God. They'll have to strap you in a coffin once you get through that. You're likely to explode.'

They laughed. But I was thinking about Joy when he said it. I took off my spectacles, laid them on the table by my Bible and excused myself to go in the bathroom. I didn't want to cry in front of Jesse. Sympathy from somebody I don't know good makes me queasy.

I was still sitting on the toilet stool with the door locked when I heard Tammy clomp the stairs and rattle about in the kitchen. I knew it was her 'cause I could hear her clearing her throat.

'Tammy,' I called out.

'Bay-bee. Pal-a-teen,' she called back.

'I'm on the toilet,' I lied. 'I'll be out in a second.' I blew my nose. 'How you doing?'

'I'm as well as can be expected.' It was hard to hear between the wall. I could just about make out what she said.

'You want me to go to the undertaker's with y'all?' I shouted. My voice sounded gruff compared to her'n which is like somebody cultured with every word clear as some of them announcers on the six o'clock news. It's hard to believe Tammy didn't go past high school.

She called, 'There's no need for all of us to be put through that ordeal. You must be exhausted.' At times she was like a mind reader and could know just how I was feeling without me saying nothing.

'Hold it a minute, Tammy,' I said and blew my nose. 'I can't hear what you say.' The cistern made a big whoosh noise when I flushed it to make her to think I'd been using the toilet. 'I'll be right out . . .' I flicked some cold water on my eyes to try to perk them up and prepare to deal with her. I wasn't comfortable 'bout her arranging the funeral 'cause I reckoned Joy wouldn't of been. But who was I to say.

The kitchen was tucked right next to the toilet and as I stepped from one door to the other I reminded myself that I'd sworn to Freddie B that I wouldn't let nothing that Tammy said or did upset me, because like or not she was bound to try my nerves, 'cause to hear Tammy tell it, didn't nobody raise her girls but her. She remembered what she wanted and forgot all the rest, leaving a tower of difference between what she claimed happened and what did.

She always loved to find something ailing folks, being a bit of a hyper chondriac herself, so soon as she saw me she said, 'Good grief, Baby Palatine! What's wrong with your eyes? They're all puffy.' She pushed my face up to the light. 'That looks like conjunctivitis.'

We didn't hug. Tammy's always been off-standish in that way. Not just with me neither, 'cause I could count the times I ever saw her hug Brenda or Joy. Though with Anndora she did a bit better. Not that I'm for all that kissy-face stuff myself, but seeing as I hadn't seen Tammy for a few years and we was both there to mourn her middle child, I reckon that to have put my arms 'round her would of been natural to me if I'd of got the feeling that it would of been natural to her. But I didn't, so I had to do with her version of a friendly hello which was to check that I didn't have no conjunctivitis. However my eyes looked, they saw her good enough.

In my mind I always remembered Tammy to be way taller than she was. So it didn't matter how much time passed between me seeing her, whether it was a month or a week or three years like it had been while we stood together in Joy's kitchen, Tammy always seemed way shorter than I thought her to be. And during them three years that she'd been living in Virginia, seemed like she'd shrunk some more. I'd guess it was the extra few pounds she was carrying till I looked down at her feet and noticed she had on a pair of flat shoes. I must of been near on three inches taller than her standing there and for some reason, it made me feel good. There wasn't no way she could look down on me, and I stood taller as she checked my left eye after she'd examined my right. With her holding my face up to the strip lights in Joy's kitchen, it's a wonder I wasn't blind by the time she finished taking a good look.

'So what's the verdict, Doctor O'Mara,' I asked though I knew that all was wrong with my eyes was that I'd had that little weep in Joy's bathroom. 'Nothing's wrong with my eyes. I just had me a good boo-hoo.' If she'd ever seen me cry it was that time I got hysterical when the police dragged my brother Caesar out my apartment 'cause he forgot to report to his parole officer two weeks running. But that had to of been over sixteen years back, 'cause he'd been dead that long. He got to be a worse drunk than my baby sister Helen, and died of cyrhosis. Tell the truth, I don't know how it ain't killed her yet.

'What's to cry about?' Tammy asked sipping on her cup of coffee. In spite of the few crows' feet by her eyes, Tammy's skin was still butter smooth and she had already made her face up. Mascara. Eyeliner. Rouge. The works. Not that I'm claiming that she had on too much, but grieving like she should of been, it's a wonder she had the wherewithal to doll herself up.'

'Crying won't bring Joy back,' she said matter-of-fact which nearly got me started again, but I wiped the corners of my eyes with a paper towel. By saying that, Tammy'd irked me already and I knew the onliest way to handle her was to stay out her way so I told her, 'Maybe I best stay here while y'all head over to the undertaker's and answer the phone 'case it rings.' Hearing myself say it reminded me how strange it was it hadn't rung once, not that Joy had a whole lot of people ringing her, but everybody's phone I reckon rings once or twice of a morning.

'That's probably a good idea. You can let Anndora in too, if she turns up before we get back.'

'Anndora!' I almost said out too loud, but caught myself. I didn't know she was coming, and while I was glad for Tammy's sake, in the back of my mind it struck me that it woulda probably of been less fractious for me over at the undertaker's than it was gonna be with me in the apartment. I didn't have no time for Anndora. And whereas I had learned to put up with her selfishness and bad manners when she was little, after she messed with Sebastian Egerton that time I was done with her for good.

'What time's she expected?' I asked Tammy trying to sound pleased the child was coming.

'Who knows with Anndora. Your guess is as good as mine. I was surprised that I didn't have to beg her to come, to be quite honest. She actually offered and I nearly dropped the phone.' Tammy laughed a little before she straightened her face up seeing that I didn't laugh with her. 'I'm sorry though that it has to be a tragedy like this that brings her home after four years. You realize, don't you, that Anndora's never even met Jesse and my whole life revolves around him.'

What was more likely is his revolved around her 'cause Tammy liked to be waited on hand and foot and used headaches, period pains, corns and everything else as her excuse to get somebody else to fetch and carry for her.

'Where's Anndora living? Joy said Milan the last I asked her.'

'Anndora'd have me believing she's a lady of no fixed address because the odd times she's called she always hands me a flimsy excuse as to why she can't leave me her address and phone number. I imagine she's living with a man.' Or maybe two, I thought to myself.

'So how'd you find her yesterday, then?' I said.

'She just happened to phone out of the blue. It was another one of those freak coincidences that remind me that the telepathy between us is uncannily strong.'

Tammy used to always make out that her and Anndora had some kinda special connection, but I didn't never hear Anndora rushing around talking about it.

I asked, 'Was she upset when you told her?' Anndora can outdo her mother when it comes to dramatics.

'She was . . . sweet . . .' Sweet wasn't a word to describe Anndora at the best of times. Anndora and sweet didn't mix, no more than quinine and Kool-Aid. ' "Mommy, I'll come straight home," ' Tammy went on, imitating how Anndora had talked. 'But I think somebody must have been in the room with her,' Tammy said, 'from the way she kept putting her hand over the receiver. Jesse offered to pay her way with his MasterCharge, but she said not to worry she would even help me with the funeral arrangements if she could.' Tammy put down her empty coffee cup and rolled her head around to loosen up, I expect.

'Well that's natural enough. All the rest of that squabbling between the girls should be water under the bridge now. That's what I mean to tell Brenda,' I told Tammy.

'Well, Anndora is grudge bearing. That's a Taurean affliction, Baby. And with her being born on the cusp, you know and I know she'll never change.' I didn't know nothing 'bout all that astrology stuff but what I did know was after all those years Anndora never forgave Joy for siding with Brenda over that group mess. And whereas Tammy should of made her do better, she always tried to make like the excuse for Anndora was her being born under a bad sign.

I didn't know how we were supposed to deal with Anndora and Brenda in the same room. They hadn't said a peep-a-ty-boo to each other in years. Not since Brenda quit the group after that article come out in the *Queen for a Day* magazine. It was one of the things I spotted in Joy's cardboard box in the cupboard and thought was better off in the trash. I don't know why in the world Joy would of saved the nasty thing anyway. It come out way back in 1977 when the girls had their first record out and was going over a storm in them homo night clubs they got all over 'Frisco. So, as that's where the record got big first, the publicity guy from the record company, Tommy Lynch, said it was a good gimmick for the girls to have 'em a big article in *Queen for a Day*. We was in LA at the time and the record was doing pretty good down there too. Real good actually. Anyway, though Brenda was the best at singing hands down, Joy was the one that shined when it came to doing them interviews. She was smart and wasn't scared to talk to nobody. A couple of them even wrote how she'd been to the Junior College and that Joy had the gift of the gab and how she had been planning to go to Nepal to work with some poor folk.

Joy was always planning to do good things like that and though she never actually did, I loved to hear her talk about it. Tommy even got her on some TV talk shows. Brenda was jealous, but like Tommy told everybody, 'Joy's a master charmer. In all the years I've been in publicity I've never known anybody manipulate journalists like she does. She's remarkable. Remarkable!' And everytime she did one of them shows, the record picked up, so all the girls was gaining benefit though her face got to be the one known. That's what made Brenda jealous and it started a rivalry. Not on Joy's part, 'cause she said she didn't care if Brenda did them interviews. But it was Brenda. Brenda said, 'Why the fuck do I break my ass up there singing and Joy's the one that gets to do all the talking with her face everywhere.' It wasn't for me to say that if Brenda'd looked and talked like Joy, them papers and magazines would of wanted her, so I kept my mouth out of it and let Joy handle Brenda 'cause she was best at it. Joy was nice about it, but then it ain't too hard to play Mr Nice Guy when you the one on the winning end.

Anyways, by mistake, Tommy had booked Joy to do two interviews at the same time. One on the radio that there wasn't no way he could cancel 'cause the station had been saying for a whole week that she was coming on, and the other was that *Queen for a Day* thing. So he tried to get Anndora to do the gay magazine, but she wasn't interested and went out with any Tom, Dick or Harry that invited her like she always did when we was out on the road. Joy said Anndora couldn't go a whole day without sex and that's why she used to slip off to get herself squared up which left Brenda to do the interview, but she's honest to a fault and Tommy didn't never let nobody talk to her 'cause he said she was dangerous to herself 'cause she didn't know what not to say.

It was the same with everyday stuff. You could say, 'Brenda, what d'you think of my dress,' and if she thought it looked terrible she'd tell you flat out. Wasn't no malice in what she said but don't nobody expect to hear the honest-to-God truth. 'Specially nowadays. And whereas Joy used to try to teach her to sweet-talk folks, Brenda was determined to say whatever come into her head. It's like the time I fried her a pork chop and gravy after a show and she mopped up the plate. I said, 'Girl, you really enjoyed that, didn't you?' 'Cause it's a pleasure to see a plate licked like she'd done. She had the nerve to say, 'Not really, but I knew before I asked you to cook me something that you always fry a piece of meat till it tastes like shoe leather.' I didn't even flinch when she said it 'cause I was used to her exasperating ways. But when Tommy set up that interview he told me, 'Watch her like a hawk; don't let her talk long. And no pictures.' He was sure good at his job and didn't nothing get into them newspapers that he didn't want in.

It was a great big sissy with muscles coming out his eyeballs that turned up for the *Queen for a Day* magazine with a tape recorder. He was wearing all white skin-tight ducks so his balls was practically out and a tight T-shirt. He didn't look bad, but wasn't what you'd call no Clark Gable even though he had a Clark Gable mustache. I don't be eyeing no white boys, but I know me a cute one when I see him and 'cause he was not too cute and not too ugly I knew right away that Brenda would get on all right with him. Especially since he had a kind of simpleton's giggly-girl laugh and didn't look serious like some of them newspaper writers did.

Brenda was shy with white folks. What my mama would of called backward, where she was slow to come forward and speak up for herself. She was the same at school. But that young interviewer guy and Brenda got on a good foot from the get-go. And I sat there with them chatting and kept my eye on her like Tommy'd told me to but that interviewer stopped his tape and asked me to leave 'em alone 'cause he said that Brenda was likely to clam up with me watching. I figured he was the one made uncomfortable so I went to sit in my own room right next to hers. I had a bunch of sequins I needed to sew back on them dresses anyhow. The record company had us staying in a suite at a hotel on Sunset Boulevard which I hated 'cause I expected it to be fancy, but they didn't even have no room service and if anybody wanted a bite to eat, I had to drag out in that heat to the delicatessen two blocks away.

Before I agreed to take my rusty-dusty behind out of Brenda's room I yanked her to one side and reminded her to talk about herself and nobody else like Tommy Lynch had said for her to do. He figured that way she couldn't say too much wrong.

Brenda come bouncing to my room a hour later when they was finished, smiling from ear to ear and even said she'd walked the boy to his car which ain't like her. She ain't never been chivalrous.

'How was it?' I asked her.

She said, 'Great. Nothing to it. In fact it's fun having somebody ask you all kinds of questions. I told you I'd be all right.' She opened a big bag of corn chips I had in my room and started stuffing 'em in her mouth. Didn't ask. Didn't offer.

'I was wondering if some hanky panky was going on,' I said as I was careful sewing and didn't have a free hand to eat nothing no way. 'He laughs louder than you do.' Of course that was a lie. She laughed louder than she sang and couldn't nobody sing loud as Brenda Bang.

Soon after that me and the girls went back to Oakland and they was so busy doing PAs and rehearsing a new band, didn't nobody think about that interview again while that record of theirs creeped up the charts to the top ten. Slow and steady. It was their first and couldn't nobody believe it was happening, but like their manager Danny Lagerfield told them, it was a crack in the iceberg. Then things took off like wildfire once they was in the charts. Everytime I listened to the radio, and not just the coloured stations neither, you'd hear 'Chocolate Chip'. Them 'Frisco DJs was crazy 'bout that song. They liked to play around with the name the girls had too and was always joking about 'Bang Bang Bang' this and 'Bang Bang Bang' that. It was Danny named 'em. He did everything for 'em but shit and sing.

I didn't take to him 'cause he was too quick to think that Anndora was the be-all and end-all of everything. I figured he was trying to get in her pants and she strung him along like Joy said it was necessary for Anndora to do, so he'd spend more time and money on the group, but I knew soon as I saw him that Anndora wasn't gonna genuinely have no time for him. Glasses and bald-headed and weedy though he wasn't but twenty-four. And acted as old as he looked, with money on his mind morning noon and night, though he claimed it wasn't making money off the girls he was interested in. He said it was the challenge that got him excited. He reminded me of a weasel and with all he did for Joy and them, I don't know why I didn't take to him 'cause with all the Jews I'd worked for including ol' man Houseman, I was used to their ways. But I suspected that Danny was there for the good times and sure enough when all the mess started with that *Queen for a Day* article, Danny Lagerfield was not a easy man to find.

Overnight wildfire turned to brushfire with folks making snide remarks or wanting to cancel bookings and record signings. It was terrible and I hoped it wasn't gonna last but a minute, but folks wanted to hash at it again and again. There was a big picture of the three girls on the cover wrapped in aluminum foil with a headline 'The Biggest Bang Goes Gay'. I told 'em when I'd heard that they took a picture like that that they was gonna live to regret it. 'Cause although Brenda was standing at the back and wasn't nothing bad showing on Joy or

Anndora, that wasn't the kind of pose I'd of been happy to show off at my church. The first bit of the article claimed Brenda wanted to join some organization that called themselves Lesbians for a Liberal Society and had Brenda saying she wanted to see a fair shake for lesbians and more lesbian bars particularly in the Bay Area. But it was that second part that was the killer with her talking about her first lesbian experience at a bowling alley. I didn't know she was no bull dyke, though Joy always said she always suspected as much. But I didn't. I ain't small-minded and I coulda learned to live with it, but Brenda'd also told how she loved to rub up against Reverend Earl's wife's titties in choir practice when she was little. He was pastor at the First Tabernacle where Brenda started up in the choir, and his wife, a big fat girl called Naomi, took charge of the choirs.

When the article came out the record company said not to worry about it 'cause they'd sue the magazine and get a retraction and that we should make the most of the bad publicity, but Brenda said what was printed was true. I nearly fainted and Freddie B said we had to move, since he was a deacon in the church and wasn't nobody there likely to be much pleased with us at First Tabernacle even though Reverend Earl and his wife had long since left. It was a real wrench to have to move from Grange where we'd been for so many years, but like Freddie B said, once that whole neighborhood got wind of the story we'd have to always be standing up for Brenda. Not that he minded that, but he didn't want no trouble if it could be avoided.

The story hit some of the regular papers 'cause the girls' record had jumped to number five by then, and some of them trashy papers they got on racks at the supermarket checkout had big color pictures and headlines for a few weeks running. They really know how to milk it, and Joy laughed about it and said it didn't bother her, 'cause a lot of people was gay and she couldn't see what all the fuss was about, but hoped the hoo-ha might push 'em up the charts to number one which it did.

But what with Brenda being kinda shy, she couldn't handle all the commotion. Some of it was ugly, and all she wanted to do was hide herself. I knew how she was feeling, 'cause I was ready to ship off somewhere to the Foreign Legion myself, and I didn't even have no part in the mess. It was hard on everybody, but it was Anndora acted up the worst. She was mad as hell about what it did, and said it ruined their chances to make the big time. Me and Joy tried to keep her and Brenda from killing each other and Tammy kept in the background. No . . . come to think of it, she left town to go spend some time at Tondalayah's and left us to it, 'cause Tondalayah was hanging out with a guy in San Francisco and was always saying anyone of us could use her place in Palo Alto when we wanted.

Anndora wasn't but small, but she was a spiteful little wench and could be as mean as a alley cat. She wanted Brenda replaced which Joy said didn't make sense since Brenda was the one won the record contract in a gospel contest at a Baptist convention in San Francisco. Joy and Anndora got signed on more or less as trimmings when the record company said Brenda would do better with some cute girls doing doo-wops for her.

Life can't stop 'cause of no gossip and like Joy told Anndora, the main thing was to keep going. But Brenda wanted to quit. She would have probably disappeared herself like you hear they do down South America, setting in a corner with a black bag over her head if she coulda done. When things got the worse she was so shame-faced and embarrassed, we couldn't get her to go out to buy a loaf of bread at the corner store. Joy did what she could to ease over things. That was her way. She was always watching out for Brenda and sensed when Brenda was erupting on and off like a bubbling volcano, ready to blow. Only Joy kept the lid tight on her, 'cause Brenda always flummoxed me, and her mother didn't have no time for her moods.

When Brenda decided to quit singing, Joy said it was okay by her and thought Brenda would start back up again when the ruckus died down, 'cause it wasn't like Brenda had nothing to go to. But Brenda surprised us all and took herself to Boston, though she didn't know a living soul there. First off, she got her a job as a ambulance driver, but she lost that 'cause she refused to drive 'round nights without having a cigarette in the van and somebody saw her and reported her. After that, she put her hand to a lot of different things 'fore she settled at the post office. Work is work right enough and how folks make a living ain't nobody's business but theirs, if it's legal. But Brenda Bang had her a calling with that voice of her'n, and it don't seem fair to waste one of God's precious gifts when you find out you been bestowed with one. That seems about ridiculous as winning the million dollar lottery and forgetting to go pick up your prize money.

Singing should of been Brenda's salvation and give her room to right all that was wrong in her life from not having no money to trying to stay happy in one job. Before they discovered at our church that she had them golden lungs, it seemed like the Lord had short changed her, 'cause she ain't got neither looks nor brains. I was beginning to think she was one of them that had to do all she could with her big bosom. Like that Carol Doda woman and Tondalayah. Some folks can make a whole career out a big bosom. And good luck to 'em I say.

Tondalayah wasn't never shamed to tell nobody her line of work and made as good a living from stripping as my husband did in the building trade. Folks say stripping ain't Christian work for a woman, and I see their point some, but I can't see no difference between working with your hands or your titties. Both of 'em's God-given. Same as Brenda's voice. All folks can do in this god forsaken world is work with what they got. And most don't get much.

It ain't no denying that Brenda quitting the group spoiled her and her sisters' chances of making big money. But singing ain't only worth doing for the money, I used to try and tell Anndora, especially. She kept up asking Brenda the same question after that *Queen for a Day* article come out. She was like a broken record. 'Why'd you have to open your big stupid mouth?' Brenda let Anndora keep on at her. One time it happened when Tondalayah was around visiting and soon as Anndora went out, Tondalayah said to Brenda, 'Girl, Stand Up For Yourself! And stop acting like there's something wrong with being a lesbian. I been one myself from time to time when there ain't been nothing else going on but the rent.' She laughed but I couldn't. Tondalayah, once billed as Tondalayah with the Voluptuous Body, a part time lesbian? It was the first I heard of it, and I nearly fainted. But I decided to stay friends with her anyway 'cause she was big-hearted and a lot of fun. She didn't never mention it again in front of me after that time. Thank goodness, 'cause I didn't want to hear the ins and outs and wasn't none of my business no way. It was '77 or '78 and I had lived a bit by then, and got used to shocking things even on the news.

Anyway, Brenda took in Tondalayah's advice about standing up for herself, so one afternoon a few days later Freddie B was sitting in our living room listening to Anndora giving Brenda what for in our kitchen till Brenda hauled off and knocked holy hell out her sister. The way Freddie B told it tickled me.

'Wasn't but two licks hit,' he said. 'I heard Brenda hit Anndora, and Anndora hit the floor.' She caught her chin on the sharp edge of our formica table when she fell and broke her jaw. It was lucky she didn't split her face open, sharp as the metal edge of our old table was. Freddie B got her over to Kaiser Hospital. Me, Tammy and Joy was shoe shopping when it all happened. Joy was supposed to meet up with her sisters at my place so Freddie B could drive 'em to a meeting over at Danny's boat in Sausalito. Instead, Joy had to lie to Danny and say Anndora fell down some stairs. Her jaw stayed wired for two months and it ended up that Danny had to cancel what was left of their promotion tour and their recording session that was booked to make a follow up record. He thought he could get away with postponing them dates, but Brenda'd flew off to Boston by the time they took the wire out of Anndora's jaw. So, as that squeaky voiced Chinese DJ at WJAZ put it, Bang Bang Bang was bang out the window.

Tammy took Anndora's side which was to be expected since she didn't never take Brenda's no way. I can understand a mother favoring one child, but it's sure rough justice on them other ones.

Looking at Tammy standing in Joy's Chelsea kitchen. I wisht I'd of slapped her face for things she did or didn't do way back when in Oakland when I kept my opinions and my hands to myself 'cause I was scared she'd move out with them kids if I aggravated her.

But I wasn't 'bout to let Tammy fool me in her old age, 'cause I'd already had me a sharp lesson in tampering with something old and rusty the time I found a old razor of Freddie B's laying on my bathroom floor . . . I didn't handle it careful when I picked it up 'cause it looked harmless, but it near sliced off the tip of my thumb.

Tammy had on a neat brown and green Harris tweed suit to go to the undertaker's. It showed that she was tired, but she still looked healthy, and once I tidied her wig at the back that was caught in the collar of her jacket, wasn't nothing on her out of place. She held her age good.

She'd always kept her hair dyed black with a blondish streak in it for as long as I can remember. It was more stylish she said than her natural color which was the same as mine. No color at all to speak of. Just near to black. But I suspected she was solid gray under that wig, and I ain't 'shamed to admit I am under mine.

The pink florescent lights in the kitchen made Tammy look rosy and that red lipstick she was wearing brightened up her color. She's always had her a nice even complexion and not many could of guessed her to be sixty-two. The only time I can recall she looked more than her age was when she was ailing that time she had the heartache over Dagwood.

I wanted her to at least look mournful like a mama should who's 'bout to bury a child that she birthed in the world, but Tammy was standing too upright and enjoying her hot drink too much.

'What's that funny smell?' she asked me. 'I didn't notice it when Jesse and I arrived.'

'What's it smell like?'

'Feet.'

'Oh. I bet it's that rag I found,' I said and went to check the sink. It was in the exact same spot I left it. 'I probably shoulda throwed it in the garbage, but I couldn't see the bin nowhere.' Trust Brenda Bang not to of bothered to move it while she was cooking. 'You think I oughta take it outside?' I didn't know where the incinerator was but anyhow I was glad for a good excuse to slip out before any more ructions started between Brenda and her mother.

'You ready to go?' I asked her. 'It's getting on.' I knew if I didn't bring it up, Brenda would.

'I don't know what the hell I'm doing. I've never had to arrange a funeral before.' 'Least she was honest.

I picked up the rag and carried it out through the living room.

Brenda was kneeling in front of that box I had pulled out the cupboard. She'd put some pictures by and had her head down digging to the bottom. I told her, 'I hope you ain't planning to pick over all the best pictures 'cause I want me some.'

I think she was trying to pass over what I'd said to her when she asked, 'What's that in your hand, Baby Palatine?'

'I found it in the back of the cupboard. Smells high, don't it? I thought it was a cleaning rag, but it's got some kinda cleaning fluid or chemical on it.' Smelled like old pickles or fish gone off in the refrigerator.

'What kinda chemical?' she asked me.

'How I'm s'posed to know . . . I wasn't the one put it in there. I only fetched it out.'

It was easy to steer Brenda away from something you didn't want to talk about. All you had to do was mention Tammy in a nice tone of voice and Brenda was ready for the warpath. 'I think your mother's 'bout ready to walk out the door.'

Tammy was taking her time in the kitchen. Stalling, I figured, but wasn't no way in the world she was going to get out of going to the undertaker's or dealing with Brenda. I couldn't do it for her, 'cause next of kin's the onliest one that can sign all them papers.

I tried to work out how to put the door on the latch so I wouldn't get shut out. Everything was so new fangled at Joy's that you about needed you a guidebook to go to the toilet, which by the way had a attachment to clean your behind, but I couldn't get it going. Not that I needed to use it.

I called over to Jesse who was sitting closest to the door. 'Will y'all let me back in please?' I got ready to put my house slippers on but decided not to bother. Wasn't nobody to impress and I wasn't gonna be walking round the hall long enough to catch cold.

'Where are you off to?' Jesse wanted to know.

'I'm taking this here rag to the first garbage pail or incinerator I can find, before it smells out the joint.'

Jesse jumped up from his chair and said, 'You don't have to bother with that. Let me take care of it.' Anybody would of thought I was the Queen of Sheba and was carrying crown jewels the way he offered like he didn't want 'no' for an answer. He come rushing at me trying to take the rag out my hand, and I figured that he was wanting an excuse to get the other side of that front door as much as I was. But I wasn't having none of it, and I held tight to the rag.

'That's okay, Hon,' I told Jesse, 'I'm able to take care of it myself.'

'No! Let me deal with it!' he said. Insistent which was about to make me agitated 'cause I was determined to get rid of that rag myself, needing it as my excuse to miss the Brenda and Tammy fireworks.

He snatched the rag out my hand, but I snatched it back 'fore he got him a good grip on it and I rushed to the door and got the other side of it 'fore he could stop me, letting out one of them deep sighs like I do when I'm at the end of my tether. Why Jesse was determined to get the rag off me was a mystery, 'cause nasty as it smelled, I would of thought wouldn't nobody of wanted to grab hold of it that didn't have to. The smell was sickening and though I was glad for the breathing space out in the hallway, I really did want to get shot of the nasty thing. It didn't make no sense that Joy had something like that laying in her clothes closet and it's a wonder that it didn't smell up all her clothes. Bal à Versailles or no Bal à Versailles.

The hallway wasn't all that big and wasn't but three other apartment doors on Joy's floor and as I couldn't see nothing that looked like a garbage shoot, I figured I was gonna have to take the elevator down to the ground and ask the doorman where it was. I didn't want to bother none of Joy's neighbors, though it crossed my mind that if she was friendly with any of them, somebody was gonna have to let 'em know that she'd passed. But I didn't reckon that was the right time for it.

There was only one door on Joy's floor that looked like it wasn't to nobody's apartment, and when I opened it, I was surprised to find it was a laundry room, and even without turning the light on, I could see wasn't no garbage cans nor shoots in there, so I had to resign myself to taking the elevator down to the lobby and doorman. He had already seen me once without shoes, so wasn't no reason in me getting shy about going down there to him without 'em a second time.

There wasn't no need for me to press the elevator button, 'cause the light was already up on the Lift Coming sign. I figured it was one of Joy's neighbors on their way up and was trying to decide while I was standing there if I should say something about Joy or not. But whereas folks all living in one building used to try and be neighborly, that stuff don't go on much no more. People locks their doors and keeps them locked, and who can blame 'em with the mess that goes on nowadays.

I was standing in front of the elevator door when it slid open, and I stepped back to let the woman in the dark mink get off. At first glance she looked like a bumble bee, 'cause she had big black sunglasses on so hardly much of her face was showing, and with the coat that was almost ankle-length covering her from the raised collar down, she looked more like a great big insect than a human being.

Soon as she said, 'Hi,' I realized who it was. Anndora's low wispy voice is unmistakable, and although I hadn't heard it for years, 'cause she didn't never bother to call me nor vice versa, I recognized it right away, even though I was slow to recognize her with her hair slicked back in a tight bun. I hadn't never seen her without it being curly and in a bang that framed her face. She looked way older than she was with it drawn off her face and them glasses hiding her pretty eyes.

'Hey, Miss Anndora,' I said trying to sound happy to see her. But why did I bother, 'cause she didn't crack a smile and stepped out the elevator like I wasn't no more than a doorman employed to greet her.

I was sure glad that I wasn't gonna be there when her and Brenda laid eyes on each other and the devil in me got to giggling soon as I stepped into the elevator and called back to her, 'Your mama's in there waiting on you and she'll sure be glad to see you.'

'Thank you, Savior, for letting me miss that,' I said to the reflections in the three mirrors that was reflecting each other. Then I did a skip, I was so happy that chance was on my side and I didn't have to be in Joy's at that moment.

My baby sister used to say that it wasn't Christian of me to have such a dislike for Anndora, and I can't say that she was wrong, but it didn't change how I felt.

In my whole life I hadn't met nobody as contrary and self serving as Anndora Bang, and I couldn't find nothing about her to like except how she looked. And even that had had its day, 'cause with the way I'd just seen her looking, though she still looked real attractive, it wasn't the sort of good looks that appealed to me. Too hard. Red painted mouth too set to be pretty, and general attitude too uppity to be worth the time of day.

But my better self chastised me, 'If she don't know no better how to act, you should.'

I was about to answer it back when the elevator door opened at the lobby, so instead, I smiled at the doorman and asked him where the garbage was.

'There's a shoot inside each individual apartment,' he said. 'You'll find a hatch in the kitchen. But give that to me, Ma'am, and I'll get rid of it for you.' It's a wonder that he was being so polite with me standing there looking such a mess.

'That's real kind of you,' I told him, 'but with the way this thing is smelling you don't want no part of it, I bet.'

He didn't pay that no mind and took it off me. I was embarrassed, and rushed to get straight back on the elevator, forgetting that what faced me was the Bangs without Joy to act as buffer. And whereas I knew it was my duty to make the most of the days I had to be stuck there with them, I knew that with Anndora in tow, it wasn't gonna be easy, 'cause she liked the world to revolve around her, and I wasn't in the best frame of mind to cater to her. She was the sort that could walk into a room full of folks she knew and stare everybody down without so much as a hello. My baby sister can be just as bad, but her excuse is the drink, at least. Anndora didn't have no excuse, and to have to tolerate her mess if you wasn't in the mood was real offputting.

Joy used to tell me Anndora didn't know she was being rude but I didn't beleive it for a minute.

'How in God's name did y'all spill out the same womb,' I used to ask Joy when I was on the road with Bang Bang Bang. The onliest way I could make sense of it was to think that each of them three girls took something different off their mama. Joy lucked up and got Tammy's bright sunny side compared to Brenda who was stuck with that thing of Tammy's feeling hard done by, and Anndora had her mama's haughtiness.

'I'm worth two of you,' Anndora had the nerve to tell me one time when she wasn't but seven or eight and I'd given her a telling off about leaving good food on her plate. I figured she'd heard that off her mama, 'cause she was too young to think to say something as rude as that to me.

Anndora wasn't just born haughty, she was born wilful with it, and there wasn't no way to handle her, 'cause she used not speaking as her main weapon.

When she was little I used to try to claim up at First Tabernacle that it was shyness. I had to make some kind of excuse for her 'cause them church members of ours was regularly put out of shape when Anndora would walk straight past all of 'em with her head in the air like she was doing everybody a favor by being there. And only four years old when I first took her. Them women don't have no patience with bad assed children and a couple times Sister Thompson told me she noticed that Anndora was quick enough to speak if she wanted something.

When I used to have to leave her at the door of Sunday school while me, Freddie B, Joy and Brenda went to the bigger church hall meeting, Miss Dickerson, the Sunday school teacher, used to want to grab hold of Anndora's hand and guide her to her seat. Some women love to get their mits in. As soon as we'd leave to go in the other door, Joy used to always say, in her sweetest way, 'Hi, Miss Dickerson. Can you please let Anndora make her way to her own seat, because she doesn't like strangers to touch her.' But since the child had been going to Sunday school all of July and August, Miss Dickerson had good reason to believe she wasn't no stranger, so she'd grab hold on Anndora's hand anyway and Anndora would howl the place down so that Joy used to have to go in and try to calm her. She was the only one could get Anndora to do anything when they was little.

Anndora couldn't stand Miss Dickerson touching her 'cause she said the woman had bony fingers like that witch in her Hansel and Gretel story book. True as it may have been, that was just Anndora's excuse, 'cause she couldn't stand none of them children in her Sunday school class neither. She could have made friends with them if she tried. But she didn't.

We had to bribe her to get her up the church at all the first time. She stuck out that bottom lip like she'd seen kids on the TV do and said she'd be happier staying home and watching cartoons, till I told her she could have her some new black patent leather shoes if she came. She wasn't even in first grade that summer and was already slick at getting her way. Joy pandered to Anndora about as much as their mama did, and maybe that's why Joy could get Anndora to do things nobody else could, 'cause Anndora was spoiled and usually did what she wanted. It seemed like they had a hold over each other, although I couldn't figure the how or why, being shortsighted.

Want for things ruled Anndora. Right from a little child Anndora knew exactly how to keep her eye on the prize. Her idea of a good time was sitting on Tammy's bed with my pinking shears and studying my old Sears Roebuck catalogs to pick out what she was gonna buy. She'd have her a big pile o' cutouts with everything from camping gear to washing machines and clothes galore. One time she got her hands on one of them Frederick's of Hollywood nightie and lingerie catalogs that Tondalayah left, and that child guarded that book like it was Egyptian diamonds or something. It was all I could do to keep her from taking it for 'show and tell' in her kindygarden class. I said, 'Anndora, that book's full of brassieres and sassy lingerie. Ain't no way you can take that up the school.' She didn't speak to me for two weeks and her mama just laughed about it.

The only time Anndora was nice to me and Freddie B was when me and him would take her downtown shopping to waste an hour while her sisters was at the children's choir practice. She was good as gold in them big department stores, and didn't never show out or even ask for nothing. At first I thought she used to get mesmerized by the bright lights with everything shining and smelling new, and the music playing over the loud speakers. She seemed just happy to be looking at jewelry, and Freddie B used to love to take her, 'cause he said she was like another child in them stores. And the fancier the store, the better she acted. It's a shame that as Anndora got older and even more beautiful she grew too conscious of it. Since I believe beauty is from the inside out, it ruined her chances of me thinking she was one of the most beautiful women in the world, black or white. She expected everybody's eyes to be her mirror, she was so vain.

Anndora thought everything was hers. She didn't ask for things, she just took what she saw if she wanted it, 'cause she believed everything on God's earth was hers for the taking, from a piece of chewing gum she'd see lying in your bag when she was little, to clothes hanging in Joy's closet as they got grown, to money laying on my kitchen counter. If you didn't know her good, you'd of thought she was some kinda klepto, but Joy said that in Anndora's mind it wasn't stealing. She needed it and so she took it. Whatever it was she needed or wanted.

If you caught her red-handed reading your mail, she didn't even try to hide it. Brenda would at least pretend that she was dusting around, and sneak her a peek at but a few lines, but Anndora wouldn't bother to put your letter down and would have the double nerve to question you about it.

But the main ax I had to grind against her was that she thought money was the be-all and end-all of everything. So I reckoned she was gonna be right in her element in her sister's apartment, 'cause what little furnishing Joy had looked real expensive. Right down to the crystal candleholders on the glass top dining table.

When I rung Joy's bell, it seemed like Brenda must of been standing by it, she opened up so quick and I wasn't inside the front door before she started a rampage about Anndora. It was way worse than I expected, 'cause while I knew that them two was gonna find something to have a to-do about, I expected it was gonna take 'em ten minutes at least. But I wasn't gone that long.

'As soon as she came in,' Brenda said, 'Mama hugged and kissed her and they headed straight upstairs like they had something secret to talk about.' She could hardly get the words out she was so mad. 'I didn't expect Anndora to say hello to me, but I was embarrassed for Jesse's sake that Mama didn't even introduce him properly. After they rushed halfway up the stairs like me and Jesse was invisible, Mama stopped and turned Anndora around and said, "Oh, darling, meet Jesse," like he was something the cat drug in.'

'I didn't mind, Brenda,' Jesse interrupted. 'Your mother's got a lot on her mind at a time like this, and Anndora and I will have all the time in the world to get acquainted when the funeral is over.'

'Well,' Brenda told me, not ready to let her mama be forgiven, 'I reminded Mama not to forget that we have to get to the Harlem undertaker by eleven, and do you know what Anndora had the nerve to say, "Over my dead body will there be a service in Harlem." Like she's the boss. "It's unspeakable." It was all show, to make me look small. So what am I?! See-through glass. I'm supposed to be included when Mama talks about Joy. I kept in touch with her a lot more than Anndora did, didn't I Baby Palatine?'

I already had it in my mind when I went out looking for the garbage to throw that rag in that I would grab me a nap. And I was wary of being drawn into what I could feel was brewing, so I quick excused myself, claiming that the jet lag had taken hold of me and went and put my head down on the sofa covered in that camel coat. I shifted my behind around a bit like I was getting comfortable in a doze and didn't mumble word-first. Just closed my eyes like I was out like a light but I was playing possum and took in their every word, wheezing every now and then to keep Brenda and Jesse fooled.

'She's sleeping,' said Jesse in a near whisper and I'd hoped he was gonna keep his voice up so I could hear them on the other side of the room.

'Baby Palatine's the one that I feel sorriest for,' I heard Brenda say with her loud self. 'Joy was closer to her than anybody, and she should have more say in Joy's funeral, but of course if she did, it would make my mother look bad, now wouldn't it.' Then she dropped her voice too, I guess to make sure Tammy couldn't hear. 'Mama's always been jealous of Baby, because Joy insisted Baby did a lot of the things that Mama thought that she should have done. Like going out on the road with us and stuff. And you know, Joy would always ask Baby Palatine first about anything important. They were ace-boon-coons, and Lord knows how Baby will cope without my sister.'

Listening to Brenda made the tears well up in me.

'There's ten times more pictures of Baby Palatine in this pile Joy's collected than of Mama. You want to look at them?'

Brenda got up and took a handful of pictures over to Jesse and he put his paper down. I think he was hiding behind them newspapers. Don't nobody read four, one after another. I bet he just kept his head stuck in them to avoid trouble, which was sly. He wasn't so dumb, and who could blame him for wanting to avoid them three Bang women.

'You want a coffee, Jesse?' Brenda made me proud of her, 'cause whereas I thought she was determined to stir trouble, there she was being thoughtful about her mama's husband. And me.

'No thanks. But I do want to get a move on,' said Jesse. When he took hisself up the stairs, I could make him out good even with my eyes squinted to look shut. Nobody'd mentioned that Jesse had him a limp before, so all I could think when he hobbled up the steps one at a time was that he'd hurt hisself. He climbed the stairs slow and careful pulling his right leg that was board stiff behind him.

'You ain't coming back?' Brenda asked him. I felt bad all 'a sudden about pretending that I was sleeping, 'cause she sounded kind of pitiful and I had to remind myself that whereas I was full of feeling sorry for myself that morning, Brenda Bang had lost her sister.

'Yeah. Sure. You must be pretty tired yourself, Brenda. Did you sleep on the bus?' Jesse asked as he turned the sharp angle halfway up them wooden stairs.

'I'm real, real tired. I had to do a double shift, which I don't mind usually but then I had to rush to the bus depot. A day and night shift at the doggone post office is a bitch. I deliver and sort as well some days. But at least it's not January. I can't stand carrying mail in all that snow we get in Boston.'

Jesse was trying to cut her short and she was trying to drag out the conversation, sounded like.

'Well maybe it'll be a good idea for you to curl up on Joy's bed and get a good sleep.' I think Jesse was also trying to find a roundabout way to get Brenda to miss out the trip to the undertaker's. He could see as well as I could that Brenda, Anndora and their mother didn't need to be standing in the same funeral parlor together at the same time.

I raised my head up and chimed in. 'I'm staying behind too.' Joy wouldn't of wanted Brenda to be left behind in no apartment by herself. And with Joy's place being what it was, about as homey as a waiting room, wasn't no way that Brenda could of made herself feel at home.

'You ought to go, Baby Palatine. You know better than Mama what Joy would have wanted.'

I knew it was the truth. But I wasn't about to claim to it nor admit it. Tammy brought Joy to the world, so she had the right to bury her own flesh and blood how she saw fit and it wasn't for me to stick my two cents in.

'Oughtn't we to put Joy's obituary in the *Pittsburgh Courier* or somewhere?' Brenda asked me. 'That way some friends are notified at least.' Joy didn't have nothing to do with her own people, so putting a notice in the colored paper couldn't amount to none of her friends finding out.

'How 'bout a music paper,' I said, and as soon as I said it I realized that I had to phone Sebastian with the news 'cause it wasn't fair him having to read it when I knew how to reach him.

Brenda agreed it was the best idea and the one that we would ask Jesse to put to Tammy while they was at the undertaker's, whichever one they was finally going to.

Laying there with my eyes half shut I noticed how bright it was outside, and Joy's big living room caught the light south and west, though I realized nobody'd switched off the overhead lights from when me and Brenda had turned them on. Freddie B won't let me have lights on unless it's nearly pitch dark. I let him get away with it, 'cause he gets such a kick outa seeing hardly no charges on our electric bill. To see his face brighten up when it comes makes it almost worth bumping 'round in the half dark. Except I hate to see him reading the Bible from that little bitty table lamp which is what's making his eyes so bad way more than age like he claims.

'Brenda, switch off the lights,' I asked her 'cause she was sitting so near that panel she'd been playing with earlier.

'Hang on . . .' She kept laying out them pictures on the table, so I got up and stumbled over to her side of the room and did it myself. I needed to go in the toilet, anyway, to try to wash the nanky smell of that rag off my hands.

'I said I was going to do it,' she said as I reached over her to turn the switch off.

'It's done.' I don't like to wait on nobody.

'Tammy's not happy unless all the lights are blaring,' Jesse said coming back down the stairs as I went to run a sink full of water in Joy's little toilet come dressing room. It was going to take more than a little scrub to clean off that smell, and I grabbed the cleanser from a cupboard under the sink. I saw that that was all that was in there and the cupboard was completely spotless. Like somebody had just cleaned it corner to corner. I hadn't never seen nothing like it, 'cept in a hotel when you open one of them cupboards and ain't nothing in it but a clean glass.

When I came out the bathroom, Jesse was still going on about the lights. 'I'm always going around behind Tammy turning them off. And you know what she does?'

'Goes behind you and turns them on again,' said Brenda. 'Contrary.'

They had a good cackle together. At least they was making a effort to get on. If Brenda would do as much with Tammy and Anndora, I thought, we might survive the next couple days.

As soon as I heard what I suspected was Anndora's high heels click on the way down the staircase, I jumped the gun on what I expected to be her bad mood.

'Hey Miss Anndora, you want something to eat?' I always did kiss her behind a little bit to keep peace when the group was going. I knew better than to expect her to say a friendlier hello, although we hadn't seen each other in ten years. Since Anndora and me hadn't never had much time for each other, it would of been silly to expect time to bring change. And it obviously didn't on her part. She didn't look in my direction nor try to muster either a smile or a 'thank you' for the offer.

'I ate on the plane.' She renunciated every one of them words indicating she was in one of her highest faluting moods, so I reckoned I was lucky that she'd answered me at all. But as I realized that conversation was gonna be our only salvation stuck up there for three days with each other, I tried to get Anndora talking. Kill 'em with kindness Joy'd taught me, so I tried to soften Anndora up with a compliment. Joy used to do it to her all the time and it worked.

'Girl, those shoes are fine,' I said. 'Where'd you pick them up, Anndora?' Black they was with rhinestones on the toe.

'Milan,' she said, just as salty as if I'd asked a fifty year old woman her age. She was standing still as a statue at the bottom of the stairs like she was in a room with strangers. And what with me knowing her most of her life, it was hard to believe she could want to be so distant.

'Well, I can see they ain't no $10.99 specials from Thom McAnn's,' I said which made Brenda fall out laughing. Her finding what I'd said funny was bound to agitate Anndora, so I tried to cover up for Brenda's big heehaw, and said, 'Milan. I know I been, but don't ask me what's there. Y'all took me to all them foreign places and now I can't even remember one from the next. I can picture inside some of them night clubs well enough though. 'Member the place in Germany where they'd advertised that y'all was singing topless so a whole bunch of the photographers came. And since nary one of us spoke no German we didn't know what all the bustle was over till that colored GI turned up and explained. He talked to them German photographers like he was a native, but he turned around and said he was from Cleveland. 'Member him?"

Brenda said, 'No he wasn't. He was from Boston. I bumped into him on Charles Street a couple years back.'

'You did! I liked him. I couldn't believe no colored boy could talk no German like that, could you? What was he doing with hisself? Still in the army?"

Anndora wasn't a bit interested and sighed loud enough to let everybody know it before she sat down across from Jesse. She still had her mink coat on like she was either fixing to go somewhere or wasn't planning on settling. She picked up a newspaper. As soon as she sat down, Brenda went silent.

'You speaking any of that Italian now, Anndora?' I couldn't think of nothing else to say and Jesse setting at the glass table wasn't no help.

'When I have to,' she spit out.

'Go 'head and say something.' No sooner than the words left my mouth I knew I'd said the wrong thing.

'Like what,' she said sounding sulky.

'I don't care. Say anything. Say "my feet is killing me".'

She reeled off something that sounded like a whole lot of 'Chef Boyardi' and I wasn't just putting on when I jumped up and shouted, 'That sounded just like 'em. Talk that shit, chile.' But I could see I got too excited for Brenda's good, so I sat on down again.

Though I can't exactly say what brought it on, I suddenly got a chill come over me from head to toe. But it wasn't like them chills I get 'cause a cold's coming. It was more one of them that comes with a scary feeling like something bad is about to happen. When we was kids, we used to say it's a feeling that comes 'cause somebody done walked 'cross your grave. Whatever it was, I got to shivering till my teeth chattered. I wisht I'd been a stranger to it but I wasn't, 'cause 'fore Caesar died I felt like it and again 'fore Tondalayah told me she had a tumor that turned out to be the liver cancer that killed her, I felt something similar. I tried to tell myself it was the quiet in the room and Anndora acting uppity that made me feel queer, 'cause it was real clammy with the music off and nobody talking right, though the odd sentence was trickling back and forth between us. But that ain't what I'd call talk, 'cause Anndora wasn't doing much but pissing out a grunt now and then. And neither Brenda nor Anndora'd tried to speak nothing directly to each other. But that's not what gave me that chill. I wanted to beg, 'Please talk y'all.' But begging wouldn't of done nothing. The problem was that without Joy, the Bangs wasn't like no family. And whereas it's s'posed to be the mama that links kids and that together, it could be said that Tammy did more than her share to keep them separate. Like she was happy that they didn't mix like normal kin.

It was obvious that Brenda and Anndora was fixing to flare up 'cause they was like to fighting cocks in a ring, and I thought maybe that was what got me to feeling funny, like something bad was gonna happen. I knew that sometimes it takes them fighting birds a while to start up, but once they get going, can't nobody stop 'em. But I wasn't really feared of that, 'cause I was more used to Brenda and Anndora cussing and fighting than not. With Joy having two floors, I figured if them two got to carrying on too much, I could always take myself upstairs to the bathroom and sleep in the tub.

In a way I was glad for the queer feeling. It's like a sign, and I appreciate 'em 'cause then can't nothing bad slip up on me too easy. But what was troubling was whereas I had me a sign to watch out 'cause something bad was gonna happen, wasn't no way for me to know exactly what it was or when it would occur. 'What's keeping your mother?' I asked Anndora. Part I was making conversation. And part I wanted to know.

'She'll be down soon,' she said. There wasn't nothing nice to her voice even though she was quiet spoken. It was like that Peter Lorre man's. When the girls were singing together folks was always surprised to find out that it was Anndora and not Joy that sung all the low bits. Anndora was slight. Looked like a good wind would blow her over, so it seemed she shoulda been the one singing up high. But she was on the bottom, not that she sang much of nothing. Just some shooby-doos now and then. Danny Lagerfield said that nobody that looked as good as Anndora had to do nothing but shake they hips anyway, and since she was hip shaking more with him than on the stage couldn't nobody argue. He let her get away with missing practice when it suited her. It's the only time I saw Joy mad at her.

'Anndora,' Jesse said, 'is Tammy still up there messing with that safe? Because I told her that I'd help her find the combination when we got back from the undertaker's. Assuming you did make a new appointment while you two were up there all that time.'

I laid there on that sofa back to playing possum and I was real glad Brenda asked Jesse what I wanted to know.

'Joy's got a safe?'

Joy wasn't never interested in jewelry or nothing fancy. She didn't have money for waste like that nohow, and all Rex ever got her was Indian jewelry and paste. I know 'cause I was always telling her that if she got some gold off of him, she'd have her something to sell when he dropped her. Of course she didn't listen. If she hadda done she wouldn't had to borrow from Freddie B when she did.

I couldn't think why Joy bothered with no safe. Ain't like the Depression where cash can't sit in the bank.

I watched Brenda take herself upstairs. It was sure sad how her personality changed from when I first got in. She fell right back to acting meek like when there was all the commotion with that *Queen for a Day* thing.

Watching after Brenda, Anndora opened her mouth to say something, but must have thought better on it, 'cause she held her tongue and lifted up her sunglasses for a close up look at another one of them pictures Brenda'd spread out on the table. When Anndora picked it up I noticed her break into a smile.

I asked, 'What's that one of?'

'Me,' she said like she didn't want to talk.

I guess I would of been surprised to hear otherwise.

'You doing what?' I asked.

'Being molested by Santa Claus.' I guessed that was meant to be a joke. She yawned. 'Bored' was always her middle name.

'Let me have a look,' Jesse asked her and leant across to have a see but she didn't pass it to him. She laid it down on her side of the table and got up.

I didn't like her look. It was too uptown for me. I liked girls natural. But there wasn't no denying that Anndora was fine. I wondered what boyfriend she had buying her them fancy clothes but I didn't bother to ask. For one thing it wasn't none of my business, and for another she was liable to tell me it wasn't.

She called upstairs to her mother. 'Tammy.' When she dropped out of high school to start singing, Anndora took to calling Tammy by her name. 'Mother dear', I use to call my mama. All us kids did. And if I'd of been brazen enough to dare call her Ruthie Mae, she'd of sure left a big hickey on my head to show for it.

Jesse chimed in the second time Anndora called. 'Tammy!' Both of 'em hollered at once and the only way she couldn't have heard was if she was deaf.

'What is it?' Tammy shouted back. She sounded agitated. 'I wish everybody would leave me the hell alone for one goddam minute. Just one.'

'Let's move it!' said Anndora. 'I'd like to get this over with.'

She was the onliest one who could get away with speaking to her mother like that and I was surprised how quick Tammy was to come clomping down the stairs. Brenda followed carrying her mama's coat which Jesse took off her and helped Tammy put on. It crossed my mind that I hadn't seen Anndora's bags when she'd stepped off the elevator.

I pulled the camel coat tighter round my shoulders and cleared my throat. 'Is the doorman s'posed to be bringing your suitcases up here, Anndora?' I asked.

'My case is at the hotel.'

Tammy said, 'You promised me that you were going to stay here. Brenda can sleep on the floor and you can have the big dressing room upstairs. There's a sofabed in there.'

'There's two bedrooms?' Brenda asked her mother. Seemed like that poor child didn't know nothing 'bout nothing.

Anndora didn't answer her mother and nobody acted like they even heard Brenda though what she said was bell clear. Anndora told Jesse, 'Ring down and tell the doorman we need a cab.' It was an order and if she had of said it that way to me, I'd of told her to ring him herself. I suspect Jesse was wanting to say the same thing, but he seemed ready to put up with anything from them three women. I couldn't understand it, 'cause it wasn't like he was mealy-mouthed. I took it to be that maybe when Jesse was a cop he got used to folks talking to him any which-a-way and had to take it.

I was still feeling that chill and asked Brenda to pass me a heavier coat out the closet. The living room was long as well as wide and the sofa was way 'cross from the front door near where the closets and the staircase was. I eyed them four who looked posed for a picture all bunched up around the door together. A motley crew. Brenda and Anndora didn't look no more related than Eleanor Roosevelt and my baby sister. Tammy and Jesse looked kinda matched okay, but not to Brenda towering over 'em, nor to Anndora. It's a good thing Brenda wasn't going with them, 'cause it's no telling what that undertaker was going to take 'em for.

'Aren't you coming with us?' Tammy asked me. 'Brenda's staying so you don't have to. She can answer the phone when it rings.'

I used my husband for a good enough reason to hang behind. 'Freddie B might try and ring me, and I don't want to miss him 'fore he goes to bed.' Mainly I didn't want to be up the mortician's with her and Anndora in case they was planning to burn Joy till she wasn't nothing but a jam jar o' ashes. I knew I couldn't stop 'em, so why should I want to be sitting there when they signed papers for it to happen? I can't trust my temper no better than the next one. Anyway, somebody had to stay with Brenda, 'cause no telling how long they was gonna be.

'Since ain't nobody gonna be needing Joy's bed, do y'all mind if I go up and lay down,' I said. 'I don't think sleeping on this here sofa's gonna hit the spot.' I wanted me an excuse to close the bedroom door on Brenda, 'cause I wanted to have a snoop 'round. I had a feeling that wasn't altogether too good. Part it was to do with my ulcer and part with me thinking that something was going on that Tammy and Anndora wasn't letting the rest of us in on.

When Brenda came over and sat at the edge of the sofa by my feet after them other three'd left for the undertaker's, she dabbed at the corners of her eyes, and I knew she was trying to hide tears.

'I told Mama that Anndora's whoring, but she won't believe me,' Brenda said, pouting like a five year old.

I said, 'If it's the truth, I don't want it out and if it ain't, it's a real mean thing to say about your sister. And you only guessing anyway.'

'It's the only reason Anndora can afford to pay for Joy's funeral. You know how stingy she's always been. Mama told me they sat up there and booked the most expensive mortuary in New York. Anndora found it through some lawyer friend of hers. Mama likes to brag, and I think she was just trying to make me feel bad, because she asked me for some wreath money and I don't have it. I can't afford to be here, let alone buy a wreath. What does Joy care, anyway? I explained to Mama when she phoned me at work that I couldn't come and do flowers as well, so she said she'd rather have me here with her for the funeral. Of course, had she known at the time that Anndora was coming, I probably wouldn't have been invited to the funeral at all.'

'Don't talk like that. You always want to think the worse and downgrade yourself, and you the one suffers from it.' I didn't want to let on to Brenda that it was the first I heard that Anndora was paying for Joy's burial. It took a load off my mind and got me to thinking that maybe Joy was right and I had Anndora pegged wrong.

'With Joy gone, Brenda, you and Anndora got to try to do better by each other. Tammy ain't gonna live forever, and you may wake up one day to find Anndora's the only kin you got left on this earth. Didn't you always see me take care of my baby sister?' I said. 'What little I can do for Helen I do. Drunk or no. 'Cause since Caesar passed on, we the only ones left outa all them children my momma spawned. That mess 'tween you and Anndora ain't nothing but water under the bridge.'

Brenda wiped the corners of her eyes and sniffled a couple times to hold back from crying.

'It's not my fault,' she told me.

'But you the eldest, so's you the one's got to take the lead. You act nice to Anndora and maybe she'll act nicer to you. See how she's doing for Joy?' I said, patting her leg all the while like I was talking to a little child.

'That's bullshit, and you know it as well as I do.' Brenda was bent over with her head in her hands and let out one of them deep down 'I'm-worn-to-a-frazzle' sighs. I tried to make her laugh.

'Bullshit's like horseshit. A lot of good grows from it.' She didn't crack a smile. I never was no good at making up jokes.

'Why don't you bring me over some of them pictures you took out the box, so I can be sure that you ain't trying to keep all the good ones for yourself,' I teased her. 'And bring me something sweet as you to eat, if you got anything in that kitchen,' I said and slapped her on the thigh. It was s'posed to be a kinda love tap, but my hand came down on her harder than I meant for it to.

'Dammit, Baby Palatine! That hurt!' she said, leaping up to rub on her leg. 'I was going to give you something really special like a chocolate cream eclair, but now all you're getting is a jelly donut for that.'

'I ain't partial to store bought cake, to tell the truth. My teeth or what's left of 'em can't stand all that sugar for one thing, and something soft would suit better. Ain't you got no tapioca?'

'You want me to make you a banana split? You used to like them when we were little and you and Freddie B would take us to sit at the counter down at Mr Houseman's son-in-law's drugstore. But I didn't buy any nuts,' she said.

'I ain't fussy. I'll take what I get. Surprise me,' I said to her and closed my eyes.

When I opened them again, there was a bowl of melted strawberry ice cream setting on the floor by the sofa. I guessed I'd dropped off and so I laid silent for a few minutes trying to recall where I was and why.

'Brenda!' I called out. No answer. So I got up and stumbled over to the kitchen, and as she wasn't there, I dragged my bones upstairs.

'Brenda?' I pushed open the bedroom door, and found her sitting on the floor. 'What ch'you doing down there? Why didn't you answer me?'

She held up a plastic bag full of white flour.

'Look at what I found,' she said grinning from ear to ear. I hadn't seen her smile big as that since she was winning prizes singing in the choir.

'What's that?' I didn't see what the big deal was.

'You don't know what this is?'

'What would I be asking you for?'

'I bet it's drugs.' She was glowing.

'Lemme have a look.' I wouldn't of known drugs if I'd of seen 'em. Though I knew grass. Hashish as well, 'cause Joy used to do all that. And pills from time to time. But I did know flour and that's all I thought it was, though I don't know why it was in a small freezer bag.

Brenda told me to lick my finger, and stick it in and I hoped when I went to put it to my mouth that it wasn't salty tasting. Wasn't no taste, but it made the tip of my tongue numb as that novacaine they give me at the dentist. But I didn't say nothing, 'cause Brenda looked too eager for me to.

'What is it?' I asked her.

'I think it's either coke or heroin, but I'm not sure which.' She was practically dancing and I hoped she hadn't tried none of it that might get her to acting crazy, 'cause her and drink had already mixed.

'What's the difference?'

'I'll call a friend of mine at work and find out,' Brenda said.

She went to pick up the telephone by the side of the bed.

'Don't do that! Brenda Bang, have you gone out of your mind! Gonna call up somebody to ask about heroin!' I wasn't ready for no jail. Don't start nothing and there won't be nothing is my motto. Brenda giggled but I didn't see what was funny, and as she kept the receiver at her ear and sat on the bed, I sat down on the opposite edge of it, and I took in Joy's bedroom.

It sure was beautiful. I hadn't seen it good when I peeped in at

Tammy. For one thing it was dim and the bed wasn't made up while she was sitting watching TV which made the place look a jumble. But sitting in it, I could see all the pretty flowering plants set by the tall window, and there was a nice view of the street down the block past the Chemical Bank and all the row of stores. The other window let in a sunbeam. When Joy was little she loved seeing the little dust fly in 'em, I remembered.

Her walls was gray and there was some pictures on them made out of some shiny stuff in little gold frames. On the bed was a fine lace cover, creamy colored, with a lot of hand work which I hardly dared touch. It looked like some table linen my mama got off a Scotch woman she used to work for before us kids was born. Everything in that room was perfect. Except Brenda sitting on the edge of the bed, and Tammy and Jesse's suitcase which was in the corner with their under clothes and whatnot piled on the top. It didn't look like no place Joy had lived before, but it had her stamp on it.

'Brenda, suppose you get Joy into trouble stirring up some mess?' I didn't want her to call nobody, and I could see she still hadn't put down the phone.

'How's she going to get into trouble. She's dead, and if all this in here is drugs,' she said swinging the bag back and forth, 'depending on what it is, heroin or cocaine,' she said them like they was religious words, 'we might be able to sell it to somebody this friend of mine knows and make a whole pile of fast money.' Brenda had brightened up considerable.

'Look child, you don't know what you doing nor what you talking about.' Neither did I on more than one account, sitting there with her. 'But you know that you can't start selling nothing you find in here. For one it don't belong to you.'

'Who's it belong to?' asked Brenda. She'd stopped smiling.

'I don't know. But that ain't for you and me to decide.'

'What are you trying to say, that I ought to give this packet to my mama. What's she going to do with it that I can't do better?' She pointed her finger at me. 'Now, let me tell you something, and I want you to listen good, Baby Palatine. If this is heroin, it could be worth thousands, and maybe it's finders keepers anyway, but I'm willing to let you in on it.'

'I don't want to be let in on nothing to do with no drugs.' And I meant that too. The papers was full of murders and robberies and all sorts by them junkies and that. I didn't want no part of it.

'Throw that away,' I told Brenda. 'You don't want to get involved with nothing like that.'

'Joy was. And I bet you wouldn't have said anything against her for having it,' said Brenda.

Rex came straight to my mind, 'cause I remembered that time Joy got into trouble bringing in a suitcase of his that had a couple of watches in it that she didn't know nothing 'bout and it ended up with her in a big mess down LA customs.

'Whosesoever it was,' said Brenda, 'it's mine now. I don't mind sharing what I get from it, but I'm sure not giving it to Mama. Because what's she going to do with it? Something ridiculous. . . Tell Anndora to get rid of it? Or stick it down the toilet!'

I wanted to get up but I didn't have the strength and stayed sat down on the opposite side of the bed. There was a desk and chair near the window where Brenda went over to stand. 'I hardly had bus fare down here and can't even buy Joy a wreath and what are you telling me? That I'm supposed to pour this down the toilet. Fuck that shit, Baby. If it is heroin, it's probably worth a whole lot of money, and I can't see the harm in getting rid of it through somebody I know so that we can make some money out of it.'

She threw me a dirty look and stuck the packet down the front of her blouse.

'Look,' I told her, 'your stepfather might know something 'bout this here drug stuff, so we ought to ask him when he comes back.'

'Jesse? What the hell's he gonna do. And what does an old fart like him know anyway. That he married my mother must mean he hasn't got the sense he was born with.' Her mouth started to twitch like it used to when she got too excitable. Brenda could be a handful when she lost control and I ain't strong as I was in the days when I used to throw her down and sit on her to calm her, 'cause big as she was as a kid there wasn't no other way to get her under control.

I told her, 'Let's think about this for a minute, before you do anything crazy. How 'bout a walk in the fresh air?' I wasn't wanting to sit up in there with no drugs.

'I thought you were the one who wanted to wait for Freddie B to phone.'

The plastic bag peeked out the neckline of Brenda's blouse. It made me sweat just thinking that I tried to get her out in the streets with that bag still on her. 'Don't you wanna put that away somewhere safe? I ain't gonna steal that off you, 'case that's what you think.'

'It's safe enough,' she said, and patted her bosom.

'But it makes me nervous, knowing you got that stuck down there. 'Fact, I don't like being in here with it.'

'Well, take a walk.' She sounded salty.

'Don't be ornery, Brenda. It don't become you.'

'All I said was why don't you go out for that walk.'

I told her, 'It wasn't what you said, it was the way you said it.'

'You're just jealous 'cause I'm gonna make some money. You ought to be glad I found it, because I bet if my mother had, she wouldn't be talking about sharing the proceeds.'

'You're grown, so I ain't gonna waste my breath arguing with you, but no good can come from that.'

'The money is good enough for me.' She brightened up like she was counting the dollar bills already.

'But s'pose that ain't Joy's. Then what?'

'Of course it's Joy's. Who else would have stuck it under her mattress?'

'Is that where you found it?'

'Right over there.' She pulled me 'round to the edge of the bed near the TV and turned back the corner of the mattress.

'What was you doing looking under there?' I thought to have a rouse around myself, but not 'neath no mattress. That seemed sneaky.

'You act like Joy's coming back,' Brenda said.

'I didn't say that.'

'But you act like it. You're forgetting that every single thing in this apartment's got to be divided up between the family. Not that we'll leave you out. You'll probably get something too, Baby Palatine.'

The whole idea of them digging through Joy's things when I know she didn't want them in her place upset me, and I got to shouting, 'I don't want nothing!' and I didn't neither. 'You acting like them old women in *Zorba the Greek*!'

'What's that supposed to mean?'

'You know. 'Member that bit when them women came in and tried to clean out his girlfriend's place 'fore she was in her grave. Like vultures they was. You was with me when I saw that picture.'

'I'm no fucking vulture.' She took attitude and threw her hands on her hips. I didn't know why she had bits of fluff from the carpet in her hair.

'Well how come you going around collecting up things and Joy ain't even buried yet. That's wrong, and you know it good as I do. They didn't teach you nothing like that up the church.'

'Oh shit, why do you always have to bring the motherfucking church into every damn thing.'

That got my dander up and I let rip and said more than I should of. 'What now? I got to put up with you blaspheming? I only stayed behind so you wouldn't be here all by yourself. I shoulda gone with your mother, 'cause I really don't want to listen to you cussing.' I was real mad. She could see it too, 'cause she said, 'I don't know why you're getting in a stink. So what if I do sell this stuff. It's not going to hurt you, is it?'

I didn't have no answer. What was in the back of my mind was that it would be just like Brenda to get caught up in another mess and have all us in it like she did before. But I knew to say that would open up a can of worms that I wouldn't be able to shut.

It's a shame that the dead can't speak for themselves. I couldn't believe that Joy was taking no drugs, so I spoke for her. 'Your sister wasn't no drug addict. I ain't sure of much, but I talked to Joy 'bout once the week and if she was high on drugs I'd of known it.'

'Maybe she was dealing. Ever thought of that?'

'Your sister was selling dope? I can't believe you'd think it, let alone say it. First you got Anndora whoring, now you got Joy a dope dealer.'

'Well, I'll tell you one thing, there's a whole lot of stuff in this bag. A whole lot. And she would have to be rich to either buy this much for herself or have it laying around for friends.'

I didn't want to let on too much, because I knew Brenda didn't know much about Joy and Rex. It struck me that he may of had something to do with the bag, 'cause I was sure that Joy didn't. She wouldn't of been borrowing no money off my husband if she had money enough for dope.

The corner of the bag was still sticking out of Brenda's blouse. 'Why don't you put that in your suitcase, if you're so scared I'm gonna take it.'

'Cause you'll know it's in there. Now don't play with me, Baby, 'cause I don't want to have to hurt you.'

'Hurt me for what? See what kind of poison that is. You ain't had it but ten minutes and already you been cussing and creating over it. And now you got the nerve to be threatening me.'

The phone rang before Brenda could answer me. It made us jump.

'I betcha that's Freddie B,' I said.

She picked up before I could. 'Hello?' A big grin came across her face when she said, 'How'd you know my voice right off? I didn't think you'd remember me!'

'Course he remembers you,' I whispered. 'We got pictures of all y'all on the mantel.' I reached to get the receiver off her.

'Well thanks, Auntie Helen. That's sweet of you to say. Joy loved you too.'

I already had a crook coming in my neck from tension, and the last thing I needed was my baby sister who was never nothing but Trouble with a capital 'T'.

Brenda put her hand over the mouthpiece. 'You think Helen might know the difference between heroin and coke?'

'Hell no.' That convinced me that Brenda had well and truly lost her marbles. 'Lord, Brenda, what is you thinking 'bout! Don't you go mention nothing like that to Helen. Give me that phone.' I tried to snatch it off her but she kept her grip.

My heart was skipping when she said 'Helen . . . I would sure like to see you too. Are you coming for the funeral?'

'Honest to God, Brenda. I'm gonna brain you,' I said, balling my fist at her. 'That's my telephone bill she's running up. Give me that telephone, please!'

'I think she's had a couple of drinks,' Brenda laughed and passed me the phone.

A long time ago I learned that the only two ways to deal with my sister is believe nothing she says, and not to give her cash in hand. I pay some of her bills direct when I have money extra which ain't been often of late.

'Hi, Helen. What ch'you doing calling?' I was exasperated before she even got to talking.

'Baby? Hi. It's me.' I could tell she had some snuff in her mouth 'cause when she's got a lip full she talks like she got a mouth full of cow dung.

'Helen, I'd appreciate it if you didn't run up my telephone bill. This is New York you calling. What you wanting?'

'I was worried about you. Freddie B told me something done happened to Joy. It's true?' she asked.

'True enough. But it ain't no use you worrying, 'cause I'm all right and there ain't nothing that nobody can do for her now.'

She paused a minute and took a big spit. 'I did something bad, Baby, and I don't want you to be mad, but Freddie B said I better had called you and let you know, 'cause he don't think it should be up to him to tell you. Ain't that right, Freddie.' He must have been sitting by her in the kitchen. Either that or she was in my bedroom.

'Is Freddie up?' He takes to oversleeping when he ain't working. 'Helen, I hope that you didn't come over juiced to the eyeballs disturbing my husband.'

'I come by real late last night. I didn't know you wasn't here, and when Freddie come back from the airport and told me about Joy I went to feeling bad and he said to stay over. So this morning he dialed your number and told me to tell you. But I forgot, so he dialed you for me just now.'

'Tell me what?' I didn't even want to hear what she had to say, 'cause drunk as she sounded she couldn't make sense out of sense.

Brenda slipped off downstairs and I was worried she might go out. When she took a mind to do something, there wasn't no swaying her.

Helen said, 'See last weekend when I come by? You know when you said I had to scrub your kitchen floor?'

'I only made you clean up that mess you made when you spilt that can of Carnation.'

'That wasn't me did that.'

'Lookahere, Helen, don't you be talking no foolishness with me now! I'm strained enough. What Freddie is wanting you to tell me? Put him on.'

She started again. 'See. When the girl came with the mail while I was standing in y'all's hall, I asked if she had something for us and she give me a black envelope. I figured it was some of Joy's, 'cause I seen you get some like it from her before. So that's when the devil got hold on it and tore it open.'

'Helen D'Orleans, what're you telling me.' To think she'd been messing with my mail made me madder than a rattlesnake.

'Well I don't know how it got opened but some money fell out. I didn't mean to do nothing. I was just borrowing it till my welfare come through. How was I supposed to know that that child was gonna keel over 'fore I got my welfare.'

'Spit, Helen.' I can't stand it when her and Freddie B talks with a great big wad in they mouths.

She said, 'Pass me that can, Freddie,' and took a hawk before she started up again. She usually starts to cry before I can yell at her. Been doing it since she was a kid. Caesar learned it off her and he used to try the same trick. I was waiting on her to start up when I told her, 'That's as good as stealing. You know better! "Thou shalt not steal." You been breaking the Lord's commandments? Now you really going straight to hell and I can't help you this time. How come you want to take from me with all I give you?' It didn't seem fair that the Lord had burdened me with so many crazy people all at once. I was really feeling sorry for myself and started weeping which made Helen weep too.

Then Freddie B come on the phone and I tried not to upset him. For all I knew Helen's crying wasn't nothing but the DTs anyway.

'Freddie B? How're you?' I was sure glad to hear his slow voice, but he hates talking on the phone and shouts like he's calling to somebody 'cross the street when he talks long distance.

'Baby, now you don't worry none. Helen didn't mean no harm. How's everything there?'

'Fine,' I lied. 'I wanted to ring you soon as I got here, but I didn't want to use Joy's phone and run up her bill. I only wanted to check that everything home is all right. Now, can you please do yourself a favor and put Helen on a bus and send her on home.'

'I don't mind her,' he said. He's too soft-hearted.

'Well I do. And she been stealing my mail. Had the nerve to take some money out of a letter from Joy. Did you ask her what she did with the letter? That's more important than the money as far as I'm concerned.'

'She say she still got it over at the rooming house.'

'Well 'stead of sending her on the bus, can you please drive her on over there and collect it. I'll be real surprised if she ain't lost it already.

In fact, put her back on the phone, please.' Then I remembered that Freddie B hadn't done nothing for me to be chewing him out about, so I said, 'Hon, I surely do thank you for helping me get here. I ain't got your armband on yet, but I'll wear it to the service.'

He said, 'Now you take care, you hear, and don't worry 'bout Helen. Here she is.'

She was coughing. 'Helen? I want you to give that letter to Freddie B. Did you read it already?' I was so mad I plum forgot she couldn't read. But she didn't never like to admit to it. I tried to get her to go to night school when she first moved to California but she didn't never want to let on that she didn't know the alphabet. She was good at simple sums, so wasn't nothing wrong with her brain, but when she was supposed to be catching up in grade school, it was the war and she wasn't wanting to do nothing but to hang around the streets with them soldiers all the time. So she didn't give no time for her book learning and my mama was too sick to see after her. I was already off married and working.

She knew just what I was thinking 'cause she said, 'I can read. How you think I know that letter was from Joy if I can't read.'

'I didn't say nothing about you can't read.'

'But I know that's what you'll be thinking. Just 'cause I can't read them big names in the Bible you try to act like you better than me, you ugly black heifer.'

I said, 'Ain't no need to start name calling.' But it was Freddie B's voice I heard answering me. He musta grabbed the phone off her.

He said, 'Go on 'bout your business, Helen! Baby? She don't mean you nothing. She just been drinking and that. That's all. The drink is talking. You know how it does. When I find that letter, I'll call you back. But it's garbage day, so don't wait in on me, 'cause I got a lot to do.'

'Thanks, Freddie B. You want to say "hi" to Brenda?'

'I'll speak to her next time,' he said snail pace and hung up. He don't like to lollygag on the phone.

It lifted my spirits to think Joy wrote and sent some money. She didn't mention it when she last called, but maybe that's why she was acting funny – waiting on me to say thanks, and me wondering why she didn't sound her usual cheerful self.

So I was practically humming and in a better frame of mind when I went down to Brenda who was sitting at the table looking bright eyed. But I spotted that plastic bag which landed me back on earth.

'Did you look at these pictures yet?' she asked me.

I sat down opposite her and she passed me two. They was of all three girls standing out in the parking lot on Grange. Summertime. I remember the day 'cause Freddie B had asked me to go clear up the gravel where them teenagers used it for a love nest and left a bunch of used up rubbers so folks could step on 'em the next day. But my mind wasn't on looking at no pictures, and I couldn't make out like it was.

Brenda noticed and nudged me. 'Don't be upset, Baby. Everything is gonna work.'

I'd heard that lie enough times before. 'Let's get one thing straight,' I told her. 'If you want to go to jail, that's your business, but do me a favor. Please don't do anything 'bout that bag till after the funeral and I'm outa here. That ain't asking much.' She sat broody and didn't answer. 'But I know I can't make you pour that mess down the drain.'

'Amen,' she said 'fore I could finish. Then she rolled her eyes at me and picked up a picture like she was studying it.

I went on. 'Doing wrong's always been easier than doing right. And what bothers me is that you ain't just planning to sell that. I can tell you thinking to have a little taste on it yourself.' I 'spect I wasn't far off the mark, 'cause Brenda didn't deny it. 'You know I ain't had nothing to do with neither drink nor drugs,' I said, 'but that don't mean I ain't been tempted as the next one to get high and blot out all the ugliness. Like my brother. 'Member him? . . . Soon as Caesar come back from Korea and didn't have the army feeding him and paying his rent, he panicked. Scared to death he was of being a Havenot. Cold-sober won't give a nigger a minute to pretend life's a piece of cake, so Caesar stayed blottoed. A walking zombie.'

Brenda said, 'Poor Caesar.'

'Poor Caesar my back ass,' I shouted. 'It was my life he puked and stumbled all over. Not his'n. Mine. He was sleeping deep with a clear conscience while I was up half the night praying for my soul, 'cause I had to be the one stealing off my husband's plate so my brother wouldn't starve. I was the one stealing from the housekeeping so I could have money on hand when the bailiffs called about him. It was my hands that was wringing the stale piss out his pants so Caesar wouldn't stink up the neighborhood and disgrace us.'

'What's that got to do with me?'

'This here, Brenda. All my life I been trying to live like a Christian and seems like I can't get far enough away from folks finding ways to drag me over to the devil's side. And you been one of the worse ones for it. You try to play Miss Innocent, but you ain't nothing but a river of destruction, and I don't aim to be nowhere near the next time you start a flood.'

'What do I ever do but get all the blame?'

'It's just you and me here now. Eye to eye. So don't you tell that mess to me, 'cause I know you too good, and Joy ain't here to cover up for you.'

'Joy this. Joy that. Joy the other. Saint fucking Joy! I didn't notice you saying Joy was wrong to have this under her mattress.'

'I keep telling you that for all you know Joy may not have nothing to do with that stuff. Firstly, you ain't sure what it is, and second it don't have her name on it no way, do it?'

We didn't speak to each other for a while. Staring off in opposite directions. I had already said more than I wanted to and the best thing for me to do was keep my mouth out the whole mess. Right enough, Brenda found that bag where it would get her to thinking that it was Joy's.

'Look around you, Baby Palatine. Take a good look.' I didn't want to, 'cause the living room was a sight. Coats thrown on the sofa, pictures all on the floor and spread 'cross the table. Records and tapes was strewed about and a beer can was sitting by them. The bowl of ice cream, the cardboard box, newspapers. Like Brenda said, Joy wasn't coming back. So what was I gonna jump up and clean it for? 'Take a real good look. What paid for all this and all those expensive clothes in the closets. Have you checked out the labels? Valentino! Dior!'

'What business is that of yours, Brenda? You're just jealous and anyway, Joy was doing back-ups,' I said. But I knew she hadn't hardly done nothing for two years.

'Session work can't bring in that much. Not to pay for this kinda place. How much do you think this put her back every week? This is the right part of town she's living in.'

'What's it got to do with you or me?' I asked her. I was real igorated. She wouldn't of said none of that to Joy. I turned away from her and put my head in both hands.

'I can't stand to see you with a long face,' she said. 'Smile.'

'What's to smile for? Joy's dead. Your mama's fixing to burn her into ashes and you 'bout to end up behind bars. For the jackpot all I need is for my ulcer to start acting up.'

'Oh God! Well all right! You win. If it'll make you feel any better, I won't call my friend till tomorrow night. But I refuse to hold off longer than that, because I have to be back to Boston the day after, and I can't ride back on a Greyhound bus with this shit on me.' She stood up and patted her bosom.

Brenda turned the music on before she went in the kitchen and came back with two bowls of ice cream and a bottle of beer. She set one bowl in front of me. I knew it was supposed to be a peace pipe. But I wasn't ready to make peace.

'I never eat the first one you give me.' It was still over by the sofa and I went to get it.

'It's okay. We can make a milk shake or something out of it.' She scratched her chest. 'This damn bag is itching me,' she sighed and pulled it out her blouse and went to lay it on the table by me but she could see my eyes glued to it.

'You should relax,' she said.

'How'm I s'pose to relax with you and that.' I didn't even want to touch it, so with the spoon she give me, I pushed it over to her side.

'I'm gonna put it away, so you don't have to look at it, but if you mention it to anybody, especially my mama, you're gonna be sorry,' Brenda said and give me a evil look.

'I don't like nobody threatening me, Brenda, and that's the second time you done it today.'

'Well I don't want you to mess up on me, 'cause if this is what I think it is and we play our cards right, we could all have a coat like Anndora's,' she said and popped her fingers 'fore she stuck a spoon of ice cream in her mouth.

I'm real sick of folks thinking that having things is the be-all and end-all of life. 'Where can I go in a mink but down to put out the garbage.' I warned Brenda, 'I'm gonna say it this one last time. If that's somebody else's, you gonna get yourself involved in a big hullabaloo and Joy ain't gonna be around to cover for you like she always do.'

'Let's not talk about it,' Brenda said with the bag settling by her bowl of ice cream and them pictures.

'Hide that,' I told her, ' 'fore somebody walks in here. Surely you got that much sense.'

'I guess you're right.' She went upstairs.

'Joy,' I said out loud. 'Joy, Joy, Joy. What I'm supposed to do now?'

No matter how bad things got, Joy could always see the fun and make me laugh, 'specially where my baby sister was concerned. Only Rex was serious business to Joy but she didn't let much else bother her. That's why every time she'd ring me, I used to feel good by the time I hung up the phone. She could tell me 'bout one of them recording sessions and get me to laughing. The last few months she was going place to place but with her borrowing money off Freddie I was worried about Joy. I told her if Rex had money for all them plane tickets, he shoulda put a few dollars in the bank for her. But I figured looking around her living room that she musta used all her savings just to pay the rent.

I took a spoon of ice cream and picked up a few pictures off the table. All of 'em was black and white. One of 'em had the three girls standing by Dagwood's car. He's sitting at the wheel but you can't hardly see him which is why Tammy musta didn't tear that one up. Joy had on a plaid dress I got for her in a Capwell sale. I recall it was red and brown. I didn't like the color but it wasn't but a couple of dollars. She didn't never want to take it off that whole summer. Brenda's standing with her belly out in a pair of bermuda shorts holding Anndora. It's a shame children got to get big. Dagwood's car had a French sounding name. A Pootoe or Poogo. Something like that. It was a couple years old, but he kept it shining like it was just off the lot. Black and green with white-wall tires that he was forever out scrubbing. I was surprised that they had any paint left on 'em.

Freddie B used to let him use the parking lot, 'cause Freddie said

Tammy paid for a space automatic as it was included in her rent even though she didn't have no car to park. When she first moved in she tried to get something docked off her rent but old Mr Houseman said everybody had to pay the same, $82 a month.

Wasn't but four apartments to see to above them shops at street level. Two at the front overlooking Grange and the two at the back that we was in. It was the shops that was the real hassle, 'cause Freddie B had to make sure they was locked up and keep a watch over them. Had him a black flashlight and he used to go round twice the night shining it in them windows 'fore we went off to bed. I did it on Wednesdays 'cause he had his deacons' meeting. He didn't think I would be no good at it, but wasn't nothing to it. It ain't like it was dangerous.

But the neighborhood wasn't nothing to look at. Mostly cheap bungalows and store fronts. It was noisy on the Grange side 'cause of them buses. But 'part from them rowdy boys that used to hang outside the barber shop, it wasn't what you'd call slummy, though somebody'd get they handbag snatched off 'em once an' again, but it was a lot safer than where me and Freddie B is now. Them thugs'll be snatching and grabbing right up in the White House 'fore we know what's hit us. The TV's full of it.

I got a girlfriend over on Quintara Street who takes her a baseball bat out with her to go two blocks over to the Safeway. Like she says, you got to have you some kinda protection when you're out.

I wish I could 'member what Dagwood's car was called. Brenda was crazy 'bout that car. Them kids used to love to sit in it when it was raining and they couldn't play out. Brenda would always be in the driver's seat, hands on the steering wheel. Just pretend. Their favorite game was "going on a picnic" after me and Freddie B took 'em on a real one. Dagwood used to let me take spam sandwiches out there to 'em, 'long as I didn't put no mustard or mayo on 'em and promised to go back out and clean the bread crumbs off his leather upholstery.

Joy's living room wasn't no place to set long by yourself. Big as the sofa was, it wasn't comfortable, and the chairs up at the table was modern and no kinder to your backside than a church bench. But the apartment really worked my nerves 'cause it was too quiet, and I was fixing to get up and turn the music on when the phone went.

I managed to pick up before Brenda could upstairs, but I heard her lift the receiver as I said, 'Hello, Joy Bang's residence.' That's how I used to answer when I was touring on the road with them and I'd get Joy's phone.

'I got it, Brenda,' I said. But I didn't hear her hang up.

It was Tammy. 'Baby, we've got a few problems here so we might be a while.'

'Everything all right?'

'I'm in the undertaker's office,' she said in her normal voice, then she dropped it down low. 'I can't really talk. We'll be back soon, but it's taking longer than he expected. The body's not left Santa Fe yet and has to make a stopover in St Louis, and he's worried that we won't get it in time for a cremation.'

'Thank you Jesus,' I said to myself and tried not to sound too happy. 'Well, don't worry 'bout us. Me and Brenda can find something to do. Can't we Brenda?' I heard the upstairs phone click. She'd hung up.

Before Tammy said 'Bye' Brenda'd come running down the stairs like she hadn't been listening in.

'Who was that?' she asked.

'You know who it was. Why didn't you say nothing?'

Brenda was always a mystery. She didn't answer but stood right behind my chair to look over my shoulder at the pictures in front of me. She picked up the one I'd just put down with Dagwood and his car in it.

' 'Member that summer?' Brenda asked.

'How could I forget?' She must of been kidding. So I played like heat and baseball was all I recalled. 'That's the year the Brooklyn Dodgers won the world series. Freddie was rooting for the Yankees and it 'bout broke his heart. He wouldn't talk about nothing afterwards but Sandy Kofaks till the football started up. It was hotter that year than I ever remember it getting even in Louisiana. But you kids didn't mind none, 'long as you had a nickel for a popsicle.'

'When I think about Mama, I never picture her in my mind like she looked today. She's always in her dark pink chenille robe,' said Brenda. She was smiling like it was a happy memory. But I recall that robe as part of the nightmare when for them five or so months Tammy wasn't dressed in nothing else, laying up in the bed, pining over John Dagwood.

Brenda said, 'It's a shame there's not a picture of her in it. But I searched through the whole box. Not one.'

'I ain't surprised. Who on earth was gonna take a picture of Tammy looking like that.' Kids can forget the bad stuff they go through so easy, that they get to being grown without no clear recollection of what they done suffered. The way Brenda was talking, she had me ready to believe that her forgetting was actually real forgetting, pure and simple, 'cause she was mooning over that old black and white snapshot like she saw her childself posed in the middle of somebody's Disneyland, when in actual fact, I knew she was trapped in the middle of her own hell.

I wanted to believe that Brenda had learned a big lesson that summer; that it taught her that when you grab something you ain't supposed to have before you're meant to have it, you always leave something else behind. And what you take ain't never worth as much as what you leave. 'Cause when Brenda grabbed at sex before she should of done, she left her sweet childhood behind.

After that mess with Dagwood, I couldn't treat her like a child no more, and seems to me that that's all being a kid is worth; having grown folks put up with what you do and act like you got a God-given right not to know nothing nor owe nothing.

From that Dagwood day on, that kindly feeling I got from spoiling Brenda with baby talk or letting her squirm on my husband's lap without suspecting what she was up to was over. It was goodbye to that.

When she set herself down opposite me at Joy's glass top table and picked up another picture, I said to keep conversation, 'Freddie B always had him a fist full of money that summer 'cause he was working a big site in El Cerrito. Bricklaying. But he could do most anything when it come to building b'cept running cranes.'

'Isn't that where the money is?' asked Brenda. She had money on the brain, seemed like.

'Didn't no colored boys get to drive no cranes down South where Freddie picked up his trade after the war. So it wasn't worth learning, and who was gonna teach 'em anyway . . . my mama?'

Brenda let out a good loud laugh. That's what the place needed. I went on, 'Freddie B bought me a Brownie camera that summer. It even come in a case, and I was scared to handle it till Joy showed me after she'd read the instructions.'

Brenda said, 'We looked a mess didn't we?' She showed me another one of her, Joy and Anndora in our parking lot and pointed at herself in the picture. 'Who put those huge ribbons in my hair?'

She had two teeny weeny ponytails that you couldn't hardly see for the bows, and her hair was skint back so tight she looked like a Chinaman. She was head and shoulders above Joy who didn't start growing till junior high and was holding Anndora.

'I don't know what ch'you talking about. Couldn't nobody get you to go out the house without your ribbons, and the bigger the better. I used to get them for you at the dime store next to the cleaner's. 'Member that woman with the gammy leg behind the counter. She used to give y'all something free everytime I took you in there.'

'I loved that store. That's where Joy and I used to buy material for our doll clothes.'

'That's right! Your mama got both of you them big colored dolls just after you moved in,' I said.

'No. Unh unh. Dagwood bought them for us.'

What she said silenced me. I took a big swallow.

For the first time in thirty-one years, she spoke Dagwood's name in my presence. I braced myself for the sky to fall but it didn't. Nor did the cops bust down the door and drag Brenda out by her hair. And there wasn't no bolt of lightning to strike us which surprised me, 'cause every day of every one of them thirty-one years, that's what I suspected would happen if either her, me or Joy breathed that man's name.

'Dagwood.' I said it. And it was like I could see the sound come outa my mouth in technicolor. It frightened me. But something dared me to say it again. Not loud. 'Dagwood.' The second time it seeped out, and I wiped my mouth with the back of my hand, 'cause it was like I could feel the poison from it still stuck to my bottom lip. But I wished that I could of hollered it, and I wanted Joy to be there so she could of too. Her and me never even whispered it each other. And as time went by I got to wondering if I imagined the whole episode, 'cause John Dagwood suffered a fate worse than death. He got unremembered and unmentioned like he had never been. Never existed.

I could see Brenda was sitting there feeling real bold like she was already rich or something. She had changed from when her mother and Anndora had been in the room. Brenda had her shoulders pushed way back like menfolk do when they wearing a uniform.

'You made doll clothes, huh?' I didn't want to make no more of Dagwood's name than she had.

'Well, it was more like we cut up the material, because we could never finish. Mama never seemed to have needles around.'

'I always had a needle.'

'I didn't say you. I said Mama.'

'You was in and out of my place as much as you was in and out of your own.'

'Joy was.' Brenda picked up another picture and said, 'I wasn't. You never invited me like you did Joy.' I knew that was true, but I didn't bite the bait.

'There wasn't no invitation needed. The door was open to all y'all and you know it now and knew it then.'

'Well to tell you the truth, I was always scared of Caesar anyway, so I didn't care if you didn't want me over.'

I thought she wanted to get me at it, so I shined on the last part of what she said. Only fools rush in where angels fear to tread, and it takes two for a argument.

'There wasn't nothing scary about my brother,' I said with a smile to keep things pleasant.

'I saw him take a knife to Helen once. Don't tell me you never saw it, because you were there when it happened.'

I had to laugh. 'Which time exactly? There was a whole bunch of 'em. 'Fact, it got so regular that when Caesar or Helen would run to my kitchen to get the butcher knife, I couldn't even get Freddie B to look up from his Bible, 'cause he said they was too lushed to know whether they was pointing handle or blade. I was more worried one of 'em would fall on the knife. They didn't never shed none o' each other's blood, but they liked all the cussing and excitement, 'specially if it was raining and they couldn't be out hanging in the streets.'

'They say drinking runs in families.' I hoped Brenda wasn't gonna start in on my family.

'Our mama didn't never touch alcohol to her lips. So it ain't her fault.'

'How about your daddy?'

'I told you enough times I don't remember him all that good and can't claim my mama knew him deep down all that good herself. Seemed to me like he didn't never do much more than leave her with a belly full of baby.'

'You never saw him?' asked Brenda.

'Yeah. But nowadays I can't recall his face. Mama said I was crazy about Daddy when I was a baby but after he left I couldn't never put a face to him. You lucky you got pictures like this here to remind you of things. I don't have none of Moth' Dear, Daddy, nor none of my four brothers. Just Helen. But I see too much of her as it is.'

'Well there's one here with Caesar in it,' said Brenda. I was so excited, I let out a yelp when she reached for the pile of pictures and shuffled through them till she come up with it. I forgot myself and grabbed it out her hand without so much as a do-you-mind.

It was of her, Joy and Caesar outside the First Tabernacle, but his back was so in the way I couldn't hardly see them or him. Still, there was enough of his face showing to make me sad. Brenda laughed soon as she noticed my eyes started to fill up.

She said, 'You're gonna cry over everything today, huh? One minute long faced 'cause there's no picture of Caesar and the next crying because there is.'

'Ain't it the truth,' I said. 'Boo-hooing about every little thing. Joy dying got me on edge.' So did Brenda trying to pick fights, but I wasn't gonna let on to her.

She said, 'Why don't I fix you something. You're the one's probably hungry now.' Trust Brenda Bang. No sooner than she got you mad and upset, she'd say or do something nice to you to confuse things. And that in itself could make me mad. I ain't nobody's yo-yo.

In a way she was the same with the Dagwood thing, 'cause I was well and truly off her, child or no child, after that, but then soon as Tammy let me take the girls to church Sundays, Brenda was the one up begging me to let her get sanctified and wanting to be at First Tabernacle the whole weekend. That's how come she signed up for the children's choir.

'My stomach's rumbling just thinking 'bout food,' I finally answered Brenda. 'But let's both cook,' I said, ' 'cause I'm sick of sitting here on my behind.' I pulled myself up out the chair, stiff as one of them old women suffering with the lumbago which reminded me to be thankful mine hadn't flared up.

'You don't mind if I cook for myself, do you?' Brenda said.

'Scared I'm gonna poison you?' I nudged her.

'There's a lot can be said for you, Sugar. but "good cook" ain't on the list.'

I fell out laughing so the tears run down my cheeks. Them laugh tears is more like what I'm used to.

I carried the picture with Caesar to the kitchen. Brenda said, 'Don't come in here with that, I'm gonna fry some bacon and you might get grease splattered on it. Put it in your purse.'

'You don't want it?'

'What're you trying to make me out to be? Hard Hearted Hannah? You say you don't have one of Caesar, so you keep it.'

'You sure?' I smiled down at that picture. 'It's worth five of Anndora's coats. Ten even.'

Brenda flipped me one of them don't ask me again looks.

I said, 'Before? . . . When I spoke bad of Caesar? I didn't mean none of that. I loved that boy. It was me raised him. And my baby sister. 'Cause my mama was so poorly after having him, then Helen straight after, she couldn't look after 'em . . . Two wine-os I got to my credit.'

'You did your best.'

'When the day came, no sooner, I may add, than I expected, to go down the morgue and identify Caesar's body, you know what I was sitting on the bus praying for?'

Brenda was bent over in the frigerator searching for something and I didn't think she was paying me no mind, so when she said 'What?' after a couple minutes, I didn't know what she was talking.

'What what?' I asked her.

'What were you praying for! Don't get senile on me now, Baby Palatine.'

'I didn't think you was listening. I was praying that Caesar was in clean underclothes.' I had a clear picture in my mind of me sitting on the 33 bus that day. It was April 12, 1961. Joy's thirteenth birthday. I was in the middle of baking her cake when the call come. Standing over the stove in a flimsy housedress, so I threw on my red jacket hot as it was, to head downtown to the morgue more worried 'bout tending to Joy's birthday with Tammy at work, than my brother.

'What did you care with him dead. They don't leave the underwear on a corpse anyway.'

'I didn't want the man to think I had something to do with a dirty. . . . Dead or alive, Caesar still shed light on me. Kin do whether you like it or not.'

'Well, nobody at the fucking morgue was paying your rent,' said Brenda.

'But I worked hard to keep my family clean. And myself. Can't nobody say they never smelled me or my clothes.'

'Smelly clothes,' Brenda mocked like I was the one crazy. 'Your BO is yours. And not a damn soul has to pay you for it, so what's it got to do with them.'

'You wouldn't know would you. . . Y'all always had a fresh dress to go to school in. I know 'cause I saw to it even when your mama wasn't bothering.' No sooner than them words come out of mouth Brenda bristled like a cat and her whole body tensed up.

'Mama was at the laundry every Sunday.'

I didn't say nothing, but I knew sure as I was in Joy's kitchen that when I wasn't washing and ironing for Tammy's girls, Brenda was. But I wasn't 'bout to say and let Brenda hedge me into a argument so I skipped it and went right on to something else.

'Caesar was sure a fine looking boy till his face got swoll' up from drinking gallons of Thunderbird.' I looked long at my brother in the picture. 'I wisht he didn't have his ol' corn cob hat on. I couldn't never get him to take it off. Even kept it on in the house, bad luck as that is, but he didn't like folks to see his gray hair, though I told him you could still see it growing in down his sideboards anyways. He wasn't but thirty-nine when he died and his whole head had changed color. But gray or not, I hated that hat and used to say, "Caesar you ain't down South now! Why you want to look like a farmer?" He would of worn brokendown overalls in the street if I hadn't of stopped him.'

Brenda had opened up the frigerator again while I was talking to take the last Colt '45 out the sixpack. Before she popped it open, she said, 'Your problem's always been minding other people's business.'

The way she said it was hurtful, and whereas a lot of times she don't mean nothing by what she say I could tell she was trying to stir things up.

'If I hadn't minded Caesar's business, who woulda done?'

She threw her head back and glug-glugged that beer 'fore she answered. 'Maybe he could have minded his own. Ever think about that?' She let out a great big loud belch and didn't even try to put her hand to her mouth, smiling like she was proud of herself.

Brenda didn't know no better. That was the difference between her and Joy. Joy would of never done something bad mannered as that and didn't need nobody to tell her. She also knew when to hold her tongue and was a perfect lady. That's why all them big shots was up in her face all the time when we was on the road. There wasn't no place that Joy couldn't go and act as good as any of them. I don't care who they thought they was nor what color. But not Brenda. The only place she was comfortable was a juke joint, but it wasn't worth saying it. Instead, I told her, 'You was too young to realize, I guess, but Caesar didn' take care of hisself. Didn't feed hisself right or nothing, and it was Freddie B and me that put the clothes on his back. Well . . . halfway, that is, 'cause we got Caesar things handed down from some of our church members. Like I did for you girls.'

'Oh God,' said Brenda. 'How will I ever forget those clothes you used to bring us. They always smelled of camphor balls, so the first few times you wore them nobody at school ever wanted to sit near you.'

Maybe she forgot something I didn't. 'Your mama didn't have money to buy new.'

Brenda let out another big belch that was way louder than the bacon sizzling. 'Yeah,' she said gruff, trying to sound like a truck driver, seemed like. 'But everytime you rushed in with that junk from the church, Mama had an excuse not to buy us any decent clothes.'

What with Joy dead and jet lag, I felt raw as a egg and there was Brenda beating on me. With neither her mother or sister to bully her, she thought she was gonna scramble my brains and serve 'em up with that bacon she fried. But I had news for her. I knew her good as she knew herself, and all her big talk was gonna dip down to a whine soon as Anndora was back. And then she'd be up in my face looking for a kind word.

So I took a deep breath and turned the conversation again to her and Joy in the pictures with Caesar.

'Don't y'all look cute in them twin suits you got on. And you can't say they smelled like no camphor balls 'cause Freddie B paid cash for them in a Capwell's sale I took y'all to for your Easter outfits. They was such a pretty color too. Kinda mustard. I sure do wish this here picture wasn't black and white.'

Brenda forgot she wanted to agitate. 'What I really like,' she laughed, 'is our hats.' While she was turned from the stove to get another look, she near burned the bacon. The smoke from the pan sent me in the hallway while Brenda tried to work out how to switch on the extractor fan. She F'd and blinded, and so I went back to set in the living room. It was hard to believe that she was the same child I remembered from the Easter Sunday picture I was still holding.

I was real proud of all three girls that Easter day. Even Anndora was on best behavior. Joy and Brenda had on everything brand new, even underclothes and socks. They was wearing straw bonnets with a bit of veil and posies on the brim and both them and Anndora had on white gloves, 'cause didn't nobody step in church on Easter without gloves. I had me a pair that nearly come up to my elbow. Still got 'em in a drawer somewhere and nearly brought 'em to New York.

Joy looked way prettier in her outfit than Brenda, but couldn't nobody steal Brenda's limelight that Sunday 'cause it was the first time she sung solo in the children's choir.

When she took her place by the organ to sing, 'Jesus is Dancing in My Shoes', wasn't nobody caring 'bout how she looked once she opened that mouth of hers. Women got to screaming and getting happy in them aisles. Anybody didn't know better woulda thought all our members was sanctified. Two deacons had to carry Miss Dickerson out, she got to feeling the spirit so. Tammy couldn't believe her eyes. Nor ears. Her and Tondalayah had both come. What with Brenda singing by herself for the first time, I even managed to get Caesar to church.

We was excited getting dressed up for church, but we was expecting that Brenda was gonna have her a sweet voice like kids do and make a mistake or two. But she had us fooled. Couldn't nobody in the whole congregation sit down once she got to about the third verse that goes

> Jesus goes climbing in my shoes
> And while I struggle up the mountain
> He's struggling up there too.

Mr Tyrell playing piano wouldn't stop playing and stamping on the pedals so Brenda kept right on singing. I think Tammy almost got happy that day. I know Tondalayah did. Them girls at the strip joint wouldn't of thought they knew her if they could of seen her get the spirit dressed in my purple hat and short white gloves and high stepping by the pulpit.

All the Sisters and Brothers was clapping and dancing and when Brenda finished singing, I feared they was gonna carry her out in the street on they shoulders. She was grinning like somebody saved and I expect she would of been if it hadn't been for Tammy who didn't want to talk about nothing but getting Brenda on a talent show on the TV. She said God didn't come into it. Arthur Godfrey was a better bet. And I guess that if Brenda had looked like Joy, television is just about where she would of ended up. Eleven years old or not.

I had cooked us a big ham that Easter Sunday, and I don't know what all else. Black-eyed peas. Rice. Collards. Biscuits, and baked a marble cake 'cause that was one of Joy's favorites, and I was all geared up for Tammy and them coming to us for dinner with Tondalayah, Caesar and my baby sister who refused to sober up enough to go to the service, but she had no intentions of missing a lemon meringue pie that I baked as a afterthought the night before.

Our apartment wasn't really big enough for all them people to set down and eat at once, but we made do with a couple of us eating off our laps and I fixed the three girls up at a card table that I borrowed out of one of Mr Houseman's front apartments. With all the hoopla made over Brenda, at the service, we'd all come back in a kinda party spirit, though to tell the truth Easter ain't supposed to be noisy like Christmas. Freddie B turned up the radio and was real proud of himself when he found us a gospel service. It wasn't no proper one 'cause there wasn't no preacher, but listening to the Jameson Sisters and the Four Gospelites and a couple of them other local San Francisco groups they had on was sure uplifting, until Tammy asked us to turn the radio off, because she claimed 'all that screeching' about God had a bad effect on her digestion.

She knew just how to bring down a party and like Toni told her but I didn't dare say myself, with all I had done for Brenda, carting her back and forth to choir practice at First Tabernacle, it seemed kinda thankless that Tammy wanted to speak against the gospel singers on the radio, while she was eating my food and setting her behind in my house. And whereas I had learned to keep my mouth shut where Tammy was concerned, Toni didn't keep her'n shut for nobody, and I knew that on my behalf she would have been quicker to cuss Tammy out than my baby sister would have been had she stayed awake. But Helen'd passed out across my bed no sooner than she stumbled into the apartment.

Anyway, to put a halt to Toni and Tammy getting into a argument, I jumped up and offered to serve up the marble cake which was a sly way to slip into the kitchen to turn off the radio when I carried the kids' plates into the kitchen with Joy's help. Little as she was, she was always on her feet and hankering to give me help whenever she could.

While she watched me stack them first few plates in the sink, Joy said, 'Sorry Mama made you turn off the radio, Baby Palatine.' Then she smiled and reached over to pat me on my arm, 'cause she could always tell when I was upset but covering up. And somehow just that one little pat from her made me want to act bright again. So her and me decided to have us a joke and we stuck six pink birthday candles I had in the cutlery drawer on the chocolate icing of that marble cake and went back in the living room singing Happy Birthday to Jesus. Though it didn't make a blind bit of sense, we enjoyed doing it anyway and Brenda and Toni joined in.

It was odd how singing something like Happy Birthday wouldn't nobody have noticed nothing special about Brenda's voice, but soon as we heard her singing them eight verses of 'Jesus is Walking in My Shoes' that afternoon at First Tabernacle, it was impossible not to hear that the child was well and truly blessed with a voice that wasn't only strong with a nice warble to it, but it had a special something that it was hard to explain. There was something wailing about her voice that was sad but still raised the hairs on my arms and lifted my spirit. Like every note she hit, reached out for God. But that didn't happen with Brenda singing Happy Birthday and whereas she was just having her a good sing-a-long like the rest of us, Tammy all a' sudden chastised her for not putting her all into it.

'That's not your best,' Tammy said to Brenda, interrupting the song. 'You must always sing out,' she said like she was some kinda authority which shut everybody up and made Brenda in particular feel rotten, I thought from the way the child went all quiet and sulky. Though it was

more like her feelings was hurt than like her sulks when she had to turn
off the TV and go to bed.

But that was just Tammy's way. She could easy put a dampener on
things and say something to make her kids wanna set theyselves in a
corner and be miserable. It's a wonder that Joy turned out as larky as
she did with a mama like Tammy, but then Freddie B swears that it was
me that kept the child's spirit up, 'cause I was the one ready with a kind
word.

Tammy showed special interest in Brenda for all of two whole weeks
after that First Tabernacle Easter service, while she went on kidding
herself that something big was gonna happen for Brenda. She said that
her little homely daughter was gonna be the next Judy Garland, but no
sooner she saw that getting Brenda on TV wasn't the kind of thing you
could do by big talk and snapping your fingers, she completely lost
interest in the poor child again.

On Brenda's part, all she wanted was to have her a fine time singing
up the church which was a nail in her own coffin, as Tammy didn't
never take no more notice of her singing again till Brenda won a record
contract as first prize for singing 'All Hands to the Plow' at that gospel
convention.

Setting there in Joy's living room while I listened to Brenda slamming
drawers and doors in her sister's kitchen while she tried to find the
extractor fan, I thought about how nice it would be for the whole family
if Brenda would sing at Joy's funeral. But I knew that if anybody asked
her to do it straight out, her answer was probably gonna be no just for
the sake of being contrary. And it was always impossible to convince
her to change her mind once she said no to something. So I hedged
around the singing thing after Brenda sorted herself out in the kitchen
and brought us two BLTs each through to the living room. While I
tucked into that great big sloppy sandwich enjoying mine almost as
much as Brenda sounded like she was her'n, I thought she looked
satisfied enough with her food for me just to sidle up to say that Joy
would of no doubt wanted Brenda to sing at her graveside.

'Brenda, you gonna sing at the funeral?' When she didn't answer, I
figured she hadn't heard me.

'Brenda . . . Hey, Brenda,' I said louder. ' 'Member that song you sung the first time up the children's choir, "Jesus is Walking in my Shoes",' I reminded her. 'Don't you think Joy would like it if you would sing that at her service.' It crossed my mind that she might of felt funny about singing at the actual graveside.

Brenda said, 'That's a kiddies' marching song.' Kiddies' song or not the way Brenda took and turned it 'round, nobody could of sung it better. The words went:

> Jesus is walking in my shoes
> Every stride I take
> My sweet Lord takes two
> Jesus is marching in my shoes
> With every step I take
> My sweet Lord takes two.

Right off the top of my head I went to singing the verse that goes 'Jesus is dancing in my shoes, And when the music plays for my sweet Lord, It's playing for me too', hoping that Brenda would start in with me. I sung one verse after the other and wished I could of had me a tambourine to play remembering how when Brenda first sang it as a girl, them other little kids had one toy tambourine each to bang and shake while they marched in a long, snaky line around the church to show off their Easter outfits while Brenda stood singing by Mr Tyrell's piano. Living proof she was that God forgives. With the whole congregation fussing over her, she was a symbol to me of the good Lord's forgiveness during that Easter service, 'cause it seemed like when Reverend Earl got to preaching about the stations of the cross that Dagwood mess got lost in the background of my mind.

That's all what was going through my head while I sat there in Joy's living room watching Brenda devour that BLT. 'Reverend Earl said you was gonna be the new Mahalia Jackson, Brenda, that Easter you sang that song.'

'So did his wife,' laughed Brenda wiping mayonnaise out the corner of her mouth with one hand and stuffing in that last bit of sandwich with the other.

'Oh dear Lord,' I prayed to myself, 'please don't let this woman tell me nothing I don't need to hear this day about Naomi Earl.' 'Cause

Brenda had already said enough to last a whole lifetime about Naomi in that *Queen for a Day* paper. My better self didn't want to hear no dirt, but my worser part got the best of me 'cause the truth is I was itching to hear the low down.

'That Naomi Earl mess sure caused a big upset at the time it come out, but I didn't have the nerve to ask you what it was all about,' I said knowing that Brenda wouldn't need no more encouragement than that to lay out the whole tale.

She'd said in *Queen for a Day* that it was Reverend Earl's wife that got her wanting a woman over a man. What flummoxed me was that Naomi truly played the part of the minister's wife, never wearing no makeup nor showy clothes though she had the money to with what her husband earned from preaching, I reckoned. So it didn't make no sense that Naomi'd be somebody to mess with the children. After all, Brenda couldn't of been but eleven when it happened, 'cause Reverend Earl and Naomi left First Tabernacle when Brenda was that age.

Naomi took charge of the children's choir and that's how Brenda got involved with her, if involved is the word.

She had a funny accent and didn't look nothing like she sounded, being from Brooklyn and kinda roly-poly. She wasn't but twenty-three, twenty-four years old, to her husband's fifty odd, and though she had a friendly face, it wasn't what you'd call pretty though she had a beautiful smile with teeth so perfect they looked to be false. She always doused herself in sweet smelling baby powder, and when she went on visitations with the Reverend she could eat a body out of house and home. Though I didn't have all that much to say to Naomi, I liked her.

I told Brenda who was smacking her lips chewing her second bacon sandwich, 'If you don't mind telling me what happened, I don't mind hearing.'

'Well, halfway,' said Brenda, looking eager to tell all, 'it had to do with how Mrs Earl smelled. She always had on some kind of powder that used to show through her clothes because she put on so much of it. Sometimes it would creep out her neckline and you could always see it if she had a sweater on. I used to love that smell if I got to stand next to her at choir practice, which is why I made such an effort to sing the solos, 'cause whoever sang solos got to stand by her side. Anyway, once only a few of us had turned up, not enough of us to actually do a full

JOY

harmony rehearsal, so Mrs Earl told everybody to go back home. I was the only one who couldn't, because you and Freddie B had dropped me in the car, so Mrs Earl said, "Stay with me, honey, because I would have had to stay after you'd all gone home to clean the toilet today anyway."

'We went down those three stairs to where the toilet was and she sat me down on the chair by the toilet door while I watched her scrub,' Brenda said, forgetting to stuff her mouth.

'Remember how First Tabernacle had two great big display windows at the front from it having been a store, and they kinda curved either side of the front door like store windows do.'

'You don't have to tell me,' I said. 'Every week somebody was signed up for church maintenance and I used to have to clean them windows when it was my turn on the rotar.'

Brenda went on, 'Well, Mrs Earl used to always arrange a Bible study display in those windows which I always thought was elaborate, but usually it was just some of the kids' drawings, and she said to me, "Would you like to take the Bible study display out the windows and we'll figure something else nice to put in its place."

'I used to love doing things like that,' Brenda said to me. 'It was like being asked to help out at school beating the erasers in the school yard. So I went straight off to do it, and felt special being by myself in the church with Mrs Earl. I could hear her singing away in the bathroom while I cleared out the window. When I went in to tell her I'd finished and to ask if she wanted me to do another job, I walked up behind her, but she was singing "Fredom in Jerusalem" so loud by then, she didn't hear me come in. She was on her hands and knees with her skirt hiked up around her thighs 'cause it was straight, and as big and fat as she was I guess it restricted her kneeling down.

'I could see her white girdle and stocking tops and her underpants,' Brenda said grinning like there was anything worth grinning about. 'They were pink and had a bit of white lace frill around the edge of them.' Brenda got so tickled for some stupid reason she couldn't hardly finish the sentence and I couldn't see what she thought was so funny about her as a child being fresh enough to be peeping up somebody's dress. 'Remember Mrs Earl's behind? It wasn't big, it was humungous, wasn't it?'

215

All a' sudden I didn't want to coax Brenda to tell no more as she was enjoying her memory of it way too much and reminded me of the child I saw standing in the bathroom on Grange the day Joy rushed in to tell me about Brenda with Dagwood.

'There was Mrs Earl with her dress up and everything showing and I didn't make a sound. I just stood there staring quiet as I could.' Brenda smiled and looked weird and sounded weird scrunching herself up to try and show me just how she did to Peeping Tom on poor Naomi. 'When Mrs Earl turned around and saw me she was startled and said, "Oh Brenda, you scared me! I didn't know you were there! Why didn't you tell me you'd finished." She came and checked the windows. "What a good little organizer you are," she told me and gave me a big kiss.'

I looked at Brenda funny.

'Just on the cheek,' she said. 'Then she rooted out some Biblical pictures she said she'd seen in some of Reverend Earl's books and we stuck the open books in the windows with a couple geraniums she brought in, and she had me print one sign that said "Jesus saves" and another that said "The truth is the light – let it shine". We put them in the window as well before she took me two doors away to the candy store and got me some penny marshmallows.' Brenda paused to think and started up eating what was left of her bacon sandwich. 'Then we went back to the church and I ate them and she played the piano some and I sang a little bit and was happier than I'd ever been in my life. I said to her, "Mrs Earl, I wish you were my mother, and I could come and live with you." And she laughed and said she wished that she had a little girl like me that could sing and clean too! As big as I was, she let me sit on her lap and put her arms right around me and, fat as she was, there wasn't any place left to put my head but on her humungous jelly breast, and I could smell that powder. She smelled just like Mrs Bailey's new baby and I just sat there putting marshmallows in my mouth while she rocked me back and forth humming that song "On the Sunny Side of the Street". Everything was perfect,' Brenda said. 'And from then on, anytime I went to choir practice I used to try to brush up on Mrs Earl, so I could just get a sniff of that baby powder and remember back how nice it was when we were in there by ourselves snuggled together. I wished that she'd have touched me again. But she never did. A couple of times she came wearing . . . you know those blouses you all used to wear back in those days that were sort of nylon see-through, so all the underclothes showed? Bra straps, slip and anything else under them could be seen clear as day.'

'I still wear 'em,' I said. 'So watch what you say.'

'Well Mrs Earl had a dark blue suit and everytime she wore that blue suit she wore her creamy white see-through blouse but always tried to keep on her suit jacket.'

'She was real modest,' I said. 'That's how come that *Queen for a Day* thing came as such a shock.'

'But one day she came and it got hot enough to take her jacket off, with all that singing and conducting. So I could see all her under-clothes . . . And I don't know, Baby Palatine, I just used to dream about Naomi Earl. Living at her house. Sleeping in her bed between her and the Reverend and her putting her arms around me and me just getting lost in that jellyroll bust of hers.'

When she finished telling that tale, I was sitting with my mouth open. It was times like that when I wondered if Brenda had all her marbles, and I wasn't sure what to think about her. I never in my life had heard no grown woman talk the foolishness that she did.

There we all was all them years imagining that Naomi Earl had been some kind of pervert to have turned Brenda into a bull dyke, and all that poor woman had done was rocked Brenda on her lap to try to give the child some comfort and kindness. And what did Brenda turn 'round to give her in return? A bad name in that *Queen for a Day* magazine.

But I tried to tell myself that I was getting too old to understand younger folks, not that I ever understood them all that well in the first place, 'cause much as I loved Joy, she used to flummox me half the time too and wasn't easy to figure. 'Cause for instance, frisky though she was, Joy always liked to keep to herself when she wasn't setting with her family or me. But I didn't see no point in Tammy getting after her about never wanting to make friends with nobody. But the odd white boy. Especially when Joy was in grade school.

I'll grant that somedays the child would have her a sort of sad far away look about her, but like I told Tammy, we all get to daydreaming and it wasn't nothing big enough for a mother to fret over. Just 'cause Joy's third grade teacher complained about the child staring off in space from time to time during lessons and not making the effort to mix with them other children, that wasn't reason enough for Tammy to take what that teacher said as gospel. 'Cause we saw way more of Joy than any teacher did, and the child was smiling and happy when she was with me, but Tammy wouldn't listen and if she got in one of her crotchety moods, which was regular, she would get on Joy about not mixing with other kids.

Brenda was quicker to keep to herself and didn't have none of Joy's nice ways with grown ups, but Tammy didn't never bother Brenda about it.

At least Joy had a friend in thàt Bernie Finkelstein boy till his family had to move to Miami when him and Joy was in the middle of sixth grade. It like to broke Joy's heart, and I'll grant she sure mooned around some extra then, though any fool should of realized why. 'Cause a best friend is harder to replace than a husband, though I wouldn't say it in front of Freddie.

But I reckoned right from when I first got to know her, that it was 'cause of Bernie that Joy took the habit of not fooling with them other children. Back then, she'd told me in secret that his favorite game during their fifteen minute school recess was for her and him to play hide and seek at the bottom of the school yard steps so wouldn't none of them other kids ask 'em to play rough games on the jungle jim and that. But I thought it sounded sissyfied on Bernie's part, 'cause Joy said that while they did the hiding wasn't nobody doing the seeking. And I figured it was his way to keep from rough housing with them other boys. Anyway, whatever was the reason for it, it didn't sound like a whole barrel of fun, but who was I to say.

It was only when Tammy got to heckling Joy for not mixing, that I bothered to put my two cents in, 'cause as usual Tammy went and confused things with a lot of big words and mean talk. She could easy do that. Just like that time Joy was in about fourth grade, and Tammy come in from that government job of her'n over in Alameda with flames practically licking out of her ·mouth, she was so mad. And about nothing it was.

She hissed at Joy, dragging the child out a' my place by the collar of Joy's blue dress. 'The school principal called me again at work about you.' Tammy was moving so fast, by the time she'd said that much, she'd slammed my front door and had yanked Joy over into their place. So I could just about hear the rest of what she said with my ear to my door.

I only listened 'cause she was in such a temper, and I was scared she was gonna hit Joy. And although I'd vowed to stay out of Tammy's way from that time two years before when we'd had a to do over Joy's missing baby pictures, I wouldn't of stood by silent while she beat on the child.

Our walls on Grange wasn't thin, but when Tammy got to screaming you could have heard her down the street anyway, and through her door and mine I easy heard her scolding Joy.

'The older you get the more you get like your father!' Tammy yelled. 'And you're either going to have to shake yourself out of it, or we're going to have to have your head examined, because I don't ever want that principal calling me again about you staring off into space and not socializing.'

I didn't see how that mattered 'cause the child always had her head in her books and her and Bernie was always neck on neck at the head of the class. Before Tammy drew breath I heard her say, 'If I'm disturbed at work again, I'll send you away so that somebody who's got the time can work out what the hell's up with you. So don't push me to have to do it Joy, because I won't excuse away with your moods the way some other people will.' I didn't know if she was referring to me with that last bit. Then she said something about psychopalogic. Or Something.

It seemed to me that them poor girls of Tammy's would of been better off with a beating 'cause the sting wears off quicker from a licking than Tammy's way of beating on them with big words to confuse them. Words that probably kept on ringing in their little ears like they rang in mine, worrying me to death. I didn't believe for a minute Tammy would of sent Joy away for real, but what was it all supposed to mean?

I remember hearing Tammy's voice that second time like it was yesterday. She'd had her a cold and was hoarse from coughing night after night, but still yelling, 'What in the hell is the matter with you!' she asked Joy. 'Are you a pathological liar!'

I didn't know what to make of that, 'cause I wasn't supposed to be listening no way. I'd heard Tammy shouting while I was sweeping the hall passage. So I had to piece together what she meant without no help and all's I could come up with was that Joy was on the path to being a liar after I didn't have no choice but to tell her mama that I'd caught Joy over the playground in lipstick and tight-assed shorts. Though I hated to, I had to tell Tammy about it, 'cause Anndora had been over the playground with Joy. I figured if I didn't tell Tammy how I'd drug 'em both home, Anndora might of done, and we'd of all three been in a big mess.

Added to that, Joy didn't never take notice of nothing I said and I reckoned that time that she needed a sharp telling off like only her mama could give her.

Joy was smart and knew she was smarter than me from when she was little, which is how come I think she was slow to listen to me. From when I first met her, Joy could read and count faster, talk on the phone better and make sense of all sorts quicker than I could. Like I couldn't never make head nor tail of them cookbook recipes till she come along and give me a hand.

So when Joy got fourteen, which is how old she was when I caught her hanging over at the playground, I reckon she still figured she was the smartest out of both of us. And though I ain't claiming that she was completely wrong, she didn't want to believe that I knew what I was talking about 'cause sometimes age teaches things that all the brains and book learning in the world can't.

From that time at the playground, when I caught Joy flaunting herself in front of them big ol' boys, I could see that without Tammy to stop her, Joy was fixing to land herself in heap big trouble. I never forgave myself for tattling though, 'cause of the mean, hateful way I heard Tammy come down on the child. But the very next day Joy said she forgave me. She was always real quick to forgive me if I did something.

Thinking back on it, maybe I shouldn't of been so worried about Joy at the time. Seeing how fast these young girls are today, maybe I was just making a mountain out a molehill.

What'd happened was that there was a whole bunch of teenaged boys in the neighborhood that run around together though they wasn't trying to be no gang. They was just boys being boys and played basketball a lot of time at the local school ground. I was mortified to hear off of old Mrs Nathan, one of my church Sisters, that from her bedroom window, a few times she'd spied Joy lolling 'round the school yard fence like a cat in heat while them boys was playing basketball. Fourteen seemed way too early for a nice girl to have a hankering for them big ol' rough boys, but I couldn't tell Joy that I knew what she was really up to when the story she'd tell me was that she was staying late after school to set in the public library.

It was just lucky that Mrs Nathan's back bedroom had a good view of the school ground.

So to be exact, it was one Saturday afternoon in June just before summer vacation when Joy went out the house with Anndora after she slipped a note under my door, like she had to do if she was going out to say they was headed for the library. With a book each in their hands, I held my tongue when I saw from my bathroom window that the black shorts that Joy had on was too tight to be out in the streets in, even though I thought wasn't nobody in the library with their head stuck in a book gonna take no notice of a child no way. But I did know for sure that Joy and Brenda wasn't allowed to wear black since Tammy thought it looked hussyish on young girls and rightly believed that what her girls wore was a reflection on their upbringing and her. To tell the truth though, I thought sometimes she was too particular about what them girls of her'n put on to step out the front door, not that I dared to say it.

Anyway, Joy walked out in a pair of black short shorts that she'd cut from a Simplicity pattern she'd bought and stitched up on my sewing machine. There wasn't enough material in 'em to call them pants. So skimpy they was that they cut right into the crack of her behind. It sure didn't look ladylike. Though by then 'ladylike' is something she said she couldn't see the point of.

But what worried me at the time when she walked out with Anndora in tow was that Joy had her head full of a chunky white boy named Max McDonald who hadn't long been moved into our street with his widowed mama and took him a job at Mr Houseman's son-in-law's drugstore unpacking boxes. Joy said Max was cute, but I couldn't see nothing cute about all them freckles and that curly red hair of his'n. Joy said he was seventeen, and wanted to become a pharmacist which is why he wanted that job in the drugstore.

Mrs McDonald, his mother, took a counter job over in the cleaner's which is how I got to know her. Freddie B guessed she didn't have no money which is the onliest reason he could see that she settled for living in a colored neighborhood. Poor white trash is how she looked to me but her talk was full of high faluting ideas about Max becoming a brain surgeon. She had her heart set on him going to Stanford to study on a scholarship, and I always got a earful from her about it when I'd take Freddie B's Sunday suit to the cleaner's every fourth Thursday of the month. I only listened to her going on about that boy of her'n 'cause I could tell from the number of times Joy'd mentioned him and found phony reasons to go to the drugstore that Joy had an eye for Max, and I wanted the low-down on him.

Aside from the fact that it wasn't the done thing for a white boy to be going with a colored girl, and aside from the fact that Joy was too young for him being practically at college, I didn't expect he'd of been eyeing Joy no way. She had grown out of her looks around that time and there wasn't much pretty left to her throughout her teen years but her long hair which was thick and wavy and didn't need straightening. She kept it in a ponytail and had her some bangs to cover up all the pimples she had on her forehead. She hated 'em.

Anyway, 'bout half hour after her and Anndora'd walked out the house saying they was off to change their books at the library, Mrs Nathan rang me like I'd asked her to if she ever spotted Joy again hanging 'round that school yard fence while them boys was playing.

It was sure lucky to have had Mrs Nathan on the lookout, 'cause if it had of been any of them other women from my church that had seen Joy, I wouldn't of never heard the end of it. Whereas I trusted that Mrs Nathan, being eighty, was a good meaning soul and not one for gossiping and spreading tales.

I was in the middle of pressing my hair for church that day when she gave me the call. So, I quick put in some wire rollers at the back and tied a bandana 'round my head, so that I could rush out to the A&P supermarket which was catty cornered to the school yard and I knew would give me a good excuse to be out in that direction. Usually I didn't never go to the A&P though, 'cause it was way too expensive, but I knew it would still give me a perfect reason for being across from the playground that was five blocks from Grange. I even took Anndora's old red wagon to make it look for real that I was out to shop for groceries. Although Anndora didn't use it no more, the wagon stayed in the little shed by our parking lot. Rusted though it was getting, she was still pernickety about it, and I always had to ask her if I could borrow it, anytime I wanted to use it for my shopping.

By the time I'd crossed the street in front of the A & P I could see Joy standing right by the fence near the basketball court and just like I thought, amongst all them six colored boys was Max McDonald, racing around bouncing the ball and pushing and shoving and shouting like the rest of 'em, supposed to be what ch'you call playing. You couldn't miss him. The onliest white one and with a carrot-top head. Joy didn't see me and neither did Anndora, and whereas I'd seen from my bathroom window that Joy'd gone out in them shorts, at least her hair had been drawn back neat in its usual ponytail. But there she was with it hanging loose down her back and her pink blouse made to look like a half blouse, 'cause it was unbuttoned halfway down so that she had the tail of it tied in a knot up under her bust. What bust she had. She had her collar pulled up and I was shocked to see that her whole belly was out. If she'd had any cleavage it would of being showing, but thank goodness, she wasn't buxom like Brenda. In fact, at fourteen Joy didn't have nothing to flaunt but her long legs, and I could tell she was trying to do her best with what little she had standing there.

I meant to look nonchalant like I just happened to be passing so I got to humming 'Joshua Fit the Battle of Jericho' to calm myself, 'cause on top of everything else, I could feel my blood pressure up soon as I saw Joy. I was wearing a cotton dress that afternoon and some old sneakers that Brenda'd throwed out 'cause they had holes in the baby toes. The school yard fence was above ground level and you had to walk up some concrete steps to get to it.

Joy had her profile to me and I couldn't believe that it looked like her lips was painted red while she was lolling at the fence posing to be seen but acting casual, like she just happened to be standing half naked there. Miss Anndora had her face pressed against the wire mesh fence and she didn't look up once as I stood at the bottom of the steps and called Joy's name out, wanting to give her a chance to know I was there and planning to make my way up them steps. I knew that she was bound to be ashamed of herself caught red handed about fibbing to me about going to the library.

'Joy. Yoo hoo, there, Joy,' I called out. But I reckon she had her eyes glued on Max and couldn't hear me above them boys running back and forth on the court and shouting and swearing at each other.

'Yoo hoo,' I yelled out again, waving my arms. A colored boy noticed me and came over to the fence above where I was. 'Could you tell that child in them shorts I want her.'

Soon as he did, she turned around. I saw that she was wearing heavy lipstick and what must have been Maybelline or eyeliner or something like it on her eyes which really took me off guard. I'd seen her playing in makeup when she was little, but the way it was applied that day at the playground looked too for real, and if I hadn't known her, I'd have guessed her to be about sixteen, maybe older, even though she didn't have much bust.

'Joy! What's that on your face, girl.' I wasn't laughing at all 'cause the Joy Bang staring back at me with cold eyes was a stranger that I didn't know nothing about. She had a frisky streak in her, but if somebody'd told me she was sneaking around the boys claiming to be at the library and wearing lipstick I'd of called 'em a liar.

'Girl, you better get ch'you home 'fore I tan your hide.' That was all I could think to say. I waited there for her to turn and come down the steps, but she just stood there looking through me as much to say 'no'. I thought I better go up them steps and grab her, but I didn't know what to do about Anndora's heavy red wagon that I didn't want to have to haul up the steps with me.

When Joy didn't answer I was glad I was wearing that old pair of white sneakers that Brenda'd thrown out, 'cause those sneaks carried me quick as a runner up them steps and I grabbed a handful of Joy's hair so that her head was pulled back before she knowed what was on her.

'Child, have you lost your mind,' I said. 'You better get your little hiney on home so that we can wash that mess off your face.' I didn't want to shame her, but I was loud enough to let her know that I meant business. She didn't just have lipstick on. She had on rouge and with the eyeliner and that Maybelline gook too, she looked a madam.

'Let go!' she had the nerve to say, trying to wrestle away from me, but

I'd got one strong grip and wasn't 'bout to let her shake loose without her leaving me with a hand full of her loose hanging hair.

'Leave you alone! Nigger, I'm here to rescue you from yourself!'

'I'm not doing anything wrong,' Joy said. 'Baby, let go . . . Baby Palatine! You're hurting me.' I hadn't never laid hands on her in all the time I knew her but it was real lucky for Joy that I didn't yank her brains out her head. I ain't never even struck my sister Helen when she provokes, so it was a sure thing that I wasn't gonna hit on Joy. Especially with Anndora and them boys watching me. Joy was a head shorter than me for a start and I knew if I held on to that hair of her'n long enough that she'd go home with me willing and not let me make no scene in front of Max. I didn't never have no temper where Joy was concerned but I couldn't believe how she was turned out and I wasn't going to stand for her twisting me 'round her finger like I was usually willing to let her do.

'You better get to stepping 'fore I shame you into it.' I noticed out the corner of my eye that the boys had stopped bouncing that ball and they was just watching us. 'Don't shame me and yourself, child. Now I ain't about to leave here without you and Anndora, so please come home willing.' I could feel it when she'd stopped resisting, but I gripped her tighter in case it was just her tricking me. But when she rubbed at her temples where the hair was probably yanked from the root, I wanted to cry I was so sorry that I hurt her.

'You've practically pulled all my hair out,' she whimpered, exaggerating to make me feel worse.

'I meant to,' I said but I decided not to say no more as her, me and Anndora walked down them steps.

Of course, when I got to the bottom that red wagon was gone and I knew the next mess was gonna be explaining to Anndora how her wagon got stole, but I was that mad that I didn't even bother to look up and down the street for it. I just walked on home with Joy following five paces behind. I couldn't care less whether she walked with me or not as long as she was walking. I didn't have nothing to say to her no way.

I couldn't even look at Anndora who I noticed had a bit of red smudged in the corners of her lips too, but not enough to say it was her wearing lipstick. It looked like she'd had it on and scraped it off, and I was willing to wager that she'd done that while I was fussing with Joy over at the playground, though I didn't have no way to prove it.

We headed up Archibald Street with the hot midday sun beating so hard on my head that the sweet smelling bergamot pomade on my hair kinda trickled down my scalp and made it itch. Of course nobody in their right mind was out walking which meant that nobody but Mrs Nathan must of seen the hullabaloo at the playground or us trailing up the street with Joy looking like a floozie and me too confounded to speak if spoken to.

When we rounded our corner I was feeling a bit calmer. 'You better come on into my place,' I said, 'so we can clean that mess off your face.' She just followed silent through the front door, but I could feel that she was mad, and Anndora said that she was going home to watch cartoons. I made straight for the bathroom and though I didn't have no cold cream left I knew that Vaseline Petroleum Jelly would do as good to get that makeup off Joy.

'Set yourself down there on the stool,' I said sharpish, 'and let me clean your face.'

'I can do it,' she sulked.

'Well I'll watch.' I was going to make sure that the job got done a hundred percent. My motive was selfish, 'cause I felt that I was in as much trouble with her mother as Joy was, if Joy got caught. Tammy was like them inspectors that come along to check up on things when you got an adopted child. They can walk in and lord over the place whenever they like.

I stood there while Joy smeared her face with Vaseline. Then I went into the kitchen to boil up some water, 'cause the hot tap in the bathroom had been broke for a week and Freddie B didn't have the right tool to fix it. Anyway it was that hot outdoors there wasn't no hurry to get it fixed. I wondered how long Joy had been sneaking out looking like that but I knew the question wouldn't bring no answer I would believe, so I didn't even bother to ask. Mainly what was going on in my head was how you can think you really know a child till you find out you don't.

While Joy was taking off that makeup, I remembered I had a icebox cake in my frigerator and took it out and cut off a couple pieces. Joy's silence was about to kill me, and I would have given a gold tooth to know what she was thinking setting there in the bathroom but I just served up the cake. I'd already done enough and was feeling bad, though what happened wasn't my fault. That came to be the way with us. Joy would do the doing, and I'd end up feeling bad.

I knew that Max McDonald was probably behind the makeup. I can't say that he forced her to wear the lipstick and them shorts cutting up her backside, but I'm sure that it was for him that she'd rigged herself up. He was always down the basketball court I figured, and that's why she'd traipsed down there.

'Max McDonald is too old and too white for you,' I told her while she was pushing a cake crumb around her saucer. 'Find somebody to have a crush on that's your own age and colored. There's nice enough boys at junior high school.'

'They're silly.'

'You're the one's silly,' I told her but I realized looking at the one tear that come rolling down her cheek that I'd said enough. That was one thing I thought was always in my favor. I knew exactly when I'd said enough and she wasn't listening no more.

She was hard work during them teen years and used to have me worried that she was gonna end up as hard to handle as Anndora. But I prayed and prayed that Joy would pull her socks up and go back to being the sweet-natured easy child she'd always been. And by high school seemed like she was happy and sunny again. Maybe them pimples disappearing is what did it.

Joy kept getting As on her report cards but still had time for them extras at school. I was real proud when she went straight from being a cheerleader for the junior varsity track team over to being a pompom girl for the varsity football team. She was so excited the day she got chosen for that, and came running home and asked me if I'd help her take care of her pompom outfit that the school had give her. It was a pink and white gingham dress with so many white crinolines under it, that that dress could stand out about a mile when I got it starched and pressed.

Tammy wouldn't of bothered herself with nothing like ironing that pompom outfit. I kind of understood that she was tired from going to work every day. But anyway, Joy got on that pompom squad, and she was real happy following the games around and whatnot, but I think she had something going with the blond halfback on the football team though.

She wouldn't let on to me 'cause he was another white one. Derek, I think was his name. He'd pick her up and drop her off, and pick up and drop off and never once did she get him to come in. I used to say to her, 'Joy, you got to start as you mean to continue. Don't let that boy treat you like no trash now. Bring him in. Let me and your mama see him.'

She'd say, 'Oh, Baby Palatine, he doesn't want to come in. He's just giving me a lift.' All them rides he give her, he didn't once take her out on no proper date but she wouldn't go out with nobody else neither and would set with me and Freddie B on a Saturday night watching the TV when them other girls was out.

In the back of my mind, I thought that's the price you pay if you don't stay with your own kind.

Whereas Joy always had her a boyfriend or a special boy who wasn't nothing but a friend, Anndora didn't seem to have no serious interest in boys till she was thirteen which sounds young, but on other accounts Anndora always acted old for her age, wearing both makeup and tight clothes by the time she was twelve. Her boyfriend's name was Malcolm, but I could never remember what his last name was, even while Anndora was fooling with him. They looked like the Bobsey Twins that come from the same womb 'cause both had the same light eyes and wavy reddish hair and light skin. He came from the fancy part of Oakland up in them hills, and his daddy was a doctor. Right from the time he started taking Anndora out to them big Cotillion Ball parties, she didn't seem to want to have nothing at all to do or say with nobody else in the family except Joy. I hardly spoke a word to her though I'd practically known her from the cradle, but she didn't never take to me and said to my face that she didn't like to come in my house nor eat my food 'cause she thought that it was disgusting that Freddie B had his spit can in our living room. Though she said it made her feel sick just to think about Freddie's lip of snuff, Helen's didn't bother her. Hard as it was to believe, her and Helen got on real good, and Freddie B used to say it was 'cause Helen and Anndora was alike.

I'd say, 'How you gonna compare Anndora to Helen?'

And he'd say, 'Well look how Helen was when she was young and look at Anndora.'

True Helen'd started out like Anndora to be a real beauty so maybe there was some kind of basic understanding between them, and while Anndora made it plain that she didn't wanna have nothing to do with me nor her Uncle Freddie B, her and my baby sister used to laugh and talk and everything. I think what started them out on a good foot was that Helen used to make such a fuss of Anndora when Anndora was dancing, though Helen didn't pop over to Tammy's much, 'cause Tammy didn't try to make her feel welcome.

That's why I had to tell Tammy one time, 'Much as I favor you and them kids, Helen's my flesh and blood and I'm all my baby sister's got, so don't be mean to her.' Drunk or not, I didn't want Helen mistreated. We'd go over to Tammy's together from time to time when Helen was sober enough and promised not to show out. I'd clean her up good and she'd sit down with just a pinch of snuff in her mouth and get to talking and even making sense. It was always Anndora that Helen would end up talking to and Anndora would answer back nicer than she ever did to me. I don't know how the conversation went the time Helen asked Anndora did she know how to dance, but all Anndora ever really needed was somebody to want to talk about nothing but Anndora and what Anndora did and what Anndora liked and she sure liked dancing and liked to talk about it. Not that ballet stuff though. But like them dance crazes, the Jerk and the Shuffle and that.

Any time Helen went over to Tammy's for a visit after that she'd get Anndora up dancing and whatnot. I knew that Anndora couldn't have been all bad but Helen saw sparkles of good in the child. She even went off with Helen down Mr Houseman's son-in-law's to sit and have a cherry coke a couple of times.

By the time Anndora turned fourteen, Joy had finished high school and Anndora didn't have her sister to follow behind so she took up with a older boy called Peter Trent from East Oakland way that used to dance on a local afternoon TV show. I never knew whether she liked him for hisself or liked the fact that he could take her to the TV studio with him and them other teenagers showing off to the hit records. I told Anndora who didn't have no clothes to be on no TV, 'Don't get started in something you can't finish, 'cause you need nice outfits to look good as them other kids and your mama can't afford that.'

Actually I was glad she showed interest in something 'cause she was near as bad as Brenda when it come to putting off homework, losing her school books and finding reasons not to go to school at all while Tammy let it slide. But then, like I said before, Tammy didn't raise them girls they just drug theyselves up with their mama letting them do what they wanted 'cause that's the easy way out.

When Peter Trent started taking Anndora over to San Francisco to another dance show called *Record Shop* televised from KGTV I knew she was cutting quite a bit of school, but her mother didn't seem to care when I told her that Anndora was missing her studies too much.

I'd turn on the TV set in the afternoons to check *Record Shop* and every once and again there would be Anndora's face on the screen dancing to beat all them other kids. She had her a nice shape and being thin and neat looking was way prettier than any of 'em on there as well as being the best dancer to my eyes.

She didn't never say it out loud but I reckoned she had her mind set on being some kind of a star and didn't care whether it was acting or singing or dancing as long as 'star' was part of it. So even when the singing thing came up with Bang Bang Bang it wasn't like she was ready to be singing for the rest of her life, I don't think. What Anndora figured was that the group could be her stepping stone for her doing something on her own as Bang Bang Bang wasn't fun to her 'specially 'cause she was never partial to Brenda even when they was little. Anndora was like she was Joy's, and though I didn't never say it, if their mama didn't make Anndora act better toward Brenda from when they was little, seemed like Joy should of done.

The onliest thing Tammy found the time to say something about something, it was to do with Anndora on that television, 'cause Tammy had all kind of big hopes for her and started buying the child expensive clothes. 'Hand-me-downs aren't good enough for Anndora,' I overheard Tammy tell Joy when Joy said Anndora could borrow a couple of her best sweaters. 'She has to look fabulous if she's going to get some place on television,' Tammy added and with Brenda working and Joy living out the house, Tammy had enough money to keep Anndora dressed up like somebody whose daddy was a lawyer or doctor or something like that. Anything that was in them fashion shop windows in San Fran, Anndora had one of. Great big knit sweaters and matching pants, Madras jackets. She had all that she could to look smart dancing on that TV, and all Anndora had to say was 'I want' and Tammy was right downtown trying to buy it for her, getting herself into debt. But it was her money and she seemed happy to do it, so what was I supposed to say about it.

Once Joy settled over at the City College her and Anndora started getting real close again. With Joy moved in with two girls up at the college, Anndora was over there all the time. I thought it was a good thing, 'cause it was just Anndora and her mama living in the apartment and they didn't get along on their own which I couldn't understand seeing it wasn't crowded in there after Joy had taken herself off and hardly ever bothered to visit her mother let alone stay over. Anndora used to go see Joy as much as possible. And Tammy used to ask me, 'Why doesn't she want to be at home? Her closet is stacked and I never get to see her in all those clothes I've been buying her.'

'She's with her sister,' I'd say. 'Joy'll be a good influence on her, so you leave her be and let 'em get on with it.'

About every weekend Anndora would borrow my overnight case and she was gone. Off to Joy's. And I would of been more pleased about it if she'd of come back on a Sunday night looking better. But the girl looked tired and worn out like she was ready for a vacation instead of being rested for school. So a couple of times I took Joy aside and said, 'Now look, that child got high school to get through. You ain't supposed to let Anndora be playing so hard at the weekends that she's like a walking zombie over at the schoolhouse.'

Joy would laugh and say, 'Yeah, yeah, yeah,' teasing me like I was a nag and then the next weekend Anndora was off and gone again and it was the same thing all over. That went on until Joy came to me in a state of nerves and told me that Anndora had got herself pregnant and that I was gonna have to help the child get rid of it, 'cause there wasn't no way in the world they wanted Tammy to find out about it.

Of course, Tondalayah was just the kind to always know where she could get something done in the back room and knew an ol' white woman from Houston who lived down Bakersfield way that could take care of Anndora's problem.

So one Sunday we told Tammy that we was gonna take a trip down to see Tondalayah in San Jose 'cause that's where she was living. Joy was driving by then and Freddie B let us borrow his new white Chevy to drive down and Tammy let Anndora take half a day off school, 'cause Tammy liked Tondalayah by that time.

I was always against them back room abortions, but what would of been worse was Anndora with a baby when she wasn't nothing but a big spoiled baby herself.

When we got to her house Toni had got everything organized and ready to go. We had to get it done on a Friday night, so that Anndora could get over the sickness at the weekend and be back for school on Monday. Not that she actually went to school much. But she was home for a whole week afterwards sick and I was scared to death we was gonna get found out.

We'd tried every kinda thing before I took her down to that woman, so couldn't nobody blame me for that abortion mess. In fact I even told Anndora about how if you jumped down seven steps about a hundred and fifty times you could shake the baby loose, and one day she stayed home from school and tried that. Thank God wasn't nobody else living in Mr Houseman's apartments at the time but me and Freddie B.

I fixed her a can of tomato soup to build up her stamina 'fore she got to jumping down the hallway steps. She jumped 'em and climbed 'em, jumped 'em and climbed 'em and jumped till she twisted her ankle. Around about a hundred and twenty she'd got to 'fore she sprained it and couldn't jump no more. Nor dance.

She was nice to me when she thought I was the one could help her but she went back to being her usual impatient and irritable self for a few days while we waited to see if that durn baby was gonna shift. But it didn't, so that's when I knew we was gonna have to definitely get Tondalayah to book Anndora with that white woman that did them abortions. It was gonna cost us $125 and I had to think up a lie to get Freddie B to give me that much cash money at one time. He wasn't all that happy about it, but he give it to me like he always did after I'd give him a excuse. I told him I wanted to buy a new refrigerator 'cause ours was making a humming sound that was about to drive me crazy. And when no new refrigerator came he didn't never ask for his cash back.

When we three got to Toni's place, I think Anndora was real impressed and Joy said she didn't expect it to be nice like it was. To tell the truth, I didn't know it was gonna be that palatial neither. It was a real big apartment that Toni had looking over a park full of trees with a

Catholic church setting in the middle of it and it had snow white wall-to-wall carpets in every room and real antiques from all over.

Luckily, that abortion worked, so I didn't say nothing to Anndora about how she got her belly full of baby and figured that that one scare would put her off messing with boys.

She went back to school but then got antsy and went and quit the next year. I was shocked that her mother didn't care and Tammy tried to tell me that it didn't make no difference whether Anndora finished in the tenth or in the twelfth.

I ain't got no education so I give it due regard and used to say to Tammy when she told me that Anndora was fixing to drop out of school, 'What's she gonna do with her life, a colored girl finishing school in the tenth grade? Anndora ain't always gonna be cute, Tammy, and that poor child needs you to tell her that if she ain't careful she's likely to end up working behind a cash register in somebody's supermarket and be lucky if she can even get that. Probably'll end up scrubbing floors. Don't let her turn out ignorant like me.' I ain't scared to admit that I didn't get decent schooling and Lord knows I didn't want to see the same happen to Anndora where somebody got to help her read a cookbook and make sense of the dictionary.

Tammy used to laugh and say, 'Don't worry. My Anndora's never gonna scrub a floor.' From that point of view Tammy proved herself right, 'cause seeing how Anndora looked in her fancy mink when she walked into Joy's to help Tammy organize the funeral, you could see that hard labor wasn't something that she'd ever suffered from in her life. Them hands of hers was smooth and manicured looking as any you'd see in a magazine advertising hand creams. Every polished nail was perfect.

Thinking back on them high school days with Tammy's girls, what didn't never seem fair was that while Anndora and Joy was getting Valentines cards and all that attention from the boys, not just neighborhood ones but them that went to school with 'em, Brenda didn't have nobody. I think that's why she stayed so interested in the church.

Ain't nobody more for religion than me and I'm quick to say I don't see how folks get by that don't have none, but too much of it in a young girl may be too much of a good thing. Brenda had the church and gospel but there was still room for something else in her life.

I think she had a hard time up the school. She got that big that buying clothes for her was nearly impossible and it was lucky that we was able to keep getting them from the church. Sister Hodge was about Brenda's size so we had most of her hand-me-downs, but she could of done with having something to brighten her looks up a bit.

Whereas on Sundays what she wore didn't matter much 'cause she could throw on them white robes the choir sang in, during school times it would have helped make her more popular, I reckon, had she looked better.

Brenda didn't much like school and wasn't much good at it since she didn't never bother with studying. Sitting still was her biggest problem when she wasn't in front of the TV, though as she got older she stopped having so much trouble with that.

Most of her time got taken up with the church, and as she'd already lost interest in books and boys, her gradually becoming star of our choir seemed like Brenda's salvation. Wasn't but about sixty families in our whole congregation, but amongst that sixty, Brenda belonged.

I was glad when she decided to take a commercial course after she finished school, 'cause typing and shorthand and that will keep a girl in work, and she proved to be not bad at it. Good enough by the time she was twenty to get her a stenography job. Tammy wanted her to work for the government 'cause Tammy said that you didn't get fired so quick, but Brenda wanted to do part-time temp so she could take off anytime she felt like, so she could go on them gospel tours that she wasn't able to miss if she wanted to keep first place in the choir.

It was Brenda who'd got everybody singing better at First Tabernacle 'cause they all got to competing with her and they was really tops which is why they all 'a sudden got invited all kinds of places in California singing. Brenda did as much as a body could to help get them singing tours organized and they would go up and around Northern California; mostly like San Anselmo, El Cerrito, San Jose, places like that, doing their bit on the last Sunday of each month when a visiting choir would come to First Tabernacle. I think Brenda was surprised herself the time they even got as far as Palo Alto singing for a charity.

She would regular come back with some kind of citation for this or that and she seemed content though Tammy said Brenda not having a boyfriend would lead to trouble. For a woman who didn't take no time with her children, she knew 'em good enough and while I didn't see no harm in Brenda never having a date, 'cause she was busy with the choir, Tammy swore blind it wasn't natural. We should of listened though I figured Brenda could have got herself squared up with some man or other had she been interested.

She was so big that there wasn't many boys tall as her to choose from 'cause by the time she hit eleventh grade she was nearly six feet. And that was her shoeless.

With Freddie B being such a string bean, I used to tell her she'd be lucky as me one day and run up on somebody tall that suited her, but she didn't have nice gentle ways to draw nobody to her.

One time I heard Helen ask Brenda why she didn't have her a nice boyfriend to take her to the movies and spend some money on her and Brenda said, 'I'm destined to be a nobody.'

I said, 'Don't get reckless with the truth, 'cause everybody got a somebody in 'em, you just got to dig around in yourself, Brenda, to seek it out. And anyway,' I reminded her, 'you got to see yourself for what you're naturally blessed with. The Lord didn't give you that set of lungs for you to be claiming you ain't nobody.'

I could tell by the way she changed the subject and wanted to talk about Helen coming to hear the choir that Brenda didn't take notice of what I said. The sad truth is that with her mama never making a fuss of Brenda's singing accomplishments nor them citations she'd bring in to show off, Brenda didn't really believe deep down that they was worth that much.

It's strange how some folks go through they whole lives trying to please their mama and don't matter if they got the whole world at their feet, if their mama don't take notice the rest of the world applauding don't mean a dickeybird.

I reckon if Tammy had thought better of Brenda, Brenda homely as she was, could of thought better of herself.

While she was still at high school I'd hoped that they was gonna ask her to sing at the graduation or the senior prom but she told me she wasn't going to the prom and I knew it was 'cause nobody had asked her. So I hinted to one of Mrs Nathan's nephews up at First Tabernacle that was in Brenda's class that it would be nice if he took her. But instead he took his big mouth and ran it all round the school that Brenda didn't have her a date which got them teenagers teasing Brenda about being a wallflower.

That's why I reckon a couple of boys off the football team made fun of what she was wearing when she was standing waiting for the bus one day after school and Brenda hauled off and hammered hell out of one of them mealy-mouthed bastards before he knew what was happening. And when he stumbled and fell, she said, 'Now laugh again at my shoes,' and kicked him in the face. The other one punched her and she's still got a scar over her left eye where he laid into her. Though it happened only three days before her high school graduation ceremony, she got suspended 'cause them boys lied and said she'd started it. So poor Brenda didn't have no proper cap and gown graduation and tried to say it didn't bother her, but I reckon it did. She just got her diploma mailed to her 'cause there was a lot of fighting up at her high school that year and the principal said somebody had to be used as a example. Scapegoat is what he meant. And had Tammy taken up the cause, no doubt Brenda would have been marching down the aisle in a blue and white cap and gown like the rest of her senior class.

I was worried that her mother wasn't gonna take the day off to go to her graduation no way, although me and Freddie B made sure Brenda knew we was definitely planning to go. But being neighbors ain't the same thing as having your mama there when everybody's showing off their family outside on the lawn afterwards.

Brenda really didn't seem to mind all that much and as she had a big gauze bandage taped above her left eye anyway, I guess she was glad to have a excuse to be off school.

I was ironing Freddie B's shirts in my apartment the afternoon it happened and Brenda came home from school with blood on her dress and down the side of her face. She was trying to hold a handkerchief to it when she knocked at my door asking if I had a bandage, but I couldn't stop the bleeding and it scared me to death.

'What in the world has happened to you?' I asked her, fearing one of them gangs that was starting up over West Oakland way had jumped her. West Oakland, where she was at school, was getting real violent.

But when she told me about them two footballers I felt like crying 'cause I knew it was my fault for telling that Nathan boy Brenda couldn't get a date. If I hadn't put my two cents in they wouldn't have been mocking her up at the school. Thank goodness, Freddie B'd come in early from his work that Wednesday afternoon and I got him to take her to the casualty over at Kaiser Hospital.

'Make sure,' I told 'em heading down the stairs together, 'that there ain't nothing gonna ruin her eyesight out of that eye.'

The doctor said the eye was fine but forewarned Brenda the cut was gonna scar 'cause she didn't get it stitched up right away. She looked like a prize fighter with her eye swelled up so and with a big square patch of white bandage above it. I couldn't understand that when Tammy came home, she didn't even ask Brenda what happened to her. Thinking back on it, I reckon Tammy was having her a mid life crisis, but didn't none of us know nothing about the likes of that kind of stuff in them days, so I just took her depressing ways as being moods, and whereas we kept expecting her to act lively, she would drag in from work strained-looking like somebody that had been toting barges all day instead of setting in the air conditioning at a typewriter like she was. She'd mumble about being tired and didn't take a minute to see how them three teenagers of hers was doing and then she'd grab a sandwich and head straight for bed. At six o'clock. And out of the girls, it was Brenda that seemed to suffer the most from her mother's strange ways, 'cause Anndora and Joy was always busy doing whatever they was doing from TV dancing to that pompom girl stuff. But Brenda's choir practice wasn't but two evenings a week and the rest of the time she didn't know what to do with herself.

She was all of eighteen and should of been past needing her mama anyway, but she was slow to grow up in that way.

But that particular evening when Brenda was setting in the apartment with that bandage over her left eye that only a blind man could of missed, it was completely ridiculous that Mrs Tamasina Bang could walk into the living room past her own daughter without taking notice. So since I happened to be setting there with Brenda and sensed that she was wanting her mama to say something about her eye, I trumped up and said to Tammy as she walked in and threw her handbag right on the sofa where me and Brenda was parked, 'We got some extra bandages from the hospital if you want to take the bandage off Brenda's eye and see the big ol' cut one of them mean bastards off the football team give her at the bus stop today.'

Without so much as looking back in our direction, Tammy said, 'I'll have to look later, because if I don't put my head down right this minute, I'll faint.' She kicked off both her high heels as she was walking and I couldn't help but see that a black straight summer skirt that she had always filled out nice was hanging off her where she'd lost weight.

Seemed like she could of at least asked Brenda to follow her into the bedroom, 'cause Brenda could of told her what happened while Tammy stepped out her work clothes which she had got in the habit of leaving on the floor for Joy or Brenda to pick up, which she claimed was what having three grown children was for. Not that she expected Anndora to hit tap at a snake.

Anyway, I wasn't surprised that Brenda bounded off the sofa and stalked off to the kitchen with her hand holding her eye and said loud enough for Tammy to hear in the bedroom that her mother was a stupid bitch.

Seeing that up till then none of them girls was either crazy or bold enough to curse Tammy before, I figured that them two words alone was gonna cause a Greater Commotion which is exactly why I leapt up off the sofa and made my way to the other side of their front door as fast I could. 'Cause it would of taken a fool to set around and wait while Tammy and Brenda got into one of their dog and cat fights.

They used to get so they threw things at each other and once when they got to arguing in the kitchen while Brenda was cutting up a chicken to fry I thought she was gonna take the knife to her mother the way she was holding it. And all they was fussing over was how Brenda had paid so much for the chicken that there wasn't no change left over from five dollars and so Brenda came back from the store without the pack of cigarettes that Tammy had told Brenda to bring her.

But that evening Brenda had got the cut over her eye, her mother's dander was not to be raised and while I stood quiet outside in the hall by their apartment door waiting for the shouting and screaming to start, lo and behold there wasn't none.

I stood in that darkish hallway for what seemed all of five whole minutes thinking that the silence was the calm before the storm, but there wasn't a whisper. I knew that would of upset Brenda way more than all the hollering and screaming in the world, 'cause what she hated the most was getting no attention, and she'd of been right to think that her mama not rising to the bait of being called a stupid bitch was a good sign that Tammy didn't give a damn about Brenda or what she had to say and was too lackadaisical to bother to argue the point.

Seemed it was from that day that Brenda finally washed her hands of her mama, 'cause whereas before Brenda had been quick to try to coax Tammy to go to her gospel recitals (that Tammy flat out refused to go to) or draw due attention for Brenda's running their household, Brenda practically stopped speaking to her mother. But I suspected that it didn't have the effect on Tammy that Brenda wanted it to. In fact, it probably suited Tammy in the frame of mind she was in.

So three days later when the afternoon of Brenda's graduation came and went, while all them other kids that had shuffled through twelve years of school had them a special occasion to remind them that they had done their duty and would suffer no more cafeteria lunches and smoking restrictions and surprise history tests that Brenda always complained about, Brenda spent the hour of the ceremony setting in front of the television soaking up commercials like she used to when she was a kid.

What she could of done with was a auntie or uncle or grand-daddy or somebody that she could call family that would take a extra minute with her. But Tammy being a orphan didn't have nobody like that for the kids to turn to and so her brand of lovelessness burnt down way deeper than it would of done if Brenda'd had some kin to fall back on.

Freddie B used to try and say that Tammy's problem was that she probably didn't never have nobody to give her no love which is how come she didn't know how to give it out, but that didn't seem like a good enough excuse for the sorry way she treated them girls. Especially Brenda.

'Cause whereas my God-sent child had me and Freddie, Brenda didn't have her nobody and it ain't no wonder that one poorly bit of a hug off Naomi Earl got Brenda off on a weird curve.

I looked over at Brenda setting the other side of Joy's big glass top table. She had two empty beer cans sitting in front of her that she had drained dry and then crushed with her hands so that they was both bent over like they had collapsed. In one curl at the front of her hair she had a bit of mayonnaise from them two BLTs she'd gobbled, and when I went to pick it off, she slapped at my hand.

'Don't mess with me hair,' she said to me.

'I was just gonna move some mayonnaise you got in it.'

'I can do it,' she said and reached for a curl on the side.

'You didn't get it.'

'Oh shit, Baby Palatine, who cares,' she said. 'Let it stay there. It's not bothering anybody.'

I took a deep sigh and wondered how long it was gonna be before Tammy and them came back, 'cause Brenda was starting to seem like hard work, and it felt like there wasn't gonna be no convincing her to sing at Joy's funeral which in itself was upsetting.

'Wouldn't it be nice if we had some of them Sisters from First Tabernacle like Sister Lucias and Sister Hodge here to help us mourn Joy,' I said to Brenda.

'What for?'

'We need for somebody to get us in a mourning spirit. After all a funeral is s'posed to raise the soul to heaven and you can't do it with a lot of folks moping around.'

'Joy's dead, sweetheart. It's not suppose to turn into a block party, is it?' asked Brenda trying to be sarcastic.

'You know what I mean. Like Reverend Earl used to laugh and tell the congregation when somebody passed, don't forget the F-U-N in funeral. And he was right, 'cause who knows where Joy's soul is headed,' I said hoping that that may have give Brenda the idea to sing for Joy if she maybe wasn't going to heaven automatic.

'At this late stage are you starting to see the light!' said Brenda. 'I thought that you were the one who always wanted to pretend that Joy was perfect.'

I didn't give Brenda the benefit of a answer. My mind was caught up thinking how sad it was that Rex wasn't planning to be there for Joy, 'cause though he had a whole lot wrong with him, I knew from all them years Joy was with him that he knew how to celebrate and Joy always said that Rex knew how to party. Sometimes she'd call me from wherever she was with him and I could hear the joint jumping, loud music and folks laughing in the background. She said he used to have everybody up singing and dancing and whatnot till sun up.

I know from living down New Orleans that them rednecks know how to whoop it up with no more than a couple crates of beer. And I expect poor folks know how to have 'em a good time don't matter what color they are.

'You should of seen how they used to bury folks down New Orleans where I come from,' I told Brenda. 'When I was a girl and there was gonna be a big funeral, folks used to turn out in the streets like there was gonna be a parade and the idea of Joy having a quiet funeral don't set right with me.'

'God, Baby, that was in the olden days. People don't do that stuff any more.'

'How do you know!' I asked her. 'Miss Smarty Pants!'

'Well how do you?' Brenda said and got up and went to the kitchen and came back with another half of sandwich for herself. 'You were always complaining that you never got to go back home while we were on the road, so how do you know what goes on in New Orleans now.'

'But that don't mean that I don't know how folks still get buried down there, and anyway, I did get home that time y'all played in Baton Rouge 'cause Danny gave me the afternoon off and I took the train home.'

'How can I forget,' said Brenda. 'You drove us all mad for about a week before you went going on and on about going home.'

'Well I was real excited about it and you would of been too if you'd of been me 'cause I hadn't been home since I'd left with Freddie B.'

'Yes you had,' said Brenda. 'You went twice while we lived in Oakland.'

'Only sort of.'

'What's that's supposed to mean,' said Brenda. 'You either did go or you didn't.'

'The two times I'd been back down New Orleans with Freddie B to bury some of his people, I didn't get over to my part of town.

'I didn't have no kin left to go to but I wanted to see our old place and Mr McDermot's farm where my three brothers burned to death in the barn.

'I took a train to the city and caught a bus to the outskirts where we'd lived. I was beside myself with excitement riding that bus home. Setting on it, I dreamed Mama was stood at the screen door and come running with a big ol' grin on her face when she seen me on the road near the house. Not that I ever saw her run again after my brothers burned up. I was too young to realize at the time it was depression that took Moth' Dear.

'It was in that dream that I saw our two-room shack that Daddy'd left us in 'cause Mama said he couldn't bear to wake up in it another day.

'Funny how if you AWOLd in the army like Caesar said he tried one night in Korea they'd of had you shot, but a man could AWOL on his family like Daddy did, and wouldn't nothing happen back then but the government would send victuals. Just enough to keep a body from starving to death. That's how come to this day I can't eat peanut butter 'cause for years that's all we was rationed to keep starvation from death's door. Peanut butter . . . that had oil a finger deep floating on the top when you opened the can and what had settled to the bottom was so bone dry you couldn't spread it like I see folks do on them TV commercials. You had to spoon it out and eat it dry . . . Peanut butter.'

Brenda laughed when I turned up my nose and made a big face. 'I hope I don't never go hungry in this life like that again, Brenda, 'cause when I left Louisiana in one piece with my brother and Freddie B and my baby sister I figured God give us a second chance in life.'

'My family didn't hardly have nothing, though I didn't mind since we had Mama who was always laughing and telling us to look to brighter days which used to make my brother Spartacus mad, 'cause he said that she'd been telling him that for years and he still couldn't see nothing but clouds.

'My mama was sure beautiful. And not just in the Lord's eyes neither. She was real dark-skinned with hazel eyes and gray hair that she kept knotted in a bun at the nape of her neck. She wasn't old enough to be gray she said but she said hers turned overnight with worry when my daddy walked out on her and us six kids.

'At first after he left Mama used to laugh when she'd say that Daddy went AWOL. I couldn't see the fun in it though and I bet she couldn't neither once she realized that he wasn't coming back. We had a neighbor I loved, a widow woman named Benjamima who always said nobody expected somebody good looking as my mama to settle with a man as ordinary as Daddy. But Mama said she didn't marry him for the how his head looked, she married him for the nice thoughts it was full of.

'When she took up with him she wasn't but sixteen and when he left her seventeen years later, she was already bent over like a old woman from years of scrubbing at a washboard to try and make ends meet while my daddy had his head muddled by big dreams and crazy notions about how to make a haystack full of money. I was third eldest and not but thirteen when he left, but I remember what he talked about better'n I remember his face.'

His talk reminded me of that mess Dagwood was always on about. Enterprise this and enterprise that. He'd learned a lot of fancy talk from the Tuskegee Institute but it didn't feed us half as much as them pennies Mama made from taking in washing.

'For a long time after he was gone Mama made me keep a regular morning lookout for Daddy 'cause he left his onliest suit and she reckoned he'd aim to slip back when he thought she was out and try to collect it. But all them days I kept my eyes glued to the road, and I didn't see nothing but poor folk marching to the fields in the morning to work and them same ones creeping back at night way slower than they was moving at sun up.

'We managed good enough without Daddy 'cause of Mama's determined ways and with her finding things to laugh about all the time. She kept our spirits higher than a lot of families who had way more than we did. But I grew up thinking that necessities like shoes in the winter was a luxury and though my feet told me I couldn't do without shoes, listening to my mama, she'd of had us thinking we was luckier to be barefoot than all them kids at our school who was wearing boots.

'Our family would of done good in the long run I reckon if it hadn't of been for the fire that broke out in Mr McDermot's barn while my three brothers, Spartacus, Napoleon and Aristotle was baling hay.'

'Lord have mercy,' Brenda laughed, interrupting a clear picture I had in my head of their three wooden coffins that sat days in our yard waiting for somebody to come and help Mama dig my brothers' graves. 'What kind of crazy names did your mother give y'all. Helen's the only one that came away with a normal one.'

I said, 'Mama said it was Daddy that made her christen every one of us after somebody famous and Helen's full name is Helen of Troy though she don't never tell nobody. Like I don't never tell that I'm called Princess Palatine 'cause to hear it you'd expect me to be a princess. Like Anndora did when she was real little and Joy went and told the child I was a princess.'

'I don't remember that,' said Brenda.

'Well I sure do! Anndora told a little Mexican friend of her'n that she knew a princess and brought that child 'round to take a gander at me one Saturday while I was sweeping down the steps.'

'And what happened?' asked Brenda.

'Anndora came tapping me on my backside while I was bent down with the dust pail in my hands and told me to tell this little girl I was a real princess.'

Brenda said, 'You mean that little girl with the long braids that Anndora always had riding on the back of that tricycle of hers.'

'Yeah, that's the one. Margarita, I think her name was.'

'Margarita! That was it. God. Just hearing her name brings back old times. Margarita and Anndora. They were a pair weren't they! Always eating the last of the chocolate Oreo cookies,' Brenda remembered.

'Anyway, I had to tell Margarita that I wasn't a real princess and Anndora didn't speak to me for a long time after that.'

'That's terrible. Why didn't you tell Mama?'

'To tell the truth, Joy was the onliest one that could handle Anndora in them days and Joy didn't like to make Anndora do things.'

'Mainly,' said Brenda, 'as I saw it, Joy liked to keep you to herself and didn't want Anndora to like you. Sometimes when she was supposed to read her a bedtime story, Joy used to tell Anndora about how you turned into a witch at night.'

'Oh Brenda, why you gon' set there at your sister's table and tell that lie on her,' I laughed thinking how foolish Brenda was to say something childish against her sister like that.

'Well don't believe me. But it's true. Joy used to say all kinds of things to Anndora to keep Anndora from liking you when she was little and then Joy didn't have to bother after a while, 'cause Anndora got so that she never asked Joy if she could pop across the hall with her when she went to visit you.'

It was all news to me and I didn't know what to think, 'cause between the beers Brenda had downed and either the heroin or the cocaine that she couldn't see that I could see stuck at the tip of her nose telling me that she was sneaking dips into that plastic bag she'd found, I reckoned Brenda could of said anything. I didn't want to get her started telling no lies about Joy, so I went back to the story of my family that had kept her quiet all of ten minutes.

'Anyways, don't you want to hear the rest about my mama.'

'Oh yeah,' said Brenda. 'Finish that.'

'Where was I?' I asked 'cause that story she told on Joy had so put me out of kelter than I didn't know where I was, wondering if it could of possibly been true that Joy had been naughty enough to scare little bitty Anndora into believing I was a witch.

'You got to the fire in the barn.'

'Oh. That's right. That's right,' I said half concentrating. 'Spartacus and Aristotle and Napoleon was in McDermot's barn baling hay when a fire started. Didn't nobody know how, though McDermot tried to tell my mama that he reckoned one of my brothers was in there smoking or playing with matches when they was supposed to of been working. That's how come he made 'em go back in the barn to let all his horses out the stables, but that ol' wooden barn fired like a tinder box and as the horses run out McDermot told Mama that the roof caved in. With my three brothers inside.'

'God. Baby Palatine. You never told me that.'

'I like to pretend it didn't never happen. It's easier to forget mess like that so you can carry on, otherwise there would be too many tears everyday of our lives.'

'So then what?'

'They didn't never find the bodies though we sifted through ashes for a whole day but Mama had three coffins nailed together anyhow so we'd have something to bury and mourn. It was her that used to say you need to see the dead. I got that off her. That's how come I'm hoping Joy's gonna have a open coffin.'

'Don't go on about Joy, please God,' said Brenda, sounding exasperated though I hadn't give her nothing to be exasperated about. 'Just finish your story.'

'Well we kept them three coffins in the yard for a week, 'fore the preacher had time to come from town with a few men from the church and bury my brothers.'

'I thought they weren't actually in the coffins.'

'They weren't. But as the days went by, it got like they really was and Mama swore blind she smelled the bodies rotting and had me believing it. Helen and Caesar was too young to understand what was going on, so I had Mama to deal with on my own.'

'How old were you?'

'Fifteen.' I sighed. 'Not but fifteen.'

I hadn't never cried when it all happened for real and never told nobody but Joy how my mama stopped smiling and laughing after that all happened. Freddie B hadn't even heard that part. And to think that the only person I ever trusted to tell it to was dead hurt me to my heart and brought tears welling in my eyes till they rolled one after another in two streams down my cheeks.

'Don't cry,' said Brenda in a soft voice like she cared I was hurting.

'I want to, 'cause I was too scared to cry at the time. Feared that if I started, I wouldn't never stop. Instead, I put on the happy face my mama used to wear and tried to take over from where she left off. For Helen and Caesar's sake, 'cause Mama wasn't never right again after that. She pined till sadness was her shroud and within two years we had to bury her. I kept watching the road while she was sick to try and give her hope that Daddy would come back. But it didn't work,' I said wiping back tears and trying to think of something that would take away the bad feeling that I remembered from them times.

'How did you manage?' Brenda asked like she really wanted to know. 'What did you do with the kids?'

'I don't know. But I kept us alive. And Mr McDermot let us stay at the shack for as long as we needed to. It was Benjamima that fed us and I took in washing and kept us going to school 'cause I know Mama would of turned over in her grave had I done less.'

'Didn't anybody try to find your father?'

'No,' I answered. 'And whereas I know the Christian thing is to forgive, I didn't never forgive him.'

'Nor me mine,' said Brenda.

'Yours died, child. He didn't desert you.'

'Yes he did.'

'I thought Tammy always said he got killed in a accident at work?'

That minute the phone went and Brenda leapt up from the table to answer it like she thought it might of been for her.

All 'a sudden I felt close to Brenda with just the two of us setting together in Joy's living room and I was glad that I'd decided to stay behind. Apart from worrying about what she would do with that plastic bag full of stuff, I was more at ease with her than I'd been since her and Joy and Anndora'd got to singing together. Those were the happiest times and whereas for Tammy it was the money part of it that got her excited, for me helping the girls get started up was the best and I always thanked God Tondalayah lived long enough to help me get Tammy's girls on the stage.

Toni used to rehearse 'em in my front room and then have 'em down in the parking lot soon as the sun was down so they got used to dancing in the dark like she said they would have to learn to. She wanted to turn the headlights on 'em of a white Chevy Impala with red leather upholstery that Freddie B had at the time, but Brenda was scared that all the neighbors and people walking down the streets would see and laugh at them. I remembered one October 31st good when we were outside and I was holding Freddie B's flashlight.

Toni'd said to the girls, 'If you young chickens can shake a leg on this doggone gravel, you'll be able to cut up anywhere. I've been on stages with holes in the floorboards and you'll probably see the same thing before this is over.'

She sure had her some wild looking dance steps and hip movements that she said she'd learned off a Irish girl that she'd met while she was stripping one time in Vancouver. She taught all that to Joy, Brenda and Anndora. It wasn't quite a bump and grind, but it was nearly.

'Don't ch'you think that looks too nasty Toni,' I said to her when she finally got 'em all up doing it in a line.

'Good! Goddammit! Nasty is how it's supposed to look,' she snapped at me before she eyed Brenda. 'S'cuse me, Baby P,' she said pushing me out her way so she could see better. 'Dammit to hell, Brenda, didn't I tell you not to bump your backside till that third chorus.' She had 'em practicing to a tune called 'Please Mr Postman' and we had the music playing in the downstairs doorway with the front door only cracked open so it wasn't too loud. 'I'm not standing out in this night air for my goddam health. Get it right now, Sugar, so I can go home and get my beauty sleep.'

As it was Hallowe'en that particular night, a couple of the neighbors' children were out knocking on doors for trick 'n' treat, so I had a great big mixing bowl full of caramels setting on a dish towel on the hood of Freddie B's Chevy for when any of them walked up to our door.

Only a few turned up. The best was the two that come dressed up as scarecrows. A ghost about three feet tall who tripped and fell on the white sheet he was wearing reminded me of the KKK and I was sure glad when he took his caramels and left. And one clown who looked real cute and had red lipstick painted on her nose stood in the parking lot for a few minutes watching the girls get their routine together. She tried to join in the dance steps before she took her five caramels and headed up the street, and Joy was quick to grab her little hand and try to show her the step.

'What ch'you supposed to be?' she asked Toni who was leaning on the car in a pair of tight leopardskin pants that the child must of thought was a costume. Toni was fit to be tied, and we all had us a good laugh about it, but Toni wanted to concentrate on what the girls were doing.

'Joy, loosen up, please! You're not supposed to look slinking like some movie star, Sugar, you're trying to pass for an R 'n' B star, now. So you may as well drop your shoulders and try to look less sedity.'

Joy was naturally elegant. She kind of moved like a cat. Toni said she was gonna have to look more streety, and Toni thought maybe her posture was too good and got Joy to round her shoulders a bit when she moved. 'This ain't the corps de ballet, Miss Joy,' Toni told her. 'You're getting ready for the chitlin circuit, honey. It's not Monte Carlo where you're singing this Thursday night, it's the Boom Boom Club on 33rd Street and those fellas'll be paying to see you shake and shimmy and look like you're having a good time. Nobody's interested in you looking like you're dancing at a Cotillion Ball, so loosen those hips, Miss Thing.'

Joy smiled one of her big false smiles like she did when she was agitated but intended going along with the program, and Toni went over and put the record on for the umpteenth time. It always tickled me when she talked like one of those finger popping fast talking DJs on the colored radio station and sometimes would say something in a rhyme if she could think of it. 'Go with the flow, and move with the groove, ladies,' she'd say and do a couple bumps and grinds of her own.

I didn't know Toni when she was young. She was already in her late forties by the time we met in that club down Bakersfield. But wouldn't nobody in the world have believed it, 'cause she had her a young girl's figure almost up to the day she died. But with all the pancake makeup and that she wore on her face, as well as the lashes and the long vinyl wig, the few lines she had around her eyes got kind of soaked up in the overall girlish effect of everything from her clothes to her barroom country ways.

Sometimes when she was over at my place and I'd watch her put on her makeup to go out, she used to say, 'I like to have some glamor with a kink in it, because no man worth a night in my pants is looking for a daisy.' I used to tell her off for talking dirty around the girls when they were little but as they got older, I could tell that they liked her for it, 'cause Toni was their favorite out of my friends, who all was mostly from the church and I only saw at Sunday meetings.

I don't know how we would have ever got them three girls on the stage that first time if it hadn't of been for Toni, 'cause I didn't know how to begin to help 'em and Tammy wasn't interested because she was mad that they were gonna sing at the Boom Boom. She said it was just a low down juke joint. Somehow, to hear her talk, the only thing she wanted to make the girls believe it was worth doing was going on the television.

Tondalayah went downtown with us to help the girls pick out a dress to wear on the stage at the Boom Boom, and I was really worried because Freddie B was laid off work and we didn't have much money to give 'em and Tondalayah took two whole days off work to lend a hand as she was the only one knew where to get gowns and things with dazzly bits on 'em. She even offered to let the girls wear some of her low cut half-dresses but thankfully Brenda couldn't get into nothing that Tondalayah had anyway. I say thankfully 'cause it would of been wrong for the girls to go out wearing strippers' clothes, skimpy as they was.

But the girls were real excited and so was we. Anyhow we went into a couple of them cut-price stores that Tammy was always going to for Anndora but they didn't have nothing fancy enough for stage, Tondalayah said, and she told us about a woman named Clydean who made stage outfits and we five went on over to Clydean's place, with not much time to spare thinking she would have to make tent dresses. But she just happened to have three dresses, silver and red, that she said she could alter to fit all of 'em. She'd made 'em for some other girls who didn't turn up. Well the one wasn't gonna fit Brenda but the woman said she could add little bits of shiny red fabric here and there and make it look like it was meant to be slightly different looking as Brenda was out the front singing lead. 'Cause Clydean and Tondalayah had been friends for a long time, she gave us a special reduced price of $35 a dress with no extra charge for the alterations. When I think back that Anndora was the size of a twig and there was Brenda, three times her size, and the woman had identical dresses to fit both of 'em, I should of known right then that them dresses was a sign of God's will and that Tammy's girls was going to the top which is exactly what happened. They went down good at 33rd and Broadway and they was a big hit in that club. Clydean had sewed a few extra beads and whatnot on the dresses and Joy, Brenda and Anndora really looked nice hip shaking on that bitty stage with not but two spotlights. Freddie B and me was sat out there in the audience with Toni and Helen, and we were so proud. Tammy vexated me 'cause she didn't bother to come, claiming that the Boom Boom wasn't nothing but a glorified bar and saying she was sorry that the girls were singing down there. Well, I thought that was a bad attitude to take, 'cause like I said, everybody got to start someplace.

Anyway, Freddie B had put on his suit, a Sunday suit, to see the girls and we went right on up there and got us a nice table not too close to the front 'cause we didn't want to make the girls nervous. It ain't like him to go down them clubs since, being Christian, he don't smoke or drink or dance or nothing and I was really excited to be sitting up there at a table with him. He ordered both of us a whiskey and when the waitress left the table I said, 'Have you gone out of your skull, man? You know you ain't never gonna drink that whiskey.'

He said, 'So. This man is running a business establishment, he didn't put these tables out here for his health. We got to drink something that costs a couple dollars.'

I said, 'And so are you gonna start to drink whiskey?'

He said, 'No, but it can sit there.'

My baby sister Helen had used Toni's boyfriend's ticket 'cause he decided not to drive from Frisco. Helen hadn't never been in no proper night club and I was scared she was gonna show out, but I finally said she could go anyway. By the time Toni finished getting Helen made up, I didn't recognize my baby sister and wished our mama could of seen how beautiful she looked in a black cocktail dress of Toni's with her hair piled in curls on top of her head.

I said, 'Well, Freddie B, I wanted me and Helen to have a Babycham.'

'I ain't stingy,' he said. 'Sure, I'll get you one. And Toni can have them whiskeys, can't you gal.'

So I sat there happy and drank three Babychams while our girls took the stage and sang a whole set of six popular songs with Joy and Anndora either side of Brenda. She took the lead with her sisters doing all the shooby-doop-wops and the dance steps Toni taught 'em with a scuffle of cha-cha and a bit of mambo, everything thrown in. And they looked really cute though Brenda's dress didn't fit right. A couple guys in the audience whistled at 'em and Freddie B looked over at me, much as to say, 'I hope this is a Christian thing you and Toni got these young girls doing.'

Seeing them that night, I didn't reckon they was going to get real, real famous but I figured they was gonna be happy doing what they was doing. And for quite a long time they was.

It was eighteen whole long months later when the day finally came for them girls to go over to the recording studio in San Francisco and cut their first record. Brenda was so nervous she almost gave herself a case of laryingitis. She hadn't never lost her voice the whole time she was singing gospel and I was afraid that it was some kind of bad sign.

I said, 'Funny Brenda that when you sing about the Lord everything is fine and now you end up singing about some hips and tips and chocolate chips and you done almost lost your voice.' She said she was just nervous 'cause she hadn't never sung in front of no orchestra before and that Danny Lagerfield had told her there was gonna be a great big one with twenty-four musicians in addition to a rhythm section of guitar, bass and drums. Neither Joy nor Anndora looked as anxious as Brenda but then on the other hand they hardly had anything to do anyway. Not only did Brenda sing the vocal up the front but she covered herself on some of them backing vocals, 'cause had them close harmonies been left up to Joy and Anndora it wouldn't have sounded bad, but it wouldn't have sounded outstanding neither, 'cause they didn't know them gospel harmonies like Brenda.

The recording studio where the girls cut their first record, 'Chocolate Chip', was over the Bay Bridge near North Beach where I'd heard all them crazy drugged up hippy children and people'd hung out in the streets, and Joy asked me if I wanted to go. I said 'no' 'cause I figured that Brenda was nervous enough as it was and she didn't need nobody else tagging on to upset her. But I sat up all night though, pacing and making Freddie B more jittery than me while waiting for 'em to come on home.

Tammy, as usual, was early to her bed and I had baked a cake and fixed a jug of mulled wine and a big pot of coffee and some rice, black-eyed peas and ham hocks so that there was something special for 'em to eat and help 'em celebrate when they came in.

It was Joy told me how the session went when they straggled back at four a.m., and got me to laughing. She said that with Brenda never being in front of no orchestra before, the sight of some of them old white men looking kind of distinguished with their white hair and glasses, sitting with violins and violas and cornets and bass violin and all that froze Brenda up. But Brenda said she just felt outta place and didn't feel like the session had nothing to do with her. Joy said, 'It was lucky that the producer, a young guy from Berkeley called Jamie Smith, was smoking a joint and gave Anndora and me and Brenda a few puffs on it, so that Brenda loosened up enough to sing. In fact,' she said, 'Brenda got a little too loose and had relaxed so much she wanted to bag on everybody and tell the musicians how to play the music. The violinists played their bit and then the oboes came in over the bass and drums which smoothed the rhythm track so that it sounded romantic behind the bass and drums. But Brenda insisted after every take that they didn't play with enough rhythm and asked Jamie to make them do it again. And again. And again. And so after the night was as tired as the musicians and she still wasn't happy, Jamie refused to make the orchestra play the part again. He said they couldn't do it any more, because it was past perfect and they would totally lose the feel,' Joy laughed drinking her mulled wine out of a china tea cup and holding a saucer on her lap. 'And Miss Brenda Bang here got totally black with him and said, "What goddam feel?" It was just that joint,' laughed Joy, and went on, 'so Jamie took attitude of his own and said to her, "The orchestral arrangement has definitely got a feel. I wrote those parts myself, Brenda." Brenda got super loose and said, "Fuck the orchestral arrangement, this is R & B." And although Anndora and I laughed, the men in the orchestra didn't look like they thought it was funny, nor did the girl playing the harp.'

I said to Joy, 'There was a harp there?'

She said, 'Yeah, a really pretty blond girl played it and she let me pluck a few of the strings. God, I couldn't believe how hard they were to pluck, could you, Brenda!' she asked her sister. 'And her fingers had huge calluses on them.' It was wonderful to hear Joy so excited, because up till then it seemed like she was just helping Brenda out for Brenda's sake.

When Brenda interrupted Joy to say she didn't think the record sounded very good and if she hadn't had that smoke of marijuana she probably would of walked out of the session, Anndora was nodding out. In fact she was yawning the whole time her sisters were telling me what happened, and she soon got completely fed up listening to both of 'em and left to go back over to Tammy's place. Not that nobody cared.

Brenda said to me, 'I just didn't think it sounded right. They played that music like they thought Nancy Wilson or Peggy Lee or somebody was coming out there to sing it. It is, after all, supposed to be dance music,' she said looking to Joy for support. But she didn't give Brenda any.

'You'll have to learn to keep your mouth shut and do what you're told, because none of us know what we're doing and however well you can sing, Miss Thing, you've never made a record before. So next time you ought to at least try to listen to what the producer says and let the musicians get on with it,' Joy told her.

Brenda burst out laughing and said she wished she had some more pot. I tried to laugh along with them and hold my tongue about the marijuana, but I warned them that, recording session or not, I'd heard enough of their talk about drugs in my place.

'If y'all want to eat something you can, but otherwise you should go home and get yourselves some shut-eye so that Brenda won't lose that voice for church on Sunday,' I said. She was still in First Tabernacle's choir after twenty years. Joy picked at the food, never being partial to pork while Brenda ate too much. And 'round about five o'clock in the morning Joy said she couldn't decide whether to go sleep on the floor over at her mother's or drive back to her apartment on the other side of Lake Merritt, but since Brenda had to work that following Saturday morning because of that Friday afternoon she'd taken off to do the recording, she said she wanted to go home, so Joy took her.

When they walked out my door together I thought how nice it was that the sisters was really together having a good time being sisters. Anndora included . . . whether she wanted my cake and black-eyed peas and ham hocks or not. 'Cause all the time they was growing up that togetherness had been missing with Brenda to one side and Joy to another and Anndora off doing her thing. Admittedly, once they was grown, there wasn't no need for them to be following behind each other like shadows but it didn't seem right that they wasn't real close like I think sisters is supposed to be, don't care what Tammy thought.

Before that record of theirs got released, Danny Lagerfield told the girls he wanted 'em on the road doing little shows here, there and everywhere to get 'em ready for the tour he hoped he could organize for them to coincide with 'Chocolate Chip' coming out as a forty-five.

I couldn't believe it when Joy said that they needed somebody to take care of their clothes and whatnot and I was glad to do it for no money 'cause Freddie B was working by then and we didn't need none.

When time came for us to load everything in a eight seater VW van and take off, I was more excited than anybody 'cause I hadn't never travelled but always wanted to. Even if it had to be in a Volkswagen bus up and down California which is just what it was at first, which is why Tammy was happy to stay home. But no sooner than we'd done a couple months in California, Danny managed to get the record released in Europe. And we was off to the races. 'Hold on for the big time,' Joy squealed when Danny told us to get our passports done at the consul in San Francisco.

So my first passport got stamps from Belgium, Germany, Italy, France, and Joy wanted Danny to get us down to work some in Spain but I couldn't take no more. I had shriveled up to a prune and was tired 'cause all that traveling wears you out and is way more work than I thought it would be. Packing and unpacking. Getting lost. Never knowing where I was nor where I was headed.

I got all them places kinda mixed up in my head. I said the Leaning Tower of Pizza was in France and the Eiffel Tower was in Germany. Sounds German, so why not? They should of give the durn thing a French name if they wanted folks to know it was in France.

I ain't one to get lonely when I'm surrounded by people but I got lonely a couple times when I was on that European tour and not able to phone home every other minute. Freddie B ain't much to look at, but I missed having him to do for and hearing his talk about Bible study, though the thing I reckon I missed the most when I was away from him was having somebody 'round to be good for. My better self don't heckle me half as much when I'm by myself as it do when my husband's 'round. That partner thing I have with Freddie B, I didn't have with nobody else in life. Makes it easier to go to bed nights and wake up mornings 'cause I know there's somebody caring one hundred percent about me that I vowed to the Almighty I'd keep caring about.

I used to try and get the girls on sightseeing tours when we was in Europe, but Joy used to make fun of me for acting like a tourist and say, 'What for?' But I thought, 'This here's the whole world in front of us, and I ain't 'bout to let my eyes and ears miss none of it.' I told Joy, 'May not be no second chance, so you best grab at Chance while you can.'

On the road, Brenda stayed in more than anybody and didn't bother to make friends with the fellas in the band, nor the roadies. And since we didn't stop in no place for more than a night or two, there wasn't time to get to know nobody else. She said she liked setting in her hotel room all day till we had sound checks before each show.

The audiences went crazy for Brenda's voice especially in Sacramento, and praise seemed to calm her down and fill her up though she still had a lot of room left for her food. Nothing eatable slipped by her without her stuffing it in her mouth 'specially when it was free, which it usually was. I finally had to tell her that I couldn't alter her dresses no more, and she'd have to quit pigging which she wasn't one bit happy about.

I thought she was gonna kidnap our hotel chef in Munich, Germany and drag him home, 'cause she loved them sausages and strudels and dumplings so. I believe Brenda thought she'd found a new kind of soul food. We was in Germany for three weeks and she gained a pound a day. Maybe more.

If by night she heard them audiences screaming and clapping, then by day she could really tuck into her victuals.

Whereas Germany was Brenda's favorite, England was a chance for Joy to hang with the Five Hundred like I noticed she liked. If anybody coulda pushed Rex Hightower out her number one spot, it would of been one of them Earls or Dukes or something. She had her head way up in them clouds when she was stepping out with one, the Earl of Zip-a-Dee-Doo-Da, I called him 'cause she didn't like me to say his name out loud. He was supposed to be Lordin' over them poor people someplace in Scotland and to tell the truth I couldn't pronounce his name all that good even once she'd said it. If he believed he was Scotch, who was I to argue, but he didn't have no brogue and sounded English to me on the phone when he'd phone Joy in the middle of the night. He claimed he wanted to follow us back to Oakland, and I had to laugh to myself 'cause I figured that he thought them girls had them some money with the way they was turned out on the stage and their record in the English hit parade. But that was all Danny Lagerfield's doing. He didn't just pay for them touring dresses neither. It was him picked them out and the girls' day clothes that was always expensive and the top fashion. Danny was a rich boy from Nob Hill and admitted he was only playing 'round with radio and managing 'cause he had a law degree from Berkeley. It was written all over him that soon as the fun ended and things got rough, he'd run home to Easy Street, but then he wasn't but twenty-four. And in a way it was a miracle he showed the common sense he did with them three Bangs and the whole band and record company and promoters to deal with.

The girls sure had their work cut out for them getting ready to go out on the road, and Danny was a lot of help. But I didn't like that he was always up in Anndora's face. He was good at the job and seemed to do right by the girls, lending them money for clothes and paying their musicians before they'd made money to pay theyselves. And Joy said, if Danny was after Anndora, it was likely he'd do better for the group. But that starry-eyed chile was awful impressionable and seemed like any ol' crazy thing he wanted her to do, right to showing her titties in a girlie magazine for publicity, she was ready. Too ready, I told Joy.

'Your sister still ain't nothing but a sprite,' I said. 'Don't let nobody take advantage of her just so y'all can get ahead. The record ain't worth it.'

'Danny's okay,' said Joy. 'Anndora could do a lot worse. And, it's no big deal that Anndora's been photographed topless in Italian *Vogue*. It's prestigious.'

He happened to turn up in London when Joy was with that Earl and Danny told her to find her another plaything, 'cause it was creeping into the society columns in the *New York Daily News* that one of them colored girls in Bang Bang Bang was toodling about with married English royalty. What bothered me was that man had him four young children Danny said.

When I found out I told Joy myself, 'Miss Joyce Bang' – I only called her by that when she was doing something she wasn't s'posed to – 'Don't you go ruining some kids' lives over no man, 'cause that stuff comes back on you and the next thing'll be that somebody is leaving you high and dry with a horde of your own little 'uns. 'Cause girl, mess up some woman's family and I'll grant you'll be messing with your own one. Then you'll be sorry and won't have nobody to blame but Joyce Clarissa Bang.' Joy had two smiles. One for work and one for real. I got the one for work after I gave her that lecture, which was a sign that she wasn't gonna take a blind bit of notice of what I'd said, and since we was staying another two weeks in England, I knew that if she wanted to see that Earl she would, 'cause the girls wasn't playing but three shows and we had us a lot of time to socialize. And Joy sure knew how to do that with them white folks who was always asking us to go out for lunches and dinners and parties. We could of gone to two or three parties a night if we'd of accepted all them invitations the girls got, but Joy only wanted to go to them high faluting ones where everybody was rich and half of 'em had some kind of title. 'Lady this' and 'the Honorable that' that wasn't no more honorable than my flat feet.

I used to tell her, 'I don't know what you getting so excited for 'cause they the same people that would have been hauling your ass on a slave ship if it was a hundred years ago.'

'Well it's not. It's today and all that slavery crap is over and there's no reason to bring it up.' She wasn't never abrupt with me even when I'd chide her about something, but she sure was that time.

Joy didn't like race talk and I figured the reason it got her mad was 'cause soon as anybody got to talking about black and white, she had to admit she was supposed to be on the black side. It didn't never make no sense that she wasn't proud of who and what she was and I was glad to hear Sebastian try to put her straight about them people that she was wanting to rub shoulders with that didn't have no more respect for her than she had for herself.

Sebastian was still working with the girls when we was in England and he said he didn't have no time for them society people. He said they had only invited Joy and them to their parties to add to the decorations and the girls wasn't no more to 'em than some extra streamers, so he couldn't see why Joy was so quick to want to hang with 'em.

'Oh Seb,' she used to say, 'why are you so up tight and aggressive. Learn how to have a good time.'

'I'm ready to party like anybody else, but I hate to see you make a fool of yourself with the Earl of Neilston. You're just this week's fuck as far as he's concerned. So unimportant that he's probably told his wife about you, her being the one with the money. And if you think that he has any intention of really going back to Oakland with you, you're completely mad.' Sebastian laughed and I could see that Joy didn't like him making fun of her seeing that Earl, but he had the good sense to quit while he was ahead.

'But it's not my business, so if you want to hang out with Lord and Lady Muck, be my guest, but count me out.'

'Don't be like that,' said Joy, 'come to the Buttercup Ball with me, I need an escort and Teddy has to be there with his wife, because his in-laws are coming down from Ireland.'

Sebastian said, 'No and no and no. Fuck Teddy and his wife and his in-laws and fuck the fucking Buttercup Piss Up. Maybe it's my being English, but I see things about them that you can't. There's an airtight caste system in this country and it makes me sick that you're so blind to it. The Earl of Neilston was bred not to give a shit about you. How can you be so naive about things sometimes, Joy?'

'What things! You're making such a big deal out of me going out with Teddy. He likes me, perhaps even, loves me,' she grinned, 'and I find him exciting.'

'You're black you silly cow, and although he may find the visual side of that attractive, you can be sure that neither Teddy nor anybody else at that fucking Buttercup Ball tonight is going to take you seriously as anything more than a good "seen and heard" story at their next intimate dinner party to which you will undoubtedly not be invited.'

I realized then that Sebastian should of taken some lessons from me about when to hold his breath, 'cause sure enough when nine o'clock rolled around Joy and her sisters and me was all dolled up looking just like them fancy streamers that Sebastian had told Joy she'd be.

Joy looked a zillion dollars or more in a white evening gown that was cut real simple but clung to her from the off shoulder neckline to the slit at the ankle. It was one of them dresses that didn't look nothing on a hanger but with Joy poured into it, it hung on her like a satin second skin. We passed Sebastian in the hotel lobby while we was heading for the Rolls that Joy had hired for the night 'cause she said she didn't think it looked right for her and Anndora and Brenda to turn up in a taxi seeing that their record was so high in the English charts, but I figured that she didn't want Teddy to see her stepping out no taxi which is the onliest reason that she bothered paying her hard earn dollars on that white car and white chauffeur.

Sebastian stopped in his tracks when he saw her, 'cause didn't matter how mad he got with her, she could paralyse that poor boy when she put her clothes on and messed with her hair which was shoulder length at the time and fell in nice tiny waves down to her bare shoulders.

'Hey Joy,' he said, trying not to look her up and down but managing to drink her in anyway from head to toe.

'Hi Sebastian,' she said and swung 'round to kiss him on the cheek leaving big red lipstick stains which she tried to rub off with her right hand that he grabbed and pushed away. A man in love with some woman that don't love him can be a pitiful sight and I looked the other way so I couldn't see the hurt in Sebastian's eyes, 'cause whereas he'd talked to Joy earlier like he didn't want her used up like a decoration at that ball, I reckon it didn't sit so good with him that not only did Rex Hightower feature over him with Joy but so did this Earl of Whatchamacallit.

I was sure glad to hear Joy tell him, 'It's not too late for you to join us if you want to.'

'No deal. I'll check you all out at the rehearsal tomorrow. My sister's meeting me here in ten minutes,' he said meaning to sound matter-of-fact and checking his watch.

Brenda and Anndora didn't wait and was already out the door, but I'd stopped 'cause for some reason seeing Joy and Sebastian together always caught me spellbound. Whatever Joy claimed about not having no love for that boy, there was a strong vibration between them like he was part of her whether she liked it or not. I half think that that's what put her off him, the combination of him drowning her in his eyes and the feeling that there was something between them even though there wasn't nothing for real.

That whole night everytime I looked at Joy, I'd get a picture in my mind of her hanging from the ceiling with the balloons, 'cause that stuff Sebastian had said about her being a streamer at the Buttercup Ball stuck in my head.

What they called a ball, wasn't nothing but a big dance with a buffet and there was a DJ playing normal music, thank God, 'cause I had imagined 'fore I got there that the whole night there was gonna be a little orchestra dressed in tails and playing minuets like I'd seen in some of them old movies. It was just like me to get to worrying 'fore we went somewhere fancy, 'cause I was always scared that I wouldn't do the right thing and would show the girls up, though Joy was sweet enough to mind out for me when she thought I couldn't take care of myself 'cause she'd studied that etiquette book and knew every fork and spoon, didn't matter how many was stuck on the table just to make more work for the poor soul who had the dishes to do afterwards. Anyway, at them big dinner parties she used to lift whatever fork or spoon I was s'posed to be eating with high enough for me to see so I could follow suit. Before we had that arrangement I was scared to eat out with them big shots from the different television stations and them night club owners that was always dragging us someplace when I would have been happier ordering up a plate of french fries on room service. But Joy Bang could sure hold her own at them fancy dinners if they was talking English.

No sooner than we'd set down our coats at that Buttercup Ball, I was wishing I could call me some room service, 'cause there wasn't hardly nothing worth eating and that's all that I'd really gone for being past the age to want to shake a tail feather.

The great big hall was in Knightsbridge and though I didn't get introduced to nobody much, I could see how the place was full of this and that and the other . . . a lot of old fogies there was, they mostly looked good decked out in all that finery and what I suspected was real jewelry. Like royalty.

When I did get to shake hands with anybody, I got introduced as the girls' manager, 'cause nobody would have said 'hello dog' if the girls had told the truth and said I was a cleaning woman who they'd drug along to make sure Brenda got up in the morning and Anndora came back at night.

No sooner than we arrived the girls gradually disappeared here, there and everywhere. I didn't like being alone in that long, high ceilinged room full of strange folk and what Sebastian'd said about being a decoration was repeating in my ears.

I was wearing a blue sequined cocktail gown I borrowed off of Brenda. It was supposed to be a midi length, but it was practically touching the ground on me and looked more like a maternity dress the way it was cut high in a umpire waist at the front. Under the bust it tied with a big fat black satin bow and I looked okay in it, though from the back I filled it out which surprised me. I would have never believed my ass was wide as Brenda's.

A few of them old men who looked like they was ready for a rocking chair had the nerve to get out on the floor to dance a quick step. I shouted to one of them fogyish ones with snow white hair, 'Watch it, you'll give yourself a cardiac, chile.'

The DJ played a lot of loud music seemed to me, considering the age group of who all was there. Wasn't no young folks and not one kid, but the music that was playing would of suited a sock hop.

About every ten minutes the girls' record, 'Chocolate Chip', got played and everybody would rush on to the dance floor like they was hearing it for the first time. It was the dance that went with the song that I reckoned got them out there every time, 'cause the Chocolate Chip was a lot of fun to do even if you couldn't keep good rhythm like most of them fossils that was out on the floor trying to hip shake.

The Chocolate Chip was what I'd call a jump and bump dance, 'cause all you had to do with a partner was take two steps to the left and grind, take two steps to the right and grind and then do a little jump before you bumped behinds. Freddie B used to say that he was shame-faced to see me doing it when Joy taught it to me at first, 'cause he said it was too sexy looking, but like I told him it didn't make no sense for me to be working for them girls and not be able to do the dance they made so popular. And anyway, I was glad for any excuse to dance.

The fogyish man with the white hair that I'd shouted don't give yourself a cardiac to must of figured that I was making a pass at him, 'cause the next time that 'Chocolate Chip' played he come over to me and pulled me out on the dance floor, and I thanked God that Joy Bang had taught me to do that dance 'cause with me supposed to be their manager that night, it wouldn't of looked right if I hadn't of known how to Chocolate Chip like them old white folks that was trying it.

I pulled down my dress that was riding up and smoothed my wig down and was ready when I got out there on the dance floor. I thought they should have shot the DJ when the girls' record started up for the umpteenth time 'cause though it was a cute catchy song I was sick of hearing it 'cause the lyrics was so simple and the tune just kept repeating. The words went

> Shake your hip, do the chocolate chip
> Shake a leg
> Get down and beg
> Stick your body to the left
> Bang your booty to the right
> Doin' it, doin' it, doin' it right
>
> Pump your hips
> Till you make me flip
> I'll be your hot hot hot chocolate chip
>
> Pump your hips
> Dip your tip
> I'll be your
> Hot chocolate trip
>
> Can you heat me up
> Can you melt me down
> Can I make you beg
> All 'round town
>
> Rock-on my choco
> Sock-on my poppa
> Choco, choco, choco chip

Though the girls didn't write the song, everybody spoke to them about it like they thought they did which was a shame 'cause I reckon it gave the impression that Joy and them had sex on the brain.

The white haired man dancing with me who didn't have no behind was sure trying his best to Chocolate Chip. His pants hung low around where his backside was supposed to be and when we went to bump behinds, I could hardly find his'n. You could really see it was flat when he took off his jacket and tossed it down on a chair at the side line. Like he was getting right and ready to shake loose and show something special though there wasn't a lot to shake.

'Go 'head with your bad ass self,' I said to get him hotted up. I don't know if he knew that was just meant to be friendly and get him dancing better, but it was as much as I could do to give him some encouragement. When he lifted up his leg like a dog ready to pee and stuck out what behind he had and shook it all over, I smiled like he was dancing real good, but not once was he in time with the rhythm. Really concentrating yet looking like he was letting hisself hang loose as much as he possibly could.

If I'd of seen him strutting around the streets in a derby hat, he would have looked more dignified than David Niven or Charles Boyer 'cause in that black tuxedo and white dickey bow tie he looked like something out of the movies.

When he got tired of doing the Chocolate Chip he twisted for a while. I laughed to myself and thought if colored folks danced that bad we wouldn't never be allowed on no dance floor.

I'm easy to sweat and after two minutes I was sweating like a pig and got scared I was gonna ruin Brenda's sequined dress, so I pulled the man off the dance floor and told him I thought he should have a rest. What would of been perfect was if Joy had of rescued me. Though I can't claim I was having a bad time till somebody farted. I didn't know what to do, and I was sure that folks would think it was me, so I said right away to the woman stood next to me, 'That wasn't me.'

'What wasn't you?' she smiled which I figured was the giveaway for her being polite when she figured I did it.

'Wasn't me that did that you-know-what,' I said 'cause I didn't like to say fart or broke wind in company and I didn't know what English folks liked to call it. It was hours later when I was laying in my bed back at the hotel 'fore I remembered that the proper thing to say was pass wind. I suspect the man with the white hair thought it was me farted too 'cause all 'a sudden he said, 'Bye now and thanks for the dance,' and swaggered off. I could see he'd had a few, but I hadn't realized as much when he was high stepping on the dance floor with me.

With all the noise and strange folks milling about, once I finished that dance, I was well and truly ready to go home. 'What are you doing here anyway,' I said out loud to myself. 'Sebastian was right,' 'cause it sure seemed that didn't none of them people have no time for me. In fact they hardly looked like they had time for each other.

My feet was hurting and I all 'a sudden noticed it bad standing there by myself, but I waited on Joy another forty-five minutes and kept walking around from one corner of the room to the next 'cause I didn't want to look lonely and out of place to have folks feeling sorry for me. I hadn't never seen so many white folks turned out in finery like that, not even when I helped that caterer serve a few times for them Nob Hill soirees.

I was wishing I could of said something friendly like 'how d'you do' to the colored man serving at the buffet, but I didn't 'cause I knew from working with the caterer in 'Frisco that if you're serving you ain't supposed to hob nob with the guests, don't matter what color they are. But he looked the onliest person worth talking to as far as I could see. Had him a smile which is more than I could say for most of them other folks standing on the guests' side of the long stretch of buffet table.

I don't know why I stopped at the buffet though, since I didn't see nothing that looked appetising in spite of the full spread. Everything was in aspic except the sausages and I didn't know how in the world them English people thought they should be eating them little poorly-looking wizened things cold. Anyhow I asked the waiter man for some potato salad which he gave me on a real pretty plate though I'd of been more satisfied with a ugly plate and some decent tasting potato salad which it wasn't. No pickles nor celery. Just onions and mayo.

I was standing there trying to eat it when Joy found me. She said, 'Where the hell is Brenda? I told her to stay with you. God, Baby Palatine, you can't be having a very nice time by yourself. How long have you been standing alone here. And didn't anybody even offer to get you a drink?'

'It don't matter none,' I said. 'But you mind if I go set in the car?'

'I can't let you do that by yourself. Knowing you, you'll get lost and end up in Manchester,' she laughed. 'Hang on, I'll come with you. Just let me go say a quick goodnight to a few people.' I figured she meant Teddy.

Joy wasn't used to having to worry about me 'cause it was always Sebastian who used to set with me if we had a big party that wasn't a set down dinner to go to after the show. I reckon that he did things like that for Joy's sake but I ain't sure she realized how he'd put hisself out for me when we was all out together.

'You been having a good time?' I asked her.

But two people come up to her just then and started talking, and I could tell that she was probably gonna be a few more minutes. As my feet hurt me too bad to try and be polite, I said, 'I hope y'all don't mind if I grab me some nice fresh air,' but didn't none of them three hear me, they was so busy lollygagging and grinning, so I just slipped off and found my way out to the car. It looked like a funeral procession out in the streets with all them big black hearses parked out there waiting on folks in the party.

I was surprised to find Brenda 'sleep in the Rolls when I finally got to it. She could sleep anywhere and truly loved dozing off in the cars we was chauffeured 'round in after she'd had herself something to eat. I tried not to wake her, but the driver made a big deal of getting out the car to open the door for me, and when he shut it behind me it roused Brenda.

'Heh, Baby P,' she said in a dopey half 'sleep voice. 'Are we ready to boogie on home?'

'No. So go on back to sleep, 'cause Joy's still in there and I ain't seen Anndora since we arrived. But it looked to me like Joy might be another few minutes. You tired?'

'Girl, you know I can take those kind of people or leave them, and I found the number of times they played that doggone record of ours embarrassing. I got lumbered with some woman who was running the charity that this was supposed to be for and I'm surprised that she didn't collar us to spend the entire evening in a corner signing autographs. I really do hate it when people supposedly invite you somewhere and then try to get their pound of flesh. Had Joy told me it was a charity, I would have never come, because they never cater them right anyway. Did you see that sorry looking food, girl, and if I had seen another cold sausage I would have thrown up.' Brenda laughed. 'How's about we get the guy to paddle this boat back over our hotel so that we can order up some room service. I could kill for some ice cream, couldn't you?'

It sounded like the perfect way to end a sorry evening, but I was worried that Joy might come out looking for the car and not be able to get her a ride home. 'Don't you think we should wait and see if Joy's gonna come?'

'Why are you always looking out for Joy, when you see that she doesn't bother to look out for you.'

'Yes she does,' I said and rolled down the window 'cause there wasn't no air in the car and it smelled of feet from when Brenda was sleeping in it with her shoes kicked off.

'Okay,' I said thinking 'bout it. 'Have it your way . . . Tell the driver to take us back to the hotel if that's what you want. I ain't the boss no way.'

The one thing that me and Brenda had in common was that we liked to set up in the bed at them hotels and play with the TV control button changing channels and eat, and I'd be lying if I said that the idea of it didn't sound just what I needed. It was nights like that that I missed my husband and wished for all the world that I could be setting with him in our own place watching the TV and drinking me a cream soda.

I liked being on tour for the most part seeing different places and whatnot, but sometimes I longed to see somebody normal that wasn't no kid or no crazy fan or nobody with their eyes hungry for what they thought that they could get that they thought we had; whether it was money or limelight or the comfort of just being among the gang of us together.

England was our last stop on the European tour Danny arranged and I was sure glad to see real food and real people when we got Stateside again even though we was stuck way over on the East Coast. For one thing, in Europe I found it too hard being with nothing but white folks all the time, and although I could see that Miss Joy was in her element, I like being with my own.

By the time we got off the plane in New York, 'Chocolate Chip' was number fifteen in the charts and the girls was getting the celebrity treatment everywhere we went which was nice for them, 'cause they was tired from all that rushing on and off planes and smiling at strangers and never getting a full night's sleep. Sleeping in hotels, even them that's first class, ain't all it's cracked up to be when you got to be up at the break of dawn for interviews and photo sessions and that, and I was as tired as the girls was, 'cause looking after them and their clothes don't sound like a lot of work, but it was 'cause I didn't have my own washing machine and wasn't in my own house to set and relax while I sewed sequins back on them dresses night after night. But all in all, I realized how lucky I was to be going all them places abroad and seeing parts of America that I had heard about but hadn't never been to like Washington, DC, and Boston and Philadelphia. Staying in fancy hotels mostly. The girls was quick to get used to doing things first class, but it made me feel kinda bad when we'd come out of one of them expensive hotels or restaurants and I'd see poor folks walking on the streets that could of made good use of that money the record company was wasting on big ol' hotel bills.

Once while we was working that time on the East Coast and was staying for three days at a real pretty old fashioned hotel in Princeton, New Jersey, 'cause the girls was playing at discos thereabouts, I noticed a tall thin colored woman waiting outside the hotel with the usual bunch of autograph hounds. She looked so out of place and reminded me of me when I'm in a washdress and ain't fit to be seen out on the streets. 'Cause the faded out floral black print dress she was wearing hardly had a design left on it and looked like it had been machine washed ninety thousand times. She had on a pair of white running shoes that was made of five and dime stuff 'cause I could see they was board stiff like they didn't have no give in 'em like decent running shoes is s'posed to have. They caught my eye the first time we passed her driving out of the hotel, 'cause they looked brand spanking new in comparison to that dark washdress of her'n.

It seemed strange to see a woman old as her lined up with them teenager fans hanging 'round for the girls outside our hotel, especially as that whole tree lined town of Princeton looked like it must of been reserved for young white kids togged in expensive casuals anyway.

With the fans screeching and pushing to get to Joy and them everytime we stepped out of the limo to go in or out of the hotel, I could see this poor woman didn't stand a chance. But I could tell she was determined 'cause she come back all three afternoons though she obviously wasn't no regular autograph hound and didn't know how to elbow and scream like a banshee to get to the front of the crowd to get her book signed. And as we, I should say Joy and them, didn't stop for more than a few minutes for signings either going or coming, only the pushiest had a hope to walk away with Bang Bang Bang signatures and their books and posters signed.

It was just as well that the poor woman was outside the hotels where the fans acted politer 'cause when Bang Bang Bang slipped out of them night clubs, those kids would knock you down soon as look at you with their pushing and shoving. Them professional autograph hounds would have as many as five pictures they'd been collecting out of magazines or from God knows where, 'cause Joy was always asking 'em, 'Where'd you get this picture from?' If she really liked it though she'd hang on to it and pretend it was one that she hadn't seen and needed her a closer look at but then wouldn't remember to hand it back.

Anyway, I took pity on this woman when I saw her still out there on our third and final day, as we was getting in the limo to head for the airport to fly out of New Jersey.

'Let me catch y'all up,' I called above the racket of the crowd to Phil the driver, a sweet natured Puerto Rican guy who doubled as body guard more for show 'cause I reckon if things ever got rough it would of probably been Brenda protecting herself and the rest of us. 'I won't be a second,' I told Phil as I slipped behind the crowd getting pushed and rustled till I got to the woman.

'They'd kill you quick as look at you,' I said when I got near enough to her, feeling like I knew her from seeing her as regular as I had the hotel night porter. But I realized from the way she shot a glance my way that she didn't have no idea who I was nor care that I thought I was on a rescue mission, 'cause she was concentrating on waving her book in the air.

'Brenda! Brenda!' she was yelling, while all the kids was screaming for Brenda, Joy and Anndora. 'Yoo hoo! Hey Brenda!' she hollered as if Brenda could hear her above everybody else. 'It's Delores Hayward from Collins Street!'

'Far back as you're standing,' I said to her, 'Brenda ain't got a chance in hell of hearing you.'

Miss Delores Hayward looked at me like I'd just been let out of the Camarillo nut house, so I added in my extra friendly voice to straighten her out, 'Hi, Hon. I seen you waiting out here every day in this heat and humidity waving that book of your'n to get you a autograph, and I can easy get the girls to sign it for you, 'cause I work for 'em.'

She looked me over like somebody would a criminal in a police line up, and I guess I did look way different from the way folks probably turn out to be traveling with the stars. I didn't look like nobody special and wasn't dressed up. I wore loose cotton slacks most of the time 'cause they was comfortable, and it meant I didn't have to bother with no stockings or girdle and could keep on my flat shoes. And hot and humid as it was in Jersey, I wasn't even bothering to put on my wig, 'cause my head sweated too much underneath it, so I just bound a bandana round my head like I did when I was a kid and went berry picking summertimes on the farm.

Delores Hayward needed some convincing that I was Bang Bang

Bang's wardrobe mistress and I didn't have time for all that, so I said, 'I got to get straight back in that limo, 'cause they're ready to shove off. But if'n you're quick with that, I can get it signed for you.' I put out my hand to take her book off her.

'You really know 'em?' she asked not sure what to do.

'Since they was this high,' I bragged showing her where Joy used to come just past my waist.

'I knew 'em when they wasn't but this high,' Delores said bending over to where my knees was to do me one better. 'In fact I was there the evening when their mother brought Anndora home in a blanket from the maternity hospital.'

'You shucking me?' I was sure glad to meet somebody who knew the girls from back when, 'cause all the twenty years I'd known 'em didn't one person turn up from their past.

'For real,' Delores Hayward said. 'I knew them when they lived on Collins Street in Newark. My family lived two streets away, and I loved to babysit for Brenda who was five and used to love for me to come over. But the twins were too much of a handful. I was the one that taught Brenda how to whistle,' said Delores with as much boast as somebody saying they'd taught Brenda to sing. 'I thought when I saw Brenda's picture in my son's music magazine that it was her, but she's changed so much.' Delores smiled. 'She's sure glamorous now. I'd bet you'd hardly believe that she was kind of homely as a little girl.'

I didn't want to tell her that Brenda still looked rough when she wasn't helped by Joy, Max Factor and the black curly wig that passed her shoulders. Not that Brenda Bang is a common name, but I wondered if Delores was getting her families mixed up 'cause there wasn't no twins.

'My last name is Merriweather now, and I work on the campus for a Swiss physics professor at the university that won him a Nobel Prize two years ago. Just housekeeping for him three days a week, you know. But when I saw the girls' picture I told my kids that I knew the girls. But they don't believe me. So, I've had a few days off and I made my boy a bet that I'd be bringing Brenda's autograph home.'

'Don't you want Joy and Anndora's?'

'Yea, okay, sure,' she said like she wasn't all that interested. 'Brenda was my favorite. Oh, oh!' she yelled all of a sudden craning her head to look to where the limo was parked. 'It looks like the car is pulling away from the curb. Didn't you say you're supposed to be in it?'

I turned and stood on my tippy toes, but Delores was way taller than me, so I couldn't see all that she could.

'Do it look as if it's really pulling out?' I asked her, scared that Phil, our driver, would be absent-minded enough to drive off through the crowd and leave me standing there amongst all them screaming fans.

'Here,' said Delores pressing her blue autograph book in my palm. 'You look honest. Take this and get the group to sign it will you. My address is in the front if you don't mind mailing it to me. Can Brenda in particular sign it for Hazel, Arbutus and Willie Jr. That's my kids, and tell her Delores Hayward is so proud of her. Imagine! Her growing up and singing like that. Who could have thought it?'

I didn't have time to get the details, and rushing through the crowd to the car the only name I remembered to tell the truth was Willie Jr, 'cause I was really panicked and wouldn't have put it past Phil or Joy to leave me there if they thought otherwise we might miss the plane.

'Baby Palatine. Dammit. What the hell are you doing mixing with those kids. Bring your ass in this car,' Anndora hollered at me. She could be as bad mouthed as her mama, and Anndora and me didn't have a lot to say to each other, 'cause of that mess that'd happened in Baltimore with Sebastian, but when we did, we didn't mince words. I'd got used to her talking to me like I was a scrub woman. Not that it sat no better with me for all my being used to it.

Before I could get situated good in the little bumper seat, I got three questions thrown at me at the same time, which was the usual since everybody expected me to do everything except wipe their behinds.

'Did you pack everything? Where's my wallet? Where are we going?'

By the time I satisfied Anndora with an answer to the first, Joy to the second and Brenda to the third, I'd already got fed up talking and forgot about Delores Hayward and the autograph book I had in my hand when I dozed off sleeping.

It must of fallen on the floor and with the rush to get out the car at the airport, I totally forgot about it until I was sitting strapped into my seat next to Joy on the plane headed for Boston's O'Hare.

'Lord! Can you believe I don' gone and lost that child's autograph book,' I said to Joy. 'And what with her not believing at first that I really worked for y'all, I feel doubly bad about it.'

Joy didn't like plane riding and was trying to settle herself in a comfy sleep position with her behind pointed in my direction as she nestled up into the window with a pillow she got off the stewardess soon as she got in her seat.

'Please don't let me forget to buy a autograph book and get Brenda to sign it.' Joy was as good at remembering what I had to do as I was about remembering for her and everybody else.

'Yeah okay,' she said like she wasn't in no mind to chitchat.

'Do you remember somebody called Delores Hayward?' I asked.

'No. Where am I supoposed to know her from?' Her eyes were closed but she wasn't really sleepy yet, I could tell.

'Collins Street, in Newark.'

'Newark?' Her body tensed like memory of it suddenly give her a sharp stab.

'Did y'all used to live in New Jersey? I promised to get Brenda's autograph for some woman that was standing outside the hotel and claimed she used to babysit for y'all. But I wasn't sure she was telling the truth, 'cause she thought you was twins,' I laughed. 'Thank God there wasn't two of you,' I went on, ' 'cause you been handful enough.' The plane took altitude as I said, 'If I'd of had to deal with another one of you filling my head up with "Don't tell Mama," I don't know where I'd be.'

As the plane took off Joy quick yanked the sickness bag out of the pocket in front of her seat in time to bring up her entire breakfast from that Princeton hotel. I hadn't never seen her do it in all the years I'd known her, and the first thing that come to my mind was morning sickness, though I hadn't seen nobody in her room but Sebastian.

The stewardess was real nice about helping us to clean up the mess though most of it went in the bag, and when Joy climbed over me to go to the toilet, I asked her if she wanted me to go with her 'cause I saw she was shaking so. But she shook her head 'no'. 'It's okay, I'll be okay,' she almost whispered like she was saying it to convince herself as well as me.

With Brenda and Anndora sitting two seats ahead of us, they didn't even realize that something had happened, and I didn't see no point in telling 'em.

'Can you please bring us some water and apple juice,' I asked the stewardess. I wasn't too good at asking for nothing for myself but when it come to asking for Joy, I was known for being demanding.

She didn't come back to her seat for a long time and with the flight only being forty minutes we was almost landing when she finally did, saying she felt woozy. I noticed she stayed pale looking and not her sunny self for a couple days after that, and oddly enough it was Sebastian she seemed to want to set with them two days which got me thinking that maybe it was morning sickness like I thought at first, though it didn't turn out to be no pregnancy and I never found out what exactly ailed her.

But bless her, in spite of that upset, Joy still remembered about Delores Hayward's autograph book and said I wasn't to worry, 'cause she would see to buying the woman another one and getting it signed. But a few days later when I went to ask Brenda if she'd had the book off Joy to sign, Joy tried to hush me up by poking me on the leg and making one of them 'keep-it-to-yourself' signals that she sometimes made to me when she thought I was about to say something that I wasn't supposed to.

Somehow I got the feeling it was more Delores that she didn't want me to mention to Brenda than Delores' autograph book, though Brenda said she didn't remember her babysitting for them all that good no way.

Them times on the road was the best I had in my life, and when I looked over at Brenda who was still talking on the telephone in Joy's living room, I couldn't fathom how she threw away all her chances for that life 'cause of a newspaper interview. It didn't make sense. And I had it in mind to tell her when she got off the phone. She had been talking over on the phone by the window with her back to me and my mind had been so busy raking over old times that I forgot to be curious about who she was speaking to till she blammed down the receiver.

'Bingo! Bingo! Bingo!' screamed Brenda like she was the grand winner when she put down the telephone right the other side of Joy's L-shaped living room. Whatever was up made her feel so light on her feet that she did a hoppity skip and then laughed and giggled another loud cry of 'Bingo!' again.

Though I was happy to see her happy, I was itching to know what had her all a' grin.

'What you so lightfooted about?' I asked, figuring that it was something 'bout that telephone conversation that got her smiling.

'Hang on,' she said. 'Let me just put some music on, and-I-will-tell-you-the-news,' she sang out her every word like a star preacher at the pulpit revving up his congregation.

The sun was coming in the window from behind her and it put her in shadow so that I couldn't see her face that good, but I could still tell that she was beaming when she bent over to choose a record from the pile.

I was surprised by what she played 'cause I figured that with her having said that she needed to forget about Bang Bang Bang, she wouldn't have wanted to hear 'Chocolate Chip' ever again in her life. But I knew straight away, from the first tinkle of a finger bell that rang out on the record 'fore the rest of the music thumped in, that 'Chocolate Chip' was what Brenda'd put on Joy's turntable. For some reason I hadn't played my copy in years, and setting there in Joy's cold looking, big white-on-eggshell-white living room, I didn't know whether I could stand to hear it with her gone. My heart swelled up so inside me with the sounds of them first guitar chords rushing me with memories that I thought my chest would bust open from the pressure. Maybe it was what folks call heartache that I was feeling. Whatever it was it took my breath away faster than anything else could of done save Joy herself opening her front door and walking into the room. And I got to wheezing.

I don't know what possessed Brenda to play that record but hearing it made me glad and sorry at the same time.

'That was Jesse on the 'phone,' Brenda said.

'What'd he call for?'

'To say that they might have trouble getting Joy's body from Santa Fe in time for a funeral tomorrow.'

'So what's s'posed to happen now?'

'I don't know. Jesse thinks that Mama might decide to do without the cremation if it's going to be a whole lot of trouble, but Anndora is insisting that she wants Joy cremated, and like I said to Jesse, who is she to decide? And what about my say so,' Brenda added before she joined in singing along with the record. 'Till you make me flip, la, la, la, I'll be your hot, hot, hot . . .'

'Brenda!' I called above her singing, 'Don't you think you got that turned up too loud. Think of the neighbors!'

She rolled her eyes to the ceiling before she turned it down and I wanted to tell her that I couldn't have been no more exasperating to her than she was to me, but instead I asked what she was yelling 'Bingo' about.

'Oh yes. . .' she smiled. 'Guess who else called.'

'When?'

'Just now while I was talking to Jesse. Guess who came through on a call waiting.'

'Sebastian?' I said, hoping.

'No, but you're close. Guess again.'

'Do I have to, Brenda, I'm too tired to be messing around with guessing games. Just tell me who it was.'

'Rex Hightower! Can you believe it. After all these years. Rex Goddam Hightower calls and is just the boy to know where I can move that bag of stuff for ready cash. Major bucks. Major, major, serious readies,' Brenda squealed like she was ten years old and about to get her a big cherry double decker ice cream cone.

'Lord have mercy, Brenda, don't tell me that you went and told that man about that bag of stuff being in this place. What if somebody was listening in?'

'Damn, you're paranoid for somebody who's supposed to be law abiding. What makes you think that somebody would listen in to Joy's phone?'

'It ain't unheard of that lines get crossed. Where was he calling from anyhow?'

'Columbus Avenue where he said he still lives.'

'He's in New York City!'

'Yeah. What's such a big deal about that.'

'Did he say that he was coming to Joy's funeral?' I asked getting real excitable.

'He didn't mention the funeral, but I told him to come straight over so that he could give his expert advice about what's in the plastic bag.'

'That s-o-b. It's probably his'n and he got Joy with it so that if anybody gets in trouble over it, it'll be her and not him, like that time he had her carrying them watches of his through customs that he hadn't paid no duty on.'

'Huh?' said Brenda swaying back and forth to the music that I wanted her to turn off 'cause it was eerie hearing it playing there in Joy's apartment knowing she was dead.

'Never mind. It don't matter. But you couldn't turn off that record player could you, or else put on something soothing.'

'I feel so good,' wiggled Brenda, 'that I might even find a Nat King Cole album.'

'Is Rex really and truly coming over?'

'That's what the man says,' said Brenda practically singing it 'cause she was still so excited.

'Did he ask if I was here?'

'How'd you know?' Brenda asked.

'Never you mind,' I said and wondered if I should of gone upstairs to the bathroom to freshen up. 'Is that all he's coming for, to look over the stuff, 'cause if it is, I think I'll go out somewhere.'

'Well to tell the truth, I do believe that he wants to see you, because he said that you have something that belongs to him.'

'What the hell's that supposed to mean!'

'How do I know. I figured it's something between you and him. Now see how secretive you are? I didn't know that you stayed friends with Rex,' snickered Brenda.

I didn't give her no reply and was wondering what I had that Rex thought should of been his'n. 'What time's he coming, did you say?'

'Right away. So straighten your wig, tighten your seatbelt and let's get ready for the ride!'

'What ol' ride! Brenda, will you calm yourself, child, and make sense. There's you all up in the air over Rex Hightower, that didn't give that poor sister of yours nothing but a hard time, and I want to know how is it that you can get so excited about him coming and not giving a moment's thought to what Jesse had to say.'

'I told you what Jesse said . . . Joy's body might not get here in time to be cremated, because there's a lot of red tape involved state to state and the body needs to be in New York State at a certain time for Joy to be cremated.'

'Thank the Lord.'

'For what?'

'Well maybe if there's a problem, Tammy will bury the child proper like she should be doing in the first place.'

'That's for Mama to decide, not you,' said Brenda sounding surly all of a sudden and changing her tune from when she'd told Jesse that maybe it should of been for me to say what should happen at Joy's funeral.

'You may think I'm gonna get in a cheap ass argument with you, Miss Brenda, but you are oh-so wrong, 'cause I done learned how to deal with all y'all, and I well and truly ain't gonna let you upset me with your ornery talk.' I figured that there wasn't no need for me to try to say no more to Brenda, and I sat there wondering if I should put my shoes and jacket on and go out if her and Rex was gonna be setting there messing with that plastic bag of stuff.

But short as Brenda's concentration was, she had already moved on to thinking about something else as soon as she sat back down with me at the table where there was still that pile of pictures laying that she had been earlier shuffling through.

My heart was pounding and I wished that Brenda had found that Nat King Cole record like she had promised instead of putting on that boom-thump-a-boom music that she had playing before she set herself down again opposite me.

She picked out a snapshot and passed it to me though I wouldn't take it off her 'cause I was mad at her for what she had said about me interfering.

'Look at this, Baby Palatine. Remember her . . . Sarah Jane Henderson. Golly, was she a goofy child,' Brenda laughed. It always annoyed me about Brenda that like her mother, she could say something hurtful to upset my apple cart one minute and then turn the conversation to something completely different two seconds later while she still had me churning over in a temper.

'Anything you wanted to know about sex you could ask Sarah Jane and she had the answer,' said Brenda re-inspecting that snapshot. 'The boys in our school called her Queen Pussy and she was really popular, because she'd go up to the back of the playground during morning and afternoon recess and let them have a feel under her blouse. She never did wear a bra. A feminist, ahead of her time,' laughed Brenda.

Listening to Brenda talk about Sarah Jane, it crossed my mind that it was probably that sorry child that had taught Brenda to do what she'd done to Dagwood, but I didn't say.

I was jet lagging and so distressed over Joy and the thought of Rex coming to inspect the plastic bag, that I didn't have strength to neither move nor disapprove of Brenda's tale though I couldn't see the point of upturning ugliness from way back when sometimes the past is best left with the dust sheets thrown on it.

Whatever Brenda said, I hated to actually think that poor little Sarah Jane Henderson wasn't no good 'cause that's not the sort of thing a Christian likes to say about a child. And she wasn't nothing but a child back in them days when she come in our place and I got one of Brenda's good cotton dresses on her after I give her a bath.

But Brenda sat there at Joy's glass top dining table and told me about how it was Sarah Jane used to steal *Confidential* magazines from the stand at the drugstore. It had all them nasty pictures with crime stories so that a few of them children Brenda said would gather together at the back of the schoolyard while somebody read the magazine out loud. And she said on days there wasn't no magazine to read, the kids would have a contest to see who could tell the dirtiest story.

'Sarah Jane always won hands down,' laughed Brenda, 'because while the rest of us were making things up, Sarah Jane could actually tell us things about her mother and her sluttish sisters and their boyfriends. One time she told a whole bunch of us kids about how a big removal truck used to park down the block from us on Grange through the night every weekend. Sarah Jane said there were some boys in that gang, remember, Baby, that hung outside the barber shop? They used to meet up odd nights in the back of the truck, using it like their hangout, smoking reefers and getting wasted on Thunderbird and whatnot with her sister Jeanette amongst them. She said her sister even went to the drive-in movies with a load of boys in that truck and did all sorts of crazy things with them like terrorize people in other cars. But the worse she told us was about how one Saturday night when a bunch of the gang got stupid drunk, Jeanette came into their house, woke Sarah Jane up and gave her a dollar to sneak out with Jeanette to join their truck party.'

'I can't believe it,' I said. 'The child couldn't of been not much more than twelve. Thirteen at most. Was this around that time that I had Sarah Jane in my place to clean her up?'

Brenda just went on talking and didn't answer. 'She told us the boys

got her in the back of the truck and offered her a ten dollar bill to take
her panties down, but before they gave it to her they pulled them off her
anyway, tied her hands behind her and put her panties over her head,
so she couldn't see who was doing what while they said they were gonna
play blind man's bluff with her. Sarah said she couldn't see and they
spun her around and around till she got dizzy and fell down on the floor
of the truck which is when one of them got down and started feeling
between her legs while she could hear her sister's voice whispering and
laughing with the boys. She thought her sister even helped them hold
her down and spread her legs open while one after the other of them
spunked in her. Can you imagine!'

'Spare me the details, please Brenda.' I didn't want to hear no more
and it made me sick to think stuff like that was going on in our old
neighborhood and wasn't nobody doing nothing about it.

'Oh come on, let me finish,' said Brenda who was enjoying the telling
too much I thought. 'The rest isn't so bad . . . Sarah Jane didn't try to
fight them off because she knew Jeanette would beat her up otherwise
when she got her in the house, but she said that it felt like they'd all had
her before her sister made her get up and sneak back indoors with the
come running down her legs. Sarah Jane was scared to say anything to
anybody about it because Jeanette said she would tell the police how
Sarah been stealing magazines from the drugstore. So she come to
school sore and hardly able to pee it burned so much and really worried
for a long time afterwards that she was pregnant. But when months
went by and nothing showed, Sarah Jane went back to being happy and
ditzy again as always,' Brenda said, fingering the picture, turning it
round and round while she talked and making me nervous.

'Can we talk about something else,' I asked. ' 'Cause can't no good
come from rehashing no terrible mess like that.'

'What do you want to talk about?'

I didn't know. Mainly I wanted to be quiet and especially not hear no
more miserable stories about the past that it was too late to right like the
one Brenda had told about the Henderson girl which left me all achy in
my joints it had tensed me up so much.

'Did Jesse have some idea when they was coming back?' I asked to
put us on another footing.

'Nope,' she said picking at her back teeth.

'You sure?'

'Yep,' she answered picking at her front ones.

Brenda started grinning off in space like she wasn't all there.

'What ch'you thinking about?' I wanted to know, 'cause I couldn't stand for her to enjoy no joke without me.

'I was picturing how I'm going to fly first class down to Phoenix to see Latrice and surprise her with a black leather coat that she eyed in Macy's last year. I couldn't get it for her at the time, because we couldn't even afford to pay the electric bill.'

'And how you expect you can afford it now?' I knew what her answer was gonna be before she gave it, but I was testing to see if she was as foolish as I thought.

'If I can lay that stuff on Rex, I bet I can grab some cash from him for it before I leave here, and then I can make quick tracks home once the funeral is over with my pockets lined with Ben Frank.' She stood up and stretched. 'God I feel like I'm on the verge of something big. Thank you, Joy. Thank you, Joy. Thank you, Joy,' Brenda sang out looking up to heaven. 'You're about to change my fucking pinchpenny life,' she laughed and run up the stairs shaking the whole apartment as she went.

When she came back down with her overcoat on, she was shoving that plastic bag of stuff down her blouse.

She said, 'I didn't buy enough beer before because I was trying to conserve my money this morning, but under the circumstances, I may as well pop over and get a whole case, don't you think?'

'You can't go out in the streets with that bag, Brenda. Anything could happen. What if you get hit by a bus or something, or fall down with epilepsy with that stuff on you. They'd throw your black behind in jail 'fore they'd think to carry you to the hospital.'

Brenda opened the front door and shook her head saying, 'Epilepsy, eh? Epilepsy! Ha! Goodness gracious, you are one crazy bitch, Baby P,' then went out. I was tempted to go shout at her in the hallway, but then something said, 'That woman is grown now, so if she gets herself thrown under the county jailhouse, it don't have nothing to do with you, 'cause you ain't kept in touch with her all these years, so there ain't no need to start fretting over Brenda Bang now.' She was always a mess and there wasn't no controlling her wildish ways, and whereas I used to fuss sometimes with Joy for not keeping better touch with her mama and her sisters after Bang Bang Bang split up, I could sure see why she didn't bother.

I went over to look out the floor to ceiling window and noticed for the first time that it was drizzling. I wondered how many times had Joy stood where I was standing and was she really happy in New York or did she just stay for Rex's sake? It didn't seem natural that somebody that had a choice and was in their right mind wanted to live day in and day out in no New York City. Not even if they was living at the Ritz overlooking Central Park where we once spent a night when the girls' record was in the charts, 'cause still the rest of New York, the scummy, degrading over crowdedness of it that kept folks from believing they was human and got 'em to acting like rats, had me palpitating even when we was high above the hubbub at the Ritz.

Luckily Joy's double glazed windows kept the dirt and the sound of the city out, as I watched both people and cars like they was some kind of a silent movie, and so it was odd to spot Brenda jaywalking across the middle of 23rd Street as she headed for the store down on the other side. She lumbered along like her feet was cramped in shoes too small and I noticed she'd lost the mannish stride she once had when she was a teenager. Instead she moved like her insides was drooping. Like somebody middleaged.

Standing there in a daze at the window I got mad at myself for waiting on somebody else to do things for Joy, 'cause deep down I knew it would take a army to get any of Joy's family to take care of her funeral like they was supposed to without her being there, since it was her that had held the Bangs together and made them seem halfway normal to me in spite of each of 'em's strange self serving ways. So I went over to my suitcase that was still laying near the front door where I left it when I first walked in.

I wanted a slip of paper I had tucked in it where I'd copied down them phone numbers from Freddie B's Bible that Sebastian'd give me so I could reach him that time before when he asked if I wanted to go on that tour of Japan. I hoped I wasn't just fooling myself thinking that he'd still have heart enough for Joy to want to make something special of her funeral, but I had to try him 'cause there wasn't nobody else. 'Do it make sense,' I asked out loud, 'that a girl beautiful and smart as Joy don't have her one true friend I can call?'

The first two numbers I dialed for Sebastian was disconnected and since I didn't have but four numbers for him anyway, I was scared to dial the last two and have to face what to do if I couldn't get him, 'cause in the back of my mind from when I boarded that night plane out of San Francisco I was expecting him to help.

So I said the Lord's Prayer twice to bolster myself up with, and then recited the whole of the 23rd Psalm so I could hear myself say the upraising bit that goes 'I will fear no evil for thou art with me' before I dialed the third. I was sure relieved when it rang and rang 'cause at least it meant it might of been Sebastian's. But didn't nobody answer. And I got scared again and that's how come I had to pace around the living room to build up my strength to ring the fourth, which had a 203 area code. I didn't know where that was, but I figured like Brenda said, I wasn't really running up Joy's phone bill 'cause she wasn't never gonna have to pay it.

When I'd mustered courage to try the fourth, it rang twice in my ear and a machine came on that played some eerie pipe organ music before a woman's spooky voice said, 'Pie-Eyed Records is out to lunch, but if you leave us a message we'll phone you as soon as we get back.'

I didn't know nothing about Pie-Eyed Records, but at least it had something to do with the music business and I was hoping that if it wasn't Sebastian's number no more, maybe somebody there could tell me how to get hold of him.

I don't never know what to say talking into them recording machines, so I hung up quick and felt foolish no sooner than I'd put the receiver down.

My better self chastised me, of course. 'Don't be backward now, woman. How can you ever expect to find that boy if you ain't even able to say a few words into a answering machine.' I felt so useless I started to cry, and wanted Joy to be there to leave a message for me, like she did twice when I had to ring the dentist and his answer machine came on. I tried to think like Joy and hear how she would of told me off.

'Baby Palatine, you mustn't be afraid to talk,' she'd of said. 'You speak just as well as anybody else.' It always made her mad that Tammy had got me so convinced that I should of been 'shamed of the sound of my voice and the way I strung a sentence together. 'Say what you want to whom you want, because your accent makes you worth no less than the next fellow. Now, let me hear you say something into the phone,' she would of coaxed before she'd of give me a peck on the cheek to show support. She used to talk to me sometimes like I was her child and I liked it.

So back at the telephone calling Sebastian, I cleared my throat and tried to stop wheezing for a minute by holding my breath, though no sooner than I started to breathe natural again, that wheezing started up. Nerves is all it was. Still, I redialed the fourth number I had for him, and when it stopped ringing, I blurted out, 'Hi, this here is Baby Palatine Ross that used to work for Bang Bang Bang and I'm trying to get hold of Sebastian Egerton, so could you please get him to call me back.'

I was that anxious I forgot you have to wait for the machine voice to talk first and only remembered when I was 'bout to hang up and something told me that I didn't say my telephone number. But when I went to put the receiver back to my ear to speak, I heard a voice saying, 'Hello! Hello! We're here, don't hang up!'

'Hello?' I said but sounded too meek and wished I could of said it again.

'Hi! Baby Palatine Ross! I know who you are! I used to hear my brother and Seb talk about you! Aren't you the one who used to sweep up the sequins after the shows,' the girl's voice laughed.

'Yeah, that's me.' I was so relieved I wasn't talking to no complete stranger, my eyes got to tearing.

'My name is Lisa. I'm Jimmy Fraser's sister. I was in elementary school when they were on the road with you, so my mom never let me come to any of the shows because she claimed I was too young, but Jimmy and Seb used to come to our house and talk about you all the time, and Jimmy still has that ashtray you gave him when he and Seb left Bang Bang Bang. Do you remember giving him an ashtray with a three dimensional picture of Christ painted on the bottom of it that blinked when you moved it?'

'I surely do.' I couldn't believe he still had that. 'How's Jimmy?'

'Our grand-dad died last Saturday and Jimmy was really close to him, so he's not too sparky at the moment, but generally he's been a lot happier since he stopped just playing guitar and started producing bands with Seb.'

'Wanting to get hold of Sebastian is why I called. Do he work there?'

'He and Jimmy own the studio, but they work out of St Lucia most of the time if they have the option.' She had a thin sugary voice and didn't sound but a teenager.

'Is St Lucia hereabouts?' I asked her.

'No, it's in the West Indies.'

'Seb's in the West Indies?' I knew there wasn't no way that he could do nothing for Joy from there.

'No. You're in luck, because he happens to be in New York to have a big meeting. But tonight he leaves for Hawaii. Anyhow I'm sure he'd really love to hear from you. He still tells great stories about the days when you guys were out on the road with Bang Bang Bang. D'you want his number?'

'Yes, please.' I sighed. The weight of the world lifted off my shoulders to know Sebastian was in shouting distance.

'He's at the Plaza using the name Mr Trevor Cambridge and his room number is 1356. In fact, if you want to hold on a sec, why don't I try to get him on the other line. He'll be really buzzed to hear from you.' She was gone before I could say thanks. She sounded so full of life and to talk to somebody that was bright spirited, made me feel better.

When she came back on the line she said, 'Seb wants your number, and he said he'll call you straight back.'

I didn't know the number and it wasn't written on Joy's telephone, so for a minute I panicked. Then it came to me that I had it in my purse on that green file card.

'Just let me get it. Tell him I'm right in New York myself.' As I rummaged through my bag for it, that piece of paper with a number scribbled on it that I'd found in the Papagallo shoe fell on the floor, so I picked it up and went back to the phone with Joy's number. I was so excited that I could hardly read it to Lisa off my card.

'He's gonna call right away?' I asked her, hoping that he wouldn't leave me waiting for a minute longer than he had to and that I could get a word in with him before Brenda came back from the store. 'Could you tell him that it's a' emergency and would he please call me straight back.'

'Yeah, sure.'

I hadn't put the phone down but a few seconds 'fore it rang. I was sure disappointed to hear an American man on the line.

' 'Scuse me Mister Whoever-You-Are, but could you call back in about fifteen minutes, 'cause I'm waiting on a real important call that's about to come through.'

'Baby Palatine,' the man said.

'Yeah?' I wondered who could be calling Joy's that would know my voice.

'Hey, Baby Palatine. It's me.'

'Me who?' I didn't have time for no guessing games.

'Sebastian.'

'This don't sound like no Sebastian. Who is it for real?'

'Honestly, it's me.'

'Sebastian Egerton ain't got no American accent.' I wasn't ready to be fooled.

The man laughed. 'Bloody hell. Do I sound fucking American? I've obviously been here too long.'

As soon as he said that 'fucking' part, I knew it was Sebastian. It made me laugh to think it was him with a sort of New York accent and it felt good to know that he was on the other end of the phone.

'What are you doing in New York? Visiting Joy?' he asked. 'God, it's weird that you should call me, because I haven't been able to get her off my bloody mind all day and at one point I could have even sworn that while I was in the shower, I smelled that perfume she used to wear. Remember? Bal à Versailles?'

I said, 'She'd buy her a bottle of that before she'd buy necessities . . .'

'How are you?' Sebastian asked. 'I'm really glad that you've caught me, because I have to leave in a few hours for Maui to meet my wife and kid.'

'You're married?' I don't know why I expected him not to be, but I guess I wanted him to be on hold for Joy forever. Whether she loved him or not.

'If married is what you can call what Jennifer and I have. It hasn't been easy, but we've managed to hang on together for nearly two years,' he sighed. 'Not that she's to blame. I think the problem is that I'm away from home too much.'

'And you got a baby? I'm real happy to hear that Sebastian,' I said. But to tell the truth I wasn't. I wanted him to be the same as I remembered him, pining after my God-sent child.

'We have a little girl. And she's beautiful. Fucking beautiful. Already has two teeth and laughs a lot. You'd love her.' He sounded so proud.

'What's she called?'

He didn't answer for a whole minute and I thought we was cut off. 'Sebastian. Are you still there? Hello?' I heard him clear his throat. 'What's the baby called?' I asked him again.

He cleared his throat a second time. 'Joy.'

'Joy,' I repeated it slow and a big lump of sadness swelled up in my chest.

'Will she be pleased that I named the baby after her?'

I managed to eke out with what little strength there was in my voice, 'Joy's dead, Sebastian,' and soon as I'd said it the clouded New York sky opened up. So what had been a drizzle poured a heavy rain on the streets like the thought of Joy being dead rained and thundered in my head making me cry along with the clouds, forgetting that poor Sebastian was still on the line.

His voice suddenly took on his old English accent and it sounded like him to me again when he said in a faint whisper, 'Oh my God. That's why you've called me?'

I stretched the phone cord to give myself leeway to set down on the sofa and I held a tight grip to my green file card and that little piece of paper with numbers that had been in the toe of the shoe. 'Yes. I'm sorry and 'shamed to say.' I tried to hold back from sobbing any more and wondered how I wasn't cried out from before.

'Why should you feel ashamed?'

' 'Cause she treated you bad at the end and I got the nerve to be calling you to come help to make something of her funeral.'

'When is it?'

'Tomorrow or the next day,' I said studying them numbers on that little piece of paper while I talked . . . 15-90-36. 'Her mama's trying to have my child cremated tomorrow but Brenda says there might be a hold up 'cause of state laws or something like that. I ain't in a clear mind about the facts, and so I can't rightly say, to tell you the God's honest truth.'

'Joy . . . oh Joy . . .' he sighed. 'Baby Palatine, I haven't been able to get her off my mind today. It was like she was standing over my shoulder with that teasing laugh of hers which made me look behind me, but of course, she wasn't there.'

I couldn't speak and he fell silent with me till he said like he was talking to hisself. 'Why couldn't I ever tell her how much I needed her?'

'I hope you got enough feeling left to mourn her like she meant something to you.'

I thought about all them times I had seen Sebastian waiting on Joy to walk her back to the hotel when she'd tell him off for not leaving her alone to get knocked in the head walking back last by herself. And while I reckon she knew he wanted her, needing was a different story altogether and I suspect that's what made her run a mile. 'Cause a man that needs you, won't never let you go.

'When . . . Listen,' he took a deep breath, 'do you mind if I call you back. I'm due at a meeting but I promise I'll get back to you before I go to the airport. And Baby Palatine, I can't tell you . . . I mean, I know how fucking important she was to you. I'm really so sorry.'

Just as Joy's front doorbell went Sebastian hung up.

I figured it was Brenda 'cause wouldn't nobody but her could have got on the elevator past the doorman. So like a fool I opened the door without asking who it was.

And got one almighty shock.


To be face to face with Rex Hightower standing more than a head taller than me the other side of Joy's front door with the rain dripping off him wasn't what I wanted. His cowboy hat was soaked and he banged it on his elbow to shake some of the water out of it. I caught the spray and automatic jumped back a pace.

'Sorry. I didn't mean for that to get on you. It's raining catfish out there, and you're lucky to be indoors.'

I hadn't seen Rex in the flesh for fifteen years, and it was dead obvious that all them years of being famous and making money bought him what help he needed to look his best though I couldn't see his face all that good 'cause of his dark gray smoke tinted glasses.

I didn't think for a minute he was decked out in black to mourn Joy and guessed he had on black jeans, pointed black alligator cowboy boots and a oversized black silky looking trench coat 'cause that was what he'd decided to put on for his own selfish sake.

When he grinned at me I was surprised his teeth looked so perfect 'cause I remembered them from years back when they was crooked and a bit buck top and bottom. But I reckoned with him wanting to be in the movies he'd got him some new ones.

Joy said Rex took to looking after hisself better once he was in them two cowboy pictures she drug me to see, which I thought wasn't nothing special like the posters for them tried to make out. Both movies was supposed to be aimed at the kiddies Joy thought, but I noticed wasn't nothing but middleaged women setting with us in the movie house when me and her went. Crazy as he made them women they was all the ones he needed to buy his records and pay to see them two films of his'n that both bored me silly. Mostly I hated it when the cavalry rushed in blowing bugles to rescue him in the end.

Rex was gonna be a modern singing cowboy like Gene Autrey or Roy Rogers or somebody that breaks out into yodeling when something extra exciting is s'posed to happen and don't. But Rex didn't sing good enough to play a smoothy like they was. He had a gravelly voice and practically talked through his songs which was all that country stuff that I can't stand.

I stared at him still standing in Joy's doorway and when he put a long chocolate brown cigarette to his mouth to take a slow draw, I noticed the tips of his fingers was stained with yellow nicotine though his nails was manicured as much as any woman's, clean and even and painted with clear nail polish. Since he'd been singing and playing his guitar since he was in his early teens it was likely he hadn't never done a day's work like nobody normal and his hands told the tale.

I remember how when she first got with him, Joy had drove me to one of his concerts, but once we got to our seats it reminded me way too much of being a child surrounded by a whole bunch o' rednecks that left me with that scary feeling I used to have living down South that anything could make 'em turn on me. And so setting waiting at Rex's concert on him to start up singing, I got that old piss-your-pants scared feeling I used to get down home.

Soon as he put out his hand in Joy's hallway to say hello and shake mine I could hear that Rex'd cleaned up his Okie accent quite a bit from when I used to talk to him on the phone while Bang Bang Bang was touring, and whereas I'd read that he had a bad drug problem two years back which was one of the worryingest things about Joy being with him, he looked pretty healthy like sombody normal standing there.

I was sorry when I brought him in the living room that he took them dark glasses off 'cause those turquoisie colored eyes of his pierced right through me and I had to look off in the other direction.

When I used to ask Joy what did she see in his pasty face, she'd say, 'I fell in love with Rex's smile.' But I was tempted to tell her that a smile ain't worth a ding-dong if a man ain't got nothing else to go with it. Though I got to admit, I could see some of what Joy could see when Rex flashed them two rows of glistening Hollywood movie star teeth at me.

Though it ain't in my nature to have no feelings for no white man, I tried to be patient with the fact Joy was different, not being from the South and a younger generation, 'cause when she was growing up there wasn't nothing but big talk about mixing and integration. But in truth, come to think of it her thing about whites reared its head the first year she and me got to be buddies on Grange, 'cause one time when she was in my place prancing about in them Papagallo shoes, I told her, 'I bet'cha you gonna be a model in *Ebony* magazine when you get grown.'

She said womanish, 'I'd rather be in those other magazines.'

'Which other magazines?'

'The ones from the drugstore with the girls in all the pretty clothes that you gave me so I could draw from them. You know the ones. *Harper's.*'

She was referring to some old haughty fashion magazines that I got off Mr Houseman's son-in-law when I saw he was using 'em as firewood 'cause they was out of date 'cause Joy so liked drawing girls in evening gowns I thought she would like 'em. But I wondered even from that time if they had something to do with what got her thinking that she wanted to be somebody she wasn't. 'Cause whereas I'd seen kids wanting to be what they couldn't, like some poor child downhome cut out for scrubbing that thought she was gonna be a nurse, or like Caesar when he was little wanting to be a architect when wasn't nothing for him but bricklaying, I hadn't never heard of no child that was black and thought she could grow up and be white.

'They white magazines, child,' I laughed at Joy, 'and it will be a cold day in August 'fore the likes of you'll be in one of them.'

'Why?' Kids can ask the durnedest things that got answers so simple it seems like everybody ought to be born knowing.

' 'Cause you ain't white and ain't never gonna be,' I explained.

'Mama says that if we work hard, we can be whatever we want. Even president.'

'Well that ain't a complete lie. But I can tell you one thing for absolute sure: whatever you grow up to be, you ain't never gonna be white.'

'Maybe,' she said looking downtrodden, with her eyes cast at her feet, like her feelings was hurt.

'Ain't no maybe in it.' I was mad at her for not having good sense, 'cause in all other ways she seemed so wise.

'Do you want to hear a secret?' she asked me.

'Yeah all right then.' I suspected that she didn't want us to have no disagreement and was gonna change the subject to tell me something about something else.

'When I grow up I have to be white like Bernie, because he says he won't marry me until I'm white.' Them whispered words burned a hole in my ear and I had to curb my temper.

'Well you tell that Bernie Finkelstein that you don't want to marry him no way, 'cause you're gonna get you a nice little colored boy.'

'But I want to marry Bernie,' she said, insistent but dewy-eyed like she was truly sorrowful.

'Anyway, Miss Fancy Pants,' I said to her, 'you ain't but eight, so what you doing worrying now about who you'll be marrying? Keep your mind on your school work proper and all the rest of that mess will take care of itself.' She slid off them Papagallos and took herself home after I said that, and although I didn't realize it at the time, that was probably the first instance I had of Joy hearing only what she wanted. 'Cause she didn't never once have no colored boy then nor after. I couldn't figure out why but didn't dare ask her for fear she'd say something against our race that I wouldn't of been able to forgive her for.

But with Rex Hightower hovering in the living room in Joy's New York apartment, it sure did come to mind to ask him finally what hold he had over that girl, 'cause it didn't make no sense that she followed him 'round the globe. Rich and famous as he was or not.

I offered him a coffee and he said looking about him like he hadn't never been there before, 'The place is pretty nice isn't it? I didn't imagine for the money that she would have so much space.' He picked up a glass ashtray and checked the heavy weight of it. 'It's not easy to find a good medium priced apartment in New York. She was lucky to get hold of this.' He gave both the living room and kitchen a quick once over.

'Didn't you visit much?' I said following two steps behind him like he belonged and I didn't.

'No. Joy had a back room at my house on 76th Street. She just kept this for tax purposes, because she needed a few deductions she said and it wasn't my business how she wasted the money. But it's not bad here . . . nice furniture. She had good taste, ol' Joy.'

If I could of hit him I would of done and wanted to ask what had happened to all them crocodile tears he was shedding when he phoned me the day before in San Francisco.

It was confusing for me to want him there for Joy's sake on the one hand but not want him there for my own, 'cause I can't respect a man that don't show respect for his woman.

He said, tapping his watch, 'Is Brenda here?'

'She just stepped out to the store and'll probably be a couple minutes.'

'It's just as well, so we can get our bit of business sorted out before she gets back, because I didn't feel comfortable about having to deal with the pictures while she was here with you anyway. Have you got them?' he asked like I knew what he was talking about and reached his hand inside his coat pocket and pulled out a big padded envelope. 'I've got the bucks.'

'That mess that Brenda was talking to you about don't have nothing to do with me, Rex, so let's get that straight right now. I'm here for Joy's funeral and I don't want no part of that plastic bag shenanigans,' I scowled. I was mad as I wanted to be.

'Okay. Okay. Keep your hat on, Ma'am,' he laughed.

'I don't see what's supposed to be funny. I think it's a crime and disgrace that you can rush over here to see about that bag acting like didn't nothing happen to Joy. 'Specially seeing as how she gave you all the best, and as it done turned out, the onliest years of her life when she should of settled down and had her a nice little family.' Once I get going I can let fly, and I was full to gagging with madness in me.

'Joy gave me the best years of her life?' he laughed. 'Did she now? And what makes you think that, little lady?' I hated the way he set hisself down back to front on a chair at the dining table like it was his, and stubbed out his cigarette that had burned to the filter before he straight off lit him up another one. 'Let me have the photographs and we can talk about the best years of her life.'

'What photographs? I don't know what ch'you're talking about.'

He suddenly sounded real aggravated. 'Look. I've brought you the money, so let's not beat about the bush and maybe we can get this all sewed up before Brenda comes back. It can be as simple as you give me the pictures with the negatives and I'll pass you this envelope with your twenty grand and be out of here.'

Rex wasn't grinning no more and when he sucked deep on that long brown cigarette of his, he had the same irritating manner of speaking like he had in that first terrible cowboy movie I'd seen him in, where he run off with a Mexican girl who had stole for him.

'I don't know what you're talking about. Twenty thousand dollars for what. That stuff Brenda found?'

He gave me too long of a good look while he filled the living room up with cigarette smoke, blowing it out both nose and mouth.

'Joy and I had a deal that you would get a lump sum of money for those pictures she's got of me if anything ever happened to her. Now,' he said talking to me slow like I was five years old, 'you give me the photos as well as the negatives. As much as I can understand your wanting to play dumb, I'm in a hurry and I want my fucking pictures, because I didn't mind playing Joy's silly blackmail game, but I won't, repeat won't, put up with the same thing from you.'

My thoughts was tumbling one over the other as he said that, 'cause he didn't look like he was kidding on, so when I sat down opposite him and tried to take in all what he was saying, it was befuddling. Joy blackmailing him for what? The idea of it seemed ridiculous, but it got me nervous to think about her doing something like that, and like somebody certifiable, I folded and refolded that bitty piece of paper that I was still holding with the numbers on it into my green file card that I set on the table in front of me. 'Repeat what you just said,' I asked him, ' 'cause I don't understand what you're getting at.'

'Then let me spell it out. Joy, having access to my bedroom, took some pictures of me that she shouldn't have one night when I was in bed with somebody not long after she and I first met. Then once when she was tight for cash it started as a joke that she demanded a few bucks from me to keep these snapshots of me out of my manager's way, but her scam on me was repeated and her scam became more and more real as time went on. And before I knew what was happening, she was practically on the office payroll. And she used those pictures for twenty years which amounted to a steep sum for her "weekly allowance". I let her get away with it, because she was a good partyer and hard not to like.'

The walls in Joy's living room could hear him better than I could, 'cause my ears was ringing with what he had said. Rex's voice trailed off. That Joy could have done something mean and spiteful like that seemed as impossible as him putting up with it for years.

'I don't believe you.'

'Believe this,' he said, emptying the envelope of money on to the table. I hadn't never seen so many bills. He had 'em in three little stacks bound with rubber bands and I tried to take my eyes off them but couldn't while he went on, 'I hope you're not planning to hold on to those pictures imagining that you can get more than is on offer, because you haven't got a chance in hell. I only played the game with Joy because it suited me to have her around for the press it brought me.'

I said, 'How y'all was living together and she was blackmailing you! Either you was crazy or she was, 'cause that don't make no sense.'

'Joy and I didn't live together. What gave you that idea?'

'You just said yourself that she was living at your place on 76th. I got ears.'

'I live on Columbus. My place on 76th is an apartment I keep for my driver.'

'She was living with a chauffeur? I refuse to believe you, Mister. I ain't never heard her tell of nothing like that. And it wouldn't have been like her to settle with no chauffeur.'

Rex fell to laughing like the joke was on me.

'Come on, Baby Palatine. You're trying to play dumb with ol' Rex here aren't you? Don't tell me that you don't remember my chauffeur. You've talked to him a few times and he's picked Joy up enough over the years.'

I figured he must of been talking about a nice looking colored fella that worked for him during the years that the girls used to sing back-up for Rex . . . Curt, that boy's name was. He had a club foot and Brenda used to always go on about how cute she thought he was. He seemed to mind his own business of driving Rex's car the two times I had to ride with him. But what I remember best about him was his girlish ways. Nice as he was, I reckoned he was a big sissy.

'You talking about Curt?'

'My one and only,' smirked Rex.

The way he said it gave me the impression that he was wanting me to think on Curt as being something to him.

'What's that supposed to mean.'

'That's my business, little lady. Now can you get me those photos so that I can hightail it out of here. I'd like to miss Brenda if at all possible.'

'What about her and that bag she's planning on selling you.' He was forgetting what he'd really come for I thought.

'I'm not interested. I never did like that second rate coke that Joy handled. I think she cut it with belladonna anyway. Greedy fucking cow . . . She could have made enough selling it clean. She sure got herself in a mess with that which is why I thought she was in Taos, but maybe I was wrong.'

'You was the one got her into that drug mess. So don't try to weasel out and put the whole blame on her,' I told him flat 'cause I didn't want to hear no trash like him call her no names nor accuse her of selling drugs. 'If you thought so low of her, why did you waste her time?' I asked.

'Joy was my perfect foil. We kept the press so busy trying to prove that I was spending my time with a black woman that they didn't notice that I was with a black man.' Rex stuck his glasses back on. 'Curtis plays chauffeur and bodyguard so that nobody has wondered why he's been everywhere with me these past twenty years, while at the same time, people imagined I was keeping Joy and seeing her behind closed doors, and that's what made Joy comfortable with me. She didn't want a man to love her. All she wanted was a safe hiding place.'

'And what you trying to say she wanted to hide from?' I asked.

'Herself, Curt thought.' Rex got up and sauntered over to the window overlooking the parking lot. 'He would come back from spending an odd afternoon at 76th Street and tell me that Joy had spent the whole afternoon doing this.' Rex let his expression go blank and turned his face to the tall window. 'She'd stare out of a window, unable to speak, unable to move, she was so traumatized, but I could never figure out from what. She was damaged goods and it got worse as she got older which is why I let her believe that she was getting away with a scam on me. I wanted to help her. Do you understand? I didn't *have* to pay her that money every week . . . You want to know how quickly I could have had her ass kicked and grabbed those pictures if I'd wanted to? But I knew that they were safe with her. She wouldn't have sold me down the river. I was her meal ticket and the only friend she had, and she didn't have that much of me.'

'You didn't never have nothing going with her?'

'Nor ever want to, but by tagging on from the beginnning she became like family to me and I enjoyed her being around. I needed friendship. The road can get lonely and the trash that wants to rub shoulders and pick up with you while your're touring is not worth hanging with. To tell truth, Joy provided a service, and in fact, she didn't screw me out of bread like she thought she did. I think I got her on the cheap. It was nice to have such a beautiful woman in tow that didn't want anything from me but a weekly allowance and most of that she spent on clothing for herself, so she looked the part to be seen on my arm when I needed for her to from time to time to lead the press on to the wrong scent.'

'But I still don't see why she had to stay with you. 'Specially if like you say, you was with a man.'

'Come on, little lady. Joy wanted the high life. And for a woman of color, that costs a whole barrel of real live money. Not only did she like expensive things,' said Rex turning away from the window so I could see him better when he talked, 'but what was more important to her was being given the royal treatment when she walked into a restaurant or a hotel lobby, and being black meant that she had to go first class to get the frills usually reserved for blonds,' laughed Rex. 'Particularly when she went with me down South. She was smart enough to realize that, even if she never completely admitted it to herself.

'Joy liked to have the doors open for her. She wanted waiters to scrape and bow when they served her. She wanted people to love her, and Curt summed her up. He said because she had such a low self image, she needed confirmation from the way people treated her that she too had a right to be on the planet. Don't tell me that you didn't know that's what all that charm was about that she played off. She always aimed to win by pleasing and never just relaxed. Joy refused to just be herself. Always smiling and laughing and cajoling people so they would want her around and no sooner than they liked her, she'd run and hide. I think that she was afraid that if she acted normal like the rest of us, nobody would pass the time of day with her. . .' Rex could see that I wasn't buying what he'd said. 'You don't have to believe me, but you come up with an answer as to why, as you yourself said, Joy spent her whole life with me. She knew that all I wanted was Curt, and she never tried to come between us in any way. She liked me being gay, because it let her off the hook . . . Anyway, Baby Palatine, that's enough about Joy,' Rex said, tapping his watch again. 'I'm here for those pictures. Are you gonna hand them over peaceful like?' He juged his hand in his coat pocket to get another cigarette.

I asked Rex if he knew where I might find the pictures he was talking about, 'cause whereas I didn't know whether he was telling the truth or not, I couldn't see why he'd lie about something as off color as that.

'She probably kept them somewhere hidden,' he said. 'You know the combination to get Joy's safe open?' I asked him. 'If them pictures you're so worried 'bout is in there, there ain't no way I can get 'em for you without a combination, and I got to warn you that Tammy's husband said he was gonna try to help her get in there. With him being a ex-cop, maybe he really knows how to do it too. Can't you find you somebody that can crack a safe?'

I didn't want his money but I just wanted to clear up Joy's mess if she made it, and I wasn't even tempted by nary one of them hundred dollar bills in the stacks. Broke as I was, they sure looked good to me, but then so do a fancy hat in Bonwit Teller's that I oogle when I go out window shopping but don't have to have.

Rex closed his eyes like he was tired, turned his head again towards the direction of the window and lit up another cigarette. I didn't have no reason to like him but that didn't stop me feeling sorry for Joy's doing him wrong, and I wanted to right things.

That's what I was thinking when I unfolded that little piece of paper I was playing with. Something said to me – 'check them numbers you found in the Papagallos 'cause they definitely had the dashes in the wrong place for either a phone number or a proper number. I knew not to wait another second and prayed to myself for God to keep Brenda over at the store, and so I fibbed to Rex that he should keep thinking about a safe cracker while I went to the toilet and I got myself up Joy's stairs quick as somebody young.

We used to have a safe to keep the rent collections in, in one of them apartment buildings we managed after we left Grange, so I knew exactly how to work a combination.

The sweat broke out on my forehead and my heart was thumping when I kneeled down in front of the two foot high by two foot wide metal safe that looked out of place in the closet in Joy's pretty bedroom. The rain beat on the window pane and I wished I was out in it, 'cause though I hate the rain I hated even more to be in Joy's bedroom for the reason I was.

Using them numbers on that paper I turned fifteen to the right, and 'round two times to stop at ninety and then 'round to the left twice to click thirty-six and when that door lightly swung open, I wanted to yell like folks do when they win the jackpot on one of them morning game shows on the TV.

There wasn't nothing in there but a brown sealed envelope and my hand went to shaking trying to get it open. I didn't want it to be them pictures of Rex 'cause I wanted him to be lying about Joy taking money off him.

But there they was.

I didn't really want to look at no dirty snaps but I peeked long enough to see him and a colored boy with no clothes on and Rex standing up against a pink wall with the boy squatting in front of him with Rex's whole dingle down his mouth.

I couldn't help but take another good gander though 'cause even at a quick glance that colored boy's sweet young face looked familiar to me. Much as I didn't want to stare at the nasty picture I had to, 'cause right off it come to me that it was Curt, Rex's driver.

I wanted to scream. But there wasn't time for me to think on how I was feeling nor why. I suspect that what made me sicker than seeing Rex naked with a boy was the idea that what Joy did to Rex was worse. 'Cause at least though I can't say I understand it, there was maybe some love in what Rex and Curt was doing.

In all, there was six pictures of Rex with Curt and the strip of negatives was with them. But as I went to put the pictures back in the envelope to hand them over to Rex, I realized there was a couple sheets of paper tucked in there and there was also another snap that was a bit crinkled and in black and white. It wasn't that sharp and I shifted my glasses down my nose a inch so I could take a better look.

I wondered why Joy had put into her safe a picture of Brenda as a little child of five standing with a little boy that didn't look much more than a year or two younger than her. On the back of the picture was hand printed in pencil, 'Delores' little friends, 1952.'

I separated that one from them that was Rex's and shoved the one of Brenda and the boy down my blouse as I slow, step by step, walked downstairs with the brown envelope under my armpit and neatly folded up the two sheets of typewritten paper figuring I'd have a chance to read it once Rex was gone. I shoved them down my blouse too.

He was standing at the bottom of the wooden stairs like I had come down at the same minute he was planning to come up.

'You were a long time,' he said smoothing back his hair.

I didn't answer and handed him the snapshots and the negatives. 'Here you go.'

'I thought you knew where these were all along.' He snatched them from me and stuck them in his coat pocket without even looking and walked over to the table and collected up the three piles of hundred dollar bills and put them back in the padded envelope that they come out of. Something 'bout the way he did it made me realize he didn't have no intention of giving me that $20,000. Not that I was bothered. 'Cause his ol' dirty money wasn't worth the paper it was printed on as far as I was concerned.

He was obviously planning him a quick get away, but a ring of the front doorbell stopped him cold and he looked like a scared rabbit, like he would of broke and run had he had him someplace to run to.

'Don't worry, Mr Scaredy Cat,' I chided. 'That'll be Brenda,' I said going the few steps to the front door.

And I was right. The water was dripping off her Jeri curl but I could tell she wasn't caring.

'Rex is here, isn't he! I saw a limo downstairs and I knew right away it was his.'

'Hey Brenda, man. Long time no see,' said Rex like she was his long lost bosom pal, but I noticed he didn't hug her nor try to take the heavy looking cardboard box off her that she was gripping in both arms like it weighed a ton. That women's liberation stuff has sure messed up a lot that used to happen natural. Like I knew a time when the lowest man wouldn't never stand by like Rex was doing and watch a woman struggle with no big box full of Colt '45 beer.

Brenda looked like she was going to drop it.

'Roll out the red carpet, Baby Palatine. The great man is here,' she said with a crooked smile like somebody back from the dentist. Her lips looked different. Kind of blubbery like they was too relaxed.

What made me saddest about Brenda I realized was that she was still noisy as a circus but that was just a boom in her voice. It wasn't that nice noise that comes from being happy from within.

'I haven't seen you,' Rex said, 'since that party that Dan Lagerfield threw after you got your gold record.'

I remembered the girls' gold record good 'cause for a whole month I had it hanging in my hallway. It was framed and backed on to dark green velvet and the plate inscription on it said 'Presented to Bang Bang Bang for the sale of 500,000 units of Chocolate Chip'.

Brenda thought the thing was real gold and when she went to quit the group, she took it down the pawnshop hoping that she was going to get a lot of money for it. But she said the pawnbroker told her that the record wasn't really worth nothing to him, 'cause who'd want to own somebody else's gold record, and so he didn't give her but fifty bucks for it. I was fit to be tied when I come home and found that Freddie B had let her take it down off the wall 'cause it was as much Joy's as it was hers'n I reckoned.

The day that they got presented with it, Anndora and Brenda wasn't speaking to each other 'cause that mess had come out in the papers about Brenda saying she was a lesbian, and Anndora had the nerve to say that she didn't want to do no publicity for the group until the mess about Brenda died down in case somebody got them mixed up and thought that she was the one that was sleeping with women. It was Danny Lagerfield that finally got Anndora to the party for it and the photo session.

His wallet had her wrapped around his little finger and in a way I was glad to see that somebody for a change was bossing Anndora instead of her bossing them all the time. I think she expected that he would take up with her permanent, but like I told her, 'Don't hold your breath 'cause that rich Jew boy won't be walking down no aisle with nothing but another Jew.' And not but a year later he proved me right of course.

The gold record was more my pride than Joy's 'cause she said what was the point of being a one hit wonder and that if they'd of had any sense they would have put out another record and made all that bad publicity work for them. She didn't think that it should have mattered all that much if the world knew that Brenda was a lesbian or not. Like Joy said, who cared. It was 1977 and seemed like everybody was claiming they was weird in one way or t'other.

I could see how harsh time had been on Brenda when I compared her to Rex and it didn't seem fair that whereas she had more talent in her baby finger than he had in his whole body, he was the one that had creamed off the top of that music business.

Brenda said, 'Rex, you look better as you get older, and the coat is bad, boy.'

Bad meant good the way she said it.

Brenda put the box down on the floor and took the plastic bag out of her blouse. She still had the rain dripping off her and wasn't bothered a bit that it was getting all over Joy's thick expensive pale carpet. It hurt me to see that she made dirty water tracks as she headed for the sofa.

'You can't sit on suede in no wet coat,' I had to remind her. 'Set ch'here,' I said offering her a plastic chair. They wasn't really comfortable but wasn't no way that I was gonna stand by and let her ruin Joy's sofa messing with Rex and them drugs.

Instead of setting she asked Rex to and then she took off her coat and draped it over the other plastic chair that was pushed up against the glass top table.

'You ready for a quick taste?' she asked him.

'Always,' Rex said. He stubbed out his cigarette and pulled out his wallet and I was glad to think that he was gonna pay Brenda right off which maybe meant he wasn't gonna stay long. But all he did was take two crisp single one hundred dollar bills out and roll them into straws, giving one to Brenda. 'Let's check it out,' he told her as she made four neat thin rolls of the white powder on the glass table. No sooner than she had used my green file card that was laying on the table to make the lines straight, her and Rex stuck them $100 straws to their nostrils and bowed their heads to the table to sniff up two rows each. It looked doggone stupid for two grown folks to be doing what they was doing and Rex caught me staring.

'Sorry Ma'am. We should have offered you a line . . . Bad manners,' he said and slapped the back of his hand.

Brenda hooted and some of the white powder blew out her nose. 'That was an expensive laugh,' she said, wiping at each nostril. She looked hard at Rex. 'What's your professional opinion, maestro?' she asked.

'I'll have to have a little think about it,' Rex told her pinching the end of his nose after two big sniffs, ' 'cause there's an abundance of classy stuff in town at the moment, and though I'd like to help you out, I can't make any promises. In any case, I don't think it's worth the sort of price I quoted you over the telephone. That's why I wanted to sample it.' He stood up and said, 'Baby Palatine . . . Brenda. My condolences.'

Brenda seemed dumbstruck.

'I'll be in touch. And even though I won't be in town for Joy's last goodbye, my heart is going to be there for her,' Rex said. 'And of course,

I'll send a bodacious wreath. She loved gardenias but it's the wrong time of year for them, isn't it?' He checked his watch, picked up his hat and bowed low before he clicked the heels of his boots together military fashion.

Then Rex was out the door and gone 'fore Brenda could say Jackie Robinson.

I knew as soon as I heard Joy's front door slam after him that I was bound to be in double trouble 'cause firstly Brenda was sure to be mad that he didn't leave her money that she already had made plans for spending, and secondly I suspected she was high if she wasn't used to all that stuff she had put up her nose.

'Fucking bastard,' was the first words that come out her mouth as she bent over to lift that box she was carrying when she came in to take it to the kitchen. 'I spent almost all my money on beer and that S of a B is stalling on a deal. Did it sound like that to you?'

'Don't draw me into that mess,' I said, 'cause I had already been through enough with Rex and them pictures and was neither ready nor willing to side with Brenda over what was to happen to the stuff in the bag.

I figured that Brenda was so high she hadn't noticed that Rex had left them two $100 straws made of bills by the ashtray and if her money was spent like she said, them two little rolled up pictures of Ben Franklin should of looked like her miracle for the day.

I took 'em in to her in the kitchen.

'Thanks,' she said. Like they was hers.

'You can sound more grateful than that. Whatever happens, that two hundred dollars is probably more than you come with, and you ought to thank the Lord.'

'Fuck the Lord,' she said.

And I jumped right in her face. 'I won't have you blaspheming in here, Brenda. What you just said is a sin and you should ask God's forgiveness.'

'God who? Give me his name and address and I'll remember to send him a full written apology as soon as I get back to the post office.'

'You get that kind of terrible talk from your mama and it don't sound no better coming from you than it used to sound coming from her.'

'And what's wrong with me believing what my mama believes. That's how it's supposed to be. With nosy neighbors or without,' Brenda laid into me.

She wouldn't have said none of it to my face if Joy'd been living.

'It's sure funny that all day you been rising up to defend your mama and when I first come in, you didn't have a nice word to say about her.'

Brenda opened her a can of beer and I knew better than to say anything to her about drinking on top of that drug stuff she'd just filled herself up with.

'Well it makes me furious when you try to talk as though you're better than Mama.'

'I never said that.'

'But you act like it.' Brenda took a long swig. 'And if it hadn't been for you, my mother would probably have been in a lot better shape when we were growing up.'

'You can't blame me for your mama taking to her bed.'

'Who can I blame?'

'Yourself. If anybody was responsible for your mama's so called sickness, Brenda, it was you and that mess with John Dagwood.' I didn't have nothing to lose by hitting her with the truth.

Brenda said, 'I may've made Mama sick, Baby Palatine. But you were the one who kept her that way.'

I wasn't in the mood to have her say nothing spiteful to me, having heard just about enough from Brenda Bang talking through her beer and cocaine, but what she said worried me and I asked her, 'What do you mean, I kept her that way?'

'You were always so much stronger than Mama so you got in her way. All the time. Doing the things for us that she was supposed to do, especially after Dagwood left. And although I guess you didn't do it with malice, you did it all the same. Butting in.'

'Brenda, everybody got a right to their own opinion and I guess that's yours, but from where I was standing I figure I did for y'all things that your mama wasn't willing to do. Raising kids ain't just about teaching 'em how to speak good English and aiming 'em in the direction of the bank. It's loving 'em every day, even when it ain't fun to love, and there was a whole lot of times when there was a lot better things I could of been doing for myself and my husband and my brother or sister, but I did for y'all instead, 'cause you looked like you was needing me.'

'Well,' Brenda said, 'like I said, Baby Palatine, I didn't say you did it with any malice, I just said you did it.' Brenda wasn't gonna be happy that day unless she got my dander up and so I went straight over there to my Bible and had a read of it to lift my spirits up so I could carry on, in spite of her hurtful words. Some folks claim God is a weakness, but I can't see how folks get by with nothing to believe in but what they see. That means all they believe in that ain't on earth is smog.

I was still reading my Bible when Tammy, Jesse and Anndora got back. And I asked right away what had happened at the undertaker's.

'We sorted it out, but for a minute they thought they couldn't get the body on a plane,' said Tammy. I pretended I was glad to hear they got the cremation sorted out.

Brenda was up on the toilet getting rid of some of that beer in her system when they came in and when she come in the living room she eyed Anndora. Sizing her up, tom cat to alley cat. It was just as well that Anndora was staying in a hotel for the night 'cause ain't no telling what would happen with the two of them caught up in the apartment too long together. What made Anndora dangerous was that she looked so harmless.

I figured it was just as well for Anndora that them girls didn't get famous, 'cause she had a haughty enough attitude without the whole world setting her on a pedestal. The thing about Anndora was that she should of been grown in the forties and then probably she could of made something special of her life like one of them Lena Hornes or somebody who didn't look colored and got by on that.

But by the time Anndora was grown it was the sixties and into the seventies and folks was funny about colored people who didn't look it. Being so light skinned you looked white wasn't a big thing no more, and like my baby sister Helen used to ask, 'Where did that leave a colored girl like Anndora that didn't look colored enough?' I felt sorry for Anndora 'cause maybe she couldn't be no better than she was, and although I wanted to think kindly about her, it was hard to because in all the years I'd known her, I couldn't think that I ever saw her do anything nice for anybody except for that very day when she had took it upon herself to make sure she got her sister buried right.

It upset me to see her and Brenda together 'cause it was pitiful sight . . . Sisters not able to speak to one another. Where was the love and sense of duty to kin I used to always tell 'em 'bout when they was on the road. Kin needs to be more than enemies to each other I wanted to tell 'em when I saw them together in Joy's, but I held my tongue and sat down at the dining room table to put my head in my arms the way I had to when I was a little child in first grade and the teacher made us take a nap called our quiet hour. Maybe if we'd of spent more time learning and less sleeping, I mighta learned something.

Next I knew, Jesse was shaking my shoulder and saying, 'Baby Palatine, go upstairs and have a little sleep before dinner.'

'Excuse me,' I said yawning. 'I didn't mean to doze off. I put my head down to have me a think.'

'You're probably too tired to think. Why not go on upstairs and lay down? I'll help you up there,' he said offering me his arm.

'What do I look like,' I asked him. 'Some kinda old fossilly woman? I can climb stairs good as you, thank you very much!' No sooner than the words come out my mouth I realized I had said the wrong thing to a man with a limp, though he didn't take offense and seemed to be somebody that didn't get rustled by nothing. Even tempered, a bit like Freddie B, and I hoped that Tammy knew how lucky she was.

It wasn't but six o'clock when I went for that rest, and just the sight of Joy's extra big bed nearly had me swooning till I saw a gun on the bed in a kinda shoulder holster like something out the movies. I screamed bloody murder 'cause I hadn't never seen one that close up for real and the thing looked alive though it was dead cold to the touch. I was tempted to pick it up but knowing me, it would have probably gone off, so I decided not to handle it.

Even with living in San Francisco me and Freddie don't keep us a gun 'cause I figure I don't know how to use it and if I did, I wouldn't wanna be up shooting nobody. Anyway, Jesse come running up the stairs shouting, 'What's the matter, what's the matter?'

'There's a gun on this here bed,' I said pointing to it like it was dead flesh.

'Don't worry,' he said. 'That's mine.'

If I'd had things my way the whole of America would have to turn in their guns, and I said, 'What ch'you doing carrying a gun?'

'Habit.'

'But you ain't working for the police now, what d'you need it for?'

'Habit, I told you, Baby. Go to sleep and don't worry about it.' He picked up the black leather holster and hung it over his shoulder. 'I didn't mean to scare you. It was wrong for me to leave it here.' He went to lay it on top of the desk and I said, 'I ain't gonna be able to sleep good unless you take that someplace else.' My voice was a bit excitable compared with his that sounded extra relaxed.

'Sure,' he said, picking it up and seeming to look for somewhere else. 'Can I get you something? How would you like a drink or a little snack?'

'No thanks,' I said. 'I just need a sleep,' and I pulled back that fluffy gray eiderdown like them ones we used to get in the hotels in Germany, puffed up thick as a pillow. I pulled that back and climbed under it. Whatever paradise feels like that bed was running it a close second. When I woke up I was glad that I managed to sleep a whole hour without dreaming 'cause it was likely under the circumstances that I may have had me a nightmare.

Downstairs I asked Jesse if he would take a stroll outside with me, while Brenda rustled up something for our supper 'cause I'm used to being in the outdoors living in the warm, and I don't like to stay cooped up in the house all day. It had stopped raining and though there wasn't no place to walk in New York City, air's air, I said to myself and dirty air's better than that you got laying in your lungs with a lot of folks blowing cigarette fumes up the house all day long.

Jesse got his jacket on and watched me struggling to get my right foot in my shoe. It was so swollen I nearly asked Brenda who was preparing something in the kitchen if she had some shoes I could borrow, but I finally got my own on. When we got out in the street I wondered what I was rushing to get out there for. New York City is sure ugly. The people look ugly, a lot of them act ugly, the streets is ugly, the tall brick buildings is ugly and I betcha some of them poor people ain't never even been out of New York to realize that you can live some other place nice. I'm sorry that that's where Joy decided to end up, 'cause when they used to talk about New York being the asphalt jungle they didn't know what they was talking about 'cause at least things can grow in a jungle. Seems like the onliest thing anybody can grow in New York is a fungus.

When I think of all the money that's gone into building them buildings and they ain't nothing but prisons, every single, solitary one of 'em, even them expensive ones that's all locks and bars and bolts, it seems too ridiculous.

Jesse said, 'Everybody, rich and poor, is locked up inside their homes scared to come out, and then when they do they have very good reasons to be petrified to walk on the street.'

Well, I wasn't scared that evening 'cause there I was out with Jesse James O'Mara and even though I could see he didn't have his gun on him, I was stepping light in the street feeling a whole lot freer than when I got off the bus to catch a cab early that morning.

It was mostly an outing to get some fresh air. But 'course, there wasn't none. We breathed in some fumes from the cars bumper to bumper that snail paced along in the rush hour.

Jesse and I didn't go nowhere special but four blocks to a nice store, had a look around and picked up a few magazines, and he said all 'a sudden, 'I'm glad you asked me to come out with you, because Tammy and Brenda are a handful. They've been barking at each other ever since you took your nap.'

We passed a donut store and we went in and ordered some coffee and two custard and two big sugar donuts with apricot jelly in them. We was ready to stay a while, and sat down in a booth by the window. Not that I wanted to see out, 'cause I would have been just as happy to pretend that I wasn't in New York City.

I realized how tired I was when I took the first sip of coffee 'cause didn't seem like I had the energy to swallow.

Jesse said, 'It's wonderful that you took the time to come all the way here from California and although Tammy has had too much on her mind to say thanks, I know she'll get around to it.'

I didn't think he was right. Tammy hadn't never thanked me for nothing and one of the things that hurt was not that she took all I did for granted but that she seemed to want to take and take and never give nothing back. Not that I wanted no gifts or nothing, but a bit of her time and the odd telephone call would have made me happy.

I guess in a way I was jealous that she went off and got hitched up, 'cause she seemed like a stranger living so far away with a man I didn't know. I looked at Jesse eating his donut with a knife and fork, and thought what nice ways he had.

'You happy?' I asked him.

'Relatively.'

'Relatively don't sound bad but it don't sound happy neither.'

Jesse ran his dark brown hand across his white hair before he said, 'Tammy wanted to tell you something, but she's been putting it off because she didn't know how you would take it. But I told her this morning that I didn't think it was fair that you should lose Joyce and not hear what Tammy has to tell you.'

'What is it? Is it something bad. 'Cause if it is, save it. Like the song say, "Don't Nobody Bring Me No Bad News"',' I said trying to muster a smile. ' 'Cause with all I done heard in the last two days, my poor ears is ringing.'

'It's not exactly bad news. It's to do with Joy.'

'What about Joy?' I perked up ready to hear that she wasn't dead after all. 'Did y'all find out there's been a mistake?'

'No, I'm sorry to say,' he said, pushing two bits of donut around the saucer.

'So what then?' It was like he was stalling.

A couple splats of water settled on the donut shop window and I saw a few women start running to get theyselves out of the rain.

I bit into a jelly donut and was well and truly exasperated to discover there wasn't hardly no jelly in it, which I was fixing to go back up to the counter and complain about when Jesse said,

'Joy was a twin, Baby Palatine.'

I stopped chewing and held my breath waiting on him to say something else but he didn't.

'What done happened to her twin sister?' I asked hoping while I waited for Jesse to answer that he was gonna tell me where I could find Joy's other half.

'It was a boy.'

'A boy? A brother? Why didn't she tell me?'

Me and Joy had a whole lot of secrets and it hurt me to my heart to think that she had kept such a big one from me and then I remembered that I had stuck that picture and the two page letter that I'd found in the safe down my undershirt.

'Will you 'scuse me,' I asked Jesse. 'I gotta go to the toilet. I'll be back in two shakes.'

'You're not upset are you?' It was sure nice the way he was always wanting to know if I was okay, and I had to smile.

'It takes a lot to shake me up, Mister,' I said and I meant it. I reckon losing Daddy and then my brothers dying and then my mama and trying to raise Helen and Caesar when I wasn't but a sprite had toughened me up for the rest of my life, which is what makes them real hard times worth the suffering.

In the toilet I reached down my blouse and was worried for a second when I couldn't find that picture and piece of paper. With my roll-on being so stiff I could of been carry a whole filing cabinet and wouldn't have felt nothing.

The overhead florescent light reflected so on the snap that I couldn't see the face of the little boy in the picture with Brenda and I angled it to get a better look before I unfolded the businesslike typed letter that was in that brown envelope I'd found in Joy's safe.

In bold face it said across the top:

*Statement Given to Detective O'Mara, Chicago P.D. by Dolores Merriweather*

It had a date stamped in ink on it but I couldn't make out what it said. It looked like June something but I couldn't tell if it was 1983 or 1985.

I ain't quick at reading so rather than standing on my feet which was pinching anyway in my red pumps, I sat my behind down on one of the two toilets.

The statement went:

Mr Bang said he only ever wanted sons. So Joy's twin brother Jackie was their father Sherman's favorite. That's why I wasn't surprised that both Brenda and Joy were jealous of the attention and presents Mr Bang brought for Jackie but not his other two. I think it was the reason Joy heckled and punched her brother all the time, but their mother thought it was a rivalry that would pass.

She was always reminding her husband that he should treat all their three little children the same. 'Especially the twins,' she used to say. 'The twins can't be shown favoritism.'

Brenda was in first grade and the twins went for a few hours to morning nursery when their mother fell pregnant. It was her fourth time. She'd had difficulties with the third birth and the baby boy was stillborn. Mr Bang was really disappointed and to make sure that there wasn't another miscarriage he made a big effort to allow Mrs Bang time to take things easy and have afternoon naps believing that minding Brenda, Joy and Jackie could be left to him. But he wasn't good at it, because he'd suffered from depressions that would slip up on him and he'd have his dark moods without any warning. Mrs Bang said it was nothing to worry about and that he'd had them ever since him and her met at their orphanage when they were in their teens.

But whereas she could normally coax him out of them, she didn't have enough energy while she was lying in pregnant, and she had to leave him to his own devices with the children. Some Saturday afternoons he took them to the playground around the corner from their house and that's where he and the three children were that May afternoon when the accident happened. I always say accident, because nobody knows what really happened.

Brenda was way over on the swings and the twins were on the big slide. Mrs Bang never let them get on the big one. She said it was too high for four year olds, but Mr Bang never watched the kids as close as his wife did. I know because sometimes I was there with my little sister and would see him reading the paper when he should have had his eye on his three.

Whatever Jackie did, Joy always liked to prove that she could do better, and Mr Bang said he was watching them out of the corner of his eye while they vied to be the first one to slide down. Jackie rushed up the steep steps of the slide first. I wondered if he had looked back to tease her when he got to the top, because I'd seen him do that a couple times on the little slide when I'd had them at the playground. I always wanted to ask Mr Bang if that was the reason Joy pushed Jackie. But all Mr Bang knew was that he saw Jackie drop head first, ten feet to the ground.

The little boy was dead before the ambulance came.

The news sent Mrs Bang into premature labour and Anndora was born that evening, but Mr Bang didn't even go to the hospital to see his wife because he slumped into a depression that he never recovered from. I had to take care of the kids that day, and I saw how Joy suffered. While her mother was rushed into hospital and her brother was buried within three days, Joy changed.

Mrs Bang said the social worker warned her that a dead twin leaves a shadow. It seemed to me that Joy suffered too much. But I was too young to say anything like that to Mr and Mrs Bang and Joy was too small to express herself. So her father's explanation as to what happened left them all to believe that Joy wilfully killed Jackie, though once I heard Mrs Bang say she didn't want to believe that Joy thought it out before she pushed Jackie off the slide.

Mrs Bang had her hands too full to see to Joy. And I don't think Mr Bang was altogether wrong when he said his wife used their new baby as a way of avoiding him. In the midst of this chaos, Joy, tiny as she was, realized that the best way to get her mother's attention was to shower love on to her baby sister, and I think love and charm grew in her mind as a form of deceit, so within a year she was as masterful as a Fuller brush salesman at sweet smiles and compliments and good manners. I also saw how Joy mistook her father's long depression as something directed at her, so she avoided her daddy.

Although the Bangs had a small circle of friends before Jackie died, Mr Bang's depression drove everybody away. I was the only person that used to go to their house and I only went to babysit, and Mrs Bang soon discovered that they only had each other, since neither of them had any natural family. Mrs Bang told me before they moved that she hoped a change of location, house and job for Mr Bang might lift him out of his depression and the memories of Jackie, and save their marriage. And she made a household rule that Jackie and all mention of him had to be forgotten. It didn't work at first and then one afternoon she got really mad and she burned every photograph that included him in it. She got in such a fury that Mr Bang didn't try to stop her rushing around the house finding every picture she could. But in so doing part of Joy got destroyed. She was in every picture taken of Jackie, and as he was erased and forgotten, part of her was too.

I spent a couple odd weekends with the Bangs after they moved to Wilmington, Delaware and life got off to a sluggish start, although both Mr and Mrs Bang found well paid jobs in a shipyard with her working as a stenographer and him as a stocktaker in the yard. Anndora went to a day care center and the two bigger girls were both in elementary school.

I think that the three little girls thrived in the house in Wilmington. They had their own backyard to play in, and even Brenda who'd had difficulties making friends found playmates in the neighborhood. But tragedy struck again after they'd been in Wilmington less than a year when a haul of cargo dropped from a lift and killed Sherman instantly. But to tell the truth I think Mrs Bang felt what I heard Anndora say, 'I'm glad Daddy's not coming home again. He wasn't any fun.'

Mr Bang had no insurance and the only compensation Mrs Bang got for his death came from the shipyard owners who claimed that he had been standing in an off-limits zone which is why he wasn't eligible for a huge settlement.

My family moved to Princeton a couple months after that but I heard that there was enough money to bury him and pay off their debts for the furniture and let her pay four months' rent in advance so she could stop work and take stock of her life.

'Mrs Bang was angry at how Mr Bang's accident had been treated so she decided not to continue work at the shipyard, because there was bad feeling about the payout on her husband's life. She always said that had he been white, she would have got more, and she took the advice from a girl in the typing pool who had an aunt in Oakland, California, who suggested that Mrs Bang make a move West, where job prospects were better. The last time I saw her she said she had enough to buy plane tickets and new clothes for herself and the children and pay for some psychiatric sessions that the school recommended for Joy who seemed happy enough, but refused to go into the playground with the other children. But I remember that to get Joy to go to school at all after they moved to Wilmington, Mrs Bang had to promise Joy that she wouldn't tell the school about Jackie. And Joy had to make a promise too. That she would be perfectly behaved and do everything she was told.

I lost touch with them after that what with nursing school and moving to Ohio and all the rest of it, so I was sure glad after I saw you in Princeton when Joy phoned me. Like I said to her, I only had one photograph with Jackie in it and I was sorry I couldn't give Joy what she really wanted which was a picture of Joy with her brother. I think it's really good that she wants to find out about her past and if you need to contact me again, I'll try to help.

I folded the pieces of paper back up and stared hard at the photograph. One of my tears plopped down on it and I was glad and lucky that it didn't fall on the little boy's face. I tried to see Joy in his smile but they wasn't identical. He looked more like Brenda.

Lord only knows what Jesse must of thought had happened to me in there and I wasn't surprised when the teenage waitress come in to ask after me.

'You okay, Ma'am? That fella you left waiting at the table for you is a little worried I think.'

I didn't answer.

I wanted my husband, 'cause I was confused and ain't nobody in the world better than Freddie B for sorting me out when I get muddled.

I smiled at the girl and asked if she would give me her arm to lean on to walk me back to Jesse. It wasn't but fifty steps but my heart was beating fast and I couldn't catch my breath good.

'Do you need a doctor, Ma'am? You don't look so good.'

I felt a hot flush come over me as she said it and I broke out into a cold sweat so that she took a paper towel and patted it on my face and forehead.

'You want some water?'

I said, 'No thanks, Hon. I'll be fine in a couple minutes. Maybe it was that apricot donut I ate, 'cause I ain't used to no store bought cakes. And by the way, ain't y'all a bit stingy with the apricot jam!'

She flushed pink.

'Ain't no use you being embarrassed 'cause you just work here and it ain't like I'm a regular customer that you got to worry about.'

We took short steps to get to where Jesse was sitting and when I got to the table, I laid down both the picture and the statement by his cup of coffee.

'What on earth happened to you? The color's gone out of your face.'

I pushed the paper and picture closer to him and he picked them both up.

'So Joy did let you see these. I told her to and that it wouldn't change how you felt about her. She was worried about that when she came to me a couple years ago and asked me to put a trace on a Delores Merriweather in Princeton. She was in therapy and said that her doctor thought that it was important for her to know something about her early childhood which she had blanked out.'

'What did it have to do with you. Why's your name on it?' I asked Jesse, 'cause as far as I knew, Joy wasn't all that taken with him.

'Joy came to visit once in Richmond, and I was asking her about when she was a little girl and she had a complete blank about her early years which worried me, because I noticed a few years ago when Tammy and I started going together that there weren't any pictures of Joy although she had a lot of her other two when they were small.'

While he was talking, I thought about that first set-to that I'd had with Tammy and how it didn't never sit good with me then nor afterwards that Joy seemed left out.

'Anyway, she told me that you had bumped into a woman somewhere in Princeton, New Jersey, who claimed to know the family and thought that Joy was a twin, but Joy was afraid to ask her mother if she knew this woman. So I put a search out on her through a friend of mine that's a detective in Newark. And one weekend, I took off and went to Princeton to speak to her on Joy's behalf, because Joy somehow was afraid to do it herself. She was a strange girl in many ways, and after I interviewed Delores Merriweather, I realized why. In part anyway, because I suppose nobody understood Joy. But the one thing that Delores Merriweather said that I'm sure is true is that the four-year-old Joy must have been devastated by the loss of Jackie without being able to reason why.'

The rain kept coming down and I sat silent with the smell of sugar and fresh coffee hanging over me and Jesse and making it seem impossible that whereas the smell should of made me feel like I was in a fairground or some kind of sweet smelling Disneyland, I was setting there in a hell that my mind and Jesse's words and that statement from Delores Merriweather had made for me.

'Joy was trying to get help and help herself, Baby Palatine which is why I told her that you of all people needed to know more about her. But she didn't want that, I guess. She said that you saw only good in her and she didn't want to destroy that illusion.'

'It wasn't just no illusion. My God-sent child was kind hearted and I saw her for what she was. I wouldn't have cared about nothing that she did by mistake when she wasn't but four. What kind of mess would the world be in if God punished us all our lives for what we did when we wasn't nothing but babies.'

Jesse rubbed at his face and shut both eyes for a minute, not like he was tired but like he was thinking deep. Then he beckoned for the tab, but the waitress was so busy pouring coffee for a young Puerto Rican couple at another table, she didn't take no notice and me and Jesse just sat stiller than still till he reached for my hand that was laying limp on the table. I was numb all over and couldn't feel nothing when he got hold of it, though I could see my hand was in his when he said, 'You didn't completely get rid of all the smell from the rag I saw you carry out to the trash this morning, did you? I'm sorry that you had to deal with that, but I had used it to wipe something up that I spilled on the kitchen floor, and no sooner than I was finished, I could hear Brenda trying to open Joy's front door. So I threw the rag in the back of the closet and made my way back to Joy's bedroom where I'd left Tammy sleeping.'

I was too muddly headed already to make sense of what Jesse was saying and that rag was the last thing on my mind, but he wouldn't let it rest.

'I was worried that Brenda would ask me questions that I didn't want to answer if she caught me with that rag. To tell the truth I'm at a loss to know why Joy had that kind of stuff in the apartment anyway.'

I drew my hand away. 'What kind of stuff?'

'A substance that drug dealers used for testing the quality of certain drugs . . .'

I could tell from the way he said it that he was fixing to harp on it and I didn't need to hear no more and flashed him one look that said exactly that. He took the hint.

'Joy loved you, Baby Palatine. That's the only reason that I think that she didn't want you to find out about her past,' Jesse said. Then he stood up and helped me to stand. 'I think we better get back home, don't you?'

Walking back to Joy's a fella passed us in the street who was in a fancy wheelchair that he must of had in high gear 'cause it was moving a pace along East 23rd Street. He was kinda fat and had on a old dirty white T-shirt and torn air force jacket and I was sorry to see that he didn't have but one arm and one foot was missing and he had a star tattooed on his forehead. He was shouting, 'The time is nigh, you bastards, the time is nigh.' He wasn't old enough to be in no wheelchair. Nor did he look like he had spent his whole life setting in one, so I took him to be a Vietnam veteran. That poor child was crazy mad. Frenzied and on the edge like folks get when they been under strain too long.

He almost drove over Jesse's foot and hollered about what he was gonna do to him. Jesse laughed at him and saluted as that poor child rode on past us, fast as a little old sports car driving up on a sidewalk still screaming, 'The time is nigh, the time is nigh', and I wanted to shout 'Amen' 'cause I knew just how he was feeling and suspected like Jesse said that he was screaming about being broke and limbless and probably hopeless.

Brenda had gone to a whole lot of trouble fixing a meal, so when me and Jesse got back, I didn't like to tell her that I didn't feel up to eating nothing which is why I set myself down at the table with everybody else.

The spaghetti and great big tossed salad and Italian garlic rolls was laid out proper, and when we all started eating, I realized that it was the first time that the five of us acted like we was all part of the same family. And even though there was a atmosphere between the three Bang women, things felt half way right.

I kept my head bowed and tried not to take no notice of the fact that wasn't nobody speaking to each other. The quiet was nerve raking, and I didn't blame Tammy for taking a long sigh of relief when Jesse piped up and said he wanted to tell about the first time he saw Joy.

He said she was in a two piece tailored gray and black herringbone suit and some black patent leather stiletto heels and black stockings. 'When she came walking through our door in Virginia I could see what Tammy looked like when she was young as clear as day. There was Joy dressed up to the nines, you know how she dressed like somebody stepping straight out of *Vogue* magazine. "Suitcases in the car?" I asked her.

'Well I went out to grab the cases and boy, that car was loaded up with more gardenia plants. So I told her, "That automobile of yours will smell like gardenias for the rest of its natural life." Joy laughed. She knew her mother loved gardenias and since Mother's Day was coming up she bought a whole lot of 'em to plant in our quarter acre. "What's the shovel for?" I asked noticing the one she had on her back seat. "I didn't know if you had one," she said.

' "Hey, daughter, I'm a gardener from way back, I haven't been hanging loose for two years of my retirement for nothing."

'As soon as I got Joy's bags in the house she asked me if I had a pair of galoshes. I said, "What for?" "So I can start digging. These poor things have been in the car for seven hours. They're dying for some fresh air and water and dirt."

' "Don't worry about that," I said. "Have something to eat first." She wasn't interested.

'Remember, Tammy?' Jesse reach over and touched Tammy's hand. 'I bet the neighbors couldn't believe it . . . Joy . . . Dressed fine as a Paris fashion model except for my size eight galoshes that swallowed up her neat feet and she got into the garden and started digging. We couldn't get her in,' Jesse laughed.

'Night had fallen by the time she'd finished. I don't know how she did it, she didn't get any dirt on that expensive suit of hers and when we woke up the next morning that front lawn looked like gardenia heaven because several of the ones she brought were already in bloom. They're still growing and flowering and when the breeze blows in that scent is so strong all I can think about is Joy. I love sitting on the front porch when that perfume fills our garden first thing in the morning. But the nicest part of that Mother's Day weekend was that Joy bought her mother a Nat King Cole album. Do you remember that, Tammy?'

'I still play it,' Tammy added.

'It was an old one of his original 1956 recordings. So when I came down to breakfast the following morning, Joy was already down there,' Jesse went on. 'She had the table laid and coffee brewing, and I asked her, "How d'you find your way around the kitchen?"

' "Pretty easy," Joy said to me, "but I can't find your stereo. Don't tell me you don't have one, Jesse!"

'She said, "I have something to play for Mama when she comes down." She put that Nat King Cole album on and played "Blue Gardenia" and it was the sweetest sound. It was the most enjoyable three days I think we've ever spent. She had such a sweet heart that girl. A heart of gold.'

I had tears running down my cheeks when Jesse finished. He was talking about the Joy I knew. Tammy was smiling too when he finished. Then she told about when Joy was five years old.

'Joy used to go out with Brenda and her father and make a choo-choo train with a bunch of cardboard boxes in the garden. You remember that Brenda?' asked Tammy. Brenda said she didn't.

'Anyway,' Tammy said, 'they used to make a choo-choo train out in the garden or a tent. As little as Joy was, she was good at making things. Making up stories was what she did best . . . But she'd make a good tent by hanging a blanket over the clothes line in the backyard and she'd pretend that they were Indians, she and Brenda. Princess Summer Fall Winter Spring, Joy said she was. You know, from the puppet on *Howdy Doody Show*? She'd sit in the tent and make up fantastic stories which she would tell to anybody. One day when she came in to have her lunch from playing out in one of those tents, I asked "What do you think you're gonna be when you grow up? Some kind of storyteller?"

' "No," Joy said to me, "I don't want to tell stupid stories."

'I said, "Well what do you think you're gonna be? A teacher?"

'Joy told me, "When I grow up I'm gonna be white," ' Tammy said.

I had to laugh at the way Tammy told it and I said, 'Joy told me the same. I told her don't hold your breath.' We all laughed till we cried. Not mournful neither which was good.

'Sherman came in from work at that moment and I told him what Joy'd just said and he laughed at her too, not in a mean way but still Joy cried herself to sleep that night. It was like I'd broken a dream of hers. She didn't ever mention it again and it was one of those stories you don't like to remind kids of when they get big, but I can see her as clear as day sitting at our formica kitchen table.

'Brenda was still out in the garden playing in their tent, waiting for Joy to come out with some cheese sandwiches, but Joy asked me to take them, because she needed to do something. She stayed with Anndora all afternoon. Playing with her and brushing her hair.' Tammy turned to Anndora. 'She always loved to comb your hair. Thinking about it, Joy never really accepted that she couldn't be white and said when she got older that white was a state of mind. Remember?' she asked me direct. 'She always lived like a white girl and believed that she could convince the world she was worth as much as any of them. That's what I thought the Rex Hightower affair was about. Joy . . . determined to notch the richest hillbilly in the world to her belt. I never believed she loved him. I guess that makes her sound heartless but I saw her charm people when she wasn't old enough to know what charm was.'

I didn't like the way Tammy's story fitted what Rex had said, but I hadn't told her yet that Rex had been and wasn't about to ruin our nice dinner by letting on.

Instead I asked if it could be my turn to tell something 'cause I remembered how good Joy had been the time a boyfriend of my baby sister's named Harold Tate had got drug out of my place late one night by the police claiming he was a Black Panther. It must of been around 68 or 69 and there was a whole bunch of them Panthers that used to hang out over by the launderette on a week night. That's where they got theyselves organized for marches and whatnot and whereas Harold Tate used to sho'nuff pop over to the launderette to swig him a drink, wasn't no way in the world he would of put on no black beret and no black jacket and that and be marching nowhere. You couldn't get him to march to the toilet let alone march down the street. All he was interested in was staggering to the liquor store. I'd of been glad to see he'd got in the Black Panthers, might have made him at least concentrate on something for five minutes. Anyway, the police realized when they got him down to the police station that they had made them a mistake. They sent him back on the bus. No apology, nothing. And so Joy wrote 'em a long letter saying that she was gonna complain to our city councilman about how Harold had been manhandled at the station and come back with two cuts and a bruise on his face.

'That letter of her'n brought him some compensation. It wasn't but fifty dollars but that was enough for him and Helen to get high for a week. And I was real proud of Joy. 'Member how she didn't stand for no mess?'

Didn't nobody laugh when I told it because I ain't no good at storytelling, but I knew how funny it was at the time that Joy got us some compensation for that old wine-o Harold.

Anndora lifted her goblet of wine high in front of her and said, 'Cheers. Here's to Joy. I hope she chokes, wherever she is,' and smiled before she took a halfway curtsy and sat down. The rest of us was dumbfounded that whereas we was telling nice stories that she could say something vicious like that.

She told about how she used to go over to Joy's every weekend during tenth grade and Joy had her fixed up with some Oakland college boys and that while Anndora said at first she thought a couple of them liked her, it didn't take her long to realize they were only interested in weekend sex romps which she provided though Joy didn't. I couldn't believe it and I didn't wanna hear it and I was surprised that Tammy sat there and let that child tell that lie on her sister. Poor Jesse was so shocked, he actually had his mouth dropped open the whole time she was talking and Tammy cleared her throat umpteen times but didn't say a word to stop Anndora so it was me that finally said, 'Anndora, why you wanna tell that lie on your sister?' I didn't see why we had to set and listen to lies.

'It's not a lie,' she said. 'It's as true as the fact that you and Joy bundled me down to Tondalayah's for that abortion thinking that somebody on the TV show got me pregnant. I knew that the only guys I had been with were the ones Joy set me up with, and did you know at the time when I got so sick afterwards that that abortion tore into my ovaries so I'll never be able to have children? . . . So fuck Joy, and fuck you for making the world think that she was so wonderful.'

When Tammy interrupted to say, 'That's no way to talk to Baby Palatine. Apologize!' Anndora came back with 'Our family was never allowed to be a family because of her.'

'Anndora, tell her you're sorry that you just said that.' Tammy looked over at me and I was biting my lip to hold back the tears 'cause I didn't want Anndora to see me upset and get satisfaction out of talking bad to me.

'I'm glad I've finally said it,' Anndora piped in, 'and why don't we drink a toast to the happiest days of my life when mother moved away from Oakland with Baby Palatine kissing Joy's behind and always treating Joy like she was so perfect so that Joy got away with murder.' Anndora got tearful. 'She and Danny Lagerfield were the ones that got me involved in this,' she said, and yanked back the sleeve of her dress. Her skinny little arm was a terrible sight of long black marks.

'Damn,' Brenda said. 'What the hell happened?'

Anndora didn't bother to answer and continued her tirade. 'You're always talking about Joy like she's some kind of saint.' She was shaking she was in such a fury and didn't none of us try to stop her. It was like them tantrums she used to have when she was a bitty girl and couldn't nobody control her but Joy. 'I've spent my whole life trying to get out of the deep shit that Joy always dragged me into for a quick dollar while you turned a blind eye to it . . . Well it's all right for your dear sweet innocent Joy who took her quick exit and left me behind to deal with this mess.'

'What mess are you talking about?' I tried to ask her but she wasn't to be interrupted and her anger threw either fear or spell over them other three 'cause didn't one of them try to shut her up which made it seem like they was agreeing with what Anndora was saying to me. Brenda hadn't been as quiet all day.

'If I'm not smiling,' Anndora smirked, 'it's because I have a right to be mad. Heart attack. What fucking heart attack! I bet I could tell the coroner in Santa Fe exactly what pills she took. Heart attack? How could she have a heart attack when she had no heart. Joy killed herself and all of you might as well hear about it now. She couldn't live with her guilt.' Anndora picked up the wine bottle and poured out the last of it into her glass. Jesse had his head in his hands.

'She and Danny got me hooked up with some guy who got me strung out and I started paying for my habit by making their European deliveries. God, was she clever, Joy, because while she watched me ruin my life she never bothered with the shit herself.' Anndora looked at me. 'If she was so wonderful, don't you think it might have been nice if she had spared me?'

I just sat there. I wasn't crying or upset or nothing. And just as I looked over at Anndora and said, 'That's a lie and it's a disgrace you could tell a bareface lie like that on your sister when we're about to put her in her grave,' something happened that I wouldn't of never expected. Brenda sided with Anndora.

'Thank God somebody has finally uncovered that lie you built up,' she told me.

'Listen y'all, I come to New York City to do one thing and one thing only and that was to see Joy buried,' I said to everybody at the table. 'I didn't come here to argue with y'all or to rake over the old ugly mess that y'all been hiding all these years. I don't see no point in even talking about it, 'cause far as I'm concerned, it don't mean nothing now.'

'Why not, because you don't want it to,' asked Tammy wincing. 'I'm horrified. You could have come to me, Anndora. I mean about being pregnant. You could have told me,' Tammy sobbed. 'How old were you?' Jesse didn't budge but stared over at his wife.

'You let Baby Palatine take over,' Anndora said, 'and I never trusted her or you, because Joy had you both so convinced that she was an angel.'

Brenda stood up. 'Okay, Anndora. Now it's my turn because I have something to say that I've been dying to get off my chest.' Her speech was slurred and I was sorry to have to see her losing control. 'We had a game called truth or consequences, dare or repeat, that we always played that first spring that we lived on Grange. Anndora was too small to play and it was usually Joy, me, Sarah Jane and a couple girls that lived around the corner. We'd sit in a circle at the back of the gravel parking lot and whoever was "it" would have to tell the truth, take a dare, take the consequences or repeat anything stupid that one of us told them to. Everybody seemed to have their regular preference like Sarah Jane used to always like to take truth, so anything you asked her she had to tell you the truth about. Like somebody might say "Sarah Jane, did you ever see your sister Jeanette sleeping with a boy?" She couldn't lie. I never understood why she liked to take truths,' laughed Brenda suddenly 'because everybody always asked her questions about her sisters and their boyfriends having sex. Being biggest I felt bravest and used to always like to take dare. Most of the time the others gave me silly dares like "go say a curse word at some old woman or other" or "steal some candy from the drugstore". But the night that school had closed for the summer we had a really long game because we were all allowed to stay out late for a change. And our little game of truth or consequences took a real heavy duty turn that night when Sarah Jane had to give me a dare and she had dared me that I wouldn't get under the sheets and suck John Dagwood's cock while he was sleeping.' Brenda laughed and I was scared to even look over in Tammy's direction. 'I think Sarah Jane had an obsession with your old man,' she said to Tammy. 'Joy was there when I took the dare. She promised Sarah she'd be the one who would watch to see if it actually happened and whereas everybody else forgot about the dare and the game, Joy kept saying to me over that whole following day, "When are you gonna do it?" Well I couldn't go back on a dare you know, because when you're a kid things like that're important, so I said, "Well, we'll have to wait till he's at home and Mama's gone", but I said that 'cause I didn't ever believe that would happen. He always took Mama to work didn't he, Mama.' Her voice went a bit husky but she sounded babyish and when she wiped the corners of her eyes I thought she may have been wiping tears but didn't none fall.

'I'd never seen Dagwood in the house let alone in the bed, when Mama was gone, and Joy couldn't wait the day Mama went out and left Dagwood. I was sitting in the living room watching cartoons on the television that morning as Mama carried Anndora out with her. I used to love those stupid game shows that came on in the morning, like the one with the heart line, remember?' Her mind had drifted off and for a second I thought she might forget to finish telling what she'd started, or was I hoping Tammy would shut her up? But Tammy was frozen, I reckon.

Brenda went on, 'Joy came in and said, "Okay Brenda, now's your chance", and I was feeling a bit chicken and I wasn't willing to do it, because in the cold light of day, kid or no kid, I knew that the game was over and the dare wasn't worth anything to anybody. But Joy said, "I'm gonna tell everybody if you don't." I wish you could have seen her face. Sometimes I think Joy was evil, Baby Palatine.'

'What you do to folks they do to you, and since I don't have nothing in my heart for Joy but love, that's all I got back,' I told her. Everybody wanted to lie on my God-sent child because she was dead. 'It's like you're all claiming now everything that's ever gone wrong with your lives was down to Joy,' I hollered. 'Anndora was selling dope 'cause of Joy . . . Anndora was selling herself 'cause of Joy . . . Anndora can't have a baby 'cause of Joy. Next thing you'll be telling me, you was born ugly 'cause of Joy.'

Brenda looked hurt and I was ashamed I had said what I'd said, but before I could get out a 'I'm sorry', Tammy took over by standing up. I figured that the mention of John Dagwood had her upset and that probably Jesse hadn't never heard the name mentioned and didn't fear it like I did.

But for a minute Tammy looked over at me like what she was about to say was only meant for me. I had already heard too much and my ears as well as my mind was numb from the terrible things that I had

had to listen to about Joy when she wasn't there to defend herself. It didn't seem fair, but I knew better than to stand up to all three Bang women, 'cause I didn't have strength to do it even when I was younger.

Tammy picked up a cigarette and stuck a filter on the end of it before she lit up. My back was to the window, but the room was so silent for that minute that I could hear the rain start up again and beat on the window. Brenda had turned Joy's living room lights to dim when she set the table, and I wanted to turn them on full, 'cause I had a feeling that it was the shadows in the room that made everybody act so strange and talk so bad and not be able to think on nothing bright and positive.

'Jesse,' Tammy said, 'I'm sorry that you've had to hear all of this, and I don't want you to think that I let all of it happen because I just didn't care about my children. Maybe the truth is that I cared too much, but I was young and alone and until I made friends with Baby Palatine, the whole thing of being in a strange town without my husband got on top of me. We had been together since we were sixteen and even though a lot of people couldn't understand why I stayed with Sherman when he was so often depressed, he was all the family I felt I had when we were in the orphanage, and I really felt responsible for him and loved him.'

She took a draw off her cigarette and looked in Anndora's direction. 'You never knew your father properly, Anndora, but in spite of what he did, I never want you to think that he wasn't a wonderful person.'

Anndora didn't look up and it was Brenda that said, 'What do you mean, what he did.'

Tammy let out a deep sigh and touched Jesse's arm. 'He poisoned my mind so about Joy, that I was afraid of her.'

I couldn't hear no more and didn't care what she had to say, and although my legs felt weak under me, I decided to get up and clear the table.

'Don't bother with those,' Jesse said to me. 'Listen to what Tammy has to say to you.' His voice was soft and soothing and I knew that whereas he meant to be nice, I was too on edge to set there a minute longer without screaming.

I moved around the table like I was in a dream and Tammy went on talking though I was going in and out of the kitchen that wasn't but a few steps away from where she was standing at the end of the table. It was a relief to be on my feet 'cause I had been setting like a zombie after Anndora and Brenda got through saying what they had.

'Because Sherman had problems, I always suspected when I was carrying one of his children that his mental anguish would pass on to one of them, and I prayed and prayed that our babies would be spared his dark moods that crippled him without any warning. So don't think, Baby Palatine, that I was godless until Joy did something that I still can't bring myself to talk about.'

Brenda threw back her head and closed her eyes and her face looked to me again like that statue that Toni had got for me at Fisherman's Wharf. One long tear leaked from her closed lids.

'When we moved to California, I was lost and didn't know how I was going to manage to do what I had promised Sherman while he lived which is that I would see to it that I'd send Joy away. To protect Brenda and Anndora he said it had to be done, but I just couldn't bring myself to do it, and inasmuch as I had grown up without a family and had lived my whole life in an institution, so the thought of any of my children having to go through that was too awful. So in spite of the procedures that Sherman had started in Wilmington to have Joy taken from us and put into a special home, I was determined after his death to keep my children with me. And I had hoped that by moving to California not only would I get rid of the social workers that were assigned to us and wouldn't let us alone after the accident . . .'

'What accident,' asked Anndora. 'Daddy's accident?'

'No,' said Tammy. 'We had another accident in our family. Is there any more wine in the bottle, Jesse?' she said and passed him her empty glass as I cleared the rest of her place, feeling empty headed and glad for the mercy of something to do.

If I hadn't of seen me that statement Jesse'd got off Delores Merriweather, what Tammy was about to say would of probably given me a heart attack, but I was readied and repeating in my head the 23rd Psalm the whole while I was lifting dirty dishes off the table which gave me greater strength than I knew I had.

'Jackie.' I heard Brenda whispering as I got to her place. Four empty beer cans was piled near her salad bowl and I figured that with all that was in her system she should of been too drunk to stand up. But she wasn't.

'Joy had a twin brother, Anndora. And I'm sorry that I was never able to bring myself to tell you about him, because he was such a wonderful little boy and we all loved him, didn't we Brenda?'

'Oh Mama,' Brenda whispered as she folded her arms around herself and started rocking, gently back and forth like you see them old women do in their porch chairs to bring theyselves some comfort.

'Jackie was four when he died and you were born that night of the accident.'

I could see that with the upset of the rest of dinner and maybe 'cause of the wine she had been drinking, Anndora looked halfway in a stupor, but she screamed at her mother, 'What fucking accident? What are you talking about?'

'Joy pushed Jackie off a slide,' Tammy managed to say, staccato like the words just didn't want to come out. 'And there was no way for us to know whether she did it on purpose or not. Whether she wanted to destroy him or not. She was so jealous of him and all the attention that your father gave him.'

'Jackie,' I heard Brenda whispering again and again under her breath as she rocked back and forth and even in the dim lights I could see, though he had his face down, that there was confusion on Jesse's face.

I knew that what Tammy had started shouldn't have been said under the circumstances of everybody being strained from the long day what with Joy's dying and the funeral, but I knew better than to say anything, 'cause from the way Brenda and Anndora had talked to me, they didn't think I was worth listening to no way.

'That's why when we moved to Grange I was so relieved when Baby Palatine took an interest in Joy. I know that you thought, Baby, that you were stealing Joy away from us, but in fact you were doing us all a favor, because I was afraid of Joy, didn't know how to handle her and the reason that I never moved from that hole in the wall of an apartment of Houseman's was because of you and the relationship you had with her. I was glad that you loved her and trusted her, because in a way you were the only one that could, knowing nothing about her as you did.'

'It was wrong of you not to tell me about what had happened at that time, Tammy,' I butted in. 'It wasn't that it would of changed nothing, but I had a right to know.'

333

'I was afraid if you knew that you would have been as wary of Joy as I was. And she needed somebody, anybody to want her.'

'What are you trying to say?' I asked her.

'That you didn't steal Joy. I was relieved everytime she walked out of our house and into yours, because I was afraid of her and what she might do to the other two children.'

I sat down and felt my stomach churn upside down 'cause I could see little Joy in my mind strutting 'round my living room in them Papagallo shoes and most times, always sooner than she was ready, I would make her scurry off across the hall 'fore Tammy got back from work. Though Joy always seemed to want to stay in my place and would hover about my apron strings and would find her any excuse to be with me and Freddie B. But it didn't seem right to keep her from her mama even though I did it anyhow a lot of the time. I used to try to send her home, after she was sat for a couple of hours in my place and it made me sick to think that whereas my mind was always telling me to hug her and hold on to her, I didn't at the time 'cause I was feared that was part of the special love she needed to get from her mama and that was her mama's territory.

'Damn, this is some heavy shit,' said Brenda getting up to go over to the record player. 'This is getting like a real life version of truth or consequences, isn't it. Anybody mind if I put on a record? God. I can't take any more of this without some music.'

'As long as it's something quiet,' Jesse said. He had hardly said more than a couple sentences through the whole of dinner and it was nice to hear his placid voice again.

I couldn't believe that Brenda decided to put on the twelve-minute disco version of 'Chocolate Chip' and judging from the sallow expression on everybody else's faces I figured they wasn't no happier about hearing it than I was.

'I liked y'all's record as much as the next person,' I said real loud to be heard above the music, 'but now ain't the time for it.'

'You're just a guest here, Baby Palatine. So you don't have a say.' It was either them beers or the cocaine that was making her bolshie all a' sudden and I didn't feel comfortable with the way she had been so sorrowful when her mama mentioned Jackie but got brighter as 'Chocolate Chip' started playing. It was like she had one of her lion to lamb, lamb to lion switches.

The sight of Brenda dancing had me mesmerized. She rolled her big behind and rocked back and forth on her feet doing the Chocolate Chip and I reckon it didn't look no better to Tammy, Jesse nor Anndora than it looked to me 'cause they refused to glance in her direction.

She said to her mother, 'Hey, Mama. I was having a talk earlier with Baby Palatine about Dagwood.' She kinda laughed and said, 'Remember Dagwood, Mama?'

Tammy was in a sort of low mood setting by Jesse and she said, 'Yes, of course, Brenda. I remember Dagwood, you remember him too, don't you? Wasn't it because of him that you turned into a little whore overnight?'

Well, it's possible that neither Jesse nor Anndora knew anything about Dagwood, because when that conversation started they didn't look particularly shocked at the fact that Brenda had spoke his name direct to Tammy. But I was stunned and scared because I could tell that there was a ugly atmosphere in the air and it wasn't just Joy's death had a bad feeling coming on me.

I looked over at Tammy and I said, 'It ain't my place to say nothing to you Tammy, but I don't think that's no way to talk to Brenda.' As I said it, though, what went through my mind was, I never realized that Tammy knew what happened, and she said, 'Shut up, Baby Palatine. Just you mind your business and shut the hell up. You covered up for her long enough, don't you think?'

'What are you talking about?' I said.

'You know damn well what I'm talking about,' Tammy told me.

'No I don't,' I said.

'Well Joy said you did,' said Tammy.

'Joy said what?' I looked over at Brenda and suddenly I wondered if they all knew something that I didn't. 'Joy said what?' I asked Tammy again.

'Joy said that you had encouraged Brenda to lie to me and that Brenda had been doing things with Dagwood. Things that a ten year old girl shouldn't have done.'

I said, 'Jesse, listen. I think all of these women done gone crazy. Maybe I'd better take myself to a hotel or someplace because the last thing I wanna do is get into a cheap ass argument. I promised my husband when I came here that I wouldn't let Tammy and these children upset me. So let me tell y'all something, Joy was the best thing that happened to you.'

Jesse said, 'Listen, nothing has ever been solved by a whole lotta arguing over something that happened donkeys' years ago. So just let the shit rest.' He got up from his chair and was standing next to Tammy when he said it and Tammy said to him,

'This is none of your business either, so stay out of it, Jesse.'

All the time that Tammy and I were talking, Brenda, went over to sit at the table and looked like she was in some kind of daze. She said in a kind of little girl's voice, quiet like, 'Mama, how long did you know?'

'Since the day it happened.'

Brenda said, 'I don't believe you.'

Tammy said, 'Well believe it. You betrayed me, Brenda, and so did you, Baby Palatine, and I'll never forgive either of you.'

So Brenda turned on Tammy and sneered, 'Maybe if you had given John Dagwood a bit of what he wanted, I wouldn't have had to.'

Tammy said, 'How dare you talk to me like that.'

Brenda said, 'Well it's the truth isn't it. I used to hear him say that you needed to loosen up a bit and be willing to try a few more things.'

Tammy said, 'What are you telling me, that you used to listen at the bedroom door?'

Brenda just laughed at her and said, 'Well, I took him higher.' She jumped up and started to sing and finger pop. 'Higher,' she sang. 'Can't you take your man higher.' Like she had lost her mind. Laughing and singing and nearly foaming at the mouth.

Jesse said, 'Brenda, why do you insist on bringing up unnecessary dead wood like this? Drop it.'

'Why?' said Brenda. 'Because I sucked her boyfriend's dick. Because I gave him the good time that she wouldn't.' She howled laughing.

I couldn't believe I was hearing none of this and what was worrying was they probably would have forgot they'd said it in a hour when it would be pricking at my poor brain for the rest of my life.

But all I could think about was Joy, Joy who had sworn on Freddie B's Bible that she wouldn't tell and told her mama anyway. I was too hurt to cry. Then Brenda started up again.

'Well, I'm sorry if you couldn't keep your man, Mama,' she said. 'He liked me just as much as he liked you,' Brenda taunted her mother.

'What are you trying to tell me, that he was some goddam pervert. I don't believe it,' said Tammy. She was standing up at the end of the glass top with her fists balled up by her sides. It was obvious that she was really mad, and her eyes were glaring.

'Wait now, y'all. Now ain't the time to rehash that mess. That's over and done with.' I stood between them. Nothing was worth the whole family arguing when they should have been feeling closer to one another in their time of grief.

'It won't ever be over,' yelled Tammy, 'because Brenda is crazy.' She moved a step closer to Brenda and it brought back to me how just the name John Dagwood turned Tammy into somebody else from the first day she'd met him.

'You had to have him all to yourself, didn't you? He wasn't supposed to kiss us or hug us or nothing. You were supposed to get all the attention. And all you wanted us to have was another fucking can of Heinz baked goddam beans. Baby Palatine knows I'm not lying. If Joy was here she'd tell you.'

Jesse stepped in. 'Listen. This can't solve anything. Why fight about something that happened thirty years ago?'

'Because we should have fought about it then and everyday since but Mama was too scared to mention Dagwood. So was Baby Palatine. But I never forgot it. Not once,' Brenda told Jesse.

'Who could face that their ten year old tried to have oral sex with a man asleep?' Tammy yelled straight over me to Brenda. I was still between them so that it was my face that she was up in and I could feel the spray of her spit. I looked around the table and noticed how Anndora looked dumbfounded. I wondered why she didn't get her coat on right then and there and rush off to her hotel like I would have done if'n I'd of had a hotel to run to.

'How the hell was I supposed to come to terms with the fact that he had to leave because of you. Ten years old and flaunting yourself like a goddam street whore in front of a decent man.' She went for Brenda who lunged at her and I caught somebody's elbow in my chest. It hurt but there wasn't time to think about how I was feeling, because I knew that if Brenda got too close to Tammy she would really do her some damage and with her being drunk, I didn't reckon Brenda knew her own strength. I was scared Tammy was gonna get hurt till I saw her pick up a ashtray, big heavy glass thing that was on the table in front of her.

'Tammy, put that down,' Jesse shouted and jumped up to hold both her arms. He wrenched the ashtray out of her hand at the same time that Brenda stretched across the table and took a swipe at her that didn't catch Tammy full on. But it made her wig sit crooked on her head and two empty wine bottles crashed onto the glass top table.

'You black son-of-a-bitch! How dare you put your hands on me,' Tammy yelled. She wasn't about to back off till I broke out wailing.

'Stop y'all. Stop! Joy's dead and all y'all is thinking about is yourselves. Ain't you got no feelings?' I hollered with tears streaming down my face. 'Just calm yourselves down till we can get the child buried. Then you niggers can kill each other if you want to.'

My sympathy went out to poor Jesse who I guessed didn't know what all he was letting hisself into when he got shacked up with Tammy. I ain't never seen a man look downhearted like he did right then. He loosed the hold he had on Tammy's arm and got ready to sit down. But soon as he did, Tammy made a grab for that ashtray again, and I knocked it out her hand so it rolled a foot from where Brenda had moved to by the fireplace and she took attitude like it was me that had thrown it at her. Brenda turned on me and I could see she was mad when she picked up an empty beer can. 'I should break your face,' she said crushing the metal can like it was made of polythene. I knew it was the cocaine talking. She had some of it caked white in the corners of her mouth like she'd been eating it.

Tammy screamed, 'Brenda are you out of your mind!' and I ducked to lurch out of Brenda's way as she made a grab for me. I was moving so quick that I didn't see Brenda was headed for the same corner of the room by the record player, so instead of dodging her we bumped into each other and she came down across my face with the crushed beer can, hitting me with such a wallop it felt like my brains was knocked sideaways. My bottom lip split open like a coconut, gushing blood into my mouth which so took me by surprise, I was gagging from it when Brenda threw me down on the floor. She jugged her knee into my throat making it so that I wanted to scream but couldn't. My mouth was open but no sound came out.

While I was laying on the floor with her knee across the side of my neck, I couldn't catch my breath and could just about see with my eyes bulging out as Jesse hobbled upstairs as fast as his stiff leg would let him, and as I heard Anndora screaming from the other side of the room it seemed like the noise that should of been coming out of my mouth was coming out of hers.

The side of my face was pressed down into the carpet and I felt something sticky and wet under it which I guessed right off was my own blood. With the way Brenda had hit on me, it was lucky I was conscious and didn't have my skull caved in.

'You dumb, stupid black whore,' Anndora screamed out. 'Let Baby Palatine go. Let her go,' she said and something came hurling across over from her side of the room and landed near my face. It was a glass candleholder with a purple candle still stuck in it that she'd thrown at Brenda. 'Haven't you done enough! You dumb bitch,' she let rip again.

Brenda jumped up and cut me loose. I watched her make a rush over to the fireplace and grab the coal stoker.

'Put the stove shaker down!' Tammy called out and I sat up as she made a lunge for Brenda who brought that shaker down so hard and fast on her mother's head that the sound registered way above the girls' record that was still going round on the turntable. And no sooner than Tammy fell from that sharp blow that made a terrible dull thud, Jesse must of seen his wife fall as he was coming back down and lost his balance running too quick down the stairs. He came a'tumbling while I was trying to pick myself up off the floor wishing I was young enough to break and run myself.

'Brenda. In the name of God, child, save yourself and rest that piece of iron. Can't you see you done hurt your mother real bad,' I called out as I almost stood up but then fell down again to my knees 'cause my head was reeling so with pain. There wasn't nothing for me to do but crawl over to Tammy whose wig had flown off her head, letting the blood spurt from her right temple like Brenda had opened up a main artery. Blood was everywhere.

It didn't take but two leaps for Brenda to reach Anndora and Jesse hollered, 'Don't do it. Don't hit her. I've got a gun, goddammit and I don't want to have to pull this goddam trigger.' But whatever he was threatening to do come too late and I watched Brenda's eyes roll back in her head as she swung that coal shaker at Anndora like she was in a ball park swinging a baseball bat. I screamed and closed my eyes. 'I'll make you beg all around town,' her voice still singing on the record was blaring and filled the whole apartment as I opened them again and watched Brenda as she hit her sister with full force so that Anndora dropped silent with that one blow before Brenda went to hit her again. Anndora's slight body crumpled like a wounded animal down on the floor. But Brenda kept beating on her like I seen my brother Napoleon do a poison rattler one time when we was kids. She brought the shaker down once, twice, three times, and I froze, scared to move closer to Tammy who had been moaning when she first fell but'd stopped.

My ears was ringing with sounds of moans and Brenda grunting and I didn't know what was piercing above all of them till a big bang went off that cut through the noise in my head to make me realize that what I'd heard was my own self screaming.

'Mamaaaaaaaaaaaa, Mamaaaaaaaaaaaaaaa,' I hollered as I watched Brenda's body take what look like a invisible blow from behind. Seemed like she did some kinda quick dance step before she toppled and I looked over towards the steps and saw that what had made that noise that swelled in my head above my scream and had cut Brenda's feet from under her was a shot from Jesse's hand gun.

Deep maroon blood was sprayed over Joy's white walls and the creamy carpet of her living room and Brenda looked way bigger than she was splayed half on the suede sofa and half on the floor with the tree sized plant laying at a angle cross her where it came down as she did.

In the avalanche of bodies dropping, that record had got stuck and Brenda's spiritual voice sang 'Chocolate chip, chocolate chip, chocolate chip, chocolate chip, chocolate chip, chocolate chip, chocolate chip' till Jesse went over and stopped it.

If I hadn't of been raised on a farm, I reckon the scent of fresh blood would have had me vomiting till today. The smell was stronger than at a hog kill and I closed my eyes and put both hands to my bloody mouth.

Jesse hobbled over from the record player back to me and from the way he moved holding his side, I figured that he had hurt hisself bad when he fell down them stairs. But I realized he wasn't thinking 'bout his own pain when he buried my head in his chest and said, 'Don't look.'

I had already seen. And I knew then that the sight of Tammy, Brenda and Anndora dead on Joy's living room floor is what I will see forever when I go to close my eyes.

'I called the police,' Jesse said. He had my whole head cradled in his hands. 'Thirty-two years a cop and I never needed to kill,' he told me quietly just as we could hear the police sirens wailing out in the street.

When the police ushered me and Jesse out, they put me in the back of a squad car and him in a black maria that was setting outside Joy's. I really wanted to go with him but the woman cop said I had to stay with her. I asked her if I could make a phone call at the station.

'I need to ring my husband,' I said. 'I only came to New York for a funeral and my husband'll be expecting me to be home in a day or two.'

I'd decided 'fore I dialed my number not to sound upset nor tell Freddie B what had happened till I got home. What good would it do him to worry?

'Hullo Baby.' Freddie sounded half sleep when I finally got put through. I could hear the TV going in the background. 'How are things going?'

'We've had a little trouble here, Freddie B.'

'Well don't fret yourself 'bout nothing, wife, 'cause I can fix me something to eat for as long as you gotta be there. Like when you had to be with Tammy's girls on the road. How's Tammy taking things, by the way?'

I didn't have heart to say nothing over the phone, so I just asked him how Helen was and told him I'd be home earlier than I thought. My plan was to head back home soon as I could catch me a plane out.

After I said goodbye to Freddie, they give me a cup of coffee and I got to make a second call, as Jesse had told them I was only a witness and wasn't to be charged with nothing.

I got the number for the Plaza Hotel off the operator.

'How much money do you think you'll need to give Joy a righteous sendoff?' is all Sebastian asked when I got through to him.

'Well it ain't just Joy got to be buried now.'

'What do you mean, Baby Palatine?'

I braced myself to tell him what'd happened.

Sebastian's limo stayed parked outside the police station for three hours with his driver waiting to take me with him to the airport after he'd paid Jesse's bail and had his own lawyer to the police station to see that things was gonna be handled right.

The street lights sparkled all over New York from behind the smoked glass windows of Sebastian's limo, and I wondered how such a godforsaken place could look so pretty to me.

Sebastian had the CNN news switched on the small TV set in his stretch limousine and I couldn't believe my eyes when a picture of Joy, Brenda and Anndora in my favorite of their stage outfits flashed on the screen.

'Bang Bang Bang,' the colored newscaster announced practically grinning, 'was found dead tonight in an elite Chelsea highrise. The pop singing African American sisters who had a number one hit in the late seventies with the record "Chocolate Chip" which started the daring dance craze were tonight murdered with their mother. Their stepfather, a retired detective from the Chicago police force, is being charged with the second degree murder of Brenda Bang, one time lead singer with the group, after she bludgeoned to death both her mother Tamasina O'Mara of Richmond, Virginia, and her sister Anndora Bang domiciled in Italy . . . Motive for the multiple murder is unknown although a large quantity of cocaine was found in the apartment,' the man said smiling like he was talking about something pleasant, 'but it enters the rising statistic of family homicide in the Manhattan area mainly due to hand guns. Neighbors in the apartment building. . .' Sebastian reached over and turned it off.

'I'm sorry,' he said. 'You don't need to hear that.'

'Is it ever too late for I'm sorry?' I asked him.

'I hope not,' he answered. 'We'd all be fucked if it were.'

# The Finish Up . . .

'Well there you was thinking you knew everything about Joy and you didn't know nothing,' Helen said. ' 'Cause seems like the thing that ruled her life was pushing that twin brother of her'n off that slide and killing him and you didn't even know she had no twin. You can't trust nobody these days.'

'But Joy was only four,' I told Helen who didn't want to understand.

'So! And part of her was still four when she killed herself, 'cause we can't never leave them baby ages behind. Three and four and five and all the rest of 'em. We just be carrying them ages 'round same as you see them ol' bag ladies downtown carting shopping bags full of rubbish they scared to leave behind. Loaded down. And with what? Nothing but rubbishy things that they done convinced theyselves is worth hauling everywhere in every kind of weather. And for what!'

'Talk sense, Helen! It sure do make me mad when you get to talking crazy. I thought you said that you didn't take a drink today.'

'I didn't,' she said and lifted her wig up to scratch at the back of her nappy head. 'You don't think that I'd have a drink when I got to go up to your child's funeral do you? I don't always do right, but I ain't evil.'

It took a minute to admit, 'Joy wasn't mine. I didn't birth her.'

'Peeing a child out ain't all there is to having one. And if that child ever had her a mama, it was you, 'cause you was the onliest one that loved her blind like mothers do wanting to pretend like their little ol' snot faced, bad assed kids is perfect.'

'I didn't never try to pretend that Joy was perfect.'

'That's a damn lie, and you know it 'cause whatever Joy did, you wanted to act like she was doing right. And from all that Brenda and Anndora told you, the truth is she was a bad actor.'

'Life made her like it and it ain't no wonder that she got more and more twisted up with Tammy trying to cover up Joy's confusion.'

Helen was already fed up with the discussion. I could tell, 'cause she got up and got to scratching like she does before she needs a drink. There wasn't but another twenty minutes to go before Sebastian had the car coming to take us all over to the cemetery in Oakland where he had organized a memorial for Joy in the open air like he thought she would like with the few gospel groups and a band and a little orchestra. He decided that if she'd told me she wanted a celebration if she ever passed that that's exactly what he wanted to give her. He had ordered five hundred silver and gold helium balloons that they was gonna let fly with some white doves when a four piece band played 'My Funny Valentine'. It wasn't like we was gonna bury my God-sent child but like we was gonna set her free.

I had me on a beautiful red dress 'cause that was Joy's favorite color and whereas she said that I looked good in pink, Sebastian said that he wanted me to go out and buy something special, like a long evening dress that was shining. But he must of seen when he said it that I didn't have strength to go out looking for no dress, so he told me he would have somebody come to my place and bring me some dresses to choose from. Which is exactly what he did, and the one I chose I knew Joy would of liked me in, 'cause it was elegant and made me feel like them women I see getting out of them black limousines on TV when they're about to walk in to be seen by billions at the Academy Awards.

It had a great big huge bow at the back that stood out six inches either side of my hips and a kick pleat. Freddie B said that with that high mandarin collar and the long sleeves I looked better in that red dress than anything he'd seen me in all the time we'd been married.

When I first picked it out, I was worried about how I was gonna sit down in it in the limousine, but the dressmaker showed me where the bow unsnapped at the behind and hung on the side so you could set when you had a mind to.

The woman Sebastian sent also brought 'round some tuxedos for Freddie B to try on, and I thought that we wasn't gonna get one to fit Freddie 'cause of his long arms, but like that woman said, they could alter that suit for him in no time.

So when the suit box come for Freddie B he took it straight to the bedroom like he was embarrassed to be seen making a fuss about what he was gonna put on. But he's always been pernickety about what he wears, though he likes to claim that he'll put on any ol' thing.

Sebastian's woman had thrown in a pretty blue iridescent cumberbun and stiff shirt and bow tie that Freddie wanted me to knot, but he knew better than me how to tie it.

Helen had one of my curly black wigs and some deep red lipstick, but since Sebastian didn't realize she was meant to be coming, he didn't have nothing sent over special for her with that woman, but it didn't matter no way, 'cause I found one of them Dior suits with a fine pleated skirt that Joy had give me that wasn't too big looking, and when I lied and told Helen that the short skirt was supposed to be as long on her as it was she was happy. The reason that I didn't never wear that suit was 'cause the skirt came way above my knees and whereas Joy with her long legs would have looked fabulous in something like that, I was way too old to have my knobbly knees hanging out.

I told Helen how nice she looked and made her take her snuff out 'fore we took the elevator down to the car. Joy would have been proud to see us stepping into the limo when it came.

Sebastian said Joy shouldn't have no proper church service 'cause it made death gloomy. He made other plans and I didn't have to lift a finger. Not that I could of 'cause the doctor gave me a sedative that knocked me out for sixteen hours once I got back from New York.

When we got to the cemetery, the four gospel choirs from the Bay Area and San Francisco that Sebastian had booked to sing was already in their white robes and grouped in place and the local radio station Sebastian organized had come to do a live recording 'cause he said that Joy would have wanted the whole world to be able to celebrate and they only could if the thing was on the radio. I was worried that that was taking things too far, but when that first choir got to singing "I Been On This Train Too Long" I realized that it was right to allow everybody who wanted to hear to have a chance.

Sebastian said it shouldn't have been no different from some of them outdoor concerts that he played and I don't know who he got to organize everything, but like he said, there wasn't nothing when it came to putting on a show that folks in the rock business didn't know how to organize with music and stages and dancers and balloons and foolishness such as that. He had it all there for my Joy's sendoff.

'Chocolate Chip' was playing over the loud speakers and lots of them folks that turned up I figured had only turned up 'cause they heard over the radio what was happening that day.

The Biggest Bang was what the memorial announcements read. And I hadn't never seen nothing like 'em nor the number. They was more like glossy programs for a show and had a lot of pictures of Joy and her sisters, and Sebastian had even included that black and white one of Brenda with Jackie. There wasn't just hundreds printed, there was thousands for all the folks that turned up I reckoned 'cause Sebastian's name was attached to the memorial service.

I patted the edge of my long glove to make sure that that note of Joy's that Freddie B had finally found over at Helen's was still on me. I was hoping that when Helen'd told me there was a letter in that envelope that she'd stole the money out, that Joy had wrote to me proper. But it wasn't but a note.

Joy had such neat pretty handwriting, and she'd used gold ink on the black stationery that she liked so much. When I showed it to Sebastian the day before the memorial service, he asked me if he couldn't have it copied and tied with red ribbon on the ends of every single one of them helium balloons that he was planning to fill the sky up with. He said that it was the best way for Miss Joy to have her own final say.

Them four gospel choirs was really good and they sang two songs each. They rang out in the warm March air with those strong mellow voices. But the balloons and doves didn't let fly till the choir from First Tabernacle sang 'All Hands to the Plow.'

That's when I looked up and saw all them silver and gold balloons catching them a bright spark each off the afternoon sun and though couldn't nobody see while they was way up in that sky that they was all carrying a copy of the message in my glove sent to me from my God-sent child, I knew. It didn't say much, but it left me feeling that Joy knew she still had me with her 'cause what she had wrote was,

> Dear Baby P
> Love is stronger than death.